Steven Bosworth, an accomplished and qualified engineering manager who has worked for several large international companies, wanted to share some of the experiences and emotions shared throughout his life. He had the idea for the main character, Dean Nash, over 20 years ago, and it wasn't until 2010 that he finally put pen to paper.

Dedication

This book is dedicated to my close family and friends for all their love and support, from the happiest days through the darkest times, showing me the way to forgiveness and giving me strength to believe in myself.

Best Regards.

Steve

S/Bell

3/9/18.

Steven Bosworth

THE BETRAYAL

AUSTIN MACAULEY PUBLISHERS™

LONDON • CAMBRIDGE • NEW YORK • SHARJAH

A CIP catalogue record for this title is available from the British
Library.

ISBN 9781787107373 (Paperback)
ISBN 9781787107380 (E-Book)

www.austinmacauley.com

First Published (2018)
Austin Macauley Publishers Ltd.
25 Canada Square
Canary Wharf
London
E14 5LQ

Acknowledgements

I wish to acknowledge all the people that have contributed towards making me into the person I am today. Their presence, if only for a few hours or years of memories together, helped me to understand a better life.

1

Living under the knife held by another man's hand fills my thoughts as the tube shudders then bangs and rattles along the track. The horn sounds, releasing my mind from this torture and bringing me back to the reality of the tedious commute to work, but thankfully I know it's Friday and there is a bank holiday weekend ahead. Sitting in the carriage, the faint aroma of joss sticks and stale sweat are briefly masked by the scent of aftershave and strong perfumes hanging in the air and my mind thinks what a pleasure, this is at 8.00 am before a long day at the office. Looking around the carriage, I see many of the regular faces on the daily commute to work and today, as ever, there are a few new ones. A young couple in their early twenties are sitting opposite me holding hands, laughing and kissing, both casually dressed in jeans and T-shirts so they must be in the city for pleasure. They look very much in love, engrossed with themselves and not a care in the world.

A grey-suited gentleman, about fifty years old, is sitting to the left of the young couple reading his paper, waiting for the tube to stop at the platform. This man follows the same routine every morning like clockwork and always tries to sit in the same seat to read his copy of the Daily Telegraph from the sports page backwards, taking small sips of his tea. To my left sits a mid-thirties black-suited man; I can tell he is a power crazy stock broker with his designer Armani suit and Rolex watch. He is pretending to read the Financial Times, but is really looking at the pretty woman sitting to the right of the young couple opposite. She is in her late twenties, playing with her iPhone and dressed in a tight fitting pinstripe light grey suit. She is slightly tanned, quite athletic and, sensing that the stock broker is staring at her, she keeps flicking her long blonde hair towards him, trying to attract attention discreetly.

Sitting to my right is a well-dressed, polite, mature lady with a friendly smile and today she looks across at the young couple with a smile of happiness on her face, maybe remembering some past love. Finally, sitting next to her, is a guy in his late twenties with a head covered in dreadlocks, looking like a mature student. He is wearing cut off combat trousers and a torn T-shirt showing the Scarface film cover with music blasting from his earphones as he looks around the carriage, not having a care in the world. The polite lady is leaning slightly away from him trying to not be offensive. The remaining carriages are full with the daily onslaught of people commuting into the city. I like people watching, but you never know who is watching you and what they are thinking.

I start thinking about what could happen today, and why this day might be different from yesterday. My thoughts drift to this weekend and things to do as the carriages rattle to a sharp stop, jolting me forward slightly. Then work projects now fill my thoughts, such as the boss offloading piles of meetings and paperwork onto me so that he can sit reading the internet all day in his office. The doors bang then slide open, triggering the mad rush of commuters being pushed and bumped along the platform up the stairs towards the daylight of the city outside. Noise blasts from the coffee shops with the Daily World news channels, stock market share prices, sports headlines with weather reports and rubbish adverts that are masked by the station loudspeaker attendant calling the next tube in his strong cockney accent. I continue walking past the coffee shops and restaurants as the smell of fresh coffee and burnt toast, along with cooked bacon and eggs, floats through the musty, stale underground air, tempting even the not hungry to want to eat.

Inside Canary Wharf station people can be seen asleep in chairs, waiting for the next tube, and past the exit doors the sun shines bright. Reaching inside my suit jacket inner pocket with my right hand, I pull out my sunglasses case. As the sliding doors open a wave of noise hits my ears with car horns blasting, emergency sirens whirling and people walking everywhere in a mad rush, shouting just to make basic conversation. I remove my sunglasses from the case as the brightness of the sunlight causes my eyes to sting and the sudden darkness of wearing the glasses brings some instant relief. Beginning to walk towards the office block along the pavement, my senses are working overtime trying to filter out the noise, smells, taste and light of the city but as always it feels as though something is missing from my life with being subjected to this abuse every day. The biggest sensation that keeps washing over my subconscious is that of someone watching me or maybe it's just the CCTV cameras placed on every building and lamppost.

People shout into their cells and bump past without a single apology. It's so formal and impersonal. In a big city I am just a person and nobody says hello, everyone feels like a stranger and my invisible boundary is constantly being invaded. Walking through the streets of concrete and mirrored glass buildings my feelings of being watched grow ever stronger until I finally reach the apparent safety of Harpers and Harpers stainless fronted entrance. It towers over all its rivals as the sun's rays reflect off the highly polished surface. I pass through the large spinning doors and, reaching the light grey marbled foyer, continue making my way to the ground floor office entrance doors past the front desk.

The receptionist, Sophie, is just answering a call and, tilting her head slightly, she looks across and smiles. She is always well dressed, polite and very good looking in her late twenties with beautiful dark brown hair and piercing blue eyes. Her intoxicating perfume lingers in the air like a refreshing mist, filling my nostrils. Smiling back, I keep to the right side of the foyer and continue down the corridor towards the main office doors where two security guards stand like statues in rent-a-cop uniforms at the end.

Walking past, I smile, saying, "Good morning, gentlemen." They both look at me, showing no emotion on their faces.

Pushing the office door open with my left hand, I walk into the large open plan area and begin to thread my way through the maze of desks towards my glass fronted office at the far right side of the room. I notice the sun's rays shining against the large windows that overlook the city. As I continue past the desks, men and women are just getting ready for their day at work by switching on computers and connecting phones, with the sound of desk drawers opening and closing resonating everywhere. If any people notice me I always say, "Good morning," knowing that good manners are the only things in life that are free. The desk phones begin to ring, signifying the start of a new day as I reach my office. Leaning forward with my right hand, I push the glass door open and continue through the doorway into the room with the warmth of the sun feeling quite overpowering. Reaching my desk, I turn and see Shaun walking over with a great big grin on his face. Strolling into my office, he collapses in one of the chairs opposite my desk.

"Hey up, Deano, how are you Gezza?" he asks.

"Morning, Shaun, and from the look on your face there is no guessing what you have been up to," I reply, smiling.

"Took Chloe from sales out," he answers with a smirk all over his face.

"Oh, just a quick drink, hey fella?" I say winking back.

"Yeah, you know me." He smiles.

Shaun is a typical single man in an office full of women, befriending as many as possible. He is thirty-two and loves to keep himself in shape and looking his best for his admiring fans. I met Mr Tantasic, as I call him, at the local gym around two years ago when I first moved to the area and we quickly became good friends. He now thinks my office is his second home after I managed to get him a job working at Harpers and Harpers.

"What did you get up to last night?" Shaun asks.

"Well, you know me, I like to keep my business private!" I smile back.

"Won't ask any more, fella, I have given up trying to work you out. Are we going to that new club Castro's tonight?" He nods at me moving his arms like an excited schoolboy dancing in the chair.

"Sounds like a good idea; it's been a hard week and it's Friday after all." I nodded in agreement.

He jumps out of the chair, turns and walks out of my office, starting to whistle the theme tune from Great Escape and weaving his way through the rows of desks as I pull my chair and shake my head at him smiling. Sitting in the swivel chair, I stare around the office walls that are covered with calendars, new project plans and presentions. Feeling exhausted already, I turn to look through the office window, trying to imagine some freedom, but the harsh reality is that unless I make a change, my life will always be the same. My thoughts begin to wish for something better than this prison cell of feeling so constricted and wasting my life wishing to see much more of the big world outside. Turning back towards the desk, I switch on the laptop which begins buzzing and whirring as the hard drive wakes up. The usual damn passwords and access numbers are typed in as I dream for a simpler life where there is no one telling me what to do and when to do it.

Now the laptop is fully booted, it shows the count of emails received over the last twelve hours and so the first thankless task begins. My concentration is broken by the big boss starting to make his way into the open plan office, strutting his stuff wearing a posh grey suit, but with no brains or common sense. As he walks along the rows of desks women either cower in their seats or sit bolt upright looking for attention. Everyone in the office knows that the cowering women are his previous conquests and after meeting his wife once it seems that his family worships the ground he walks on and this is how he repays them.

The other women sitting high hope they will be shown the Promised Land. He will deliver nothing and take everything. What an arsehole. I hope one day he gets his comeuppance, thinking that time will tell and people always stand and fall by their actions. He can be quite a bully at times and is not well liked by the staff, but the directors in the company love him, confirming that people in power always try to abuse the situation for their own good and never give anything back, but fate always has a hand in balancing any situation and thankfully this is his last week before he moves to a new company. The thirst in my throat highlights that I haven't had a drink yet this morning, so standing, I leave the cell of my office and start to walk towards the drinks machine, speaking to few people at their desks as I pass by.

Reaching the machine, money is taken from my right trouser pocket and inserted into the slot, then after pressing the coffee option the machine begins to whirl into action. Looking across, the boss has now reached his office as his assistant chases after him, carrying a freshly made drink. The sound of running water being poured into the cup can be heard followed after a few seconds by a bleep. Taking the cup from the dispenser, I lift it to my lips and the smell of freshly mixed packet coffee hits my nostrils. My mind starts to drift away to a distant memory of a small coffee shop with freshly ground coffee, but I can't remember who is with me. My thoughts are shattered by the sound of the boss storming out of his office, shouting at his assistant, Racheal, and talking to her like a piece of shit. Turning in disgust I walk back to my office, thinking what a pleasure it would be to tell him a few home truths. Reaching my desk the cup is placed on the top and, sitting, I look across to the laptop screen where a new email has been delivered.

****

Date: 27/8/2010 09:02

From: Sophie.Roberts@h&h.com

To: Dean.Nash@h&h.com

Subject : Tonight.

"Hi Dean, I hope you are okay? You looked nice this morning. I am planning to visit the new club Castro's tonight with VIP passes and was wondering if you would like to join me?"

****

Reading the mail words on the screen for a second time, being a little shocked but also surprised, I thought she may have been informing me of a visitor at reception not asking me to join her at a club. I try not to mix business with pleasure and have tried keeping myself to myself, but having spoken with Sophie a few times, she seems to be a nice person so I send back a reply.

****

Date: 27/8/2010 09:08

From: Dean.Nash@h&h.com

To: Sophie.Roberts@h&h.com

Subject : RE Tonight.

"Morning Sophie, thanks for the complement, seeing you at the main desk brightened up a dull Friday in the office. How are you? I normally meet Shaun tonight for a drink straight from work. Who are you planning to go Castro's with?"

****

I press send and after a few minutes a reply shows in the inbox.

****

Date: 27/8/2010 09:10

From: Sophie.Roberts@h&h.com

To: Dean.Nash@h&h.com

Subject : RE Tonight.

"I'm going with a few girls from work. We are planning to have drinks in a local bar then make our way to the club. We could meet somewhere if you would like to?"

****

I start to think that maybe this is a joke and she is not being serious. Equally though, being single I have no commitments and the thought that somebody of the opposite sex who you are attracted to is contacting you always make you feel warm inside. However in the back of my mind the pain from the past burns deep and hangs heavy in my head and heart. I manage to override my lustful and nervous thoughts then lean back in my chair, looking out into the office for inspiration, deciding how to write a reply.

****

Date: 27/8/2010 09:18

From: Dean.Nash@h&h.com

To: Sophie.Roberts@h&h.com

Subject : RE Tonight.

"Shaun and I normally have a few drinks in the Irish bar O'Neill's on Muswell Hill, Broadway then hit the clubs afterwards. We could meet at O'Neill's about eight thirty pm if you would like?"

****

In no time the return message is sent from Sophie.

****

Date: 27/8/2010 09:19

From: Sophie.Roberts@h&h.com

To: Dean.Nash@h&h.com

Subject : RE Tonight.

"Okay great. I will meet you there and am looking forward to seeing you later XX."

****

Trying to avoid thinking about whether it's a joke or not, I attempt to blank out the thoughts and continue with my usual day of a mad rush of meetings, phone calls and mountains of paperwork, but thankfully before long seven thirty pm finally arrives and Shaun can be seen walking over to my office.

"Ready, pal? Let's see what tonight brings." He pretends to dance and strut his stuff, shaking his backside as he walks in.

"Yeah, let's have a good one." I smile to myself, thinking that if Sophie turns up with a few other girls he will be shocked.

As we walk out of the office building I quickly stare across to the front desk but Sophie has already gone. Passing through the doors, the air is filled with noise everywhere from cars horns, people laughing and shouting along with aircraft and helicopters flying over. I look across the street and see a big black Mercedes suddenly drive away from the pavement on the opposite side. We carry on walking toward the Irish bar with people everywhere in the city talking on mobiles and rushing through the crowds trying to get the tube journey home. It's a bright, sunny evening and people are sitting outside at the bars and restaurants having an evening drink or dining on the terraces, making the most of the late summer sunshine. Shaun and I notice the crowds of smartly dressed women looking fantastic, but secretly I'm thinking about Sophie and how much I want her next to me.

We see the guys dressed in the latest designer clothes then start to discuss our motorbikes and the next trip we have planned for Europe later in September. A Ferrari drives past revving the engine and our conversation changes to the latest super cars and if we had the money what would we like to buy. Walking along the bustling streets, the bars are full with people standing and sitting outside with different music being played everywhere. This noise is not my scene, but in a big city there are not many quiet places to have a drink and relax. Finally reaching the Irish bar, I open the door for Shaun and he walks straight in, heading towards the bar as my nose is instantly filled with the scent of stale smelling beer and cigarette smoke everywhere. Following Shaun to the bar, he winks at his favourite barmaid, Kelly, who is about twenty-five with green eyes and auburn hair, pretty and politely spoken.

"Two bottles of bud when you're ready, gorgeous," he shouts at her confidently with his strong Essex accent.

The bar noise is so loud with music playing and people laughing and shouting, letting off steam from their week at work. This is the first time I've lived in a city and sometimes it's too much for me. I prefer a local bar with a few friends having drinks and a laugh. Kelly turns and reaches for the two bottles of beer from the refrigerator underneath the spirits counter and flicks off the tops, giving Shaun a seductive look. Leaning on the bar, my sixth sense tells me that I'm being watched and looking into the large rectangular mirror that hangs over the bar I glance from my left to the right to see if anyone is taking any interest in me, only noticing a man in his early fifties casually looking around the bar. The entrance door opens and Sophie, with her three friends, walks into the bar and my heart suddenly feels warmth inside. She glances across at me with her beautiful blue eyes and smiles. Her wavy brown hair floats gracefully as she walks with her tanned athletic body complementing the short cut black dress and black high heels looking absolutely stunning.

"Hi Dean." She smiles at me saying, "Fancy meeting you here?"

"Well, good evening Sophie. Yes, it's a small world," I reply.

Shaun is still speaking to Kelly, the barmaid, and stares into the mirror, seeing me talking to Sophie and, looking over his right shoulder, says, "I'll let you get on with your work, Kelly. Call me later if you like, hun?" He is distant from her now.

"Yeah, that would be great; I'll look forward to it," Kelly whispers over.

Shaun now sees new women and bounces over in two big steps, almost not touching the ground. "So what's happening here then?" he announces with a big smile on his face, winking at me constantly.

"Hi Shaun, we are just talking. These are my friends," Sophie replies smiling. "Chloe, Grace and—"

"I'm Wendy." Leaning over the two other girls she says, "Are you boys buying the drinks then?" Wendy shouts over the music.

Seeing Sophie's eyes rolling towards me smiling, Shaun looks at Chloe and Grace, winking. Chloe is about twenty-six with blonde hair, blue eyes and is wearing a short low-cut red dress and may be Shaun's date from last night. Grace looks a nice girl about twenty-eight with brown hair and eyes, dressed smart in a two piece casual suit. Wendy has dyed bright red hair, is about six feet tall, attractive and medium build, wearing a very reviling one piece skin-tight bright green dress.

Shaun shouts, "What you drinking then, girls?"

"I'll get the drinks, Shaun," I reply. "You keep the girls entertained," I said, looking across at Sophie.

"My pleasure, fella," laughs Shaun.

Asking the girls what they want, both Chloe and Grace order white wine spritzers and Wendy shouts out in large cockney voice, "I'll have a Double Vodka Red Bull." Very fitting drink I think.

"What would you like, Sophie?" I ask, looking over to her, smiling.

"I'll have a white wine spritzer too. I'll help." She looks back at me.

Walking over to the bar, I can sense that Sophie is behind me with her perfume floating in the air hiding the stale smells from the bar. Stopping at the bar, I shout the orders to Kelly, who doesn't look happy with Shaun talking to the other women, and suddenly I feel a hand on the lower part of my back and then a voice whispers in my ear.

"I'm glad you're here, Dean."

Sophie's breath touches the back of my neck, causing the hairs to stand up, sending an electric shock down my backbone. Turning and looking straight into her gorgeous blue eyes, I lean across, whispering back, placing my hand on her waist saying, "Me too."

After paying and collecting the drinks we walk back to the others who have found an empty table and, handing the drinks around to everyone, we join into the talk and laughter that is starting to flow quickly with Shaun's full charm working tonight, firing on all cylinders. He is a laugh to watch when he is chatting up girls and seeing their reactions when they are not interested is even funnier. Sophie and I talk about life outside work and interests such as music, films and past holidays in the world along with visiting family and friends.

Sophie suddenly asks, "Why are you still single, Dean?"

I reply, "Who says I am single?" See looks a little shocked.

Smiling back I reply, "I've just not met the right girl to settle down with."

The answer isn't quite true, but I don't think Sophie would want to hear about my disastrous past love life tonight. Shaun looks over, nods his head and gives me a big wink of approval. I can read him like a book. After a few hours of drinking, laughing and chatting we decide to move from the Irish bar over to Castro's.

Wendy, struggling to stand to her feet, nearly falls back down into the seat and shouts out, waving the last of her drink, "Are we going to this new club? Sophie has some VIP tickets so let's move."

Shaun gulps the last of his beer and looks at the door, gesturing. "Well, you first, Wendy, you walking in those high heels I've just got to see!" he instructs.

Standing, we thread our way through the packed bar towards the door and, stretching out my right hand, I open it by pulling it towards me. Wendy stumbles through first, followed by Shaun, Chloe, Grace and finally Sophie. Reaching the pavement outside, the city is now shrouded in an orange glow from the street lights and the occasional flickering of neon tubes from advertising bars and restaurants. I can still sense I'm being watched and look both up and down the street for any possible threat, but only see parked cars and taxis queuing, waiting for fares. Groups of men and women are laughing and walking towards the next bars with drunken voices filling the night air that is only broken by a car driving away into the distance with the rear tail lights fading into the darkness. I briefly stand, thinking that maybe too much drink has made me paranoid.

Sophie links my arm. "Come on you, help me reach the club?" she whispers in my ear.

We all walk along the pavement drunk and slurring, trying to sing, until the red neon lights and signage for Castro's invite us to enter. The entrance to the club is on my left hand side and has a bright red carpet with a gold rope attached to polished posts segregating the people with music blasting from inside. Behind the entrance is a large covered outside area where people are drinking and socialising. Above the sitting area is a top balcony with more men and women leaning against a glass balustrade. Turning to my right, the road outside the club has taxis parked everywhere, dropping off more people who are walking to the main entrance.

Sophie lets go of my arm and finds the VIP tickets in her purse and we all start to make our way along the red carpet. She shows the tickets to the four burley bouncers standing in front of the entrance who stand to one side, allowing us to pass. One of the bouncers pushes the door inwards, allowing us to enter, then suddenly a shockwave of loud music blasts through the open door, making even the drunkest person instantly sober as we head towards the first lower room with a bar across the right side back wall. To the left are patio doors that lead towards the outside covered area. The music being played sends vibrations through my whole body as we make our way towards the bar where the tiled floor is sticky from spilt drinks. Drunken men and women are everywhere, laughing and leaning against the bar, and it feels like being in a cattle market.

Wendy slurs, "It's my turn to buy the drinks, vodka Red Bulls for everyone?"

Leaning over the bar and staring at one of the bar staff, he quickly starts to prepare the drinks because of how loud Wendy is shouting and probably hoping she will disappear. Taking the drinks from the bar, we start to walk around the club towards the staircase in the far left corner. The bright white walls have pictures painted on them and the tiled floors now changes to light pine wooden flooring that is still slippery underfoot from the spilt drinks. Around the edges of the room are small cubicles with tables encircled by settees full of people. In the centre of the room there are several small high tables with sets of chairs where men and women stand or sit around them. Dry ice lingers above the dance floor and hovers into the air with the latest chart and dance music blasting through the speakers placed all around the club. The lighting is subdued but gives enough illumination to show where we are walking as a white strobe occasionally breaks through, filling the room with beams of light. I can see Shaun already heading towards the staircase and VIP lounge with Wendy, Chloe and Grace following close by. Sophie is still next to me as we make our way towards the stairs then, slowly walking up each step, we wait behind the small queue of people. At the top of the stairs a waitress offers champagne in flutes with pieces of strawberry floating inside the glasses.

Shaun leans over to her and shouts, "You can keep the fruit until later." He winks at her and she looks at him, giving a fake smile. Wendy laughs out loud and looks across to Chloe and Grace trying to support her actions.

I look at Sophie and, gesturing with my head, ask, "Are they both okay?"

Sophie leans over saying, "I've not got the heart to tell Shaun, but Chloe is already married and Grace is engaged."

"Next you'll be telling me that you're married too with kids?" I laugh towards Sophie.

"What makes you say that!" she replies quite sharply.

"I can't believe that you are still single," she repeats from the earlier conversation.

Not replying, I simply smile back as we walk into the VIP lounge and instantly it can be seen that this room is darker than downstairs with light grey walls and dark flooring. Here there are no drinks spilt on the floor and to the left are patio doors that must lead to the upper balcony I saw from outside. Directly in front is a smaller bar, with subtle blue lighting and in the centre of the room, is a recessed small dance floor encircled by large black settees. Softer music is being played which hangs gracefully in the air. As we walk deeper into the VIP lounge, there are people standing around talking and drinking, sitting around in the large chairs and settees.

Everyone seems so fake and it looks like they are all putting on a show for the opening night. The women, dressed like stunning models with fabulous figures, lots of jewellery and suntans, stand draped onto the arms of smartly dressed men in expensive suits and watches, observing us. Feeling uncomfortable, I reach the patio doors and continue outside to the edge of the balcony with the music still ringing in my ears and look down at the people that can be seen queuing to enter the club. Sophie joins me, linking my arm.

At that moment the well-dressed man I noticed in the mirror at O'Neill's earlier walks over towards us.

"Good evening, I trust you are both having a pleasant time?" He speaks with a very strong English accent. Sophie turns to face him.

"Oh, yes, thank you. We were just admiring the view," Sophie answers politely.

Feeling more uncomfortable by the presence of this stranger, my mind works overtime. Who is this man? Why is he watching me? I continue to look at him and it's evident he has lots of money, with his slightly tanned face, tailored suit, Rolex watch and, being athletic for his age, you can see he looks after himself.

"I hope you both have a pleasant evening and hopefully we will try to speak later," he says as he turns and walks away.

I watch him walk over towards a group of men and women, who are all looking over in our direction, knowing somehow they are talking about us.

Turning back to look at Sophie, I ask, "Let's get another drink and try to find the others," as she nods her head in agreement smiling.

We walk back into the lounge and head towards the bar and order our drinks. Sophie turns to me and says, "Let's find the others later; I want to enjoy our time together."

I smile and we take a seat next to the bar on our own and continue to talk about travelling, holidays, music and what we want in life. Looking across to the dance floor a few couples begin to dance closely to each other.

It's late in the night and looking into Sophie's beautiful eyes I ask her, "Would you like to dance?"

She looks across at me smiling saying, "Yes, Dean, that would be fantastic."

We both finish our drinks and make our way to the small dance floor in the centre of the room. Walking down the two small steps onto the floor, Sophie is linked to my left arm and it's evident everyone is staring at us. Making our way to the middle of the floor, I turn her so she is looking at me and, as we start to dance, our bodies gradually begin to touch. Men can be seen staring at Sophie, talking about how beautiful she looks. Yes, she is very stunning and I'm very glad to be here with her. First it was quite relaxed with some distance between us, but then we start to get closer. She lifts her left arm and places it on my right shoulder and I place my right arm around her back, feeling her body underneath her dress. It feels so soft and warm. Lifting my left arm over her right shoulder, Sophie slides her arm around my waist, touching my lower back and a feeling of excitement rushes through my body as I'm glad she is here with me. Pulling Sophie closer, I start to kiss the right side of her neck and begin to get aroused. She senses it and continues to rub against me. Dancing against each other, we look into the other's eyes and start to kiss passionately.

It feels so fantastic to finally kiss her and I haven't felt this happy for years and being here with Sophie feels so magical. We continue to dance and kiss, rubbing against each other provocatively. *Bang.* The music stops and the lights are suddenly switched on and the magic of the night is over. As we gradually stop dancing, we look across at each other and start to walk off the dance floor towards the stairs, ready to leave the club with Sophie linked onto my left arm, hugging it tightly. The well-dressed man from earlier in the night on the balcony walks over in our direction.

"Would you like to join my friends and I for a last drink?" he asks.

"Well, what makes you think we will get served?" I reply quickly.

"Well, I am the owner after all," he answers back confidently.

Looking at Sophie I ask, "What would you like to do?" A fear begins to flow through my mind about why he would like to buy drinks.

"I would like another drink with you." She smiles at me and hugs my arm.

Turning to the man, I reply, "Well, there's your answer. Yes, we would like to join you for a drink."

The first thought rushing in my head is what does he want? The second thought is wishing to leave, but Sophie wants to stay and have another drink with me and I don't want to upset her.

The man holds out his right hand and says, "My name is Nick." I hold out my right hand and handshake with him, having a firm grip.

"Hi, I'm Dean and this is Sophie," I reply back.

"A strong handshake that tells me a lot about a man," Nick replies.

We walk towards the back of the lounge, past the bar, and I can see some light coming from another room through a doorway. Sophie grips my arm even tighter as we reach the doorway that leads to the back room.

Sophie turns to me and says in a whispered voice, "I've changed my mind. Shall we look for the others?" It's too late.

We enter the back room that has similar lighting and soft music being played. I quickly look around the room and count ten men with six women standing by them in the middle of the room.

Nick turns and says, "Your friends went about half an hour ago. Sophie, you knew that!"

Suddenly looking at Sophie, then Nick, I ask sharply, "Is there something going on here I should know about?"

The door closes behind us; Sophie is holding my arm so tight it feels like the blood will stop. Suddenly starting to sober up fast, my senses are working in overdrive and my mind is full of, "Why did I decide to come into this room? What made me decide to come to this club tonight?" My heart is banging in the chest like someone hitting it with a sledge hammer and then, feeling slightly faint, I don't know what to expect or what to think.

Sophie whispers to me, "I'm so sorry, Dean." I look at her, not certain what to think. Nick walks over to a centre table in the room and sits in large leather swivel chair.

"Don't be afraid, Dean, we won't bite." He points across at two other chairs.

How does he know Sophie? What's happening here? Thoughts are racing through my head. Sophie starts to walk towards the chairs so I decide to walk with her. The waitress who was handing out champagne at the top of the stairs of the VIP lounge earlier in the night is there giving out drinks. I wish Shaun hadn't said anything and I bet she is laughing to herself now.

As we reach the table all the other men slowly begin to walk across and start to stand in an intimidating gesture behind Nick.

"Sit. Sit," Nick repeats with an excitement in his voice.

Sitting down, the waitress walks over and hands Sophie and myself a drink as I look at this man, wondering who he is.

"I know who you are, Dean, and that you work at Harpers and Harpers," he explains to me.

My mind begins to absorb his words and deep inside I begin to think. What is going on here? How does he know all of this? What's Sophie got to do with this?

"You have a particular set of skills that I want and I know you are willing to work with me." He is gesturing with his hands.

Continuing to digest his words, my brain plans the next questions. What is this, a job interview? Is he offering me a job? I've never had a job interview like this before – head hunted, yes, but not this.

"What can I offer you, Nick? What do you want from me? What skills are you talking about?" I ask.

"All will come with time, you don't realise your potential and I'm the person to show you." Nick smiles back at me.

He waves his left hand, pointing at the men behind him. They are all wearing tailored suits, smart, clean-shaven like military or police officers.

"What do you want from me?" I ask again more sharply and aggressively.

I can always tell a person by their eyes and Nick's eyes seem cool and calm today, but I sense underneath that there is something sinister behind them. Maybe it's the place and not the person. My throat and mouth are so dry I need a drink. Lifting the glass with a slightly shaking hand as the coldness of the champagne flute touches my lips. Sophie looks across at me, trying to smile. The first thought instantly turns to whether the champagne could be poisoned or drugged, but in my present emotional condition and not really caring I take a sip and the coolness of the liquid in my mouth feels good.

Gradually swallowing, the champagne bubbles moisten my throat as 'not dead yet' enters my mind.

"I've never had an interview like this before, Nick?" I ask nervously.

"That's because it's not an interview, Dean, it's a life changing opportunity that you will never get again" Nick continues.

"I've been watching you for a long time, Dean, and the skills you have will give you the chance to earn wealth beyond your dreams, if you know how to use them."

I look over to Sophie. She has said nothing since we sat down and, gesturing across towards her with my chin and a simple head movement, I ask, "What does she know? What was her role in this, to set me up?"

Quickly remembering back to my first day at Harpers and Harpers and the first time that I noticed Sophie sitting on reception, being so polite and kind, fills my thoughts. I wouldn't have thought two years later we would be sitting in a room drinking champagne. Wondering if we will leave this place alive, let alone together, I take another sip of the champagne for courage, preparing to ask another question.

"So what are you guys, the police, military or gangsters?" The room goes silent from the general chit chat being heard from the women.

Nick moves back into his seat and looks across to one of the women standing talking, beckoning her over with a casual hand gesture. From the corner of my eye I see she is a stunning six foot blonde, dressed in a red skin-tight dress and matching high heels. Her long blonde hair hardly moves with all the hairspray as she walks over gracefully to Nick, swinging her hips seductively.

"Christina, can you please take Sophie home? Her work here is done for tonight," Nick instructs.

There is seriousness in his voice, as though I have hit a nerve mentioning gangsters. Sophie looks across at me with her smile long since disappeared. Her eyes are wide open, beginning to redden and fill with tears.

Feeling protective of Sophie, even though I also feel betrayed, I blast out, "I don't want her hurt, even if she knows something."

"Dean, be calm, don't worry. Sophie, dear, would you please ring Dean in the morning so he knows you are safe?" Nick speaks calmly.

I'm thinking, "How can she call me? We have not exchanged numbers yet." But after being set up maybe I don't want her to call me, my head is so confused.

"Yes, Nick, I will ring Dean in the morning." Sophie's voice has a strong nervousness to it. She looks across to me and tries to smile, but I can see she is fighting back tears.

Christina looks at me smiling, with bright red lips, and helps Sophie stand then begins to walk towards the exit door. As I watch them leave, Sophie turns around to look at me with a tear running down her cheek. Reaching the door, it is opened from the opposite side and Sophie, looking around again, quickly turns back, exiting the room and almost being pushed through the doorway by Christina. Suddenly I now feel very venerable on my own.

"So what's next?" I ask as the door closes shut, leaving me on my own.

"Now, Dean, we are going to discuss what I want from you." Nick leans forward in his seat as he is talking to me.

"Have you heard of the roulette run?" he asks.

"No. Why? Is it a game show?" I reply, trying not to laugh.

"No, Dean, it's when all the takings from the Ketton's Casino Group are transferred to the Pearson money sorting house. After the holiday weekend the money is washed before being distributed into high street banks and it will be a big payday."

"Don't tell me you're going to steal the takings!" I smirk at him as reply.

"You are everything I was expecting, Dean, clever and straight to the point," he replies. He leans closer towards me. "You are going to help us rob the money after it has been deposited." He smiles back at me.

"Me? Why me? I just work in an office; I'm not a robber," I reply back.

"What makes you think we are robbers, Dean?" Nick asks, speaking in a strong voice with his eyes wide open.

"Well, stealing a load of money from a sorting house isn't exactly a normal nine to five job, is it?" I answer, looking straight at Nick.

My champagne flute is empty and he beckons the girl over. "Alice, be a dear and bring Dean another champagne," he orders.

He leans forward even more and puts his left hand into his right inside jacket pocket. What's he going to do, pull out a gun or a knife? Just then he pulls out a big cigar tube and box of matches, placing them on the table in front. He then reaches back into the pocket and takes out a cigar cutter and places this next to the tube and matches. Nick lifts the cigar tube with his right hand and twists off the plastic cap with his left and in doing so tilts the tube and tips out a large cigar. I can smell the freshness of the tobacco as he takes the cigar in his left hand and rolls it under his nose, breathing deeply and enjoying the scent. He places the tube back on the table and lifts the cutter, now bringing both the cigar and cutter above the ashtray. In one quick action he slices the tip from the end of the cigar and replaces the cutter back on the table. He places the cigar in his mouth and with his right hand lifts the matchbox and slides the tray open. With his left hand he takes out a match and strikes it against the box with a single action and lights the cigar. Four big inhales engulf his face with smoke as he starts to enjoy the cigar.

"I'd offer you one, Dean, but I know you don't smoke," Nick announces, looking at me through a mist of smoke.

Alice brings over another champagne flute and places it on the table in front of me and looks across to me with sad eyes. She looks worried, I can sense it from her body language.

"Thank you, Alice, that will be all for tonight. Please order a taxi from outside and ensure the bill is sent here." Nick shows some compassion in his voice.

Alice smiles, turns and walks out of the room towards the door where Sophie departed from. Nick sits back in the chair, taking a large inhale from his cigar and looking at me until Alice reaches the door, passes through the doorway and closes it behind her.

Nick waits until she has left before he speaks. "Dean, I can assure you that we are not gangsters. I can't tell you who we are yet, but I will in time."

"So what happens from here, Nick?" I ask.

"Well, Dean, once you have said yes and I know that you will, we can finalise the plans. There is a lot to finish!" He flicks some ash from the cigar into the ashtray in the centre of the table between us.

"You still haven't said what I have got to do in this robbery yet, Nick," I reply back, shrugging my shoulders.

"I can tell from your questions that you are interested and you want to say yes." He smiles back at me. "You have not said no and I know you love adventure and this will certainly be an adventure from here onwards, Dean." Nick is smiling even more at me as he is speaking.

"I wouldn't class being on the run for the rest of my life, if I survive, as being an adventure," I say in a slightly raised voice.

"You won't be on the run, Dean, we are far too professional." His answer sounds as though he has done this many times before.

"Once this job is done we won't be hurting you either, if we wanted you dead it would have been three years ago when your previous company reported some of our offshore accounts to the government," he answers sharply.

Quickly thinking back three years ago, I try to remember what he is talking about as my thoughts are suddenly refreshed. I had been employed at a large law company called Bennett's. I had been working there for about twelve months and still recollect that, when sitting in the office on just another normal Thursday morning, police officers and men dressed in long black trench coats suddenly started entering the main office area with the security team. Managers and directors were rounded up like sheep through the departments and herded into the large conference room. I remember that during all this activity the office staff were just sitting at their desks and carrying on as normal as though nothing was happening. Not sitting on the senior management team then, I was lucky. Many board members and senior management were interviewed by government and police internal affairs officers over allegations of money laundering and shadow companies funding military operations units for the government.

I remember hearing a guy in the office that afternoon saying, "Well, just another day at Bennett's. I hear the old man on the board had it bad this time."

It was after this police raid that I decided to move to another company. "Three years ago, I was never involved with that investigation; I had nothing to do with it," I reply back sharply.

"Well, you seem to know about it and that's not the information I was given," he answers back with a strong pitch in his voice.

I can sense my body starting to tense and I begin to feel very uneasy. "The police raided everyone in the office, not just mine!" I quickly reply back.

"Dean, look, it's all in the past and it's good you decided to moves companies anyway." Nick speaks again with a calmer voice.

"Well I was head hunted to come and work here," I reply.

"No, Dean, I arranged for your job at Harpers and Harpers," Nick answers.

I look at Nick in shock. My head is so confused. This job with Harpers and Harpers was offered through an agency and I moved away from friends, family and someone I loved to make a new start.

"How do you know all this, Nick? Why is it so important that I am here?" I ask curiously.

Nick replies, "We need your inner skills to carry out this job we are planning and I know that you will say yes. I know you are probably confused, but we must know yes or no tonight."

My throat is dry as my heart races in my chest, full of both excitement and nervousness. "It is beginning to sound as though I don't have much of a choice!"

Confusion fills my mind over how Nick can know so much about me and what he wants from me, but deep down I think that seriously getting some cash quickly and bailing out from this shit life may be good for me. I sit there looking across at Nick and scan towards the bar at the other guys standing. The other men just stare back, either smoking a cigarette or takings sips of their drink with nervousness and tension hanging heavy in the air from these guys because Nick is asking me to join his crew. These guys look like major professionals and I'm just an office manager but the thoughts of the money and what this could do for my life fills my head with thoughts of new houses anywhere in the world, holidays, cars and most of all freedom. My thoughts start to drift, imagining what a prison cell could be like, but the thoughts of death fall into misty clouds of insignificance against being stuck in this rat run life. I have always enjoyed adventure and this is sounding like it's going to the biggest one of them all. Sometimes you have to take a risk to get what you want in life and this could be my opportunity. After what appears to be hours, and with the constant pressure being applied, I look at him and nod my head in agreement, not sure whether it's the right answer or not.

"So it's yes then, Dean?" Nick shouts out loudly with a big smile on his face, jumping to his feet.

"The man has come through. He knows what he wants. Finally the last piece is of the jigsaw is together, the clock is ticking and we have a lot to do."

Nick walks to me with his right hand extended and, now standing, we both shake hands with a strong grip feeling like I have just sold my soul to the devil but it also feels great. All the other guys walk over, shake my hand and we all make our introductions. My head is buzzing that much that I forget their names. The women walk over and kiss my cheek. I've never been so popular.

We continue to drink and talk until the early hours of the morning. I don't know why but this part of my life has been missing for such a long time and it feels so right, as my thoughts keep turning back to my last job that Nick mentioned. It was such a bad time for me, leaving people behind, making sacrifices and starting in a new place, not knowing anyone. What are these skills that Nick keeps talking about? I'm just a button pusher in an office with profit and loss accounts, nothing more. I wonder if he wants me to arrange for the money from the heist to be laundered and cleaned.

Nick then shouts over one of the men, "Lloyd, can you take Dean home? He's got a busy day tomorrow."

He looks over to me and says, "Mum's the word. We all have to trust each other here, you know what I'm saying? I'll be in touch later so we can all have a meal."

Lloyd starts to walk over. This man must be nearly seven feet tall and looks like seven feet wide, and I've never seen such a well-built man of this size before.

"Walk with me, Dean," he orders in a strong African accent.

Now I'm thinking about what will happen. Is this it? Is this when I get whacked, thrown into a car trunk and dropped off a bridge in a black bin bag? We walk down the back stairs of the club, heading towards the car park. The dawn is just starting to break and you can smell the fresh, clean air of a new day. The sunlight is just starting to reflect from the office windows, casting shadows everywhere down the city streets.

"So, Lloyd, what car have you got?" I ask.

"Audi R8, just a toy for me." His answer is short and sharp.

Reaching the carpark, at least I know I won't fit in the trunk unless they chop me up. The car unlocks automatically as we walk over towards it. It looks fantastic in highly polished gleaming black and with his license plate 'LLOYD R8'. Making my way over to the passenger side and standing by the door, I look back to see Nick staring from the balcony at us. He gives a final wave and walks back inside as I turn, looking at Lloyd on the opposite side of the car. I lower my right hand towards the door handle and click it open. The door opens with a solid built feel and my nose is filled with the scent of fresh leather from the seats and interior. Lloyd opens the driver's door and quickly slides into the seat. Fully opening the door and looking inside, the driver's side of the car appears to resemble the cockpit like something from an aircraft with dials and gauges all set into the dashboard.

Lowering myself into the seat, the coolness of the leather seeps through my clothes, touching the skin and, as I finally look across at Lloyd, the door is pulled shut with a positive sounding 'click'.

"You sure about this new guy?" a voice from inside the dark lounge says.

Nick replies angrily, "Look, Vernon, I am never wrong, just keep your focus on the job and let me deal with Dean. Anyway, we have a card in the game now and we may have to play it. You know me, I never take any chances." Nick takes a sigh. "Let's leave it for now, Dean's time will come and when it does god help anyone who's in his way."

Nick replies and turns, starting to walk back into the lounge. Nick reaches inside the lounge and looks at everyone staring at him. "Have you people not got homes to go to? It's time you were all gone. Meet here at 8 p.m. tonight." Nick starts walking straight through the lounge and down the stairs towards the main entrance.

2

Driving down the high streets of the city at dawn is a magical time as the colours of the morning sunlight are all bright and fresh, the delivery trucks dropping off newspapers, bakeries opening, and the start of a new day and what will happen next. I feel like I'm floating and not sure where I will land, never feeling like this before. I look over at Lloyd and can't believe a man of his size and strength can fit into the bucket seats of this car, let alone drive it.

I try to break the silence with him. "So how long have you known Nick? How long have you been working with him?"

He slowly turns his head towards me and stares for a few seconds and then turns his head back to carry on looking through the windscreen as he drives and says, "I've known Mr Nick for some time; he's a good boss and a strong leader who's not afraid of getting his hands dirty."

Lloyd then speaks again. "You'd die for a man like that if you had to."

I can tell that Lloyd would follow any command to the end from Nick. I want to ask him about his role in the crew, but I know he wouldn't tell me. As we leave the city limits and head towards the motorway, he suddenly opens the throttle of the Audi R8 and we explode down the on ramp of the dual carriageway like a missile and the force of the acceleration pushes me hard into the seat as the engine roars. Lloyd is driving hard and fast, passing cars on either side of the motorway and not bothering with lane markings and road laws.

"Are those flames on the road or just your tyre marks? You're certainly not hanging around, Lloyd." I speak a little nervously, trying not to upset his concentration with a slight smile.

"Enough questions for now," he snaps back.

We pull off the carriageway after one junction and continue along the road that leads to the Chelsea harbour where I live. We pass the local school, a supermarket, clothes shops and the local bars. Lloyd turns down the main road for my apartment, finding it strange that he has never asked me any directions for my address but I'm not even going to ask. It's 6 a.m. by now. Lloyd pulls up outside my apartment block. I wonder if anyone will see me getting out of this car.

"Thanks for the lift, Lloyd; I'm glad we could talk," I say sarcastically.

He just turns to me and says, "I'll pick you up at 8 p.m. tonight. Be ready. Wear a good suit, Mr Nick expects it."

Opening the door to get out of the car, Lloyd has already engaged first gear and begins to increase the revs. I climb out of the tight fitting bucket seats and, as my feet touch the pavement, I turn and 'click' the door shut as Lloyd is already starting to move away and accelerate up the street like a rocket. I watch him turn and disappear, still hearing the noise coming from the engine as he drives back towards the motorway. I turn and walk towards the lobby of the apartments. I can see Rahul, the security night man, fast asleep by the main desk. I walk over to him.

"Morning, Rahul, good dreams you having?" He nearly falls off his chair.

"Oh, oh, good morning, Mr Dean. I was just resting my eyes." He is still half asleep.

"You're going out early, sir. Or are you just coming home?" He laughs.

He is a family man, originally from Brazil, with his wife and two children now living with him. He wants to give his family the best opportunities working the night shift. He is slight built, around five feet ten inches tall, with longish, wiry hair and a small goatee beard. He is wearing a typical jobsworth private security uniform in navy blue.

"Well, that's my business," I reply to him, winking, and then ask, "Have you seen Shaun this morning?"

"No, Mr Dean, but a parcel came for you during the night," he replies, reaching under the counter to pick it up.

"A tall European man with brown hair and blue eyes delivered it, I couldn't quite tell from the accent but it sounded German and he asked me to give this to you."

"Maybe Mr Shaun stayed out too like you, Mr Dean?" he looks and laughs at me, handing me the parcel.

"Yeah, he must have. Thank you, Rahul," I answer, wondering what is inside the light brown A4 size parcel and noticing the words 'Dean Nash' written across the front in black pen.

"Where is Shaun?" I think. I look at Rahul, who is standing smiling at me. I smile back and start to walk towards the lift, touching the parcel I can tell that it feels like papers or documents. Pressing the call button for the lift, the doors open and, walking inside, I turn around and look at the control panel on the right side of the lift. I select the button for the twelfth floor and as the lift starts to move my mind is filled with thoughts of Shaun and what happened last night. After a few seconds of travelling the lift stops on the second floor and the doors open, allowing a woman to enter who then turns with her back to me and stands on the left hand side of the lift. I don't take much notice, still engrossed over last night with Nick and Sophie. Shit, what a mess. My head is buzzing and feels like I have been punched and kicked in it. The lift stops again, this time on the fifth floor, and as the doors open a man walks inside.

He stands next the woman again with his back to me and, as the doors close, I glance across to the back of their heads and something catches my eye. I notice a small earpiece in the man's ear that looks like a hearing aid but with a wire trailing down the collar of his shirt. I quickly look across and see the same device in the woman's ear and my heart suddenly starts to beat a little faster. I look again, just to make sure I'm not seeing or imagining things. After all, it's been a long night. Feeling a little delirious, I recheck but it's not my imagination. Are they here for me already? Are they police? Have I been set up? Thoughts are racing through my head. What should I do? Nothing? Lash out? Think, Dean, what should I do? Nothing has happened yet so why panic? What should I do next? I can get off at my floor and go down the stairs back to Shaun's apartment on the tenth or even escape down the exit stairs.

The woman asks the man, "Excuse me, would you mind pressing the button for the tenth? Thank you," with a strange American accent.

"Yes, no problem, that's my stop anyway," replies the man with a broken German dialect. Now I am starting to take a lot of interest.

The woman looks around forty-five years old and is smartly dressed in a black two piece suit. She has a hard face and dark hair and eyes. She is around five feet six inches tall, slim built with just enough make up to cover her age. The man is around six feet tall with a sharply cut suit and a figure that looks quite athletic. He has a balding head and well weathered face with lots of wrinkles and a slightly tanned complexion, around fifty years of age. My mind is in overtime; I'm thinking these must be government agents, police or something like that. The lift stops at the tenth floor and the doors open. I have to stay in the lift otherwise it will look strange since I had already pressed twelve and it would look wrong if I got out sooner. Are they going to see Shaun to question him about me? Is Shaun back at home? Was Rahul wrong? Who knows? Shaun is a mate, but self-preservation is what's filling my mind and at this moment and it's starting to take full priority. I decide to go back to my place. I'll try ringing Shaun on his cell to warn him, hoping he is still out somewhere.

Watching the man and woman walk out of the lift, I hear their footsteps echoing in the silent corridor as the lift doors close and then I take my cell from the right trouser pocket. I lift it up towards my face, looking at the screen. No signal, that's strange. The lift stops at the twelfth floor. The doors open. I lift my head, looking through the open doors to check the corridor to my apartment is clear. Nothing seems out of place so, taking a step forward, I quickly glance to the right then left with everything usual. Completely out of the lift, the doors close behind and the mechanical noise of the lift starting to disappear down shaft can be heard. I start to walk along the well-lit corridor towards my apartment at the end and, still holding the envelope now tucked under my left arm. I think about whether the man and woman are near to Shaun's apartment, or are they heading back towards mine, was it a trick? I recheck the cell. Still no signal. My heart is starting to beat faster. I reach my apartment door and, placing the key into the lock, I start to turn the key with my heart beating so fast it feels like it will fall out of my exploding chest.

My mind starts to think about whether anyone is the other side of the door. I slowly turn the handle downwards as the locks 'click' open and I push the door inwards. The morning sunshine can be seen reflecting onto the white marble floor tiles. I continue to push the door fully open and walk through the doorway, trying not to make any sound. Fully inside the room my head is so dizzy, making me feel sick and faint with excitement all in the same time as I turn close the door behind, continuing to walk into the apartment towards the front room. Dropping the keys and envelope onto the glass topped coffee table, thinking that if there was someone in the apartment it might startle them, I have my cell in my right hand and looking again at the screen it still has no signal. Beginning to walk around the apartment to see if anything is out of place or missing, I check pictures, drawers, cupboards and even the position of the furniture. I'm starting to feel so paranoid. Walking back into the main room, I head towards the large bi-fold doors that lead onto the outside balcony and as I reach the doors I unlock them and push them open, allowing the fresh morning air and glorious sunshine to float into the apartment. I walk outside onto the balcony and look at the landscape around. What a great view. That's why I live in this place.

I can hear the birds singing and I take some deep breaths of the morning air. It feels so good and refreshing. My head is full from last night and everything that happened. I keep thinking about Nick and what he was talking about and can see him in my mind saying these words again and again. Suddenly the silence of the morning is broken by the sound of sirens in the distance heading towards this area. My heart sinks. I take a deep swallow. They must be here for me, what do I do? Where do I go? The sirens are getting louder and louder. I look over the balcony and see two police cars roaring down the street towards the apartment block. What do I do? That is the question. Just sit here and wait for them? Or do I run? I haven't done anything yet and besides, it's too late now, they would catch me. No, I will wait and see what happens. I will tell them nothing, since I have done nothing yet. Just then, *knock-knock* on the apartment door. Shit, this is it. What do I do? My heart is beating so fast it feels like it going to burst. *Knock, knock* again.

I turn and decide to face the music and see who it is. I walk in from the balcony and head towards the apartment door. My head feels so fuzzy and light with my heart beating so fast. The focus of my eyes seems blurry, with stars and halos around objects as I pass through the front room, placing the cell on my coffee table. I reach the door and start to lift the door handle with my hands shaking from the amount of adrenaline rushing through my body.

I ask, "Who is it?" Silence. Suddenly police cars can be heard outside and officers start shouting instructions to people to clear the area.

Just then, a familiar voice from the other side of my apartment door! "It's Rahul, Mr Dean – don't be worried, police have found an illegal immigrant on the ninth floor, and I'm just telling everyone."

There seems to be nervousness in his voice that is unusual for him. My pulse starts to slow down and, placing my hand on the door handle, I pull the door open to see Rahul's face sending a comforting emotion.

"Thanks, Rahul. Thanks for letting me know." I sigh with relief.

"I tell you first, Mr Dean, I know you are a good man." He smiles at me.

My mind replays the words 'yes' coming from Nick's mouth and then if only you knew a few hours ago what I was doing. Smiling back at Rahul he turns and walks away down the corridor to the stairway. I watch him disappear then, after closing the door, I turn and walk back into the living room, starting to wonder how Rahul had managed to walk up twelve flights of stairs, getting my apartment first? Was he tipped off? Did he tell on the immigrant? There are so many thoughts in my head I don't know if they are real or imaginary. I continue to walk back outside to the balcony just as the two people from the lift are walking out of the apartment block towards one of the waiting police cars with another woman handcuffed in front of them. She is walked to one of the other police cars as a police officer opens the passenger rear door and then manhandles her inside. The door is closed and as she sits in the back seat I look through the door window at a complete loss for words. My throat goes dry imagining myself in that situation soon enough if we get caught in this robbery.

My mind is full of what ifs. What if I die? What if we get caught? What if we escape, where will I go? What will I do?

I try to clear these thoughts from my mind with the focus turning to the envelope and what could be inside. Sitting on the dark brown settee, I reach with my left hand, lifting the package and with my right unpeeling the top flap. Once the flap is opened I tip the contents of the envelope onto the top of my clear glass coffee table with all different pictures and photographs appearing. I start to shuffle them around and try to arrange them into something of an order with pictures from last night when Sophie and I were kissing on the dance floor in Nick's club. One picture shows Shaun and me last year when we went on a motorbike trip around Europe and a few pictures of me from Vietnam three years ago on holiday. There are pictures of my family and friends when I was growing up and pictures of someone I once loved, bringing back memories of why I had to leave her and move to work here in the city.

There are pictures from when I went to school with classmates and other pictures of people who I don't know but somehow seem so familiar, like long lost relatives you see at weddings or funerals. Continuing to shuffle through the pictures one shows a military unit and from the clothes and guns it looks like it is from the Second World War and a few pictures from the 1950s judging by the clothes, with couples sitting around a large dining table at a dinner dance. I am looking at photographs of couples holding babies that appear to be from the 1960s and 1970s with young children in playgrounds and parks wearing clothes from that era. Nothing seems to register in my head instantly, but I seem to sense some history from all of these photographs. My head seems so full and confused; it feels like it will explode. These past few days have been like a whirlwind of emotions in my head, with feelings and thoughts that I wished had gone forever but all these pictures have relit the fire inside me and things that have been done in the past.

My cell starts to ring and vibrate on the top of the coffee table, resonating through the glass. This must be Sophie after Nick instructed her to call me. I pick up the cell from the coffee table and look whose number is on the screen. Seeing 'number withheld' I decide to answer the call and push the answer button.

"Hello."

"Where the hell did you get to last night, fella, you must have had a good night, hey?" Shaun's reassuring voice is heard.

Thank god. I sigh in relief and it feels like a great weight has just been lifted from my shoulders.

"Hey up, Shaun. Yeah, had a great night," I reply, not acting concerned.

"We got lost in the club. Sophie and I ended up stopping in the VIP lounge," I say.

"Well, I managed to lose all three of them and went home with Kelly. Anyway, I saw Chloe on Thursday and have had my fun with her this week." He is laughing.

"So you and Sophie? You kept that quiet, pal, you are a dark horse. What other skeletons do you have in cupboards?"

If only you knew, I am thinking. I pretend to laugh and humour him.

"You know me, I keep my business private," I reply, laughing.

"You little beauty. Catch you later, pal. Got to go, Kelly is calling." He rings off.

I put the cell down and walk to the kitchen. I lift the kettle from its base holder and take it over to the tap and fill it with water then turn and place it back on the base holder, clicking on the power switch. I'm still thinking about how someone has taken all those photographs with me not seeing them. I decide to go at take a shower, freshen up and see what happens next. Walking from the kitchen into the bathroom, I click the light switch that automatically operates the extraction fan and walk back into the bedroom. I begin to remove my clothes firstly by unbuttoning my shirt then sitting on the bed and leaning forward. The shoelaces are untied and my black shoes are removed. Taking off my socks, I stand and unzip my trousers and finally, after climbing out of my underwear, I look at myself in the mirror, thinking how much I look like shit not having a shave and my hair a mess. I need to hit the gym this week, but with all my work at the moment it's going to be tough.

I step into the shower, close the door and switch on the hot water tap. Standing in the shower, the warm water hits my body and it feels so relaxing, it feels like the constant stream of water is washing away all the problems and the warm moist steam feels so refreshing. Reaching for the shower gel bottle with my right hand, I squeeze some liquid onto my left hand and start to wash my body. The gel starts to lather and I can see it running from my body down the drain hole in the bottom of the shower cubical. I start to wash off the remaining lather and then *knock, knock, knock*. Was that someone at the door or just me? I feel so paranoid at the moment, anything could be true or not. *Knock, knock, knock.* No, it must be someone at the door. Who is this? Maybe the police? Maybe Rahul again? Maybe Shaun?

I switch off the shower, open the cubical door and grab the closest bath towel. I dry myself off quickly and then wrap it around my waist.

"Just a minute," I shout.

Walking from the bathroom through the apartment to the front door, I reach and ask, "Who is it?"

A soft voice the other side of the door confirms, "It's me. Can I come in? I so want to see you."

I pause and wait, one part of me wants to see her so much too and hold her, kiss her, but the another part of me wants to shout 'get lost and leave me alone'. After a few seconds I decide it would be best to speak to her and understand her part in this plan and why she has set me up.

"Okay," I say, starting to open the door.

As the door opens I can smell her perfume drifting through the doorway and wanting to see her so much even after what happened overflows my emotions and being set up last night disappears with her presence calming me. With the door fully open I look at her standing in the doorway wearing a pair of tight jeans, red high heels and red casual top slightly hanging off her right shoulder. She looks so good after this morning. Her blue, piercing eyes are wide open and slightly red and I can tell she has been crying. Her wavy brown hair glows in the morning sunshine and standing to one side I allow her to pass into my apartment, not really being surprised that she knows where I live. She smiles as I walk past and close the door behind her. We continue through into the living room.

I gesture at the settee, saying, "Take a seat. I thought you were just going to call me today?"

"You know I just couldn't do that, Dean. I want to try and explain to you what happened." She has a quiver in her voice and she is shaking slightly, not quite looking me in the eyes.

"I know what happened, Sophie, you befriended me and tricked me," I snap sharply at her. I sit down opposite her on one of the other settees.

"No, Dean, that's not quite right. It wasn't my intention." She looks at me with a tear rolling down her left cheek.

"Is that so? Well, it felt and looked like that," I say to her, shaking my head.

"Please, Dean, let me explain. I did want to go with you last night to the club. God, I wish now we hadn't. I really enjoyed our time together and wish we had gone before ending up in the back room." There is a lot of upset in her voice, but I still feel as though I've been set up.

Starting to calm my voice, I say to her, "So how do you know Nick? That would be a good start."

48

Sophie then starts to explain. "About two years ago my friend Alicia had been in a relationship for a few years with a guy called Keith who was very jealous and would violently abuse her. When Alicia finally split up with Keith, Alicia and I started to go out at weekends and one night we were out having drinks when we first met Nick. So we started to meet Nick and his friends every week for a few drinks and we all became good friends over a couple of months." Tears start to fill in her eyes. I lean forward slightly in my seat. I feel a little guilty now but still don't know if it's a show.

Sophie continues, "One night I let it slip accidentally to Nick about Alicia and how she had been abused by Keith. She still fears that Keith may come back and how unsafe she felt. Nick promised to solve the problem so Alicia would never have any more trouble again and she would always be safe." Sophie looks straight at me with her blue eyes all red and swollen with tears running down her cheeks.

"I assume that Nick would just try to scare Keith off with a few hired helpers. Hey, or arrange for Keith to have a good kicking?" I reply back.

Sophie starts to cry, her voice is all crackly and difficult to hear. "No, far worse than that. A few days later Keith went missing. Nick arranged to meet both Alicia and me in one of his bars. He then started to tell us the story of what they did to Keith it was terrible, and I feel sick just thinking what he told us."

"So what did he do to Keith?" I ask.

I was curious to see what Nick was like and what I had let myself in for.

Sophie explains, "Well, Nick told us that some of his guys went around to Keith's house, threw him into the boot of a car and took him to the local forest where they started to beat him and kick him."

I look at Sophie, shaking with fear as she goes on to explain, "During the kicking Keith's heart must have stopped and he died out in the forest. So Nick and his mates arranged for him to have a car accident.

"Nick just turned to us both and said, 'I don't think Keith will worry you anymore, the foxes will feed well tonight'.

"Through all of this Nick was just laughing. I couldn't believe it," Sophie said.

I look at her. Not fully sure what to feel but sensing she needs some comforting, I lean over, giving her a big hug. It feels so good to hold her and can feel her body shaking with her crying. I could tell then that it wasn't a story. What type of man would tell two women about something like that? What I had got myself into?

"So what happened with the police after Keith was killed? Surely there was an investigation into a person killed and with Alicia being his ex-partner she would have been questioned?" I ask.

"That is the strange thing. There has never been anything. I know Keith was a single child and both his parents where dead so I guess not," answers Sophie.

"Yes, but with both of you hearing that you could be linked into the murder as accomplices?" I look at her.

Sophie places her head by my neck and kisses it, and then she whispers, "Yeah, I know, but now you know why I couldn't say no to Nick."

"What do you mean?" I ask.

Sophie says, "I was out shopping a few weeks ago and saw Nick. I had not seen him for about eighteen months since Alicia and I cut all contact after they had killed Keith. We got talking and he was asking how work was and if I had met someone as though nothing had happened. I mentioned work was going well and that I quite liked you. When I said your name his eyes changed from calm and collected to that of fear, which I had never seen in him before."

I lean back slightly and, with amazement, say, "Fear? Why? I haven't met him before last night!"

"Well, all I can say is that once I mentioned I knew you he completely altered. There is something he is worried about, I could tell he seemed shocked that I knew you and he made a hasty goodbye," Sophie replies as she looks at me.

"Strange. I can't get my head around these past two days. Something is in the back of my mind but I can't put a finger on it," I answer.

"So did we go to that club because you knew Nick was the owner?" I ask Sophie.

"No. Far from it, a friend at work gave me the tickets and if I knew Nick owned it I wouldn't have gone there," she answers.

Standing up I say, "I know you're enjoying the view but it's a bit cool this morning and I need to put on a few clothes." I look at her, smiling, and she smiles back.

"The water has just boiled if you want to make a drink?" I say, pointing at the kitchen.

"Okay, I'll make a drink," she replies.

Walking from the front room through my apartment to my bedroom, Sophie can be heard in the kitchen opening and closing cupboard doors and drawers. I hear the sound of two coffee mugs being placed onto the work surface then the noise of the kettle being switched on. I open my wardrobe door and flick through the rail of clothes, selecting a pair of shorts and polo shirt then, walking through into my en suite bathroom, I change and walk back through into the living room just as Sophie places the drinks on the coffee table and suddenly notices the pictures.

The top picture is from last night when we were kissing in Nick's club. I see her pick up the picture just as I reach her. "Where's that come from?" she asks sharply.

"I don't know, I got back this morning and all these pictures and photographs had been delivered overnight," I reply, shrugging my shoulders.

Sophie sits on the right side of the three piece settee and I sit at the left side of her. She starts to pick up all the pictures and starts to look through them.

"Who are all these people? Where are all these pictures from?" she sounds surprised, looking at me.

"I honestly don't know, Sophie; I was just starting to look through them when you arrived. One thing I do know is that some of the pictures are of friends and family, so it must be someone who knows me."

We continue to look through the pictures, talking and drinking our coffee. I slide a couple of pictures over to Sophie. "I'm not sure of all the pictures, but some seem so familiar."

I pull out certain other pictures, such as the army pictures, the pictures of young couples with babies, and the photographs of people in parks with young children.

"Why has someone given these to you, Dean?" Sophie asks.

"I don't know, Sophie, but they must mean something and I must find out what," I answer.

I start to collect the pictures together and put them back into the envelope and place it back onto the coffee table. We then start to discuss last night and what happened at the club between us and how good it felt. It feels like a part of me that was dead is starting to come back alive, an inner warmth when you know you have met someone special. I lean towards her and place my arms around her waist and she does the same to me. We hold each other again and start to kiss. The taste of her lipstick and tongue in my mouth feels so fantastic. Her lips feel so soft and her tongue is so gentle in my mouth and mine in hers. I can feel my body start to warm and feel myself starting to get aroused. I lower my left hand and place it on her left leg and start to stroke her thigh. My other hand is still around her waist. I lift my right hand and place it next to her neck beginning to caress it. I can sense her starting to relax and become aroused and can hear her quietly moaning with pleasure. We continue to kiss more and more intensely as my pulse starts to rise. We start to rub each other's bodies together. Suddenly Sophie stops kissing me and tries to lean away from me. I stop caressing her neck and pull away from her mouth.

Sophie looks at me. "Dean, I must stop before we do something, I'm not ready yet, I feel too constricted. Please stop, it's too soon for me. It's not you, it's me and talking this morning I just feel too vulnerable. Dean, I must go, I have so many things to do, but I will call you later."

Sophie is already standing and is trying to make her way to the door. I can tell she wants to get out of my apartment as soon as possible. It feels like I have been set up again.

I stand up from the settee in complete shock saying. "Yeah, I understand, don't worry."

Sophie reaches the door with me following, and lifts her left hand out to grab the door handle. She turns her head over her right shoulder, looks at me, smiles and says, "Dean, I like you so much. I want to see you again soon, please give me a little time."

"Look, it's fine. Don't worry," I reply, feeling deflated.

I am not sure how to feel, with one big part of me wanting to sleep with her and another big part saying it's not the right time. I feel so used and abused, both with last night and today. Sleeping with her might have made me feel better to begin with, but I don't think I can trust her yet and trust is very important to me. I smile back at her as she open the door, still looking at me and beginning to walk through the doorway.

Reaching the door, I watch her start to walk down the corridor to the direction of the lift and, as she presses the control button, so she turns back to me saying. "Goodbye, Dean, I will see you soon, promise."

I look back at her, smiling. She smiles back and at that point I know she is lying. The feeling of betrayal makes me feel cold inside, tying my stomach into knots. The lift doors open and Sophie walks inside and like that she is gone and the feeling of loss begins to take over. Closing the front door, I walk through my apartment towards the balcony and watch her walking out of the apartment block along the street. She casually glances back towards the building but knowing she can't see me gives some form of defence as my feelings inside keep giving me mixed signals of loss and comfort. Maybe I'm too soft and having someone else back in my life who looks as though they will hurt me again instantly builds invisible barriers of self-defence against being hurt with a lack of trust and honesty. Sophie continues walking until she reaches the top of the street and turns left. Just as she reaches the corner a black Mercedes with tinted windows drives past the end of the street in the same direction that Sophie has just walked. A coincidence maybe.

My head is so full of last night, this morning and Sophie. Walking back into the front room, I make my way over to the Denon Micro Stereo and switch it on. Opening the CD drawer, I turn to my right, looking at the racks that hold the CD collection. I start from the top and look through the vast range of music choice from rock, dance, soul, classical, easy listening and some chart compilations. I prefer to buy CDs as they are more personal than a download from the internet. Finally deciding to listen to some Moby, I remove the sleeve from the rack with my right hand. Unclipping the cover, the disc is taken out and placed on the drawer of the player and the close button on the stereo is pressed, followed by play.

The sound starts to emit from the speakers and, deciding it's too loud, I turn the volume down slightly. The sleeve is returned back to the rack in its original place as I walk towards the settee. I decide to try and rest so hopefully listening to the

54

music can help me to relax and take my mind off things. Stretching out along the settee with my head on one of the cushions, the music starts to send a calming influence and makes me close my eyes and start to picture the events from the last twenty-four hours, starting from seeing Sophie, Nick and Shaun. The pictures from the envelope begin to appear, playing in my head like a film as I fall asleep.

3

Meanwhile, in a dimly lit government committee room, a team of anti-terrorist agents including Special Branch, British Secret Service, the home secretary's assistant, military intelligence (MI6) and Interpol are currently being briefed over an urgent report of a possible terrorism situation unfolding from intelligence information being gathered. In the centre of the room are twenty dark red leather covered chairs encircled around a large dark brown oval table. Above the table are a series of round lights suspended from the ceiling on long white cables. The table has green leather writing pads by each of the seating positions with bottles of water and stacks of glasses in the centre. The plain white walls are covered in large city maps of London, Manchester, Birmingham, Liverpool, Scotland and the South along with maps of Europe, Russia, China, and America on a complete global map.

The room has a deep musty old smell from the thick dark green Axminster carpet, but new air fresheners have been used to try and hide the aroma after weeks of being closed. Standing at the head of the table is Intelligence Director John Wagstaff who finished his military career at the rank of colonel after having his left leg blown off during a sweep and clear exercise in the first gulf war. Now at nearly sixty years old he is one of the world's experts in counter intelligence used to combat terrorism and has contacts all over the world following his years of army intelligence through Northern Island along with the Falklands and Bosnian campaigns. He supported gathering intelligence before the first invasions for the gulf war and helped America after the Twin Towers terrorist attacks. Standing smartly dressed, he starts the meeting with seriousness in his strong Scottish accent.

"Okay, people, good morning. I will be fast over today's briefing, so listen as I will not be repeating myself. US intel has information over a possible hostage situation that could be happening in the next two to four weeks in the UK." Wagstaff speaks confidently and calmly, looking around the table of people.

"So has anyone around the table got clear intel as to who the group could be responsible for this action and if it is home based or overseas threat?" There is complete silence from everyone.

Wagstaff looks across the team of agents and with a single deep sigh suddenly shouts across at everyone.

"Are you trying to tell me that there is a potential threat to the UK and we have absolutely no idea about who is behind it?" Wagstaff stares at the people sitting around the large conference table.

The agents sitting around are just looking at each other, speechless. George Hastings, the home secretary's assistant and old tie friend from Oxford University, speaks out in a posh English voice with a smile on his face.

"How real is this information from the US? It could be a hoax you know, old boy,"

Wagstaff leans over the table and screams, "Look, Hastings all the people sitting around this table take any form of intel pretty fucking seriously and I don't like your loose attitude. But to confirm this intel information let's speak to the US directly."

Hastings sinks back into his seat with the smile disappeared and some red blushing showing around his face. Wagstaff leans over to his desk telephone and lifts the receiver, places it to his ear and mouth, staring at Hastings with seriousness in his face, he says, "Amanda, please could you secure a hard line and transfer a call through to CIA headquarters? Langley Virginia, I would like to speak to Deputy Director Vincent Adams."

"Yes, Mr Wagstaff, transferring you immediately," replies Amanda, Wagstaff's assistant.

Wagstaff is holding the receiver in his hand and is looking around the table of people and you can tell he is furious and Hastings's words haven't helped.

The phone goes quiet for a few seconds, then an American lady's voice is heard on the line. "Transferring you now, sir," The phone buzzes.

"Good evening Vincent, how are you? How are things in the US?" asks Wagstaff calmly.

Vincent replies, "Well, good morning, John. It's a dark, late night over here, but I'm always glad to hear your voice. How are you this morning?" replies Adams in a strong American accent

Wagstaff replies immediately. "Vincent, I am just holding a briefing with the UK intelligence team over intel received from the US this morning and the connection over possible hostage situations in the UK, can I transfer you to speaker phone?"

"Yes, John, no problem," replies Adams.

Wagstaff flicks the switch for the speaker phone and places the receiver back onto the main set.

"Can you hear okay, Vincent?" asks Wagstaff.

"Yes, you are loud and clear, buddy. Okay, earlier this morning we received intel from one of our agents that there could be a possible terrorist action in the UK. We have no clear intel as to which group could be responsible or from where they are based, but we don't believe that they are Middle or Far East origins. Our agent believes that it could be a possible European based group," replies Adams.

"Vincent, are you at liberty to disclose where this intel has come from or is it classified from you side?" asks Wagstaff.

"John, unfortunately at this time I can't give you the name or location of the source due to the depth and intelligence operations we are working on, but we have been using this source for a few years now and all previous intel that has been passed to ourselves has been positive," replies Adams.

"Vincent, we have the home secretary's assistant here, along with Special Branch and MI6. We must brief the PM over this threat immediately. If we can't find who this group is, we may require additional information and support from the CIA and your source, can you confirm if requested what the US stance will be?" Wagstaff has nervousness in his voice.

"John, I will need to check security clearance from the White House through Homelands and whether the president will allow the transfer of information. We have undercover agents based deep within terrorist factions around the world and these personnel could be compromised. I don't see that additional support will be a problem, but I will need to ensure clearance is given," Adams replies with softness in his voice.

Wagstaff, still standing, leans closer to the speaker. "Vincent, I fully understand and, as you know, all the team here, including myself, will be asked questions and we will need the answers quickly. Are you at liberty to tell us if the intel has come from our Inter Agency Task Forces (IATF), or has the intel come from a US based black ops team?"

Adams coughs to clear his voice. "John, all I can tell you at this stage is that the intel has not come from the IATF team, but I can't comment as to where the intel has come from. We have already checked all the IATF teams and no agents have reported any advancement in terrorist factions, so this threat is new and from a new group."

Wagstaff leans back slightly. "Vincent, thanks for the intel and if anything else appears please send what you can immediately. And obviously the PM will no doubt be in touch with the president once we have updated him. I will keep in touch with you personally over this matter as always."

Wagstaff remains quiet as Adams replies, "John, will do my best for you, old buddy, and will keep the lines of communication open with the transfer of what we can when we can. Speak soon, goodbye." Adams rings off.

Wagstaff clicks off the intercom speakerphone and then with his deep strong voice says, "Well, people, you have just heard that we may have a possible terrorist group that could be acting in Europe and we know nothing about it. The biggest problem here is that we only have two to four weeks to find out who they are. Do I need to tell any one of you what we need to do and how fast we need to get things moving?"

John looks across at MI6. Both men are in there early thirties with grey suits, typical agent looking with sharp eyes and brown hair, clean cut and shaven.

"Gentlemen, I recommend that all airports, train stations, ferry harbours and border crossings are placed on high alert immediately, with full restricted access. Official procedures recommend that you start background checks on all ground staff, maintenance teams, security, catering companies etc. along with any delivery staff, ensuring that one hundred percent security checking and verification starts."

Wagstaff then looks across at the two inspectors from Interpol, a man and a woman. The woman is in her early thirties and well-dressed, slightly tanned and well built. The man is a section chief and in his early forties, slightly scruffily dressed. Wagstaff has had issues in the past with Interpol's lack of information and lack of dynamic reaction time.

He smiles across at them and says calmly but very firmly, "Well, you lot haven't done much to help the campaign so far. You should be the first to know about any European activities, so if you have no idea about this new group, you had better collect some intel from whatever source you need to get it as soon as possible. I am not impressed with this lazy, unorganised approach."

He looks across to Hastings and says, "Hastings, do you want to brief the home secretary over this possible situation or shall the expert do it?"

Hastings looks up and, in a weak submissive voice, says, "I can brief the home secretary and the PM, sir. I can see you have plenty of other things to do."

Wagstaff starts to walk around the table, smiling. "Well, finally the Whitehall boys have grown some balls. You see, people, miracles happen every day, even in front of your eyes."

The meeting concludes and everyone leaves the room apart from a man and woman. Wagstaff walks to his chair and sits behind the large table desk, leaning back with his hands behind his slightly balding head with his two agents standing close by.

"Preston, you and Wilson both start to investigate some of our old contacts to see which unit boys are still active at the moment and where."

"Yes, sir, no problem. Who do you think is the best to start with?" Preston asks in a strong, masculine London accent.

Just then Amanda rushes into the room, breaking the heavy atmosphere with the look of shock on her face. She leans over towards Wagstaff and whispers in his left ear. The change on his face along with the look of horror don't need much adding together.

Wagstaff takes a deep breath and, taking a sigh of disbelief, says, "Well, Amanda, I was hoping not to hear that name, but deep down was half expecting it! Okay, Amanda, that is all for today."

Amanda walks out of the room.

Preston and Wilson lean forward with eagerness on their faces as Wagstaff continues. "Start with Burns."

"Burns, sir?" Wilson asks sharply.

"Wilson, we are possibly coming under a terrorist attack and we haven't got any ideas who could be behind it, but Burns may be our only source of information. We are sitting here like lost ducks on the water and with the forthcoming G8 summit around the corner, along with the Taliban breathing down our necks, Burns may be our best option at the minute."

Wagstaff continues, "Start a trace on his known accomplices and if we are lucky, something may come off."

"Sir, we always track a few of his old team, but there are a few new boys around town at the moment." Wilson speaks in a calmer feminine voice.

"Burns could be our best friend or worst enemy so be careful and report back as soon as possible." Wagstaff looks back at Wilson.

Preston speaks. "Burns has been talking to a new guy called Nash, but I can't find anything on the records for this person."

"Hmm, that's interesting. Well, maybe we had better speak with Mr Nash first, make an introduction to find out who he is, hey!" Wagstaff coughs.

"Okay, sir." Preston and Wilson both leave the room looking at each other.

Wagstaff leans forward in the chair and, muttering to himself, can be heard saying, "Burns, of all the people to ask for help at this time?"

Buzz, buzz, buzz. As my cell vibrates on the glass coffee table, it takes me a few seconds to wake, slightly confused, not fully knowing where I am and what time is it with the music long since stopped. The wall clock reads 7.15 p.m. and, suddenly remembering that Lloyd is collecting me up soon, I sit up on the settee and lean towards the coffee table to reach the cell, just as it starts to vibrate again. *Buzz, buzz, buzz.* Picking up the cell with my right hand, the screen displays 'number withheld'. I don't normally answer withheld numbers, but in the present circumstances you never know who it is.

"Hello," I say, still half asleep and feeling a little groggy.

"You have not forgotten dinner tonight, Dean?" the voice asks.

"No, Lloyd, not at all. Just getting ready now!"

"Will be outside at 8 p.m. prompt," Lloyd commands.

"Yes, no problem, just deciding on which suit to wear. I will be downstairs."

Lloyd knows from the tone in my voice I'm lying. God, I must have been out for hours and not woken up. Walking from the living room towards the bedroom, I open the bedroom door and continue inside towards the direction of the wardrobe and opening the left side door, I begin to flick through my clothes, looking for my Hugo Boss mid grey suit. Lifting it from the rail and placing it neatly on the bed, I turn back and continue to flick through the clothes until my light blue dress shirt is found and lifted from the wardrobe and lowered onto the bed next to the suit just to check the colour matches. Finally a pair of black shoes are lifted from the shoe rack and placed next to the bed. Selecting some underwear and socks from the drawers, the socks are placed next to the shoes and I walk into the en suite bathroom carrying the underwear and switch on the light with my left hand as the extractor fan starts with a faint buzzing noise. Removing the polo shirt and shorts, the underwear is pulled on and then turning, placing my hands each side of the sink rim, I stare at myself in the large dressing mirror hanging above the sink with my light brown eyes looking back, clearly seeing I need a shave and quick wash.

Switching on the hot water tap and closing the plug, I reach for the shaving foam from the shelf then I shake the tin as the sink begins to fill. Shaving foam is sprayed into the palm of my right hand and the tin is returned to the shelf and the water turned off as steam begins to rise from the warm water. The foam is applied to my face with both hands and the remains washed off in the warm water. Reaching to the right for my cut throat razor blade, I start to shave whilst looking at myself in the mirror and can feel the blade cutting through the hairs and brushing against the skin on my face. After each stroke with the razor, I dip it into the water to wash off the excess foam and cut hairs. Finally finishing around my chin, the shaver is rinsed off and replaced back into the holder. Lowering my face closer to the sink full of warm water, the excess shaving foam is rinsed from my face and then, reaching for the hand towel hanging at the side of the sink with the right hand, my face is dried. After falling asleep my hair clearly needs some hair gel and, reaching for the gel tube on the surface, some gel is squeezed onto the palm of my right hand. I can feel the coolness of the gel against my skin as the tube is placed back on the surface counter.

Rubbing the gel between both my hands, I apply it to my dark brown hair while looking into the mirror and I spike my hair slightly just to get the right look. Next the deodorant spray tin is shaken and blasted under each armpit, filling the bathroom with scent. Taking a short breath, I cough slightly and then look through the different makes of aftershave, deciding that some Prada is suitable for tonight. Again using my right hand I depress the plunger that sprays some aftershave on my face. The aftershave stings the skin on my freshly shaven face then, picking up my polo shirt and shorts, I walk back into the bedroom. Looking through the window of my bedroom, the evening sunshine changes the sky all different colours from purple, pink and red as the sun lowers behind the apartment buildings.

What a fantastic sight, something you can't buy no matter how much money you have. Thinking about if you can see the sun rise and set every day you are having a good day no matter how bad it is. Thoughts suddenly slip to how much I miss friends and family that have died and that would never share this time again. Placing the polo shirt and shorts on a chair by the side of the wardrobe, I lift the shirt from the bed. I check the time on the clock. I see that it's 7.45 p.m., better get a move on sliding my arms into the shirt and beginning to button it up. The suit is lifted from the bed and the jacket and trousers taken from the hanger. Pulling on the trousers, I reach across to the bedside cabinet for my belt and pass it through the loops on my trousers and fasten it. Now sitting on the bed, my feet are slipped into the shoes and the laces tied. Finally standing again, the jacket is pulled on as I walk over towards the large mirror in my bedroom by the wardrobe door and look at myself up and down, checking the cut of my suit and how much I enjoy looking smart and not bad for a guy getting close to forty and that gym work certainly keeps me in shape.

Walking from the bedroom into the living room, I make my way to the coffee table, lifting the cell with my left and keys with my right from the glass surface and placing them in my jacket pockets. Finally I lift my wristwatch up from the table with my right hand and click it around my left wrist. I look at the face and see the Omega logo, remembering the sentimental reason behind why it is worn. Reaching the balcony, a car engine roaring can be heard in the distance with the time on my watch reading 7.58 p.m., so this must be Lloyd en route. Back in the living room the bi-fold doors for the balcony are closed and locked shut and, as I walk towards the front door, the envelope of pictures is noticed still on the coffee table. Reaching the coffee table, the envelope is picked up with my right hand and taken over to one of the drawers in the sidewall cabinet for safe storage. The drawer is opened then closed with my left hand as my cell starts to vibrate in my pocket. Reaching the door, it's opened with my right hand as the cell stops ringing. Walking through the doorway into the corridor, my keys are taken from the left jacket pocket and the door is closed and locked. Placing the keys back in my pocket, I take out my cell and see that Shaun has been trying to ring me.

Starting to make my way down the corridor towards the lifts, I press the button activating the return call as the cell is lifted to my right ear. The ringing can be heard, then the sound of a familiar voice. "Hey up, fella, how you doing? Where the hell have you been all day?" he asks.

"Sorry, mate, I have been busy today with one thing and another," I reply.

"Busy, I take it, with Sophie, hey fella?" Shaun asks, laughing.

"Told you before, mate, I keep my business private," I say, laughing back.

"Fair do, fella, what you up to later?" Shaun asks.

"I am just on the way out Shaun; I have some business on as you do!"

"That's a shame, fella, I was feeling lucky tonight," he laughs,

"You always feel lucky, Shaun. If anything changes I will let you know," I reply.

"Okay, fella, no problems. I will be out somewhere." Shaun rings off.

The lift arrives and the doors open. I enter the lift and press the lobby button. The doors of the lift close and it starts to move downwards. As I'm standing there I'm thinking about tonight and what will be happening. The lift reaches the lobby and the doors open. I walk out of the lift just as Lloyd roars up outside. I walk through the lobby, past the main desk and towards the doors to see Lloyd's car parked outside. I reach the car just as a black Mercedes drives past with tinted windows, looking very familiar to the same car from this morning when Sophie left my apartment. It drives past but I can't see who is inside as I stare across to it, it's traveling at a slow speed as though they are looking for something or maybe someone. In the late summer evening sunshine the light glistens over the polished black bodywork of the car and reflects from the tinted windows.

I open the door and, climbing inside, Lloyd snaps, "You okay, man? I never thought you were going to open the door."

"Sorry, Lloyd, I keep seeing a black Merc, it's just drove past," I reply.

"Yeah, man, I've just seen it, but we haven't got time to see who it is, Mr Nick requests us so we must go," he replies almost like a robot.

I get into the car and we blast off down the street in the same direction that the Merc had just travelled. My head starts to fill with the excitement of what tonight will bring. What's going to happen? Who will be there? The biggest question in my head is who left the pictures for me, and why? Thoughts then move towards the black Merc car and who is inside and how long it has been following me. We fly down the carriageway like a missile with the faint glow of the city lights in the distance. Lloyd doesn't seem concerned over speed limits and traffic laws at all and just cuts from the left to the right across all the lanes of the dual carriageway, using it like his own personal racetrack. I look across at Lloyd and you can see the intenseness in his face as he is concentrating with his driving, but you can also see a smile on his face that he is enjoying it so much. Suddenly he turns the wheel to the right and starts to blast down the off ramp. As we reach the end of the ramp Lloyd presses the brakes and I lean forward in the seat as the energy is absorbed in the brakes.

We turn off the deceleration ramp and continue towards the city. It feels like we are leaving a past life behind us. We travel past retail shops, restaurants and bars with people standing outside; it's a beautiful early summer evening with just a whisper of chill in the air. While we have been travelling we haven't spoken a single word to each other. Lloyd is so quiet and controlled and I decide to break the silence.

"What's the plan tonight, Lloyd, where are we going?"

"We are going to Mr Nick's club. It's safe, no walls with ears and no loose lips to talk." Lloyd's replies are always sharp and quite abrupt.

When Lloyd talks it feels so controlled and measured and almost like having been programmed what to say with just enough being the correct amount. We reach Nick's club and drive past the main entrance doors towards the car park where we had left this morning. Lloyd turns his head to the left and looks at the doors of the club. I can also see him looking all around the entrance as though he is checking out if anything unexpected is there. We turn into the private car park and Lloyd reverses the R8 back into the same space from last night as though it has never been missing. The rest of the car park has a range of cars on it with all being top class performance and quality cars but not as many as last night's showing. We both get out of the car and start to walk towards the main entrance of the club. The sun sets below the horizon, and the sky changes to that first level of darkness as the orange glow from the street lights intensifies. I look back briefly along the street then we enter Nick's club.

Walking through the left doorway, we continue into the main reception area of the club. It looks very different from last night with emergency lighting around the main ground floor bar, showing just enough light to pick out tables, chairs and settees. I can hear people talking and the noise of glasses and bottles being placed onto shelves behind the bar. There is very faint music playing and the light from the fridges behind the bar illuminates the rows of bottles on the optics. Lloyd turns and looks at me, pointing at the stairs up towards the VIP lounge. I can remember from last night holding hands with Sophie as we walked up the stairs and I can imagine being with her now, giving me some support and reassurance, but also still thinking that she set me up and betrayed me. My mouth is so dry with the excitement of what will happen tonight. Who I will meet? What will be discussed? I can feel my heart beginning to start racing with all types of emotions and thoughts starting to enter my head. Are you doing the right thing? Why are you doing this? What if things go wrong?

I can feel my whole body begin to shake with adrenaline and I can feel butterflies in my stomach and my heart pulse beating quite fast. The other thoughts start to kick in that say, "Fantastic, finally something new and exciting, different from my everyday mundane life, something challenging and life threatening." Someone once said to me 'do something exciting every day, it keeps you alive', but for some reason I can't remember who and when they said it. I remember something I saw on a car sticker once, 'One Life So Live It'. Well, I will certainly be doing that. Lloyd and I start to walk up the stairs towards the VIP lounge. As we continue up the stairs I can hear men's voices talking and laughing. Lloyd reaches the door of the VIP lounge first and pushes the door inwards towards the room and continues to walk through the doorway holding the door for me. I walk through the door, way past Lloyd and into the room. Lloyd releases the door and it closes slowly behind me.

The lounge is similar to last night with casual music playing in the background. The lighting is subtle but you can clearly see people's faces and reactions as I walk into the room. The waitress, Alice, is there again from last night, holding a tray with flutes of champagne.

Nick comes walking over, confidently and calmly holding out his hand to shake ours and says, "Gentlemen, I am glad you could make it, please come in and take a drink." Nick shakes my hand first with a strong grip smiles at me confidently.

He then turns to Lloyd and shakes his hand.

"Lloyd, Dean, please have a drink," expresses Nick.

He points at Alice and beckons her over. Alice walks over with the tray of champagne flutes on a silver tray, making sure not to spill any or, worse still, drop the tray. I didn't really notice her last night, but today I see she is around mid-twenties with dark brown, straight, shoulder length hair and green eyes. She is quite natural looking and doesn't wear lots of make-up but is quite pretty, has a nice smile and seems a very quiet person. Lloyd and I both take a glass. I look around the room and there are only men in the room apart from Alice and four other waitresses. All of them look like university students and are all wearing the same white blouse, black skirt and black short high heels. None of the model wives, girlfriends or arm side attractions are here tonight so it must be a gentlemen's night.

Nick starts to walk towards the large circular table in the middle of the room. As he walks over towards the table he requests, "Lloyd, Dean, come and sit next to me."

As he reaches the table the four waitresses and Alice are already around the table, pulling out the chairs and waiting for the men to sit in them before they lift and push the chairs under them as they sit down. Nick sits down first and Alice ensures he is happy before anyone else starts to move with Lloyd sitting to Nick's right hand side and with this one action seeing that Lloyd is his number two. All the team acknowledge this fact as they take places at the table in subordinate levels, leaving me sitting next to Nick on the left side, being the newest guest. I have seen this type of culture in China where people sit in certain places whether it is at work or pleasure.

Beginning to sit, Alice pushes the chair under me and, turning to my right, smiles, saying, "Thank you."

Just then a hand touches my left shoulder.

"I sit next to you, Dean, yes?"

I turn my head from the right the left sharply and see the figure of a man standing on my left. He has a very strong

German accent with brown curly hair, slightly balding and blue eyes, around six feet tall and in his early forties.

"I am Thomas. It is pleasure to meet with you," he replies.

"Yes, that's fine, Thomas," I answer back.

Just as he sits next to me, as I'm looking at him, I remember Rahul saying this morning that the person who delivered the parcel had a strong German accent and dark coloured hair. I wonder if he took the pictures in the club last night then delivered the parcel afterwards. It would make sense. I decide to wait and see if can find out later. Thomas sits and starts talking to the man directly on his left. I start to look around the table, and I can remember all of them from last night in one way or another. I can hear all of them talking and laughing and seem to feel a little out of place. It is clear that these men have worked together for a long time and are very close. Today I am fully sober and I can pick out more detail from each of them which I couldn't last night. All of the men seem to have that military or police disciplined background and all look as though they have been taught how to sit at the table and how to dress. None of them seem relaxed at the table but are happy with each other's company. All of them seem to have similar haircuts which are neat and sharp and all are clean shaven with no visible tattoos or scars of any type which seems quite strange for a group of ten men.

Registering that Thomas has stopped talking, I turn to ask him, "Last night was such a rush and things were quite intense, would you mind just telling me everyone's names again?"

"Yes, I do that for you, Dean. Sit next to me is Vernon, then it's Greg and Paul. Sitting opposite is Ramone and Carlos. The man next to Lloyd is Josef."

Thomas then goes on to explain, "Vernon, Greg and Paul are English and have worked for Nick for a few years. Ramone and Carlos emigrated here from Brazil ten years ago and have worked for Nick since then. Josef and I, as you can tell from my accent, both from Germany and contractors for Nick."

Looking at Vernon, Greg and Paul they all seem to be well built typical army men. Both Vernon and Greg have brown hair and eyes with what seem to be quite athletic well-built bodies and they look very similar, almost like brothers. Paul has black hair and dark brown eyes and is well built. They all seem to be in their late thirties and are a small crew together. Ramone and Carlos seem quite slender in their build but seem to have toughness in how they sit and look at the other men around the table and I sense that they have had a hard life back in Brazil and will not take any prisoners. Josef looks to be in his late thirties and, like Thomas, appears to be more managerial than heavy handed like the others. Lloyd is speaking to Nick and mentions the black Merc. I can hear Nick whispering something back but can't make out what he was saying. Alice continues to ensure everyone has plenty of drinks by bringing out two bottles of wine, one red and one white, and starts walk around the table asking each of the men what drink they would like. The waitresses then start to bring the food out: smoked salmon, caviar, tiger prawns, asparagus, snails, scallops, monk fish, blue fin tuna, lobster thermidor, fillet of beef. There is no expense spared.

I continue to speak to Thomas and ask him, "So what is your main role in the plan?"

He replies, "I collect intelligence information and will work on surveillance during the heist."

I suddenly snap at him, "So was it you who left the parcel for me last night at my apartment?"

Nick sharply turns to me and replies, "We know about the parcel and probably what it contains, if we had that information, I would have given it to you for the offering. There are other interested parties after you, not just ourselves. The big difference is that we found you first!"

"So who are the people in the black Merc I keep seeing?" I answer back quickly and aggressively.

"We are not sure yet, but one thing I will guarantee is that I already have people investigating who they are." Nick looks at me and smiles, but I can tell he is concerned.

The meal continues. The drink is controlled and managed. You can tell Nick, even when he is relaxed, is managing everything and listening to what everyone is talking about.

We finish the meal. Nick then stands and says, "Gentlemen, let's discuss the final parts of the plan."

Whilst he is talking he points over towards a table at the back of the room and everyone stands and begins to walk over. Noticing that the alcohol drink has made me a little light headed, I stand and try to remain focused on what we are going to discuss. Reaching the table, Nick pulls off a dust sheet covering a roadmap plan of the city with models simulating strategic buildings and vehicles. Nick starts to point to sections of map, explaining the route of the armoured trucks from the casinos and where the money trucks continue to the point where the heist will take place at the money sorting warehouse. There is a detailed internal plan of the money warehouse. We will group at the warehouse at 8 a.m., so we can hit the place at 8.30 a.m. sharp.

Nick explains, "Thomas and Josef will be in the tall building next to the central control traffic command centre to ensure our easy getaway along with the camera and security systems in the money sorting house and finally some high level background sniper support."

Josef speaks. "I have finally hacked into the mainframe central road network system and can control whatever sequence is required."

"Excellent, Josef. Thomas, have you finally carried out the hacking of the police and federal security network and the surveillance systems at the sorting house?" replies Nick.

"Yes, Nick, I completed the trace and now can monitor all security systems including radio frequencies. For money house I tapped into the camera and alarm systems and can disable when required. This company does not even have any time lock devices. I have full schematic layouts of the main building," answers Thomas.

"I trust that all schematic plans used are untraceable as are any tracking devices?" asks Nick.

Thomas nods his head in agreement, confirming with, "Yes."

Nick then starts to discuss the plan to attack the sorting house. "We will have three minutes, men, from when the alarm is raised. Vernon, Greg and you are planned to set the charges on the wall, what explosives have you managed to source?"

Vernon replies, "I have managed to get some low grade C4 that should have all blast power to implode the wall but will not cause any fire or damage to the insides."

"Greg, what have you got planned for the money marking system in the building?" asks Nick.

"Well, I've managed to disarm both the paint marking and GPS tracking used in the vehicles that in turn renders the building systems un-activated. So the vehicle will look as though all is okay, plus Josef can also now track the armoured trucks en route," replies Greg.

"Good work, Greg," replies Nick with a smile on his face.

"Paul, are the vehicles prepped and ready?" asks Nick

"They are all fine, sir. I have managed to acquire four Range Rovers, all are clean and untraceable, and the suspension and engines have been modified as you requested. The first vehicle has got the strengthened front end with welded cross bars," replies Paul.

Nick looks to Ramone and Carlos. "Gents, you will be at the first vehicle so power straight through the security house. Taking out the main control room computers, we can disable them just before. Cover any security and possible police personnel approach. Load heavy, I think this will be the route the police will try to block us out."

Nick speaks with boldness and confidence, pointing at the plan of the building.

"Get the stingers down guys, that's critical for the escape so make sure you leave enough room to turn the vehicles."

Nick then looks across in the direction of Greg and Vernon. "You guys will be in the second vehicle. Drive as close to the outer wall and set the charges. The wall must be down in thirty seconds." Nick taps his Rolex watch on his left wrist.

"Lloyd, you and I will bring up the third vehicle and park next to the wall. Paul and Dean, you follow on with the fourth. Once the wall is down, Vernon and Greg move inside and start to round up the hostages and take out any guards if required. Lloyd and I will move inside and start to bag the money with Paul joining. Remember we have to get the cash loaded quickly into the vehicles so Dean, you can manage that." Nick now has seriousness in his voice.

"Worst case, we may have to kill a few people and possibly some police to escape, so get your serious faces on. If pedestrians get in the way, send out some warning shots, but by then it could be too late. Lloyd, did you manage to source the missile launchers?" Nick continues.

"Yes, boss, all with heat seeker devices."

"Good, ensure each vehicle has one ready for use," requests Nick.

"What about weapons, Nick?" asks Vernon.

Nick replies, laughing, "Do you doubt me, Vernon? I have managed to source enough MP5s and Beretta semi autos, none traceable of course, for everyone and a couple thousand rounds each. And the final cherry on the top, a couple of Barrett 50 cals for Thomas and Josef to give high level cover. All are with me and will be handed out before we start."

Listening to Nick you can tell that he has done similar work in the past but none of it seems to scare or concern him at all. In fact he appears to be enjoying the planning as he moves into his next statement with excitement in his voice.

"Okay, so once we are loaded up and on the road we must split up quick. Drive fast but not stupid, there will be enough problems elsewhere so the police could be slow to respond, what with the bank holiday football matches among other things. We will head down separate roads highlighted and get out of the city as soon as possible. Don't use the motorways, you can be blocked out. We will regroup at the expeditor warehouse, unload the cash, change the cars, collect together all the clothes and weapons. I will then burn out any remaining vehicles and evidence afterwards."

Nick finally asks, "Has anyone got any questions?"

My head is full of questions but I feel if I ask what I am thinking all the others will either laugh or stare at me in shock. My heart is beating so fast and my head is full of 'why am I here?' and 'what do I know about this type of work?' My body is shaking with adrenaline, excitement and fear. I can sense the other members of the team are thinking about me and that I must be way out of my depth.

Nick can sense the same and then speaks out. "I can sense some of you around this table are thinking 'what is Dean doing here?' Well, I want it clear from now, nothing is going to change and Dean stops in this crew. I have never let any of you down before and I'm not starting now, does anyone have a problem?"

He is quite sharp and firm with his words and actions, staring at each crew member with nobody answering. He looks back across at each of them, expecting a response and all of them shake their heads to say no they don't have a problem.

"Look, we keep our cool, remain focused and we will be millionaires very soon." Nick's voice changes to a calm suggestion.

Lloyd asks, "What type of figure are we talking, boss?"

"Well, Lloyd, if the information I have received is correct, we are looking at around fifteen to twenty mill total and, guess what, it's Monday morning!"

Everyone suddenly has a smile on their faces.

"Gentlemen, people are starting to ask questions so the heist must be on Monday, it will be the best time for several reasons, so the bar is free, have a good night and remember no loose lips."

Everyone starts to move away from the table, talking to each other and laughing. Looking at Nick, I can't believe that it will be so soon and I am completely shocked, not sure what to think.

He beckons me over to the table where we were sitting last night and as I reach the table Nick points to a chair, "Please sit, Dean, I am sure you have lots of questions but you didn't want to ask them in front of the others, am I correct?" asks Nick.

"You're right, Nick. I'm not sure what I can do in this heist. This is nothing like I have ever done before," I reply.

"Hmm, it's your skills after the heist I want, we will have some loose ends to tidy up and that is where I need your help! Let's get the heist out of the way then things will become clearer. It has taken me a long time to find you and I imagine your head is full and confused." Nick can have quite a calming voice when he needs it to be.

"Yes, my head feels like a punch bag of emotions and I can't believe that I'm involved with this, but just tell me one thing, how did you know about the parcel?" I ask.

"Dean, I have friends all over the world, some in very high places and some in low parts, information comes to me from everywhere. I have a few ideas about who sent the parcel and why they have done it. Now, you have to remember that they are not just watching you, they are watching all of us, especially me. I have a lot of enemies." His reply is very sharp.

"They want people like us to disappear, free thinkers who make our own choices in life, people like us who need freedom and hate being told what to do. I imagine you have felt all your life that something is missing and it tears you up inside because we all feel the same, am I right?"

I answer back, "Yes, it feels like there is a huge hole in my life and the excitement of this heist is so intense."

"Dean, I have to go now, but please stop and have a drink with the crew. Lloyd will take you back when you are ready and see you Monday."

Nick then stands up, looks at me, nods his head, turns and waves at the others standing by the bar and walks towards the lounge door, opens it walks through the doorway and closes the door behind him. Turning back, I look across towards the bar and see all the team staring at me and at that point I never felt so unwanted with eight pairs of eyes burning holes into me.

Lloyd stands up, beckoning with his hand. "Come get a drink with the crew, we won't bite."

Standing up, I walk over towards the bar, just as the music in the nightclub below suddenly starts to blast away causing the floor to start vibrating. Taking a quick look at my watch, I see the time is 10.30 p.m. Reaching the bar, Lloyd hands me a big vodka and tonic as we start to exchange some small talk, but I can sense the tension and curiousness in the others over why Nick has selected me. Lloyd starts speaking more than I have ever heard before. Maybe it's because Nick is not there, but I think he is trying to break the ice. There is quietness in all the crew that seems unreal, but with Lloyd talking and laughing, the tension starts to reduce and the other men start to speak more freely becoming more open.

Trying to talk with other members of the crew, it is a little difficult to break the ice and walking over towards Vernon and Greg, I sense some friction from their body language and can tell that they are inseparable. Thomas and Josef seem fine but they are contractors anyway and are not part of the main team. Ramone and Carlos also seem very close and keep staring at me, trying to work me out as the drinks continue to flow. The tension with every empty glass seems to reduce and the team begin to relax, but the curiosity in the crew as to why I am here oozes with every minute. What do I have to offer? The strangest thing is I feel so far out of my depth, but deep down so comfortable like it is just another day at work and standing drinking with these guys just feels so right. The morning is fast approaching and I can tell Lloyd is looking through the windows at the start of morning daylight.

Lloyds turns to me and asks, "Are you ready to go, Dean?"

"Yeah, Lloyd, I have to go church on a Sunday morning away," I say, laughing at him.

Lloyd is standing on my left side and looks back at me with a strange expression on his face, not knowing whether to believe me or not. Thomas and Josef look across from my right at me, so giving them a wink from my right eye, we all laugh together as Lloyd and I leave. Repeating Saturday morning we head off in Lloyd's Audi back towards my apartment with him blasting his way along the roads without a care in the world until he is pulling up outside the apartment building, slamming on the brakes like he is carrying out an emergency stop.

Getting jarred forward with only the seat belt stopping me going through the windscreen, I turn to Lloyd and say, "Thanks, Lloyd, thanks for tonight. I know it must be difficult for you to accept me in with the rest of you?"

Lloyd looks at me and says, "Dean, Mr Nick has a reason for you to be in this crew and he has explained some of your background to me so I'm glad you are with us. The important thing for me is that you are here and it's Mr Nick's request. I'll see you on Monday morning at 6 a.m. I will pick you up from here."

I look at Lloyd and say, "Lloyd, I feel so far out of my depth with all of you, it's reassuring that you have support for me." I lift my left hand and open the door of the car. I have never heard Lloyd speak like this before and it feels like quite a serious conversation is starting.

"Dean, just remember when it's over, you must be very careful, we will be some of England's most wanted and anyone will sell you out for a quick buck."

Lloyd by now is looking at me with his dark brown piercing eyes staring straight at me. I look to my right and smile back then stand, turning and closing the door, watching Lloyd start to blast off down the street like a rocket. It's 6 a.m. and the sun is just breaking over the horizon filing the sky with a yellow haze in the sky. The tiny amount of warmth from the morning sun feels so good on my face, and the smell of the fresh new day washes all the fears away. I turn and look at the apartment block and start to walk towards the main doors. Even in my part drunken state I can sense that I am being watched, these sixth sense feelings seem to be increasing and they are stronger when I am part drunk. Maybe it's due to the body lowering down all its emotions, and I can feel more openness since a drunken man never lies.

4

Walking towards the automatic doors, they slide open and continuing into the lobby, I look across at the main desk, but Rahul is missing. Continuing past the desk along to the lifts, I press the number twelve on the control panel and can hear the lift moving in the elevator shaft. As it reaches the ground floor, a ping is heard as the doors open. After the incident with the agents yesterday, I now stand at the side of the doors and not directly facing them, this way visually seeing inside the lift and the people inside can't see me.

Entering the lift my head is still so full of the heist and what we will be doing. As the doors close my thoughts turn to what is going to happen and never being a bad man, but this feels so exciting and good then thinking about the team and what they must be thinking about me and how far out of my depth. As the lift rises up the shaft, I start to think about Sophie, the envelope full of pictures with everything beginning to be too overpowering and needing to escape for some time away fill my thoughts. Ping. The twelfth floor arrives and, standing at the left side of the lift, the doors open. Gradually, looking down the corridor towards my apartment for any signs of people or changes, I begin to walk with my hands in my pockets, searching for the door keys. Taking out the keys, the door is unlocked and I immediately walk inside. I sense that something is different and that someone has been here last night. Starting to panic slightly, I begin to quickly walk around the apartment rooms looking for anything different, checking doors, wardrobes and windows but all seem okay. The only place that seems different is the front room where the pictures in the envelope were placed in the drawer unit. Noticing that the drawer front is slightly open, I begin to question my own action. Did I leave this open? Sensing that the parcel has been touched, goosebumps start to rise on my skin.

Still holding my door keys in my right hand, I push them into my right pocket and open the drawer, lifting the parcel out with my left. Opening the envelope flap with my right hand, I notice there are two more pictures that have been left inside. Lowering my right hand into the envelope, I lift out the two new pictures. The first picture is of me getting into Lloyd's car tonight and the other is an old friend from where I had worked previously before Harpers and Harpers. Feeling again like my space has been violated, the whole place feels dirty and unclean and walking back towards the front door, I reopen it and look at the lock that hasn't been damaged. I begin to inspect the door frame for any signs of evidence from tools or screwdriver marks, but nothing is evident. Making my way back into the apartment, closing the front door, I rush across to the balcony doors, flicking the key in the door lock with my left hand and gripping the handle of the door with my right.

A thorough check shows that there is no damage to the lock and door frames. Who has been here? And more importantly how have they managed to get in without doing any damage to the doors? Thinking out loud, the only way would be with a set of keys and only one person has a spare key to my apartment. Shaun! Storming back through the apartment, I almost rip the front door from its hinges, slamming it behind as I make my way heading for Shaun's apartment on the tenth floor. My mind is full of why Shaun could have done this, or maybe it's a mistake? Reaching the lift area, I press the down button with my left hand, standing to left side of the doors opening. The lift reaches the floor and with a ping bell noise as the doors open. I pause for a few seconds to ensure no one walks out and, knowing it's clear, I walk into the lift, standing to one side and pressing the tenth floor button on the panel. The doors close and the lift starts to move downwards, then stops at the tenth floor level. Ping. The doors open. Again I wait for a few seconds to make sure no one rushes in; these past few days are making me paranoid about just simple tasks. Starting to walk out the lift, I look down the corridor to the right where Shaun's apartment is to see the morning sunshine beaming through and illuminating the floors and walls from the window at the end of the short corridor.

Light at the end of the tunnel comes to mind and, hopefully, I will find out some truth as I continue to walk down the corridor. Then, at ten metres away from the front door, I sense something is wrong, noticing that the door is slightly open and the lock is broken. Avoiding touching the door with my fingers or hand, I gradually push the door open with my left elbow and in a sweeping action, slowly walk through the open doorway into Shaun's apartment. The whole place is completely upside down with clothes, furniture, papers everywhere. The curtains are hanging from the rails, allowing sunshine to light areas of the apartment with corners still in the shadows. Watching where I place my feet, I continue to walk into the apartment with the smell of different aftershaves floating in the air where bottles have been smashed. The front room looks like a party has gone wrong in there with pictures smashed off the walls and clothes ripped all over the floor. I know Shaun isn't very house proud, but this takes the piss. My cell starts to vibrate in my trousers pocket. Using my right hand to lift out the phone, I see an SMS message has arrived. Operating the pin-unlock code, the message is opened and it's from Shaun.

It reads, "Hey fella wtf have u bin up 2 went out with Chloe from Friday. Catch u lata."

I let the message sink in then decide to try and ring him, pressing the call button and lifting the phone to my right ear. *Ring, ring, ring.* The phone connects. "Hey, fella, how was your night?" asks Shaun.

I reply back, "Sorry, mate, had some business on. Look, mate, what time are you coming back? Because there are a few things we need to talk about."

Shaun quietly replies, "Look gezza, got some business on of my own here at the min, I will be back later today."

Do I tell him about the apartment or not?

If he has set me up then no way, if he is genuine yes!

Shaun whispers, "Look, mate, there was shit last night. Chloe's old man came round my place and started kicking off and went crazy. I have got to go, will call you later, fella."

Breathing a sigh of relief and feeling guilty for doubting him, I reply, "Okay, mate, no problems, have just come round to see you and found your place like a bomb site. Will catch you later."

Shaun rings off. It feels like a weight has been taken off my shoulders, but it still doesn't explain who was in my apartment. Placing the cell back in my trouser pocket, I continue to walk around Shaun's apartment towards the kitchen and notice his key rack. Walking over, I start to look through the hanging keys, but can't find my spare key anywhere. Maybe someone took the key after they saw the door open, but why would anyone want to do that? Then comes the harsh reality that maybe Shaun is the guy taking pictures, it would make perfect sense.

He was there last night, he may have seen me get in Lloyd's car. He knows bits about my past, and maybe this whole story of Chloe's husband trashing the apartment is a cover. What I can't understand is that Shaun is a strong guy with a short fuse when he gets fired up and I can't believe that he would let someone smash up his apartment for a girl he has only seen a few times. Something doesn't seem right. I've been out with him in the past when he has smacked another guy in the face just for looking at him in the wrong way, so why does this feel so different? Feeling disappointed, I decide to go back to my apartment and begin the walk back through the bomb site, reaching the front door where I use my shirt sleeve to open the door handle just in case, to leave no prints. The sunlight fills the corridor and this time I decide to have some exercise by using the stairs back to my apartment. Closing the door behind, I start to walk down the corridor towards the staircase exit.

Reaching the door, I push it open and walk onto the stairwell that smells of musty air and has no natural light, only florescent tubes hanging from the ceiling sections. Making my way up the stairs, my head is full of what has happened the past few days, last night, this morning and what's going to happen on Monday. Walking past the eleventh floor and finally reaching the twelfth floor doorway, I pull the door towards me and make my way back along the corridor towards my apartment. Taking out the keys from my trouser pocket, my mind begins to think about Shaun's place and someone who has been in mine, trying to solve the puzzle. Opening the door, I make my way back inside the front room and closing the door behind, walk towards the coffee table, placing the keys and mobile onto the glass surface. Taking off my suit jacket, it is placed onto the nearest armchair, as I walk into the kitchen, but my appetite has suddenly disappeared with all the thoughts rushing through my head. Feeling confused and completely exhausted, I decide some rest is long overdue and continue back from the kitchen towards to bedroom. Dropping onto the bed, I quickly fall asleep.

After a few hours, the warmth of the sun's rays touching the right side of my face wakes me up. Seeing it's a fabulous day outside, it's too good to be wasted spending it in bed. In an instant I decide to get up, get dressed, have a shower and take my motorbike for a blast to the coast. This will help clear my thoughts and maybe make the most of my last few days of freedom if we get caught during the heist. Beginning to undress, my shirt and trousers are removed as I make my way into the bathroom for a shower. The glass shower door is opened and the round dial is turned to switch on the shower, letting it run for a few seconds to warm up. Now fully undressed, I step into the shower and feel the warm freshening water hitting my body, waking me up. Shower finished, I dry down my body with a towel and, wrapping the towel around my waist, walk back into the bedroom to fetch my clothes from the wardrobe. I reach for some underwear from inside the wardrobe drawer and also the base layer T-shirt and leggings to keep the wind chill out. Pulling them on, I walk towards the other wardrobe to take out my leathers from the rail where they are hanging. Reaching inside the cupboard for my crash helmet, boots, neck cover and gloves, I turn around and place them on the bed.

Unzipping the leathers, I climb into them and then suddenly feel as though I am being released from everyday life with the close fitting material. Sitting on the bed, my feet are pushed into the boots and the zips pulled up to close them, giving support around the ankles. Finally reaching for the gloves and neck cover, they are stuffed inside the upturned crash helmet.

Standing from the bed, my crash helmet is lifted and I make my way into the front room. I walk from the bedroom and stop at the coffee table to pick up my keys, wallet, sunglasses and cell phone. Placing them into the inside pocket of the leathers, I continue towards the front door and open it with my right hand. Walking through the doorway, I turn around to look at the apartment, having a strange feeling that I may not be coming back here, but maybe it's paranoia from the last few nights.

Closing the door and making my way down the corridor to the lift, I press the button of the control panel with my right hand and as ever now stand slightly sideways. The lift reaches the twelfth floor and door opens with a ping and I slowly walk into the empty lift. The stainless steel covering the inside walls shines with the reflection of me in my black and red bike leathers. I turn and press the basement button inside the lift. Standing slightly sideways, I watch the lift numbers decreasing down to the B level and as the lift stops it ping its arrival on the basement level and the doors open.

There is not much light in the underground parking lot under the apartment building with no natural light apart from beams of daylight managing to reach the exit and entry ramps. Making my way through the open door, the darkness of the basement engulfs the vision and with limited illumination from the basic florescent tube lighting flickering and buzzing with broken starter switches. My motorbike is parked at the far side of the basement level and starting to walk out of the lift, the smell of musky air hangs in the basement along with the dampness from the concrete structure that almost feels like it's touching my face. Walking towards the motorbike storage zone, mechanical noises can be heard from the lift as it starts to move in the lift shaft. My heart starts to beat a little faster knowing there is no escape from this level, and with all the things happened this weekend the distance towards my motorbike feels like an eternity.

The tough rubber soles of my boots click against the concrete floor and my leathers creek as they rub together. The basement is completely silent apart from a faint dripping noise of water at the opposite side of the garage. In the distance one of the florescent tubes flickers as the starter is failing, casting shadows across the already dimly lit floor. The emergency exit lights glow a bright green and the water sprinkler system pipes have a dim red colour. I continue walking towards where my motorbike is and finally reach the far corner. My motorbike is completely covered with a dust sheet. I grab the dust sheet with my right hand and slowly drag off the cover, revealing my Ducati 1098 motorbike. The bright red bodywork and black wheels shine even in this darkness of the underground basement. Placing my helmet on the single seat, I roll up the dust cover with both hands and turn back to the bike, carrying out a few basic checks of tyres, engine oil, chain tension and brake fluid levels, then taking the key from my helmet with my right hand, I insert it into the ignition barrel.

Having placed my left hand on the handle bars and pulling in the clutch lever, I turn the key with my right hand. The clocks illuminate, showing the gears are neutral. Placing my right hand on the throttle, I flick the engine kill switch off and press the engine start button. The starter motor fires twice and the engine kicks into action with an almighty bang. The silence of the basement is instantly killed with the roar of the engine as the headlight now illuminates a tunnel of light into the darkness. I let the engine tick over a few seconds until the engine settles then I give the throttle a quick blip. The noise from the engine is so loud, resonating through the stainless racing exhaust system and sending vibrations through the quiet basement area.

As the engine ticks over the gloves, sunglasses and neck cover are taken from the helmet and placed on the front seat. The helmet is then gradually replaced on the back seat as the neck cover is starting to be pulled over my head and tucked it inside my leathers. The suit is zipped closed to my neck with the press stud clicked on the neck collar sealing out the wind. Grabbing my crash helmet, it is pulled over my head and again clicked into position with the chin strap. Lifting up the visor, the sunglass arms are fed through the opening and over my ears, as the faint light from the basement suddenly becomes even darker. Finally reaching for the gloves, these are pulled onto my hands, ensuring the Velcro and press studs are clicked firmly in place. Climbing over the seat and standing each side of the bike, the weight is taken between my legs and with the handle bars pointing straight, the side stand is flicked up and the clutch depressed so that first gear can be engaged with my right foot then I swap feet and hold the bike from moving with the footbrake. Giving the engine some revs and now sitting on the seat, the clutch and footbrake are gradually released and the bike starts to move forward towards the light of the entry exit ramp. Sitting back into the seat, I begin to enjoy the ride. Reaching the top of the exit ramp, the brightness of the sunny day is a fabulous feeling and already the sun's rays hit the dark leathers, sending warmth into my body. I turn up the ramp, heading towards the main road and the freedom that can only be felt with a motorbike on the open highway.

I turn left onto the main road and open the throttle, heading away from Chelsea Harbour. The force of the acceleration pushes me backwards into the seat and the roar from the exhaust and engine sounds fantastic against the corridor of buildings. I change gear into second and blast away towards the pleasures of the twisting and turning country lanes heading for the coast. The sun is already high in the sky with lots of people walking around in shorts and T-shirts. As I fly past people on the street they turn and stare as though I am some type of anti-Christ making noise on a Sunday morning. I notice the time on the main church clock tower, it's just 11 a.m. Continuing along the main high street, I turn off towards the country lanes and the cool fresh air along with the noise of the bike engine feels fantastic and so freedom from this rat race of life. The scent from the fresh cut harvested crops of wheat and barley fill my nostrils and with the cold hard winter not far behind and pleasures of the late summer evenings are just around the corner. The nights begin to grow longer as the days become darker and cooler with mist hanging in the air. My mind is fully focused on the road ahead and the sweeping bends begin to pull me into the curves that make motorbiking such a pleasure. There are the typical Sunday drivers travelling towards the coast at a snail's pace, but with a motorbike you can just cut and weave between the cars with ease and safety.

In the faint distance a few more bikes start to join me on the same road to the Sunday blast to the coast, sounding like a race day at a Moto GP competition and I look in my side mirrors to see five sets of headlights glowing bright catching up fast behind. Suddenly they blast past me at speeds well over a hundred miles an hour, one Honda Fireblade, two Yamahas R1s, and two Suzuki Gixxer 750s with all the guys dressed in full race leathers of their track heroes. My leathers are simple enough for me and suit the Ducati. I normally travel at the speeds or faster of these guys with the raw power of the 1098, but today I'm just enjoying being out in the fresh warm spring air. In the back of my mind are the thoughts that this could be my last ever trip, so I want to make to most of it.

Continuing along the country lanes, making sure of police speeds traps in thirty miles per hour zones, the time soon passes and my mind is completely free of any thoughts other than me and the 1098. The bike is so responsive as you feel the tarmac surface, the pull of the corners and the camber of the road through the handlebars and the seat. Riding a motorbike is not like driving a car where you can almost drive on autopilot with the music blasting and not remember where you have been. On a motorbike you need to be more controlled and prepare for every corner with your senses running on overdrive, reading all the situations and junctions watching car drivers. You seem to develop a sixth sense for how people react towards junctions, corners and can almost judge what they will do next. Riding along, the roaring noise of a supercar behind me starts to fill my helmet, with my side mirrors filled with a bright yellow Lamborghini Murcielago convertible. Sensing the closeness of the car, I see they want to race. Today I would rather let them pass and enjoy the view of the gorgeous blonde woman in the passenger seat. We are starting to approach a small town area where the speed limit drops to thirty miles an hour. The police have already set up a speed trap system, so I drop the 1098 down a gear to slow down. The Lambo starts to overtake and suddenly pulls back in. The black guy driving is so engrossed in trying to race me, as well as speaking to someone on his cell, that he hasn't seen the police trap.

Having a grin to myself, I notice that there is a set of traffic lights for a four-way junction. I continue past the police at the correct speed and flicking up my visor, stare across at them through my Oakley sunglasses, heading towards the junction. I head towards the centre line to control the junction and also to see if the Lambo will line up for a race, and sure enough he does. As we stop at the red light, I look across the junction and see cars stopping on the opposite side. Looking right I see the traffic moving and then finally look across to my left to see the black guy and his woman staring back at me. The driver begins to rev the Lambo engine and, with his knuckles protruding in the skin, I know he is tensed and ready to race. The dry clutch of the 1098 clicks and bangs, sounding like there is a handful of spanners in the gearbox. I look back in front towards the road junction and shake my head, laughing in my helmet. The guy gets even more agitated and revs the engine again just as a police car stops at the left hand side junction. The lights turn green and he blasts away in the Lambo and instantly draws the attention of the police car as he flies past. I simply pull away from the traffic lights at the right speed and see the police car starting its blue lights in pursuit of the Lambo.

The driver of the Lambo has already noticed his mistake and his blonde Barbie doll is shouting and staring at him as they stop with the police car behind them as I ride looking at the 'oh fuck' expression on his face. Continuing along the A12 heading towards Colchester, then onto Clacton-on-Sea, the countryside begins to appear from the town area as the roads begin to snake and twist, unwinding towards the south east coast. The road is full with lots of cars, but the power in the Ducati makes easy work of the traffic on this sunny morning. One thing is evident on this Sunday morning ride out, I keep getting the sensation that someone is following me. Looking in my side mirrors nothing appears, but my sensations are working in overdrive. Riding past a lay-by I notice a black Mercedes parked with blacked out windows and the engine running. As I pass the car, it pulls away from the lay-by and begins to follow me at a distance of two hundred metres.

Observing my side mirrors, I see that there is a man driving and a woman in the front passenger seat. The car appears to be the same vehicle from Saturday and it feels as though I am being followed. Deciding to provoke an action, I decide to slow down gradually to see if they keep the same distance or try to overtake. In slowing down I continue to look in the side mirrors and also notice that they are still keeping the same distance as before. My heart begins to beat a little faster knowing they are clearly following me and after the last few days who they could be. Noticing a sign for another lay-by parking with no other vehicles evident, I decide to pull over to see what happens. Switching the indicator lever, I look into my mirrors and notice they are doing the same and my thoughts now instantly fill my brain with the decision either to stop wanting to see who they are or to carry on and blast back home and to safety. This pressure is beginning to cloud my normal clear judgment, but the thought of not knowing overtakes my ideas to escape and starting to slow down, the bike is pulled up to a gradual halt with the black car following behind. Sitting on the bike with the engine still running, the visor is opened on my helmet and I continue to look into the side mirrors, watching for any reaction from the people inside.

My body is now beginning to shake with fear and apprehension as to what is going to happen once the car doors finally open and after a few seconds of waiting, the bike engine is stopped and the side stand kicked out. I lean the bike onto the side stand and climb off. Continuing to look at the car, I remove the helmet to notice that both the man and woman who were sitting in the front have now opened the car doors and are standing alongside the Mercedes. The man begins to walk over calmly and from his stance I can tell he is carrying a shoulder holster pistol, forcing his jacket to hang slightly different on the left side.

Reaching ten metres away he stops and shouts out, "Dean Nash?"

Looking back at him, I nod my head and confirm with, "Well, I hope so. You have been following me for long enough."

The silence is broken when two cars pass by on the main road and, as he continues to stare at me, the rear passenger door begins to open and an old man climbs out and leans against the car. He takes out a packet of cigarettes, opens the box and places one into his lips, and after a few seconds, lights it then leans his head back slightly, blowing the smoke into the air.

"Mr Wagstaff would like to meet you." The male agent gestures to the old man.

Continuing to walk in the direction of the car, the old man stares across at me with dark, sunken eyes, continuing to smoke the cigarette. As I pass the man he turns and continues to walk parallel to me as the woman, now standing by the front of the car, watches my every move. The man and woman are around forty-five years old and smartly dressed in a dark grey suits, and the old man is around sixty and smartly dressed, wearing a black suit and with a slightly balding head. The woman agent has dark brown hair and the man short cropped blonde hair with a receding hairline. The older man finishes the cigarette and tosses it to the ground, stamping on it, sending out a shower of sparks as I reach him.

"Dean Nash, hello, my name is John Wagstaff, Director of Intelligence," he says, presenting his right hand.

Shaking his hand and in shock, I reply by saying, "Hello."

"Mr Nash, or may I call you Dean? Would you like to sit in the car or stand in the fresh air?" Wagstaff asks.

"Dean is fine, and standing outside would be better for me," I reply.

"Dean, let us walk a little." He limps along slowly, trying to support his left leg.

"Dean, you don't know anything about me, but I know quite a lot about you so I'm going to start by asking you a few questions starting with what is your relationship to Nick Burns?" Wagstaff asks.

Looking shocked, I reply, "What, Nick Burns from Castro's club?"

"Yes, that's the man, Dean!" Wagstaff snaps sharply.

"Well, I met him Friday and he invited me for dinner Saturday at his club. Why, is there something wrong?" My heart now starts to race faster and faster.

"Mr Burns is a man of interest to me and the government of this country, did he not tell you that?" Wagstaff coughs.

"No, why? What has he done? He seems a pleasant guy to me," I ask.

"Dean, I can't tell you all the facts since its top secret, but what I can say is that he can never be trusted and anyone who has ever trusted him in the past has either died or disappeared." Wagstaff takes a small brown envelope from his jacket pocket and passes it to me.

"Dean, please open this and take a look at what your new friend does to allies." He passes it across as we reach the end of the lay-by.

Opening the envelope, I notice pictures inside and, taking them out, I'm instantly shocked by the scenes of death and destruction. One picture shows a man with his throat cut, another picture shows a woman beheaded and there are several pictures of cars blown into pieces with a final picture of a complete family shot in the head. All the pictures have 'MI6 Top Secret Eyes Only' in red ink stamped across them.

"These were some of Nick Burn's old friends." Wagstaff takes out another cigarette and lights it, blowing smoke into the air.

"Dean, you need to be very careful with this man and anything he has told you will be of great importance to me." He hands me his business card.

Looking at the card and trying to remember the images on the pictures, I can sense that Wagstaff knows something is happening with me and Nick. I try to build up a convincing story in my head that can throw him off my scent. "Mr Wagstaff, I'm an accountant at a large firm in London and

have no business with Mr Burns other than a new friendship."
I take a calming breath and continue.

"I don't know why he invited me to dinner Saturday but the evening was pleasurable with no threats. In fact the only threats seem to be coming from you."

"Dean, Nick Burns is a man I have known far longer than you and trust me, it would be better for you to simply walk away. He will stop at nothing to get what he wants." Wagstaff turns to walk back in the direction of the car.

"Mr Wagstaff, you may know Nick, but I have no business with him other than one meal on Saturday night," I reply back, still in shock.

"Dean, please call me John. If anything changes then let me know, I can help you if you help me!" Wagstaff sounds a little concerned as he throws the cigarette to the floor.

"I would prefer to call you Mr Wagstaff and if this man is so dangerous then why haven't MI6 stopped him?" I ask.

Wagstaff seems a little shocked by my question, "Dean, we need to catch him in the act in order to stop him and as of yet he has kept evading us."

"Mr Wagstaff, I find that a little hard to imagine. If the government wanted him gone, he would have been killed or assassinated by now," I reply back sharply.

"Technically, Dean, that's true, but Burns has always seemed to evade us." Wagstaff appears to be lying from the tone in his voice.

Seeing this as an opportunity to find out more about Nick, I stick my neck out by saying, "I think Nick is still employed by the government and because of that fact you can't just kill him, you need evidence and you want me to spy on him to give you that. Am I right?"

The man and women are already sitting back in the car with the engine running as Wagstaff opens the back passenger. "Dean, if you help me I can help you. Burns will manipulate and twist you into something else to suit his needs and you will not be able to deflect his actions. I am only saying this to help you."

"Mr Wagstaff, I understand but I have no business with Mr Burns." I start to hand back the envelope of pictures with my hand shaking slightly with adrenaline.

"No, Dean, you keep the pictures, so you can remember who your new friend is and what he is capable of doing." Wagstaff climbs into the car, closes the door and opens the window.

"Mr Wagstaff, thank you for the advice. I will think it over," I reply calmly.

"Dean, remember, you help me and I help you by keeping me informed." Wagstaff closes the window as the car drives away.

Watching the car drive onto the road and into the distance, I begin to walk back to my motorbike with a head full with the images from the people in the pictures and realise that what Sophie had told me about Nick begins to ring true and now I see he could have done these things. He does have a nasty side to him that I have seen in his eyes. Pulling my crash helmet back on, I start the engine, climb on board and kick up the stand. Then I engage first gear and start to pull off the lay-by onto the main road back in the direction of London. Riding along the roads back into the city centre, my mind is full of the pictures and Wagstaff's talk keeps playing over again like a stuck record. Heading towards the apartment parking area, only a few people are seen walking around and the traffic is surprisingly calm for Sunday. Turning onto the down ramp for the basement, the engine burbles as the noise from the race exhaust system vibrates against the walls, generating a deep echo as I ride through the gradually darkening enclosure. Beginning to slow down past the rows of parked cars, a black Audi can be seen nesting amongst the other vehicles near the motorbike storage area and, flicking up my visor to stare, it's evident there is nobody inside. Finally pulling into the bike storage zone the engine is stopped and the side stand is kicked down.

I climb from the bike and remove my helmet and gloves before throwing the coversheet over the bike and closing what feels to be another possible chapter in my ever changing complex life. Continuing to walk back through the basement, I look back across at the Audi R8, confirming that the license plate reads 'LLOYD R8'. Now I know Lloyd must be here somewhere waiting for me as I head for the lift doors in the dimly lit basement. My senses are pulsating, trying to find anything that resembles the huge figure of Lloyd waiting amongst the parked cars. Finally reaching the lift doors, I press the call button and the down arrow appears. Mechanical noises can be heard as the cables stretch and move, bringing the lift to the basement. The lift reaches my level and ping, the doors open with Lloyd standing inside.

Standing shocked I look at him saying, "Lloyd, what a surprise, I take it you are after me?"

Lloyd, standing casually in the lift, places his arm across the door sensor and replies in his deep voice, "Mr Nick is waiting in your apartment."

"Oh really, does he have a key?" I answer back sharply.

"Mr Rahul on reception helped and Mr Nick is concerned," Lloyd replies as I walk into the lift.

Lloyd looks at me and asks, "Where have you been on the crutch rocket then?"

Looking back at him I reply, "Just a blast to the coast for some fresh sea air."

Lloyd pushes the button for the twelfth floor as the lift doors close and my journey to meet Nick begins. I know he will not be happy with me for riding out today without keeping him informed and thinking his operation may have been compromised, but the pleasure felt from the excitement of true freedom experienced with the bike on open roads can never be missed. Lloyd continues to stare at my bike leathers and from his expression I know he has never ridden a bike so I decide to ask.

"Hey, Lloyd, have you ever tried a crutch rocket or are you just a car man?"

"No, man, something that makes you cold and sometimes wet with rain doesn't sound like fun to me. I would rather have a roof over my head and leather seats," he grunts back.

"A house on wheels, must be a Rolls Royce you're talking about?" I reply back.

Lloyd pretends to give a smile as the lift stops and pings for the twelfth floor. My heart begins to beat a little faster as the lift doors slide open, revealing the corridor that leads to my apartment and possibly a pissed off Nick. Walking down the corridor, the size of Lloyd's body casts a large shadow against the walls, even when he is behind me. The noise from my television can be heard softly echoing through the gap from the slightly ajar door of the apartment. Reaching the door, it is pushed open with my right hand and I begin walk into the room. Inside Nick is sitting on one of the dark brown leather armchairs holding a TV remote in his left hand and a cup of coffee in his right. The television has a sports channel showing results from today's football matches in the premier league.

"Well, that's another fifty grand lost today. Oh well," Nick announces.

"Sorry, Dean, I didn't think you would mind if I made myself at home. Nice place." Nick turns, looking in my direction.

"Thank you," I reply, a little nervous.

Nick turns back, looking at the TV, and then asks the question I was dreading. "Where have you been today? What have you been up to?"

"I decided to have ride out on my bike and went out towards the coast near Clacton-on-Sea." I continue to walk towards the direction of the settee.

"Have you spoken with anyone today?" Nick stares at me with eyes on stalks.

Placing my helmet on the settee and then beginning to unzip the top section of my bike leathers, I remember the conversation from earlier in the car on the lay-by. The answer to this question could end my life, standing here right now as I begin to sit on the settee, placing my door keys on the glass table.

With a deep breath I open my mouth to speak. "Yes, Nick, I will not lie to you, a black Mercedes began to follow me and after a few miles I stopped in a lay-by where the car pulled in behind me."

Nick continues to stare at the TV then asks, "Who was in the car?"

Leaning forward slightly towards him, I answer, "There were two men and a woman from a government agency and the older man gave me a business card and some pictures."

Taking the business card from my inside pocket along with the envelope, I hand them over to Nick. He takes the card and reads out the name printed. "John Wagstaff, well there's a name from the deep dark past."

"What did he want?" Nick asks as he starts to flick through the pictures.

"Wagstaff asked if we were friends," I answer quickly.

"What was your answer to Wagstaff?" Nick asks as he looks across to me.

"I explained to Wagstaff that we met in a nightclub on Friday then you invited me for dinner on the Saturday." I leaning back into the comfort of the settee.

Nick leans forward and continues to speak, handing back the pictures. "Dean, I told you Saturday that there would be other parties after you and clearly this is the start of it."

"What did Wagstaff want you to do if we made contact again?" Nick asks with confidence in his voice.

Taking the pictures from Nick, I explained, "He said that it would be in my interests to keep him informed of any contact, do you know what he meant by that?" I ask submissively.

"As you see from his card he is intelligence director and will be sniffing for any information. We have a past together and he occasionally tries to make contact through external people like you." Nick continues.

"He's harmless, don't worry about it. He will follow you for a few weeks to see where you go and who you meet and try different scare techniques such as those pictures."

"With him following me, will that affect tomorrow?" I ask nervously.

"No, the best bet is for you to stop with Lloyd tonight and that way you will be lost from any surveillance. Make sure you leave your cell and anything that sends a digital signal in this apartment and they will think you are still here." Nick stands and places the TV remote and empty coffee cup on the glass table.

"Lloyd, you stay here with Dean and then take him to your place, I will meet you there later. I need to go and see a man about a dog." Nick begins to walk towards the door.

"Yes, boss, no problem." Lloyd reacts to the instruction.

"Who are the people in the pictures, Nick?" I ask nervously.

"Well, Dean, Wagstaff is correct I did kill them all, but they were friends who were sent by the agency to kill me in cold blood. The one point that Wagstaff missed out was that he sent them!" Nick replies with anger in his voice.

"There is one other thing, Nick. The other man and woman that were in the car, I have seen them before?" I ask, standing looking at Nick.

"Where, here in the apartment block?" Nick still looks at the door not turning around.

"Yes, how did you guess?" I say with a look of shock on my face.

"I know Wagstaff and he will use intimidation techniques first, they probably broke in and left the pictures in here, but nothing is bugged yet, Lloyd and I swept the apartment when we arrived. In the next few days, though, everything you use like your bike, apartment and even office computer will be bugged and monitored." Nick turns around and looks across at me.

"Nick, if this is going to be a problem for you, maybe it's best I don't get involved," I say, hoping that he says no, but also knowing that it's too late anyway.

Nick then begins to walk back in my direction and as he reaches me, he lifts both his arms and, placing the hands onto my shoulders, I can feel the weight of his body as he pushes slightly against me. "Dean, it is my dream to have you with us tomorrow and these fucking bastards are not going to stop it from happening, you being there tomorrow means more than anything."

With a warm glow inside and feeling important, I smile back at Nick and say, "Why do you want me there tomorrow so much?"

"Dean, patience, patience my boy." Nick removes has hands from my shoulders and turns, starting to walk back in the direction of the door.

Lloyd looks across and from the expression on his face I can tell he is shocked with Nick's actions and words to me. As he begins to open the door he looks back at Lloyd, smiling. "Don't look so worried, old friend, I have complete trust in you too and want you there as well."

Nick has such a calming influence on people that helps build their confidence, trust and respect with only a few words and expressions. As Lloyd said before, you would do anything for him and already I feel that Nick is a true leader who can mould and form people to exploit their potential for his own goals and that of the team. There is, however, another side to Nick from the words of Sophie and what can be sensed when he is around. As the door closes shut, Nick leaves.

"Lloyd, you may as well sit down, it's going to take me time to get changed and collect a few things together," I say, gesturing to the settee for Lloyd to sit down.

I pick up my helmet and gloves and make my way to the bedroom as Lloyd walks over and takes a seat. Reaching the bedroom, I open the wardrobe doors and place the helmet and gloves inside then bending down, I unzip the boots and pull them from my feet. Removing my leathers, I rehang the suit on the rail and drop the boots inside, taking out the small holdall and placing it on the bed and opening the zip. Walking around the bedroom, I collect underwear, socks and a T-shirt and drop them inside the bag. Next from the bathroom I take a toothbrush, toothpaste and deodorant and back at the bag unzip a small side pocket placing them safely inside.

"Has Nick got his own car here, Lloyd?" I ask, trying to make conversation over the TV volume that Lloyd has turned up.

"No, Dean, he was with me, but that's what Mr Nick is like," Lloyd replies.

Taking off my base layers and pulling on a pair of blue Hugo Boss jeans and red Paul & Shark polo shirt, I lift the bag from the bed and start to make my way back into the living room to see Lloyd engrossed in a boxing match being showed on the sports channel with the remote in his right hand pretending to jab at the TV. Leaving the bag near the glass table, I check what type of shoes Lloyd is wearing and walking towards the shoe cupboard, take out a black pair of semi casual shoes from the rack, closing the door shut with a positive click.

"A few training ideas, Lloyd?" I ask as I walk past with the pair of shoes.

Lloyd looks across, smiling, saying, "Guns solve it quicker than boxing."

Placing the shoes next to the settee, I sit and slide my feet inside, tying the laces and then stand, saying, "Okay, ready to go if you are?"

Lloyd looks across to me, then clicks the 'off' button on the remote instantly silencing all the noise that was floating through the apartment. He stands quickly and turns towards the direction of the door. Reaching Lloyd, I quickly look around the apartment including all the pictures of my family, with a strange feeling that I may never come back here filling in my mind. Bending down to pick up the holdall bag with my left hand, I lift the door key from the glass table top with my right and, casually looking around, notice the drawer with the envelope of pictures is slightly ajar, so someone has been in there today since it was left fully shut earlier before I went out on the bike. Walking over to the drawer unit, Lloyd stares across at me and notices the drawer.

Pushing the drawer shut with a firm thud, I make my way to Lloyd still standing by the door, not saying a single word, but his body language says otherwise. We both knew what my actions meant and even with no words, Lloyd looks at me and then, nodding his head slightly, acknowledges that they have been caught out. Not making a big issue, the door is opened and, gesturing to Lloyd to go first, I take a final last look around the apartment and then I walk into the corridor. The door is closed and what feels to be another chapter in my life ends as the lock clicks shut. We start to walk down the corridor in the direction of the lifts and my mind is full of whether the agents are already here and what would Lloyd do? We reach the lift doors and Lloyd pushes the down arrow button then turns gradually, looking at me. He can sense that I'm tense over the situation and tries to give a calming smile, but he is not as convincing as Nick. Ping, the lift doors open and we make our way into the lift with Lloyd again pushing the button for the basement parking level.

As the doors close, the cables begin to creak as the lift descends to the basement with Lloyd and me being completely silent, trying to stare into the future. Lloyd must be wondering why he has to babysit the new guy and, even worse, have him stay at his place with government agents involved. He stands completely at calm as the lift stops and the doors open to the basement. Both walking out of the lift in the direction of Lloyd's car, I sense we are not alone and look around the basement for any possible signs of life with nothing evident. Reaching Lloyd's car, it unlocks automatically and Lloyd makes his way to the driver's side, opening the door and sliding into the seat. On the passenger side I lift the handle, unlocking the door, and lower the bag into the footwell. Then I lower myself into the seat, pulling the door firmly shut after seeing Lloyd's driving before. The engine is started and Lloyd reverses out of the parking space, turns the wheel, engages first gear and blasts towards the exit ramp with the engine roaring as we go.

The Audi drives up the ramp and the headlights of another car suddenly appear in the side mirrors. Lloyd turns his head slightly and looks into the rear view mirror to see the car and, without even blinking, pushes the accelerator hard and almost launches the car from the ramp. The force pushes me hard into the seat as it hits the main street with the wheels spinning, generating a screeching noise from the tyres. The other car starts to accelerate, but no way can keep up with the power and handling of the Audi combined with Lloyd's precise high speed driving. Looking back towards the apartment through the ever decreasing daylight is the silhouette of a man standing around twenty metres away from the exit ramp and what appears to be a cigar being smoked who watches the two cars making their way along the street. The shape of the headlights confirm the car is a Mercedes and under the reflection of the street lights, it has a dark colour and appears to be the same car that followed me earlier with the agents. Lloyd continues to push the Audi harder with the speedo reading over eighty miles per hour on the narrow city streets as the engine roars and barks with every gear change and corner. The Mercedes following begins to back off as Lloyd heads for the dual carriageway and the signs for the motorway.

"We need to ditch the Audi somewhere safe, these guys are following us. They will already have done a PNC check on the car, but it's not registered in my name or the address where we are going." Lloyd looks in the rear view mirror and continues.

"I have a less conspicuous car in a safe place." Lloyd, at the last moment, turns away from the motorway entry slip road and heads back towards the city.

Blue police lights can be seen heading along the carriageway in an attempt to try and cut us off, but Lloyd has already turned down a dark narrow lane. The Audi headlights illuminate rows of lock up garages all having different coloured doors. Near the end of the lane, Lloyd stops the car, but keeps the engine running and, opening the door, he slides out of the seat and walks over to the last garage. Taking a key from his pocket, he opens the padlock and pushes the door sideways, disappearing inside. I hear another car engine start and then lights glow from the darkness of the garage as a silver Audi A4 Saloon begins to appear from the garage as I still sit waiting in the R8. Lloyd parks the car, pointing in my direction with the sidelights just illuminated.

He jumps out and walks back to the R8, opening the driver's door, saying, "Okay, Dean, go get in the A4 Saloon, I will join you."

Climbing out of the R8, I walk towards the Saloon as the roaring sound of helicopter rotors fills the dark sky as a police chopper begins to circle over the carriageway around five hundred metres away from us as the R8 disappears into the lock up garage. Lloyd reappears and pulls the sliding door shut and, after closing the padlock, he begins to walk over. I open the passenger car door of the A4 and instantly notice the smell of damp, musty air as though the car has been standing for a long time with the windows covered with condensation on the inside. The rear passenger door is opened and the holdall bag placed on the rear seat as Lloyd reaches the car. Closing the rear door, I climb into the car and feel the dampness of the seats against my jeans and wait for Lloyd to join me. Lloyd switches the heaters on full and takes some cloth from the front door bin to rub the wetness from the windscreen as I pull the front passenger door closed and try to rub at the condensation formed on the windows as the warmth from the heater begins to take effect across the glass surface. Lloyd closes the door and, with the headlights on full, we make our way back into the city and in the direction of Lloyd's place to rest for the night before tomorrow's robbery.

Driving along the streets, I start to think about the heist and now begin to look forward to the life changing events that are unfolding in front of me, never thinking twelve months ago I would be involved with a plan to rob money and escape a millionaire. It feels completely unreal, but then reliving the conversation with Wagstaff today, my future plans seem to come to a complete stop. Wagstaff mentioned far more than I told Nick about and the type of person he was, along with the things he had done in the past, but after what Sophie told me there was no surprise. My biggest fear is what Nick will do after the heist because I can't imagine he will simply disappear over the horizon, never to be seen again. Remembering the expression on Wagstaff's face, I could tell he absolutely hated Nick with a passion and would do anything to stop him. He kept on about the nasty side of Nick and how he treated people and the pictures of dead men and women flash through my mind. Looking at the total commitment of someone like Lloyd and how he respects Nick, there is clearly a different side to him and Wagstaff probably has some unfinished business. I never told Wagstaff anything about the robbery tomorrow and Nick will have picked up on this today since he never asked me.

Lloyd drives casually and calmly through the streets, heading for the suburb of Crawley West Sussex where finally we reach a detached house on St Catherine's Road. The car pulls onto the drive at the end of the street and, stopping the engine, Lloyd gestures. Both getting out of the car, I open the rear passenger door to take out the bag and in doing so gradually look around at the houses in the dimness of the street lights. I see different vehicles ranging from SUVs, Porsches, Mercs, Beamers and Audis parked on the driveways in true posh suburban life. Lloyd makes his way to the front of the house, opens the door and walks inside. After switching off the alarm system, he beckons with his right hand and then continues back into the house. Closing the car door, I walk up the pathway and reach the house, following Lloyd inside. The front door is closed shut with a solid thud and I begin to walk along the light oak laminate flooring of the entrance hall, staring at the plain white walls. Leaving my bag near a coat stand on the left side of the hall, the noise of running water filling a kettle can be heard in what appears to be the kitchen at the end of the hallway, so continuing to walk in the same direction, I pass three more white closed doors, two on the left and one to the right.

Reaching the kitchen, Lloyd has placed the kettle onto the black granite work surface and, clicking the switch on, it gradually murmurs into action as he turns around, saying, "Tea or coffee?"

Casually glancing around the high gloss white kitchen, I reply, "Coffee would be good."

"I had better give you a quick guided tour," Lloyd announces.

Walking past me we start down the hallway. "Okay, the first door closest to the entrance is the downstairs toilet. The next door leads up the stairs and the one opposite is for the living room," he says as he points at each of them.

Lloyd walks to the first door and opens it, showing me the living room with just a light grey leather settee with two matching arm chairs, a huge plasma TV on the wall, and simple glass coffee table in the middle of the room. Closing the first door, he then makes his way to the door opposite, opens it and clicks the light switch to illuminate the straight gloss white staircase leading upstairs. Walking up the stairs, each step makes a slight creaking noise and as we reach the landing there are five more doors, all closed.

Opening the first door in front of us he says, "This is the office," as we walk fully inside. The room is pure white and has a single laptop and printer sitting on a dark oak desk with a black swivel chair pushed underneath.

Still standing by the office door, Lloyd then points with his right hand at the other doors in sequence. "The next door is your room for tonight, the third door is my gym room and the fourth door is the main bathroom. Finally, no guessing my room is at the end and I don't want any visitors tonight." Lloyd smiles at me.

"Okay, make yourself at home and I will finish the coffees." Lloyd turns and makes his way back down the stairs towards the kitchen.

Walking back down into the hallway, I lift my bag from near the coat-stand and quickly make my way back up the stairs. The second door is reached and, opening it, I feel for the light switch and on the right wall it is felt and clicked to reveal a simple double bed against a side wall, two white bedside cabinets and a chair in the corner of the room near the window. Walking to the chair, the bag is placed onto the seat and then, closing the window blinds, I turn and make my way back downstairs after switching off the light and closing the door. It appears that all the rooms are painted plain white with the same laminate flooring throughout. Reaching the kitchen, Lloyd is finishing making the coffee and is carrying a cup in each hand. Seeing me, he extends out his left arm, offering me a cup. Taking the cup, we both walk into the living room and take a seat on each of the armchairs.

Lloyd sits on the chair closest to the door which has the TV remote resting on the right arm with the coffee cup in his left hand. I sit in the other chair and collapse with a big sigh. As Lloyd looks across he lifts the remote and, clicking on the big sixty inch plasma TV, starts to flick through the channels as people do in a hotel room, looking for anything to watch. Settling back into the boxing match he was watching earlier at my place, I can see he is totally engrossed with the two boxers hitting each other round after round and shows no signs of any emotions, almost like a robot. My eyes are looking at the screen, but my mind is full of the last few days and especially today with the words of Wagstaff along with the pictures he showed me of Nick's actions.

The strangest emotion was that Nick's actions didn't worry me and it even felt as though I was part of it, visualising the acts of terror. Perhaps it's just me dreaming and hoping to be accepted by all the team making visions from different Hollywood films or maybe there is something more. I continue to think about Wagstaff. His words were so sharp and aggressive as though he had lots of anger locked inside from the past and perhaps Nick was the explanation for all this. Starting to think about Sophie, a warm glow begins to be felt inside as an image grows in my head from her blue eyes looking across at me smiling. I sense her kiss and can almost taste her lips against mine with Dolce & Gabbana perfume floating in the air.

Then reality starts to kick in with the robbery tomorrow and the fact that Sophie could be a distraction when things happen in the future. It's been a long time since I have felt like this about anyone, and why does it start now of all times? Maybe it's a sign to cut her loose and move on, since finding commitment is very hard after being hurt. Trusting people is always difficult when you're hurt by people who you love, it's hard not to be defensive when things start to get complicated and when feelings take over what's inside your heart and their slightest actions annoy you. No person should be alone, but certain people like me may have been damaged too much in the past that it can't be repaired and are afraid of trusting other people because of being hurt again. Loners generally have baggage left over and have decided that a lonely life is a safe one and understand well that they may never find that special person to share life with.

KNOCK, KNOCK, KNOCK. All our thoughts stop abruptly with the sound of someone hammering on the front door. Lloyd jumps out of his seat and makes his way into the hallway, clicking along the flooring as he goes. Noise of the front door being opened can be heard along with muffled talking.

After a few moments, the door is closed and two pairs of footsteps echo down the hallway, getting ever louder in the direction of the living room. Nick appears at the door and makes his way to the settee. Lloyd continues into the kitchen and the kettle starts to boil again. Nick, now sitting, looks across at me, staring, then turns and looks at the TV.

"Is everything okay, Nick?" I sense that something is wrong.

Nick blows out a big sigh and answers, "No, Dean, we have lots of heat on us at the minute and it's not just you, Ramone and Carlos are being followed too for a few days now."

Lloyd walks back in with a cup of coffee for Nick, hands it to him and asks, "Is the job too hot at this time, Nick?" Lloyd sits down on the settee.

"Lloyd, we have a plan for tomorrow, so let's assume that we are under surveillance right now. There is only one way to lose these bastards." Nick continues to speak, looking at his wrist watch at the same time, then he takes the cup of coffee.

"Okay, it's 8.30 p.m. now and a bank holiday weekend so let's plan a vacation for tomorrow. Lloyd, pull up Skyscanner on the laptop and check last minute cheap flights for six of us." He rests the coffee cup on the arm of the settee and reaches inside his pocket, handing over a six passports and a credit card to Lloyd.

"Use these IDs and credit cards to book the flights." Lloyd jumps from his seat and races up the stairs with the noise of thumping as his feet touch each step.

Nick, lifting the coffee cup, looks across at me, saying, "These bastards have been tracking some of us for years, but only recently with Ramone, Carlos and now you. It's quite clear that I will need your help after this job is done to tidy things up. How are you fixed?"

Still holding my coffee cup, I stare back at Nick, saying, "Whatever, Nick, to help." I have no idea what the tidying up will be, but I can't imagine it will be anything dangerous.

Lloyd shouts from upstairs, "How about a few days in Prague? A flight leaves at 10 a.m. from Gatwick tomorrow with EasyJet and they have six seats left."

Nick replies back clearly and concisely, "Perfect, Lloyd, book it now!" then he takes a sip of coffee and reaches into his jacket for a mobile phone then places it next to me.

"Dean, use this phone it's clean." Nick instructs.

Nick then starts to speak again with anger in his voice. "This will be the last time these bastard agents stick their noses into my business. I will make sure this never fuckin' happens again. Who the fuck do they think they are messing with?" Lloyd re-enters the room with a piece of paper showing the flight detail and passes it to Nick.

Taking out another mobile phone from the black leather jacket he is wearing, he then starts to type out a message. After a few seconds both Lloyd's cell and the new mobile burr as a message arrives reading: "Gents, the bank holiday plans are booked for Prague, so we meet at Gatwick Airport at 6.50am ready for the 10.00am flight so plans have changed, due to the heat in Spain, don't forget your fancy dress. Flight number EZY5493."

"Sure this room is clean?" Nick asks, looking across to Lloyd as he sits in his chair.

"Yes, boss, the door sensor was clean and no motion has been detected," Lloyd replies with a look of shock on his face.

Nick places the cup on the floor by the side of the settee and stands holding the cell in his right hand. He walks to the door, closes it and begins to move around the room, waving his arm in a sweeping pattern close to the wall. The screen appears to have what looks like a small radar chart illuminated in green and bleeps at a constant pitch. I can tell Nick is sweeping the room for any possible bugs before he will talk any more. After what must feel like an eternity for Lloyd, Nick sits back down and continues to talk.

"It's clear that someone has talked!" He stares at the TV with a pissed off face.

Lloyd and I look at each other with shock on our faces and turn to look in Nick's direction.

"When I find out who has spoken, they will wish they have never crossed me!" Nick has anger across his face and in his voice, not seen or heard before.

"Loyalty, respect and honesty are the only things I value in life and all of these have been broken today, but at least I know you guys haven't said anything which means a lot to me." His voice begins to calm slightly.

"Whoever has crossed me is a fuckin' dead man walking and will never see another day once I find out who it is," He looks across to Lloyd then over towards me with deep sunken eyes.

My body begins to shake with fear from the look that can be seen in his eyes and as I begin to imagine some of the things Wagstaff had told me earlier. Nick is a machine who will stop at nothing until he gets what he wants. Looking over to Lloyd, I notice he is also in shock and from his face he has never seen Nick like this before. Thankfully Wagstaff was never told of the heist tomorrow from me, but I could sense that he was after information so somebody in the team must have spoken since it was too much of a coincidence.

"Who else is joining us at the airport, boss?" Lloyd asks.

"Ramone, Carlos and Josef. The other guys will meet us at the rendezvous." Nick continues as he begins to stand and looking across to Lloyd.

"Pick me up at 5.30 a.m.; there are a few things we need to sort in the morning before we meet at Gatwick."

"I will contact the other guys on another cell from the club to tell them to meet at 6.15 a.m. at the airport; I want to be long gone before any agents arrive tomorrow." Nick opens the living room door.

"Yes, boss, no problem. Pick you up from the club?" Lloyd asks.

"Perfect, Lloyd. Have a good evening, gents, and see you tomorrow." Nick looks across to me smiling and standing, wishing him a good night. We shake hands as he leaves the room and then the sound of the front door opening and closing in the distance can be heard.

Lloyd and I then sit back down in the chairs and just look at each other, wondering what tomorrow will bring as the time clicks over to 9 p.m. We watch the next boxing match live on the TV, but both of us are thinking about tomorrow and what will happen. We know deep down it could go either way when we walk into the airport. Nick's confidence is so inspiring it feels as though bullets could slide past and throwing Wagstaff off our scents feels exciting with a big risk thrown into the deal.

I need to break the silence so I ask Lloyd, "Have you and Nick done anything like the robbery before?"

He turns and looks, replying, "Not in this country, but yes."

"Really, Lloyd, where did it happen?" I ask, excited.

"Don't repeat to Mr Nick, but we got into some trouble once over the border in Poland and needed a quick escape route. We had no money so robbed a small local bank for some cash."

"Obviously you guys escaped but were there more of you?"

"Only two more guys but this sorting house is much bigger with lots of moving variables. The Polish bank was just a late Friday afternoon hit and bit of fun."

Not being surprised at Lloyd's answer and knowing these guys have done this before, an inner calm makes me more comfortable as the time quickly clicks over to 10.30 p.m.

Lloyd, noticing the time, stands, saying, "That is me for tonight. A big day tomorrow so I need some rest." He turns and walks out of the room.

"Right behind you," I say as the TV is switched off. Following Lloyd out, I click the light switch, sending the room into darkness.

Climbing the stairs, I reach the spare bedroom doorway and look across towards Lloyd's room as the light disappears. I walk into the bedroom and touch the bedside light that illuminates the room enough to return back to the landing and, clicking off the light, I turn and reach the bedroom.

After closing the door I undress and climb into the bed with my mind racing over and over about the airport and what will happen during the robbery, in the darkness of the night after the light is switched off. Inside my mind images and conversations with Wagstaff, Burns, Lloyd, Sophie and Shaun all appear as though they are in the room with me as I finally fall asleep.

5

Earlier in the evening at the main entrance doors of MI6, the figure of a limping man can be seen entering the building and starting to make his way through the security check point inside. As usual his artificial leg sends the metal detector flashing and buzzing. The police realise who the man is and stand at ease with machine guns held on safety. The man continues through the maze of corridors to a small room with intelligence surveillance signage on the dark wooden door. Opening the door, three young men can be seen inside, staring at computer screens. Two of the men are wearing headphones and are listening to recordings of conversations, trying to understand key code words and voices from the digital information.

Wagstaff limps over to the man not wearing any headphones and asks, "So, Peter, what do you have for me on a Sunday evening at 9 p.m. that couldn't be said over the phone?"

"Sir, we intercepted a message that was sent from an unknown mobile in the Crawley area of West Sussex to some of the suspects on the list you asked us to monitor," Peter replies.

"How many people received the message? Who were they? And most importantly, what did the message say?"

"Sir, the message read, 'Gents, the bank holiday plans are booked for Prague with EasyJet, so we meet at Gatwick Airport at 6.50 a.m. ready for the 10 a.m. flight so plans have changed due to the heat in Spain. Don't forget your fancy dress. Flight number EZY5493.'" Peter looks at Wagstaff.

"Damn, Burns is onto us somehow?" Wagstaff shows frustration in his voice.

"The suspects included Lloyd Farrell, Ramone Juan and Thomas Müller. Another person received the message but we can't trace that mobile."

"Get agents Preston and Wilson on the phone now," Wagstaff instructs.

The phone begins to ring and a woman's voice can be heard. "Wilson speaking."

"Please give your badge number," Peter asks.

The woman replies, "4824DOB11021971."

Another phone line rings and a man's voice can be heard. "Preston speaking."

"Please give your badge number," Peter asks.

The man replies, "5759DOB24081968."

Both the agents are connected onto a speaker phone. "Wilson, Preston, Wagstaff here, the op is blown. Burns confirms code tonight instructing the team we are following them; the team will be at Gatwick airport from 6.50 a.m. tomorrow morning. Do not intercept, hang back and follow. The team's plans are to fly to Prague with EasyJet at 10 a.m."

"How many other agents are cleared for observation, sir?" Preston asks.

Wagstaff replies in a strong voice, "Six in total are authorised and will be waiting at the main on ramp to the airport in three cars at 6.30 a.m. Two agents have been cleared to be stationed on the EasyJet counter as baggage staff. Do not, repeat, do not intercept any of the suspects. Is that clear?"

"Yes, sir," Wilson and Preston both reply.

"Okay, good evening everyone and Preston, pick me up at 5.45 a.m. I want to be there early to see my old friend Burns."

"Yes, sir, understood," Preston answers in a subdued voice.

Wagstaff clicks the speaker phone off and starts to make his way out of the small room and back through the maze of the main office without another word being spoken to anyone. The expression on his face says it all with a deep frown across his forehead and eyes sunken behind his frameless glasses. Wagstaff knows what type of character Burns is and will stop at nothing to catch him. He continues to limp out the through the main doors, past the security guards, and then, standing on the pavement, waves down a taxi as he does every time he leaves the office. The time on his old battered leather strap wrist watch reads 10.05 p.m. and, with deep thoughts of what will happen tomorrow, he opens the rear door of a black taxi cab and the car drives away, weaving its way on the busy streets of London.

The dawn breaks on the start of a new day and the sun rays shine through the vertical window blinds of Lloyd's spare bedroom, casting shadows all around different surfaces. The reflections of the daylight bend around the bed, away from the bedside cabinets and the chair legs with light and dark silhouettes. Continuing to look around the room, I didn't take much notice last night, but today it's evident there is no clutter, no pictures and no feeling of soul or family in this house being very cold and almost clinical. Lying in the bed I think about the loved ones in my life and particularly the girl that was left behind and how much I will always be madly and deeply in love with her, but we could never be together. I start to think about how much I want to wake next to her every morning and feel her naked breasts next to me, her touch sending shivers down my spine and the pleasure of that first look at each other in the morning from each other's pillows. My mind starts to remember our first kiss and the magic of the electricity and chemistry that was felt rushing through my whole body and the warm glow inside.

The first touch of her naked skin against yours and the first time you made love and how much pleasure you felt inside and the addition of wanting to feel that experience again and again. Reality starts to kick in and the realisation of being that much in love with someone that you would do anything for them, sell your soul and your life for theirs. The realisation that you shared a love with someone that intense that when you were away every SMS, email and phone call ignited a flame back in your heart that glowed that kept you warm at night. Finally, though, the reality that she was married to someone else with a family of her own and that no matter how much you loved each other and no matter how much you wanted to be together it would never be, so you make the biggest and probably the worst choice in your life when you had to say goodbye. Goodbye, what a word to say to someone you love, whether it's every morning when you go to work, hoping to see them later that day and missing them before you have even left the house. Goodbye to someone when you break a relationship or, worst, the final goodbye when someone dies.

Breaking a relationship is sometimes a form of bereavement when your heart feels like someone has stuck it with a dagger and possibly knowing that you will never see that other person again. The feeling that you are back on your own in the big, wide world and the feeling that maybe you will be alone for the rest of your life. The feelings of how much you want them back and would do anything to just see them, feel their touch or to kiss them again, but knowing deep down it has run its course and should never have gone on as long as it did. This sadness in your heart feels like there is a great big black hole that once had the love of that someone special who was so precious to you. That feeling has now gone and after all the pain and heartache comes the resentment and why you split up, why did you let them go, and why didn't they want you back? The thoughts then change to maybe this was not meant to be and fate played a game with you, just to let you experience love and pain, preparing you for losing someone special and how to recover from it. Self-preservation instantly tells you to build barriers and walls to prevent this pain and hurt from happening again, to protect yourself. This pain, though, seems to change with time and never really goes away, but changes to a tolerable ache.

The ache allows you to remember that person for who they were and what they gave you and showed with affection, caring and a sense of being loved. The thoughts then change to the new adventure and what today will bring, what will happen during the heist suddenly fills my mind. Lifting my right hand, I wipe away the tear that had started to roll down my right cheek, not wanting to show Lloyd my soft side. I need to be focused and hard, but the mind fills with 'what if' scenarios such as, what if the police show up? What happens if the money isn't there? What if people are shot and wounded? What if I'm shot and wounded? What happens if I'm caught after the fear felt from yesterday? Maybe it's the tearful start to the morning and thinking about the past, but as my pulse begins to increase, I must learn how to control these new feelings and emotions otherwise I will be useless to the team, but how is the biggest question. Noises can be heard in the house as Lloyd starts to move around and the bathroom door opens then closes. The sound of the toilet being flushed and a tap is switched on for a few seconds.

Deciding to get up from this bed of depression and face the world today to see what will happen, I begin to remember the words of Nick from last night and the fear felt. After a few more minutes Lloyd can be heard walking down the stairs and then the front door is opened and closed with a firm thud. Looking at my watch, the time clicks around to 5.15 a.m. Not knowing fully what to expect today, I make my way into the bathroom and complete the usual shower, cleaning teeth and preparing for the day ahead, but my mind is full of what could happen and as more emotions rush through my body, I begin to shake with both fear and excitement at the same time. Walking back into the bedroom, the clothes are pulled onto my part naked skin and I make my way down the creaky stairs towards the kitchen. The cups and spoons from last night are still in the sink unwashed, so I take the cup used from last night. It is washed along with a teaspoon then a scoop of coffee granules is taken from the jar and placed inside the cup.

The kettle sitting on top of the beech effect worktop is checked for water level then switched on and immediately begins to burble as the element inside starts to warm the water. Looking around the kitchen the smoked glass dining table is clear of any placemats or papers and the black leather chairs are neatly arranged, pushed under the surface. As with the rest of the house the room is clean and undisturbed by any forms of personal items. Steam fills the air from the boiling water so, walking back to the white kitchen, the coffee drink is made and the milk carton taken from the barren fridge only storing an opened can of baked beans, a box of eggs and a small amount of butter in a covered dish. Replacing the milk carton in the fridge, I make my way past the dining table to look at the rear garden through the patio doors. The garden is on one level and consists of a large section separated by a straight path built from block paving. The blocks are completely overgrown with weeds and it's difficult to see the boundary between the path and grass. The perimeter of the garden is protected on the remaining three sides by unpainted fence panels that are all twisted and beginning to break apart. I'm sure Lloyd's neighbours love his gardening attempts, but at least the garden is full of songbirds taking seeds from the heads of the yellow uncut grass gracefully swaying in the morning breeze.

Watching the grass, an area on the left side of the path begins to sway faster than the remaining section and a black cat appears holding a dead mouse in its mouth. It looks at me, staring at it through the large glass doors. Suddenly turning, it makes a few quick steps towards the side fence, jumps up the panel and disappears over the top into the neighbour's garden. My thoughts begin to be filled with the feeling of the cat in the garden hunting the mouse and the hunter after its prey and what is clear from today is that we will become the mouse and the agencies will be the cat hunting us to what feels like no escape. The silence of the house is suddenly broken with the opening and closing of the front door followed by the familiar voices of Nick and Lloyd returning. Turning, I make my way to greet them and ask if they want a coffee. Nick is standing in the hallway dressed in casual blue jeans and T-shirt, dressed similar to Lloyd. Immediately it is noticeable that the tension from last night is no longer hanging in the air as the two of them have small smiles on their faces, looking very calm and relaxed.

"Morning sleepy head, how are you today?" Nick asks.

"Morning, Nick. I'm well, how are you?" I reply.

Nick returns a smile and Lloyd speaks. "Hey, a breakfast wasn't part of the accommodation costs!"

"Well, I would have offered to make breakfast but the fridge and cupboards are bare, Lloyd." I return a sarcastic smile.

"Cheeky bastard," Lloyd replies with Nick laughing.

Today the atmosphere is very refreshing. Maybe this is Nick's way of making sure people don't make mistakes under pressure, or it could be part of an act with the lull before the storm. Either way it feels better. Looking at my wristwatch, the time reads 5.45 a.m. so Nick must live close by to Lloyd.

"We have your fancy dress for today, Dean." I notice Nick holding a bag.

"Oh great, what am I, Cinderella?" I reply back quickly.

"Nothing that fancy, Dean." Nick holds out the plastic bag for me.

Taking the bag, I look inside and notice a pair of grey tracksuit bottoms, white T-shirt and New York blue baseball cap.

"Okay, Dean, this is the plan. We will all travel in Lloyd's Saloon to Gatwick. Lloyd will stop near departures and to drop me off. He will continue for the parking and inside the building on F5 stop for you to get out and finally leave the car on F6. You need to make your way to the check in using the fake passport in the plastic bag. Remember, take out the black Nike holdall from the boot, but don't check it into luggage cargo" Nick orders.

"Yes, no problems, Nick," I answer back calmly.

"Lloyd will then make his way to check in and, once we are all sorted, I will finally make my way in and complete the check in of the group, to check how many agents are following."

Nick continues "Once we have checked in before security check, each of us will gradually make our way to the toilets and change into different clothes from the plastic bags and then return back to the parking where two other cars have been placed in zone F4. The cars are a white VW Passat and grey BMW 5 Series. Both the cars are estates and have fifty-seven plate registrations being identified by a sticker of a green flag in the top left corner windscreen. Chose any of them to wait inside."

"I don't understand why we are going to the airport, Nick," I ask.

He replies, "There are several reasons for using the airport. One, we can clearly be seen checking in with the CCTV coverage. Two, I can check how many agents are following us. Three, police surveillance can't fly over passenger airport routes. Four, the job will be completed before the flight even takes off, so we won't be missed until it's too late. Now is that what you call a plan or what?"

Lloyd and I both nod in agreement, but my mind begins to think that some of the team in the same place at the same time is a big risk for the agents to grab us and stop the robbery before it even starts.

Nick then continues, "You both probably think that this is a bigger risk, but that's part of the fun, showing these bastards how fucking stupid they really are. So grab your party clothes and let's go," Nick instructs.

"Nick, are we all meeting at the airport?" I ask.

"No, Dean, I only managed to get six passports and, besides, I have used them for the people Wagstaff is following, that will fuck his plans up." Nick laughs.

Lifting the bag we make our way out of the warmth of the house into the freshness of the August morning and towards the parked sliver Audi A4 on the driveway with our breathe leaving a very faint smog in the air from the moisture. The housing estate has an eerie sound of silence on this holiday morning so no cars rush away for the daily commute. Nick and Lloyd scan all around the parked cars and houses, checking for any possible signs of movement or sound, but the only noise that can be heard is coming from the birds singing in the trees, enjoying the start of the morning, defending their boundaries from rivals. The peacefulness is suddenly shattered by an aircraft passing overhead, leaving large white vapour trails against the clear blue morning sky.

Reaching the car, Lloyd clicks the remote central locking, opening the doors, and makes his way behind the driver's wheel. Nick sits in the front passenger seat and, knowing the size of Lloyd, I opt for the seat behind Nick, hoping for a little extra room. I climb inside, throwing the plastic bag on the back seat. The inside windows of the car are instantly covered in a mist from our breath touching the freshness of outside, and Lloyd starts the engine and heaters trying to clear the moisture. The warm engine quickly begins to clear the mist from the windows, gradually exposing the parked cars and houses nearby. Finally, after a few minutes, we are on our way to Gatwick with my body is shaking almost uncontrollably from the fear of what will happen today.

Nick senses I am nervous and turns and looks at me, saying, "Dean, don't worry about today. Everything will be fine. Trust me, there is nothing here today that you have not seen before. Just keep clam and don't lose your nerve."

"Thanks, Nick, but I have never held guns before, let alone fired any and I don't know what to expect," I reply.

"Dean, have you ever used a PlayStation or an arcade game?" Nick asks.

"Yes, of course. Why?" I answer, a little shocked.

"Well, imagine your own PlayStation game and imagine using the weapons as you would to shoot the enemy. What we will be doing today is not different, in fact it is even better since it's real." Nick looks back through the windscreen, smiling.

"I hardly call what we're doing today like a PlayStation game, Nick," I reply with a sarcastic tone.

"Dean, trust me, if any action starts, your body will react as though it is second nature, and I have seen it before." Nick turns back to stare at me.

"Nick, where have you seen this before?" I ask sharply.

"Dean, all in time. Don't worry about today, just stay close to Lloyd and he will take care of you, okay," Nick commands.

"Yes, okay, whatever you say," I reply with a deep sigh.

The car clock ticks over to 6.05 a.m. as we begin to reach the departures zone at the airport. Every minute of this morning feels like an hour with every single piece of detail being remembered and my senses on overload as my emotions are ripped into pieces. I don't know what to cling to for some level of sanity check. Sitting in a car with men planning a head to head standoff with government agents, then a robbery before lunchtime, is a different lifestyle than I normally live. My mind doesn't know what is right or wrong anymore and the agents appear to be the bad guys stopping us from getting our money. The stomach is twisting and turning in knots with an excited yet nervous feeling and my whole body begins to start shaking again.

I know what we are doing is so wrong but why does it feel so right? Maybe it's another way of saying 'screw you' to the rat race and those people with boring lives. I have made several mistakes in my life, but this will definitely be the biggest and possibly the worst if we get caught. Nick's confidence flows like a fast moving river, engulfing everything in its path, and knowing he is in charge feels like once we are swimming he will protect all of us. It's the type of strength and support that I haven't felt for many years and it feels so reassuring.

As Lloyd pulls the Audi over into the drop off zone, he applies the brake but keeps the engine running. Nick gets out of the car and walks around to the back and lifts the lid. The noise of plastic bags being ruffled can be heard and then I notice he takes out a small black overnight bag. Nick closes the boot lid with a firm THUD, rocking the car slightly and, without even looking back in our direction, he makes his way through the crowds of people dressed in shorts, T-shirts and flip flops, dragging huge suitcases into the terminal building. Through the crowds of people, Nick can be seen standing near the outside smoking area holding a newspaper, lighting his usual Cuban cigar. Lloyd continues to drive through the drop off zone and follows the signs towards the parking area. More people are seen crossing the road in front of us and amongst all the holiday-dressed crowds are several people dressed in suits and smart casual wear. In the sea of faces my brain picks out certain details and begins to pull together the pictures. Ramone suddenly appears and walks along the pavement towards the direction of Nick, followed by Carlos a hundred and fifty metres behind.

Ramone walks closely past Nick, who has moved near to a metal rubbish bin, and an envelope is quickly taken from the top of the bin that probably contains the fake IDs for Ramone, Carlos and Josef. A man in his late forties wearing casual jeans and a T-shirt, showing several days of facial stubble, starts to walk slowly behind Carlos. From his body language and actions he has no intention of any holiday plans, but is clearly watching Carlos. Another two men dressed in sharp dark grey suits get out from a black taxi cab and, taking small suitcases from the boot of the car, begin the short walk into the terminal building past Nick. Lloyd turns into the airport multi-storey parking and stops at the barrier to collect the ticket, throwing it into the door bin, and then continues to drive up the ramps through the different levels. As he reaches zone F4 he slows down to check the two escape cars and, noticing the green flag stickers in the front windscreen, confirming the position, I breathe a small sigh of relief. Bringing the car to complete stop on level F5, Lloyd gestures to me to get out. So opening the door, the first thing rushing through my mind is there's no going back now as nervousness and excitement begin to rush through my body.

Grabbing the plastic bag, I climb out of the car, close the door and make my way towards the boot. Opening the lid, I notice two black holdalls, one with Nike and one with Adidas writing. Reaching inside, I take out the Nike bag as requested by Nick, but what is inside rushes through my brain as I close the boot lid and start to follow the signs for departure check in. Walking towards the main entrance of departures, the bag has almost no weight and, reaching the entrance, Nick can be seen standing holding a newspaper, smoking the large Cuban cigar. Walking past him, I head for the check in counter. I look on the big screens, trying to find the flight to Prague, EZY5493 at 10 a.m., with people everywhere and my body still shaking slightly. My vision is a little blurred but finally the check in counter numbers are found.

My heart is beating so fast it feels like it will explode in my chest as I reach the area for EasyJet counters. The six check in counters have people everywhere, with noise coming from the tannoy system announcing flight departures. Kids scream and cry as their parents try to carry and drag them along with luggage to the check in points. The six counters have four men and two women with two counters having additional men standing nearby supporting with luggage transfers to the belt. These two men instantly appear to be agents due to their build and how they try to handle the luggage in a clumsy manner.

The agents are already on the ground and I begin to shake with fear, knowing that this could possibly be the worst day of my life. Starting to join the queue for flight number EZY5493, Ramone and Carlos can be seen at separate check in counters. The two men trying to move the luggage pretend not to take any interest, but from their body language it's clear they are receiving instructions from the earpieces. The brothers act so calmly and know they are being watched as they hand over the fake passports and booking information. People begin to push and shove behind me as I observe the agents watching the counters.

Suddenly one of the agents stares across at me, speaking into the small speaker attached to his clothes, and my heart sinks into the pit of my empty stomach as the harsh truth of me being spotted at the airport finally hits home. Not knowing what to do, I begin to breathe a little heavier as the feeling of suffocation from the complete airport closing in around me takes over. Looking around, the brothers have completed their check in and start to walk away from the counter. Feeling inside the plastic bag for the fake passport, my hand shakes more and more with the main voice running through my mind, "I must remain calm and controlled otherwise the counter staff will notice something is wrong." Gradually following the line of snaking people, I reach the front of the queue as the two agents notice somebody making his way towards the check in counters as Nick appears. Observing the row of counters there is a fat couple struggling to load their luggage onto the weigh scales, two girls dressed in short skimpy clothing trying to impress one of the male staff, and further down the line is a man standing by a counter trying to speak with the young girl from check in staff and then finally an older couple move away from a young man on the end counter. Quickly walking across, I hand over the passport, having already memorised the name, date of birth and valid from and to dates.

"Good morning, sir, can I help you?" asks the man behind the counter.

"Good morning, I am on the flight to Prague," I reply, checking out his name badge. 'Paul'.

"Okay, sir, let's have a look. Yes, returning on Thursday?" Paul replies, tapping away on the computer.

"Ahh yes, a group booking, a few of the party have already checked in. Anything special, sir?" Paul asks.

"Yes, it's a mate's stag party. As always, in Prague, hey," I reply.

Paul looks back at me, smiling, as in the background one of the agents still stares at me, but also tries to find Nick in the crowds of people. "Mr Adams, we have you in seat 22E, is that okay, sir?"

"Yes, that's fine, thank you," I reply, still nervous of being caught with fake ID.

"Hand luggage only is it, sir?" Paul asks.

"Yes, that's correct, only a change of clothes and a toothbrush for me." I try to laugh. I stare at Paul and check out his face and body language to see if he is genuine staff or an agent.

Paul presses a button and a whirring noise can be heard as the boarding pass is printed off. He places it inside the passport and hands it back to me. "Have a safe trip, sir." He tries to smile back.

Taking the passport from the counter, I turn, making a huge sigh of relief as though a great weight has been lifted from my shoulders. I see Lloyd just reaching the front of the queue with Nick standing near the back, avoiding any eye contact. Continuing past them both, I walk over to the toilets that are situated near the entrance doors of the airport and, pushing the door open, I walk into the toilet block and begin to look for an empty cubical, but all are taken. My mind is full of what will happen once we leave the airport and meet later at the warehouse. I carry out a quick headcount of the people that are involved with the airport run today, Lloyd, Ramone, Carlos, Nick, me. That leaves one more person that I haven't seen. A toilet flushes and a cubical door opens as Josef suddenly appears from inside. He looks straight at me, but we do not acknowledge knowing each other just in case any CCTV is monitoring our movements.

Just then the sound of a police radio cracks behind me. "Crr Alpha Tango Foxtrot 7463, please give your status and position?" A woman's voice can be heard on the radio.

"Crr Alpha Tango Foxtrot 7463, just carrying a sweep of toilet block two Beta by the main entrance. No sign of any suspects control. Over and out." The young man's voice can be heard.

Josef walks past me and makes his way to the washbasin as the radio crackles again. "Okay, Alpha Tango Foxtrot 7463, proceed through to the main check in hall Yankee five, control over and out." The woman's voice instructs.

"Confirmed and understood, out." The policeman turns and walks from the toilet block.

Making my way to the toilet cubical, my heart is beating so fast, it's hard to breathe. Managing to take a few large gulps of air, the pungent smell of cleaning liquids causes me to cough as the taste of chemical vapour clings in my throat. The door is closed as the taps stop running and the sound of rustling paper can be heard followed by the noise of faint footsteps clearly indicating that Josef has walked out of the room.

Leaning against the door, the lock is clicked closed and, lowering the Nike bag to the floor, I begin to remove the clothes from the plastic bag and start to exchange the clothes.

Mine are placed into the plastic bag. I take another deep breath and lean back against the cubical door in an attempt to try and compose myself for the next part of this journey to the car park, but first I must see what is inside the Nike bag. Lifting the bag from the floor, I focus on the long zip and, gradually pulling it open, I notice that the bag only has some more black canvas bags inside. Wondering what these are for, I close the zip and then, picturing the next stage, more thoughts race into my mind. What happens if the agents follow me? What happens if I'm left here? What will happen today? The thoughts keep filling my mind over and over again. I feel dizzy and faint and begin to start sweating as I click open the door lock.

My vision is slightly blurry again, probably from high blood pressure, and my head feels so light and out of balance. Reaching the washbasins and placing the holdall bag on the floor, I begin to throw some cold water on my face. I stand with my hands resting each side of the basin and continue to take deep breaths, slowly trying to clear my head and focus myself for the day ahead. Then I stare into the large mirrored wall by the basins. Wiping off the cold water from my face with some paper towels and now feeling a little better, I begin to notice more of my surroundings with the white tiled walls of the room glimmering from the florescent tubes flickering as the tannoy system announces another final call. The heavy grey toilet door is hard to open with the counterweight broken as my ears are filled with the humming noise from the crowds of people talking that hangs in the air like a thick blanket smothering everything else. The noise begins to reduce as I walk through the departure hall towards the direction of the main automatic entrance doors. Looking briefly across, Nick can be seen at one of the counters with both of the agents staring at him. Even from this distance the tension in the air is so thick it could be cut with a knife, but Nick remains calm and calculated, not even rising to the fact that the agents want his head.

Reaching the entrance, the feeling of freedom is overpowering as the doors slide open and the brief silences from people's voices is now filled with the roar from engines as aircraft blast down the runway and take off with the time on the main clock over the doors showing 6.32 a.m. I make my way towards the escape cars and see a silver Ford Mondeo and Black BMW 3 Series are parked together near the drop off zone with four men standing by them. Just from the body language it's clear that these guys are agents as two of them smoke cigarettes and the other two look at skimpy dressed women going on holiday. A familiar black Mercedes suddenly arrives and all the men try to look bothered and interested in the work today. In the distance Wagstaff climbs out from the back of the Mercedes and even from this distance I can see he is not amused, giving all the men a few choice words.

Wearing the baseball cap and casual clothing, I manage to take a wider route, sneaking past the guys as Wagstaff gives them a stern telling off. The flaky green painted door is opened and I begin to climb the concrete steps of the multi-storey car park as my nostrils are filled with the smell of damp musty-filled air. The yellow door for zone F4 is pulled open and I begin to walk in the direction of the escape cars. The exhaust gases can be seen rising from two of the cars just as a Silver Mondeo passes by me with two men inside.

Quickly glimpsing the car, I notice the men are dressed in sharp suits and, looking at the registration plate, I notice it is the one from near the drop off zone so this is probably two agents looking for us. The car slows for a split second, but then accelerates and speeds past the two escape cars and heads back down the exit ramp. With every footstep my heart races faster from the excitement of today as the agents are given the slip before we head towards the warehouse. I feeling so curious over what will happen today and hope that my actions don't let Nick down after everything he has said. Reaching the escape cars, the brothers are already sitting in the BMW and Lloyd sits in the Passat, gripping the steering wheel. He indicates across to me to join him in the car as I hear the staircase door swing shut with Nick quickly walking up behind me. Looking across at him briefly, I throw the holdall onto the seat then, climbing into the back of the Passat, I casually touch Lloyd on the left shoulder as a sign of success. Nick stands opposite the front of our car and scans all around the lines of parked cars looking for anything suspicious and indicates with a subtitle hand movement for Ramone and Carlos to go. As they pull away Josef can be seen climbing into the back of the BMW, closing the door quickly.

Nick walks over to the Passat and opens the passenger front door and in doing so continues to observe any movements within the building. With nothing looking out of place he quickly slides onto the front seat, closes the door and indicates to Lloyd to move. Lloyd engages first gear and calmly starts to drive through the car park, following the exit signs until he reaches the exit and stopping behind a blue Ford Fiesta just starting to drive under the raised barrier. Opening his window, Lloyd reaches into his pocket and, taking out a parking ticket, draws forward and stops by the machine. Sliding the ticket into the slot, the machine whirrs. Agents can be seen standing by the black BMW as the sliver Mondeo re-joins them with the other agents walking behind Wagstaff, making their way to the departures hall. After a few seconds and what feels like hours the barrier raises and Lloyd casually drives away from the car park with the brothers already at the next barrier gate waiting for it to open.

"Now, Lloyd, I've seen your driving before, nothing crazy until after the raid, okay?" Nick instructs.

"Yes, boss, of course," Lloyd replies with unhappiness in his voice.

"You see, Dean, no problems, hey?" Nick looks back at me.

"Well, for a minute I thought it was going to start when those two agents saw you at the check in," I reply, smiling.

"Hmm, yes, I saw them too, but I could tell they were not fully aware. But it was strange that none of us were stopped." Nick turns to look through the windscreen.

Lloyd has a look on his face that he doesn't know what we are talking about as I ask Nick, "Do you think Wagstaff instructed agents not to stop us?"

Nick replies, "Almost definitely, but why is the interesting question."

I can see he is deep in thought as Lloyd drives away from Gatwick towards the direction of the derelict Blue Prince mushroom farm near Horley where the warehouse is located. There is an eerie silence in the car with Nick and Lloyd both deep in thought, imagining how the events will happen today. Nick's attention to detail is unmissable and for him this is just another day at the office with government agents being a minor distraction. Lloyd will, of course, follow Nick everywhere and will not question anything he instructs, but there does appear to be nervousness in his face that I have not seen before. For me today feels so exciting with butterflies floating around in my stomach and then nervousness that I am doing something wrong and terrible, overtaken with Wagstaff's words beginning to haunt my every thought. Until now I could have gone back, but sitting in this car the thoughts of now being a criminal begin to take effect and a tear begins to fill my eye. My entire upbringing from early childhood by my parents has taught me to be kind, thoughtful and never to act in this way, but I have always felt as though something was missing deep inside and what happens today will change my life forever. The thought of taking money from a bank sorting house does not feel the same as breaking into a person's house and stealing their personal possessions, but theft is theft and if we get caught the key will be thrown away from the prison door.

"Are you ready, Dean?" Nick's voice breaks the silence.

"As ready as I will ever be, but not knowing what to be ready for is quite difficult," I reply with nervousness in my voice.

"Dean, remember, stay close to Lloyd and he will look after you." Lloyd can be seen nodding his head in agreement.

"If all things go well we will be in, out and gone quickly and peacefully, but you need to expect that if shit happens, it will happen fast." Nick seams composed and calm as ever.

He continues, "The only things that could go wrong are either a 'have a go hero' security guard or staff member or if a silent alarm is triggered. Josef and Thomas have the alarm system covered, so 'have a go hero' can be stopped quickly with a bullet to the head."

I look at Nick with shock on my face as Lloyd drives the car into what appears to be an area with warehouses and factory units. Reaching the warehouse, Lloyd parks the Passat in front of to the large roller shutter door as Nick operates the remote. The mechanical doors spring into life as the air is filled with the sound of metal creaking and scraping, gradually exposing a blackened space. Lloyd drives the car through the expanding opening and into the large empty warehouse as the others follow in the BMW. An arc of dark coloured Range Rovers are parked with two metal benches seen in front of the vehicles as Lloyd drives into the warehouse and stops the Passat opposite the benches, the time clicks over to 6.50 a.m.

Everyone climbs out of the cars, closing the doors behind, which sends a mechanical thudding echo through the quiet empty building. Pigeons fly around in the roof space, sending occasional feathers floating to the ground.

Looking around the warehouse, it is old and derelict, having broken windows and smashed glass everywhere, with parts of the roof hanging down where it has collapsed. The dull white paint flakes off the walls, exposing the grey concrete blockwork up to two metres high where the sections of bent and twisted metal window frames hang until they reach the sloping roof. White paint flakes and hangs from the roof in large sheets like a person has hung washing out to dry and the metal frame lattice structure has an off yellow colour from the rusty metal underneath. Water can be heard hitting the floor running from broken pipes. As a third car, a blue Vauxhall Insignia, arrives with Pete driving, having Vernon, Greg and Thomas inside. Nick remotely closes the roller shutter door, then Lloyd walks around to the back of the Passat and, after opening the hatch, he starts to lift out large green holdall bags, placing them onto the heavy metal benches. All the guys start to walk over to the benches as Lloyd makes his way over to the BMW and clicks the boot open. Nick begins to unzip the four bags that were placed on the bench surface top and starts to take out the black overalls, latex gloves, over boots and ski masks. Lloyd brings across two more bags and then walks back to collect the final pair from the same car. It is evident that the last four bags are heavy and make a slight clunking noise as they touch the hard surface.

"Gather round, gentleman, and take a set of each," Nick instructs as he lays the clothes into neat piles.

The air is silent with nobody talking, but looking around them, they are fully focused on the job in hand today. We begin to pull the overalls on over the clothing Nick gave us for the airport change and zip close the front. The noise of guns and magazines can be heard as Lloyd begins to empty out the weapons for everyone wearing a pair of latex gloves.

"Okay, there is a pistol and MP5 for everyone," Lloyd announces.

"Josef and Thomas, the 50 cal are in the back of the Insignia with a hundred rounds and are zeroed to seven hundred and fifty meters, that way you can both give cover when instructed." Nick looks across at them.

I pull on a pair of gloves and begin to walk over in the direction of the weapons neatly laid out on the bench top. Lloyd sees me and lifts up a pistol and slides back the top action, pointing the gun to the ground away from everyone. The gun clicks and Lloyd releases the top slide by slowly depressing the trigger and hands it over to me.

"PlayStation game, okay," he leans across and whispers in my right ear.

I take the weight of the pistol in my hands and can feel the coolness of the steel through my fingers. Lloyd then lifts another handgun of the same make and repeats the process, pointing the gun at the ground. He then looks at me, lifts up a magazine from the table and slides it into the butt of the handle with a positive click and finally pushes on the safety lock, replacing the loaded pistol back on the bench. Lifting a magazine, I repeat the same actions and instantly notice the difference in the weight of the gun as I lower it back to the surface.

The thought of holding a loaded pistol suddenly begins to feel like second nature to me as though I have done it before. Lloyd then reaches for an MP5 and holds it with the rear handle as he clicks the top bullet exhaust slide port open, then closes it with a firm push on the spring door. The trigger and safety lock are applied and a loaded magazine is pushed into the middle feed slot. Looking at the black machine gun, I pick up the MP5 with my right hand on the rear handle and complete the same actions as Lloyd with the other gang members looking at me.

"I have played call of duty before, guys!" I smile at everyone.

Nick begins to laugh and the silence is finally broken. Everyone then begins to talk amongst themselves, discussing the jobs they have done in the past. The smell of fresh gun oil and triggers being clicked fills the air as the team get to know their weapons.

"Remember that smash and grab we did in San Paulo?" Ramone asks Carlos.

"How could I forget, you shot the fuckin' getaway driver," Carlos replies.

"I hope that doesn't happen today, guys," Nick stares at them.

"Greg, remember that jewellery raid in Manchester when that guy tried to stop us?" Vernon looks across at everyone.

"Well, Vern, he didn't move after that sawn off blew half his head away," Greg answers back, stroking his MP5 and clicking the trigger.

"I hope you know how to use that, it's not your misses," Paul asks.

"I'm sure it will come back right, Dean." Greg looks across to me.

"Well, it's better than in resident evil that's for sure." I laugh with a fake smile.

Nick, picking up his MP5 and magazine, looks across to me and says, "Dean, walk with me a minute."

Nick begins to walk to the far left side of the building and stops around fifty metres away from the wall with me following behind. "Dean, do you know how to use one of these guns?" he says as we both stand together.

"Nick, I have never used one of these before, no," I reply.

Lifting the gun and turning it slightly pointing at the wall, he shows me the trigger settings indicating a little black lever. "See this switch? This changes the gun from single shot to either semi or full auto."

"Once the mag is pushed home, this spring loaded exhaust door needs to be cocked to load a round into the chamber." A click can be heard as Nick loads the magazine and then, cocking the exhaust port, he fills the chamber with a round.

Clicking the switch to single he hands me the weapon, still pointing it away from us. "Now pick a point on that wall, maybe that red paint mark, and take a shot holding the gun by the grip close to the front of the barrel and the rear handle."

I look at him in complete shock and begin to lift the gun up to my shoulder to look through the sights at the red mark about one and a half metres high on the wall. Pulling on the trigger, I tense my body to absorb the shock, but nothing happens.

Nick laughs, "You forgot the safety catch, everybody does it the first time." He points to the gun and shows me where the catch is by the trigger guard.

"Now this time don't tense up so much or snatch at the trigger otherwise it will affect how you take the shot. Look straight through the front and rear sight at the red mark and pull the trigger smoothly." He stands next to me smiling with reassuring words.

Clicking the safety catch off, I lift the gun to my shoulder again and, staring at a large red paint mark on the wall, take aim through the round sights. I begin to shake with adrenaline as the cross hairs move across the mark as trying to compensate the aiming becomes difficult. My heart begins to beat faster and then, remembering what Nick said, I begin to relax and, feeling comfortable, depress the trigger slowly. *BANG* echoes through the empty building and the recoil causes me to lean backwards as my nostrils are filled with the smell of gunpowder from the explosion of the bullet leaving the barrel. An empty 9mm bullet case pings on the ground with a small line of smoke still rising from the open end. Pigeons begin to fly everywhere and the team stops talking as the building falls into an eerie silence.

Nick looks across to me saying, "Bullseye. Well done, Dean, easy, hey."

Lowering the gun slightly, I look across at the red mark, seeing a bullet hole has hit the red mark on the wall almost central, chipping off some paint and blockwork. Clicking on the safety catch, I lower the gun completely and feel the rush of excitement from firing the round hitting the target first time and firing an actual real gun and not one from a PlayStation game. In the distance other guys in the team begin to talk again, breaking the silence.

"You see, the man can shoot after all," Nick proclaims with a smile on his face, looking across at the others.

"Now, Dean, switch the lever to semi auto, but this time don't lift the gun to your shoulder. Hold it at waist height and lean into the gun, ensuring you hold the barrel parallel to the floor." Nick shows me with a stance.

"How will I aim and target?" I ask.

"Pick the red paint spot on the wall and imagine that you have a stick pointing at it." Nick simulates.

"Now when you have that imagine clear in your mind, slowly depress the trigger and see where the bullets hit," he says as he stands back upright looking at me.

"Remember this time that you will need to lean a little harder into the recoil since three rounds will be fired one after the other and you will have a tendency to lift the gun trying to compensate the aggressive recoil." He crosses his arms and stands looking at the wall.

I click the safety catch off as Nick instructed and, leaning further into the gun, try to hold it parallel to the floor. Finally, imagining a stick to point at the mark on the wall, I depress the trigger. *BANG BANG BANG* can be heard as the recoil from each round echoes through the building and causes the gun to move slightly in my hands, making me lift the gun, trying to control the violent action. After the small amount of gun smoke clears three bullet hole marks can be seen on the wall in a straight line with the first shot being around half a metre away from the red mark and the last round hitting the top of the wall near the remains of the broken window frames.

"Not bad, Dean, but you need to hold the gun a little tighter to control the recoil. The first round is about half a metre above the red paint so hold the gun more towards the ground and try again," Nick instructs.

"Easier said than done, hey," I reply, lifting the gun back into position and holding it more firm.

BANG BANG BANG echoes again through the building as three more bullet holes appear on the wall, this time with a closer grouping around the red paint mark to half a metre.

"Better, Dean, a lot better and that will be fine for today; the machine gun is only used for close self-protection that delivers multiple shots for defence."

Nick continues, "Okay, click on the safety and push that small lever above the mag housing and pull the magazine clip to remove it. Now remember there is still a round in the chamber so you need to re cock the spring ejector door to eject it."

As instructed, the safety catch is applied and the lever depressed to remove the magazine clip. Then pulling back the ejector door the gun is made safe as I look at Nick asking, "Okay, so what's next?"

"Next we will try your skill with a pistol, but looking at the marksmanship with the MP5 I'm sure there won't be any problems. Place the MP5 by your feet and take this,"

Nick hands me over a pistol that he had in the pocket of his overalls.

"Now the safety catch can only select fire or safe so pointing the gun at the wall, pull back the top slide, this will engage a round into the chamber and press that small black button by the trigger guard, this will make ready the gun." Nick stands staring at me.

So following Nick's instructions, the top slide is activated, loading the round into the chamber, followed by making the gun safe. I ask the teacher for the next command. "Okay, so what's next?"

"Now take the pistol, click off the safety and point the barrel at the wall and, using the front and rear sights, line up the red paint mark and fire. Don't try to compensate at that distance so shoot straight." His words are so confidence building.

Clicking off the safety lever, I lift the gun and point it at the red mark on the wall, trying to line up the front and rear sight. Holding the weight of the gun with one hand is much harder than a plastic gun used on a PlayStation game and my hand begins to shake and as with the MP5 I try to compensate. *BANG* echoes through the building and another bullet hole appears, but away from the red paint.

"Relax, Dean, relax and gently squeeze the trigger. Don't snatch at it." Nick speaks with a calming voice.

Trying again, I lift the handgun and aim at the target through the sights, but the weight of the gun with the arm at full stretch is quite difficult. Determined not to give up and look like an idiot in front of the other guys, I begin to relax and the gun stops shaking so aiming becomes easier. *BANG* rings through the building once again as a bullet hole now shows near the red mark target.

"Not bad, Dean, that will be okay for today. For the firepower that we are all carrying, MP5s will be the better weapon today, the pistol is only for back up if we run out of mag clips." Lloyd casually makes his way over.

"What's he like, boss, can we hire him?" Lloyd laughs, then sees the bullet holes and continues, "Fuck, we should have had this guy before if this is the first time he has used weapons." He turns and quickly walks back to the other guys.

"It's not the first time, hey Dean? But remembering what you were taught will soon return." Nick takes the pistol from me and then bends to collect the MP5 from the ground.

Nick begins to walk back to the other guys as I continue to stand looking at the wall as the achievement of today begins to sink in, then the reality that I have just learned how to shoot two weapons that not only will protect me, but can easily kill people. This sickening thought then begins to sink in my mind. The thought of killing another person never entered my mind before and thinking that I could be responsible for somebody's death is difficult to contemplate. The truth of this crime now begins to take another direction, not only stealing money, but injuring or killing people had not been connected in my brain before now, but finally this link is made and, as a twisting sensation begins to fill my stomach, all the excitement of the last few days and the ego boost from firing guns suddenly disappears.

Nick's voice begins to register in my brain, "Dean, please join us."

"Each of the cars has black holdall bags in the boot. Dean, as you load them, make sure we have plenty by the wall." I nod in agreement.

"Nick, where's the C4 so I can check it over?" Greg asks.

"In the back of dark grey Range Rover the C4 shaped charges are prepared with detonator cords passing through them." Nick points across at Greg and Vernon as they begin to walk over and open the boot lid.

Turning around on the spot, I begin to walk in the direction of all the guys standing staring across at me. The movement of each footstep feels like an exit from my old life and entry into a new darker one. I have no understanding of what will happen in the future. My life up to this point has been planned and organised with education, study and hard work, but the last few days have felt like everything will now be given to me on a plate with the money from the robbery altering my life forever. Nick gives me such a high level of confidence and just his few simple words have me wondering what he knows about me and how this will alter my life. The buzz from firing the guns and the ringing still echoing in my ears begin to disappear as I reach the table with all the other guys. On the table there is a combat vest left and it's clear that this one is mine to wear with eight MP5 mags and four pistol clips lying next to it. Lifting the vest I place my arms through the holes and pull it over my shoulders, clipping the front buckle shut, then looking at the other guys, I start to fill the vest pockets with mags and pistol clips.

Nick reaches inside one of the last holdall bags and begins to hand out smoke grenade canisters for everyone. "These are just for escape purposes and must not be used in the money house, otherwise the sprinkler system will be activated, causing the emergency services to attend." Nick stares at everyone, giving clear instructions, and then lowers his head to look at his wristwatch.

"Okay, guys, lets synchronise watches. The time now is 07.05 precisely. Now Josef and Thomas, you take the blue Insignia and start to make your way to the building next to the road control centre. The laptops and 50 cals are bagged and ready to go. Make sure you bring the laptops and guns with you when I give the signal."

Nick continues. "You guys need to be in place and ready for eight, so I recommend you start off now following the pre-programmed navigation that Vernon has set. We hit the money house at eight thirty sharp."

"Okay, as discussed Ramone and Carlos take the dark blue Range Rover and take out that security hut, then cover the right road with stingers and have one ready to pull out on the left exit road to cover our escape, giving any cover for the road." Nick leans across the bench, staring at everyone with a heavy atmosphere hanging in the air.

"I have strengthened the dark blue Rangee with the bull bar welded to the chassis to take the loading," Paul replies as Nick nods his head in agreement.

Nick points across to Greg and Vernon. "You guys get as close to the outer wall as possible and set those charges ASAP. Remember, I want that wall down in thirty seconds."

Vernon replies, "C4 is checked and detonators set for fifteen seconds."

"Lloyd and I will bring up the third vehicle and park level to the second Rangee and wait for the charge to blow. Paul, you and Dean follow on with the fourth and park parallel to us." Nick taps his fingers on the bench in a drumming action, making an irritating noise.

"Remember, guys, even with the alarm systems disabled, I want to be in and out in three minutes, so we need to move fast. Those hostages and guards need rounding up quickly and any sign of aggression, take them out. Lloyd and I will bag the money and Paul can carry the bags to the wall, passing them through to Dean, who will then load the bags into the cars." Nick's voice has a serious tone.

"Worst case, a few hostages and maybe some police will need killing to escape, so get your game faces on and any pedestrians will soon run with some warning shots over their heads."

Nick continues, "Dean, can you fetch the Nike bag from the Passat, it has the empty money bags inside."

6

Josef and Thomas turn and walk in the direction of the car and as I reach the Passat the sound of the doors opening and closing can be heard from the Germans as they enter the car and start the engine of the Insignia. As they drive away with the tyres squealing from the violent acceleration, I turn and stare at them racing towards the exit, only slowing slightly as the closed roller shutter door begins to creak open. The rest of us then collect all the final equipment and make our way to the designated Range Rovers, climbing inside and waiting for the signal to move. Looking across at Paul, scars are now evident on his face and hands that hadn't been noticed before, but it's not the right place to ask which battle he earned them in. I can't believe that after the last few days we are finally en route to the robbery and my body keeps shaking with excitement and nerves. As Lloyd starts the engine first he then turns sharply, accelerating in the direction of the roller shutter door with Ramone, Vernon and Paul all following in convoy with their passengers.

The feelings in my mind are so mixed at the moment. Now sitting in the car with Paul and not knowing what he and the others think about me makes me nervous and out of the comfort zone that has been established until now with Lloyd and Nick. Lloyd takes the lead and begins to drive slowly from the old warehouse as we drive along the A23 in the direction of Croydon, knowing that the money warehouse is situated near to Beddington on an industrial estate just off Croydon Road. Travelling along the roads at normal speeds, Ramone follows close to Lloyd with Vernon holding back around a hundred and fifty metres and our car a similar distance gap. The lead car can be seen slowing down slightly and makes a sharp movement to the left as the driver's window opens and an arm appears as Lloyd waves Ramone to pass him as we drive past the signs for Purley Downs Golf Club.

"Oh Christ, this is it. We are getting close now!" Paul smiles across at me as Ramone speeds past the lead car.

Continuing along Purley Way, Ramone's car takes a sharp left turn and the Range Rover continues along a Croydon Road, with the tension in our car so intense not a word has been said between Paul and myself and my heart is beating so fast from the rush that is happening. Then suddenly the lead car makes a sharp left just past Cherry Hill Gardens and now begins to accelerate along the small industrial estate road, causing the tyres to squeal. All the other cars are taken aback from this action and have difficulty keeping up, but it can be seen in the distance that the car blasts through the security cabin at the front gate, knocking out the central controls and rendering the factory alarm systems useless. Lloyd's car drives through the single barrier arm and sends fragments of wood flying into the air as they continue in the direction of the main building with Vernon's car and ourselves following close by. Vernon overtakes the front car and quickly draws level with the wall of the warehouse and as the remaining other cars arrive Vernon and Greg have already climbed out and are just beginning to attach the charges on the wall in a circular pattern. Nick reaches inside the vehicle and, taking out the Nike holdall with the large black bags inside, waits for the signal.

Vernon shouts, "Fire in the hole."

Quickly taking cover by the front of the cars, Nick stands next to me and, with a huge smile on his face, gives the nod to Vernon to detonate the charges. A *BANG* suddenly echoes through the buildings and as the shockwave from the explosion hits, our bodies begin to vibrate as sections of the concrete wall fly into the air and a huge cloud of dust can be seen. In a few seconds it begins to clear, leaving a hole around one and a half metres in diameter, exposing the inside of the warehouse.

With the ringing of the explosion in our ears Nicks leans across and says, "Fill my vehicle first, followed by yours, okay."

Nodding in agreement and still in shock from the explosion, everyone begins to move quickly and silently, knowing exactly what to do with Nick, Lloyd, Vernon, Greg and Paul all climbing through the hole.

Before I reach the back of the cars, the familiar sound of gunshots rings out and shouting voices can be heard from the other side of the wall inside the building. As I look down towards the smashed gatehouse, Ramone and Carlos are already preparing the stingers for deployment across the road. Beginning to only imagine what could be happening inside the building, a black bag covered in concrete dust begins to appear from the hole in the wall and as I start to lift it from the fractured concrete the weight of the money inside can be felt. Lowering the bag to the floor, another bag already begins to appear and, quickly taking the second bag, I turn and place it into the boot of Nick's Range Rover as instructed. A third bag is quickly being pushed through the hole and, moving back to the wall, I take the third bag with the sound of a fourth already scraping its way along the dusty cracked concrete. Reaching for the fourth bag, I place it next to the others in the boot of the car and then quickly lift the first bag from the ground as the sound of police sirens can be heard echoing in the distance.

Placing it next to the other three, the boot is full so the split tailgates of the Range Rover is closed as a sinking feeling begins to develop in the pit of my stomach. My heart begins to sink as the excitement of the heist now drops to the new level of fear and the chances of being caught now start to become a reality. Screaming and shouting can be heard from inside the building and then the sound of a single gunshot echoes, followed by the rapid fire of three rounds from a machine gun. Two more bags are pushed through the wall and then another volley of machine gun rounds can be heard as I begin to lift bags into the first car by the wall. The scraping sound of a person can be heard and a body begins to appear from the hole and as they begin to stand the familiar shape of Lloyd is recognised. A seventh and eighth bag appear from the wall and then another person follows through the wall. It's Nick. He stands, lifts the bags from the ground and, as he hears the police sirens in the distance, quickly points at Lloyd to start the car.

Vernon and Greg follow behind him, appearing from the wall, and Nick shouts to Greg, "Take the car by the wall. Change of plans, we will drive in convoy." Nick throws the last two bags inside, closing the tailgate, then points to Vernon to take the outer-end vehicle.

Quickly moving across to me, Nick instructs calmly, "Dean, you ride with me and Lloyd, Paul got shot from a guard inside so Greg and Vernon will take a car each. Good work with the bags."

As everyone jumps into the vehicles we begin the high speed drive away from the side of the warehouse towards the security gate with the tyres squealing, just as Ramone begins to open fire on two police cars that are starting to approach from the right side road, answering the raised alarm and stopping short of the first stinger with the volley of rounds that Ramone is firing at them. Carlos runs along the road dragging the second stinger to cover our exit.

"Keep moving, Lloyd. Turn to the left and head for the main city," Nick starts to open the car window.

"Forget them bastards and follow us, boys," he instructs Ramone who immediately begins to run for their blue Range Rover with Carlos waiting for us to pass, holding the metal spiked end of the stinger.

Lloyd drives around Carlos who is standing on the road and quickly makes his way to the left exit towards the A23 and continues towards the centre of London near St James Garden where the second warehouse is situated, but we need to cross the River Thames over tower bridge with the other cars following close by. Carlos finishes the second stinger, tying it off around a lamppost base, and quickly climbs into the final car leaving a trail of destruction behind. Three more police cars start to weave quickly around the other parked patrol cars in an attempt to catch us and drive straight through the stinger, which takes out their tyres, sending bangs and dirt into the air from the explosions. Looking through the back window, the police officers are getting out of the cars, holding their heads completely shocked and dazed and beginning to try speaking on their radios, informing control command of our direction and requesting help.

Nick's personal radio begins to crackle as Josef's voice can be heard giving instructions. "Okay, route is blocked to A23 with police, continue left onto Croydon Road, look for the Plough pub and then a right onto B272 Beddington Lane."

Lloyd stares through the windscreen, looking for the pub. Turning by the pub Josef gives more instructions. "Okay, should pass a Shell fuel garage on the right and continue straight with green lights all the way. You need to see the sign for the sewage works."

"Okay, Josef, confirmed," Nick acknowledges.

"Keep going straight, past Beddington farm on the left then at the roundabout go straight." Josef continues to give instructions as Lloyd checks his mirrors for the other cars.

"Four lane junction on the left, keep going straight, should cross over a railway line and look for signs. Mitcham common right and golf course left."

"Got it," replies Nick.

"At the crossroads go straight along Windmill road until you see a roundabout."

"Turn sharp left then right along Manor road. Look for supermarket."

"Any news updates on police movements?" Nick asks.

"Yes, all police on high alert and heading in our direction but keep straight along Northborough Road and signs for the A23. Police are in other direction."

"This seems a fucking long way?" Lloyd asks Nick in a concerned voice.

"Okay, continue on London Road A23 towards Brixton."

Nick lifts the radio and pushes the call switch. "Josef, they will plan a blockade and at these speeds we need immediate call commands," Nick replies.

"Wait, police radio frequency confirming that a helicopter is being scrambled along with a planned blockade near to Stockwell Road," Josef confirms.

"Lloyd, we have no choice. Head along the A23, we will have to shoot our way through it." Nick has aggression in his voice.

The tension in the car is so intense with radio communication between Nick and Josef with Lloyd having a deep look of concentration in his face, throwing the Range Rover all over the road in the attempt to escape listening to the driving instructions. Threading our way through the general public's traffic at high speeds, overtaking on both sides of the road and driving head on towards oncoming cars and buses makes me feel a little sick. Then, with headlights being flashed both by Lloyd and other drivers, this feels like the scary part of the escape from my old life. It's bank holiday Monday and the sunny day means lots of people are everywhere in the city with crowded pavements and roads. Our convoy of cars is travelling at break neck speeds and it feels like every pair of eyes in London watches our progress as suddenly a police car appears on the left side of the road, trying to join the chase. Lloyd simply forces the car sideways into a line of stationary traffic and the police car crashes into the back of the last parked vehicle. The impact sends glass and plastic debris flying into the air, scattering it all over the road like a bag of marbles being spilt. Lloyd, following the instructions from Josef, throws the Range Rover around the corners, causing the tyres to squeal with the weight being exerted on them as we continue to drive through Brixton heading towards the River Thames.

Josef's radio instructions to Nick are clear and concise. "Pass over railway crossing and take first left along Stockwell Road."

Lloyd continues to drive at speed when Josef gives the bad news. "Police blockade at the end of Stockwell Road." Nick sighs and Lloyd takes a deep breath as the blue lights reflect across the houses.

Lloyd looks across to Nick and says, "Boss, we may not get out of this."

"Be calm, Lloyd. All is well. Don't panic, just head straight for them. They won't expect it." Nick looks to me and says, "Dean, load heavy. This part is going to be messy."

Lifting an MP5 from the back seat, I check the magazine and ensure that a round is loaded into the chamber as the blue lights from the police blockade in the distance fill my vision. The four cars are lined out blocking the complete road with police officers standing behind them with handguns as Nick gives the command.

"Thomas, use the 50 cal and take them bastards out!"

Suddenly huge explosions can be heard as the 50 cal rifles start to punch holes through the police car pealing back the thin metal, sending metal particles and glass fragments flying into the air along with body parts of the officers and, as they begin to fall, Nick gives an instruction. "Lloyd, drive though and don't stop."

Lloyd, as instructed, heads for the a small gap between the pavement and the police car to the left and, driving for the kerb, mounts and manages to pass by the car as pedestrians all try to run away with fear from the fast moving cars. Greg follows in the second car and Vernon drives through as one of the officers manages to take a few shots with a handgun, breaking the back window. Vernon can be seen dropping slightly in the seat as though he has been hit. Ramone and Carlos drive though as Thomas takes out the officer with the 50 cal, hitting his arm and sending it flying into the air with blood mist spraying everywhere.

Vernon's voice can be heard on the radio. "Nick, I'm hit in the neck."

Nick replies, "Keep with us, Vernon, we can sort you soon. We must keep moving."

Dodging around cars of the general public that have all stopped in the confusion of the shooting, we head out towards Stockwell Road, heading for the A3 when suddenly the road in front is blocked by another row of police cars. Lloyd continues to drive at high speed towards the blockade as Nick tries to access the threat; my heart sinks deep into my stomach, knowing this must be the end.

"Lloyd, pull next to that bus and stop. These guys won't fire, but we fuckin' will. Thomas, Josef, start open fire on these fuckers, everyone else out and open fire. We need to shoot our way out from here." Lloyd pulls the car behind the red London bus and we start to open the doors.

The police have a handheld loudspeaker and one officer tries to give instructions. "Okay, place your guns on the ground, you are surrounded." He is taken out with the first 50 Cal round.

Suddenly the air is punctured from the sound of gunshots and the supporting fire from the 50 cals raining from above. As the police start to open fire it's clear that they are massively underpowered and are very nervous to take shots with all the general public everywhere. Nick and Lloyd begin to move forward in covering fire, hitting cars and police with deadly accuracy. Climbing out of the car, I notice Greg has stopped and run over to assess Vernon's condition and it's clear he is alive but in a bad shape, holding his neck. The brothers are also out of the car and are working along the right side of the road with more covering fire hitting the police cars and knocking down officers. The gunshots echo through the tall buildings and people can be seen watching us from the safety of skyscrapers. The whirr of helicopter blades can be heard in the faint distance as the gunfire continues. I begin to move forward, following Lloyd and Nick with my heartbeat running at normal speed as though this feels normal to me as I continue to dodge between cars as bullets are fired from the police.

Snipers then begin to work their way around some of the smaller buildings, but Nick has already seen them and requested Thomas and Josef to alter targets. Clouds of concrete can be seen as the 50 cals bullets start to hit the top of buildings but a police sniper manages to take an accurate shot at Lloyd who falls to the ground. Running forward in covering fire, I reach Lloyd as the emotion begins to well inside me that he is hit, but the sound of bullets flying through the air continues as the gang members and the police trade gunfire through the cars and pedestrians cower on the ground for cover. Nick looks across to see me holding Lloyd and, without a single thought of his own life, runs over screaming what appears to be, "No," in slow motion. Beginning to lower Lloyd to the ground, I start to stand as Nick reaches our position on the road. Dropping the MP5 onto the ground, Nick quickly checks Lloyd's pulse, but already he knows Lloyd is dead.

Black mist clouds erupt from the tarmac road surface with pings ringing out as the police bullets continue to hit the ground around us. Nick casually looks across to Ramone and Carlos, seeing they have managed to punch a hole through the centre of the blockade and are already on their way back to the cars.

Nick waves across at them shouting, "Come on, let's get the fuck out of here."

He looks down at Lloyd, saying, "Goodbye, old friend, every day was an honour serving with you."

As Nick picks up the MP5, he turns and ejects the empty magazine. Pulling the final full mag from his body vest he begins to spray the police cars with an aggression I had not seen before and clearly he wants to try and avenge Lloyd's life as five more officers fall to the ground. These bullets seem the puncture through body armour as though the police are not wearing any. Lifting my MP5, I continue to spray arcs of covering fire into the cars as the sound of the police helicopter can now be heard circling above. Staring across at the pavements, people can be seen standing with cell phones videoing the whole event from what little protection they can find with other crowds of people standing in apparent safety behind the line of bullet-ridden police cars, watching the action unfold with people either curled into balls sitting on the ground trying to protect themselves from the destruction, or standing with cells being held videoing the whole event.

Nick shouts an instruction. "Dean, get to the fucking car, we are losing escape time here. We can drive through the battered cars in front."

Reaching the car, Nick shouts out another order, "Dean, just fetch the sidewinder missile launcher from the back and kindly blow that fuckin' police chopper from the sky, it's affecting my thoughts." Nick smiles.

Lowering the empty MP5 to my side, I lean into the back of the Range Rover and lift the hand held launcher from the parcel shelf. Then standing upright outside the car I rest the short barrel on the roof. Looking through the range finder scope, the helicopter can be seen reaching ever closer to our position and, without a single thought of remorse, I press the red fire button as the cross hairs of the sight lock onto the helicopter body.

With a whoosh, the missile erupts from the end of the barrel and I watch the projectile track its way through the sky in the launcher scope towards the direction of the target. As the smoke from the firing charge begins to fill the air where I stand, the missile strikes the main body of the chopper with a massive explosion that rings through the air The shockwave can be felt through the ground as the chopper instantly bursts into flames above the crowd of people below. The people's screams are suddenly silenced as burning debris falls to the ground, covering them with ignited aviation fuel. The explosion is followed by a huge heat wave that washes its way through the narrow city street with larger parts of the rotor blades hitting buildings and sticking into the softer road surface tarmac below. The noise from the heat wave roars as it passes by where we are standing, followed by the remains of the blast so intense, it feels as though my hair and eyebrows have caught alight, but the overpowering smell is coming from the burning people underneath the wreckage.

"Fucking hell, Dean, way to go. That is payback for Lloyd." Laughing, he turns and shouts across to the other guys.

"Come on, let's move now," He slides onto the driver's seat of the Range Rover.

Nick looks back to Greg and shouts across, "How is he?"

Greg replies, "He is done for."

Nick shouts out, "Drop a grenade in the footwell and follow us!" He waves.

Ramone and Carlos go forward first as a battering ram against the police cars.

The brothers are already beginning to move as Nick begins to rev the engine of the car for the escape and Greg can be seen pulling the pin from a grenade and dropping it into the car he runs for his car, which still has four bags of money inside. Slamming the rear passenger door, I jump into the passenger front seat as Nick starts to move forward, following Ramone's vehicle in the direction of the burning cars and helicopter. The air is full with the smell of burning flesh, aviation fuel and molten plastic as black grey smoke bellows into the atmosphere. Clicking my seatbelt into the clip and finally closing the door, Nick drives the Range Rover directly behind the front vehicle as the fire grenade detonates with Vernon already dead inside the last car. Ramone and Carlos hit the small gap between the two pulverised police cars and, with a large crash, push the cars sideways as the Range Rover bashes through, partly jumping in the process. Nick follows and hits one of the police cars slightly, which causes the car to list sideways and launches the car into the air past the obstacles hitting the tarmac with a sharp thud.

The brothers' vehicle is badly damaged so, taking the lead, Nick turns sharply right down along the A3 towards the direction of London Bridge. As he drives at speed, making his way through the crowds of people, with some running in the direction of the warzone and others trying to escape, the narrow streets have cars parked on both sides next to the pavement and only enough room for one car to pass. Two police cars can be seen in front of us with blue lights flashing as the two escape cars follow. Nick, without any reaction, drives straight into the direction of the two police cars, pushing both of them towards the pavement and causing them to hit parked cars, sending glass and broken plastic flying into the air. He looks into the rear view mirror to make sure the other guys are following and quickly turns down Stockwell Park Road and then back along the A23 to Brixton Road in a desperate attempt to flee the ever encircling police. Turning left, then right, and finally with signs he begins to recognise, he breathes a quick sigh of relief and looks across at me, smiling. Steam begins to emit from under the bonnet of the Range Rover and warning lights begin to appear on the dashboard as the damage from the two accidents begins to show with Nick continuing to drive at an aggressive speed along the street. The car and my clothes are impregnated with the smell of burning flesh and aviation fuel from the blast overwhelms my senses but Nick continues regardless.

Ramone's voice comes through on the radio. "Nick, come in, repeat."

"Yes, what's the problem?" He continues to drive against oncoming traffic.

"Boss, the car is fucked and won't run anymore," Ramone replies.

"Yes, I saw it fail. Leave the guns and other equipment inside and drop a fire grenade inside, then disperse and mingle in with the other pedestrians. Make your way to the tube station at Stockwell. I will contact you later once we are all clear."

Nick continues, "Thomas and Josef, make your way to the escape warehouse and we will meet there for debrief and depart."

"Clear, boss, over and out," Josef replies.

"Greg, are you okay?" Nick asks.

"Yes, boss, fine, but the police are trying to break through. We have got to ditch these cars and find something else," Greg replies with tension in his voice.

"Yes, that is clear. Head for Pure Gym in Kennington, I have another car ready there and we can ditch these, they are way too hot now." Nick turns sharp left into a narrow alleyway between a sports and electrical shop and heads for the small chain link fenced car park of the gym.

Driving through the small metal barrier, smashing it against the bonnet of the car, he parks the Range Rover next to a large light blue Volvo estate car and jumps out. I climb out, seeing all the steam and smoke still rising from the broken engine, and follow as he takes some keys from his pocket and unlocks the rear hatch of the boot. As Greg reaches the car park, I am opening the back of the Range Rover and already beginning to hand the bags of money to Nick, who quietly and calmly begins to load them into the boot space. Greg parks next to our vehicle and jumps out to open the boot hatch of his car, then begins to reach inside for some of the money bags as the air vibrates with the sound of sirens from the emergency services attending the injured and dying people.

Greg hands over two money bags to Nick and returns to his vehicle. As I lift the last two bags from our car and pass them towards Nick, he has already begun staring across towards Greg. The look of disgust on his face is clearly evident as Greg reaches his car. Nick walks across and, without even hesitating, takes out a silenced pistol and fires a single bullet round into the back of Greg's head, covering the inside of the car with blood and brain matter. As Greg's body slumps forward, Nick pushes him to one side and removes the two final bags of cash, placing them on the ground. In shock, with my hands shaking, I force my two bags into the boot space of the Volvo, then turn and watch Nick quickly lift and push Greg's body into the boot of the Range Rover as thoughts rush through my mind that I am next. Nick closes the tailgates of the vehicle, turns and lifts the bags from the ground, beginning to walk in my direction.

Nick walks past me and, as I stand shaking with shock, he speaks, "Something went wrong today, Dean. I was betrayed. Don't worry, I know it wasn't you. Come, let's gets out of here."

As he closes the estate hatch he throws me the keys and says, "You can drive."

Quickly walking around to the driver's side and opening the door, I start the engine and in that moment the escape fills my every thought, but also knowing Nick has just killed Greg without a blink of an eye, taking me would be easy. Taking a deep sigh over what I have got involved with, I engage reverse and begin to move backwards out of the parking space. Nick can be seen walking over to our Range Rover and, reaching inside a small black bag, he takes out two fire grenades. After opening the rear passenger door that holds Greg in the boot, he pulls a pin from the first grenade and throws it inside the car and closes the door, then removing the pin, he quickly throws the next grenade into the other car and closes the hatch with a large slam. Then he runs for the Volvo.

"Okay, Dean, drive carefully and get us to the safe warehouse, I will tell you which way to go." Looking through the rear view mirror we are around a hundred metres away when the explosion and fire engulf both of the cars as we slowly drive towards the direction of the warehouse.

Driving at a casual speed, we make our way back along the A23 and continue in the direction of Tower Bridge. Just before the Thames we turn onto another warehouse area district near to the Bermondsey Spa Gardens with all the factories closed due to the bank holiday. As we pass different packaging, logistics and production units my mind begins to drift back to some of the events today and how comfortable I felt firing machine guns along with the excitement felt from the bullets whizzing through the air. My body is still having a massive rush from the past hour, but there is a feeling in the pit of my stomach that there will never be any turning back from the death and destruction that has been caused. Nick indicates to turn left with his hand and I drive up to a roller shutter door of a factory unit MP Projects and underneath the words International Expeditors. Nick climbs out of the car and walks over to the small wooden side door to unlock it and after a few seconds he walks inside. Even from inside the car, the mechanical noise of a chain being dragged past metal sheeting can be heard as the door gradually begins to open.

The body count for the team today is already Lloyd, Paul, Vernon and Greg as the blue Insignia with Thomas and Josef arrives. Will Nick now whack these guys too since the alarm systems should have been immobilised, or will he wait and see what happens? With the roller shutter door now finally open, Nick stands in the doorway and stares across to the blue Insignia, then beckons it over along with myself. Beginning to drive into the unit, my heart begins to race as I know that Nick now has all the money in these eight bags and if he kills the three of us he will be home free with a lot of cash and no witnesses. But instead he walks away from the side door towards a small glass office at the back of the unit and begins to unlock the entrance door. Inside the unit is a white Ford transit van with no plates and a white VW Passat parked to the left side. Looking around the unit I can see the walls are painted white, a long time discoloured, and there is some simple racking against the right wall. Stopping the Volvo next to the Passat, Nick can be seen walking inside a small glass fronted office and switching on the florescent light, which flickers into life.

"Bring the bags from the car, guys," he shouts, leaning against the office doorway.

Opening the door, I walk around to the back of the car and begin to lift the hatch open as Thomas and Josef join me.

"Things went bad today, Dean!" Thomas asks.

"Yes, we lost Paul, Greg, Vernon and Lloyd." I didn't mention that Nick executed Greg.

"What happen to Ramone and Carlos?" Josef asks as he lifts out two bags.

"Their car was damaged and they left it and escaped on foot," I reply, reaching for two bags.

"Oh, okay," Thomas answers, lifting out two more bags.

Taking the weight of the bags of cash and then walking over towards Nick, my heart is still beating so fast. Once we are in the office he can quickly take us out so selfishly and, trying to protect my own skin, I walk a few steps behind Thomas and Josef just in case he wants to kill us and maybe there's a chance of escaping after seeing how Nick shot Greg. Thomas reaches the doorway first and begins to walk into the office as Nick can be seen bending and pulling at something as Josef starts to push his way inside. Looking through the window, Nick can be seen opening the door on a heavy metal safe, indicating for the men to drop the money bags on the ground. He unzips the first bag then begins to stack the cash into piles inside the safe and he instructs Josef to fetch the last two bags.

Walking inside the office, we all begin to remove the overalls worn during the robbery and push them into a black bin bag, then Nick asks the question I was expecting, "What happened there today Thomas? How did an alarm get triggered? I thought you had that covered?"

Thomas stands looking at Nick, loading the cash into the safe, and replies, "I was hacked into system and silent alarm was immobilised, there must be a second system not on plans."

"Well that answer is very convenient. I suggest you find out what really happened after I have lost forty percent of the team today." Nick indicates for me to lower the bags to the ground as Josef reappears at the door with the final two bags.

"Is there problem?" Josef asks.

"A problem! Too right there is fucking problem with a forty percent death rate to my team. This is not acceptable." Nick looks across to me to make sure I don't mention Greg.

"Nick, we apologies for what happen, was not our fault." Josef lowers the final bags and stands back next to Thomas.

"You two guys came highly recommended as being professionals and what happened today in my books was a bunch of amateurs." Nick continues to stack the money into the safe and after minutes of absolute silence he stands holding a big pile of cash.

"Your end for this job was two hundred and fifty thousand each. Here, take your money, unload the equipment from that car and get the fuck out of my sight. I don't want to hear or see you guys ever again and may I remind you that you need to forget everything that has happened here, because I will never forget." Nick hands them over a bundle of cash.

Josef and Thomas, with the look of disappointment on their faces, turn and walk out of the office, heading towards the car and mumbling a conversation in German, clearly not happy that they have been called amateurs. They begin to unload the rifles and laptops from the boot of the car and place them on the floor as I look at Nick, staring at them as they drive away. Placing the last of the money in the safe, he closes the door and spins the dial to lock it shut. We begin to make our way out of the office and, as we reach the door, he activates the alarm system.

"Nick, how could you let them just walk after what happened today? Clearly they must have known something about the second alarm system," I ask

"Dean, not everything is at it seems, if these guys have set me up, the first thing they will do now is go back to their handler and quickly leave the UK. Those guys are wanted criminals and just being linked with them is a huge risk for me. Besides, their time will come when I am ready." Nick switches off the light and starts to walk out of the office with me following.

"Dean, I will take you back to your flat and then just continue with your normal life until I make contact with you again. If Wagstaff suspects us, then that may throw him off your scent."

As I begin to digest Nick's words, my brain finally realises that the events of today were not a movie, but an actual day in my life and what felt like actors from a film set were people being killed and hurt. Suddenly becoming overcome with nausea, the feeling of sickness begins to dwell deep inside and then being overcome with emotion I snap back at Nick. "Normal life! Are you fuckin' serious? How the fuck can tomorrow just be a normal day after what has happened?"

Nick, stopping in his tracks, realises what he said and quickly tries to retract his words. "No, Dean, I understand that, but what I was trying to say is that we both need to act normal, avoiding any attention, otherwise Wagstaff will be on to us all."

"Wagstaff is probably on to us all anyway and acting normal is what he would expect." I shake my head as I reply.

"Come, Dean, let's go from here. Maybe you need to spend a few hours with your mate Shaun?" Nick places his arm around my shoulder.

"Yes, I'm sure Shaun would love to hear about my day and what happened?"

Looking across to Nick, the tone of his voice seems comforting and calming, clearly showing that he cares, but the emotions inside feels like a knife cutting at my insides trying to escape from this new life already.

Nick, clearly seeing that I'm confused and upset, tries to give comforting support by placing his arm again around my shoulder. "Dean, please give me a few days and I will make sure it will work out."

Walking to the Passat, we load up the equipment left by Thomas and Josef into the boot, along with the black bin bag of overalls. Nick opens the driver's door and climbs inside, starting the engine. After opening the passenger door, I slide onto the seat and look across to Nick, who still has seriousness in his face. Closing my door, we drive out of the building and, once outside, Nick stops the car. Climbing out, he runs back into the building to close the roller shutter door. I continue to stare through the windscreen into nothingness with the noise of the steel door scraping down the framework. After a few minutes, Nick slams the side door of the warehouse and runs back towards the car. He climbs inside and as we drive away from the building, my mind now works in overdrive, playing over the events of today again and again. Nick, driving at normal speeds on the empty roads, quickly reaches the street to my apartment building and, stopping a hundred and fifty metres away, pulls in by the pavement.

Switching off the ignition, he looks across to me and says, "Dean, I know what it feels like to be where you are today and know the pain you feel inside, but don't let things get on top of you and remain calm. Remember, today was the start of your new life, the life that you have been dreaming of."

Now feeling even sicker from the car journey, I smile back at him, saying, "I just didn't think it would hurt this much inside killing all those people."

"Dean, remember it was either them or you and I for one am glad you are still here today."

Smiling back, I climb out of the car as Nick begins to speak again. "I will be in contact in a few days, but please try to switch these emotions off. They will tear you up inside."

Closing the door, I cross the road and begin to walk in the direction of the apartment with the air still full of emergency sirens and helicopters transporting people around the city. Making my way to the swinging doors, I hear a car engine start and, casually looking into the mirrored windows, I see Nick drive past on the road behind. As I push my way through the revolving door, the emotion of now being alone takes over and, as I walk into the lobby of the apartments, Rahul can be seen staring at me.

"Mr Dean, Mr Dean, are you all right? It is so terrible what has happened, I was so scared you were injured." His words seem so distant although his voice is all muffled and distorted.

Feeling completely disorientated, I look back in the direction of the voice and reply, saying, "Hi, Rahul. Yes it's terrible out there, better to be safe in here, hey."

"Mr Dean, Mr Shaun was asking for you earlier, but told him I have not seen you."

"That's fine, Rahul, I will try to catch him later. I'm sure he is fine."

Walking away towards the direction of the lifts, I never thought that I would be coming back here, but having nowhere else to go, my options are limited. Still feeling completely disorientated, I make my way to the lifts and, with my subconscious senses on overtime, I press the twelfth floor button automatically. Walking into the lift, the doors close and, after what appears to be only a few seconds, the lift quickly travels upwards, stopping at the top floor. As the lift doors ping open my body, still running on autopilot, instinctively begins to walk in the direction of the apartment. Stopping at the door, I sense something is wrong apart from now realising my door keys are not in my pocket. Looking at the apartment door, it is instantly noticeable that the frame has some damage near the lock and the door is slightly ajar with a very thin bead of light seen. Just then a noise can be heard inside of someone coughing. Will today never fuckin' end is the first thought that runs into my mind, then taking a deep breath with my heart beating so fast and my legs feeling like jelly, I gradually begin to push the door open, trying to look inside at the same time to see who is in the flat. My senses are instantly drawn to the noise of running water in the sink, then a glass being filled from the direction of the kitchen.

As the water stops running, I begin the walk slowly towards the direction of the kitchen and my mind quickly runs through what I could use to attack the person and protect myself inside my space, but the only possible weapons are in the room where the intruder waits. Continuing to walk in the direction of the kitchen, my head feels so light from my heart beating so fast and then suddenly I remember a small pair of scissors that were placed with the pictures in the drawer of the display unit near the wall with the dining room then kitchen beyond. Quickly and silently I reach the display unit and, slowly pulling the wooden drawer open, I feel inside the box for the scissors. After a few seconds, the coldness of the steel blades make contact with the fingers on my left hand and, taking a firm grip, I lift them out just as the steps can be heard resonating on the laminate floor in my direction.

Only having fractions of seconds and quickly reaching the end of the wall, I stop and wait until the person passes me planning an ambush. The footstep touch the laminate floor echoing through the silent flat with my heart rate now at a pace that makes my hands shake as I hold the scissors in a stabbing position. The footsteps on the flooring now become more pronounced and the air is suddenly filled with a familiar scent of perfume and instantly I realise it's Sophie in the apartment and as her image begins to appear from around the wall I begin to loosen my grip on the scissors.

Allowing her to continue past me, I watch her walk seductively into the room wearing black high heels, tight blue jeans and a white polo shirt with her hair floating freely. Feeling both angry and happy to see her after today and being in my apartment, my emotions are undecided how to approach her. Gradually placing the scissors in the back pocket of my jeans, I wait for her to begin to sit on the sofa and as she places to glass of water on the coffee table.

"Boo," I whisper.

Turning around quickly, startled, she replies, "Oh Dean, you scared me."

"What do you expect walking around my apartment uninvited?"

"Dean, I was so worried about you after today and had to see you." She stands looking at me.

"Really, Sophie, and how did you get in?" I begin to move away from the wall.

"The door was already open when I arrived."

"Hmm, and how did you get past reception?" I am standing about two metres away.

She begins to walk closer. "Rahul recognised me from Saturday and allowed me through," she continues. "Isn't it terrible what has happened today? Where have you been?"

"What's with the one thousand questions? What are you doing in my flat?" I snap at her.

"Dean, I was worried about you and wanted to make sure all is okay after hearing nothing yesterday."

"Yeah, well, I've been busy yesterday and as you see I'm fine." I still feel betrayed that she came into my flat unannounced. I feel I can't trust her.

"What are your plans for today, Dean?"

"Relax and chill," I reply sharply.

"Would you like to have lunch somewhere? I'll pay," Sophie asks as she places her hands around my waist.

Not knowing how to react to her actions, I stand away slightly.

"What's wrong, Dean?"

"I could ask you the same, Sophie. Only two days ago you didn't want to get close and now you're in my apartment asking about my wellbeing and wanting to go out for lunch as though nothing has happened!"

"I don't understand, Dean, I thought this is what you wanted?" Sophie stands back slightly as her eyes begin to redden with tears beginning to develop.

"Sophie, there is a lot going on at the moment and I can't deal with these hot and cold emotions. I'm sorry."

"Hot and cold emotions? I have only asked you out for lunch and wanted to make sure that you were okay."

"That's just it, Sophie, you left here Saturday wanting time and now when it suits you, after two days, I find you here in my apartment and for me it's too much!"

"Too much? What do you mean? I thought this is what you wanted?"

"How do you know what I want? You have never asked." Sophie sits back on the sofa with a look of shock.

"Look, Sophie, after these last few days things have changed and maybe it's best that you distance yourself from a man like me. I'm not the type of guy you want in your life."

"Dean, you're so wrong. I realise now that it's you I want."

"Sophie, you may want me now but in the future things will change so it's best if we stop it now before either of us gets hurt anymore."

"Dean, I don't understand how we were so close Friday and now it's over before we get started. Are you afraid or is it something to do with Nick?"

"Sophie, I've never been so afraid my whole life, but it's not you, it's me, and at this time it's better for us both if we go our separate ways. And no, Nick has nothing to do with it." I wonder why she mentioned his name.

"Separate ways? Are you punishing me for Saturday?"

"No, Sophie, Saturday is over, but what I'm saying is that things have changed and I don't want you in my life any more with this type of relationship." Sophie begins to cry.

"Is there someone else?" she asks.

Pausing for a few seconds in my reply, the brain and heart now begin to fight against each other with the head wanting to protect her from what could happen if I get caught and my heart wanting to be with her. Deep down, though, I feel that she should have told me before we went to Castro's about Nick and feeling betrayed by her actions is never a good start. Now getting mixed signals from her it's clear she can't decide or there is something more behind her relationship with Nick.

"Dean, is that it? Is there someone else?" She stands with tears beginning to roll down her cheeks.

"No, Sophie, that's not it at all. You're way off the mark."

She begins to walk in the direction of the door, still sobbing.

Reaching the door, she stops and turns, saying, "Dean, I came here today to possibly begin a new life together with you and now I feel it's already over and I don't want to leave this way."

Looking back at her I stand and say, "Sophie, I'm not ready to commit at this time and maybe it's better if you leave."

"Well, fuck off then, Dean, if this is how you treat someone who really cares for you. I deserve better than this anyway."

Opening the door quickly, she walks through and slams it behind her in anger as her heavy footsteps begin to echo along the corridor as she quickly makes her way to the lifts and like that she walks out of my life. My heart instantly takes over the feelings from my brain and hearing myself thinking *what have I done?* as the emotions of loss and loneliness begin to overwhelm all my thoughts. Beginning to feel slightly afraid, emotional tears start to well in my eyes, but the thought of having Sophie in my life at this time is not an option. Walking into the kitchen, still shocked by her actions, my senses begin to take over and I instantly notice that a few things have been moved. The coffee cups from Saturday morning and one of the cupboards is slightly ajar.

Taking a glass, I fill it with cold tap water and walk back towards the living room. Now I instantly see the corner of a piece of paper lying on the floor underneath the display cabinet where the envelope of pictures was being kept. Quickly walking over the cabinet, the glass is placed on the open shelf as the scissors are taken from my back pocket and replaced back in the drawer. Lifting out the brown envelope of pictures, I then grab the piece of paper that has fallen out and, seeing the writing on one side, I take everything along with the glass from the shelf and walk back to the sofa. Placing the glass next to the remains of Sophie's drink, I empty the pictures from the envelope, scattering them out around the coffee table top.

Reading the piece of paper, the hand written words say, 'Seek and you will find the reasons behind your life'. Placing the paper on the surface, I begin to look through the faces on the photographs, but nothing has changed over whether anyone is recognisable. One thing is clear, the pictures from Friday night with Sophie and I dancing have now gone along with a picture of Shaun and me on a motorbike trip, so it's clear now that someone has been in the flat and from her reactions it's evident that Sophie is to blame. Taking a quick sigh, the feeling of my own space being invaded begins to overwhelm my emotions and, after enjoying a quick sip of water, I stand and walk through into the master bedroom only to see that one of the wardrobe doors is open, confirming another room has been invaded.

Pushing the door fully open, I begin to look inside to see if anything is missing, but I only notice that the clothes have been moved on the hanger rail. The feeling of my private space being abused is too much for me to bear after everything that has happened today and, feeling both angry and annoyed, aggression starts to rise from deep inside, similar to the emotion felt when I realised that Lloyd was dead. Uncontrollably I slam the wardrobe door shut, almost breaking it from the rails. Having never felt this type of aggression before, it's clear that the events from today are beginning to affect my normally casual behaviour and personality. Not knowing what to do with myself, I walk back in the living room and make my way onto the balcony for some fresh air, but opening the doors only confirms my worst fears as the air is still filled with the sound of emergency sirens. Finally at that point I realise that no matter what happens now I'm trapped with nowhere to go and tears begin to fill my eyes. Everything now begins to collapse around me as the emotions of today, Sophie, Nick, Lloyd and all those people start to feel like a huge weight across my shoulders.

"Why did I decide to carry out this stupid robbery and get involved?" I'm speaking to myself.

"Why did I get involved with Sophie? I should have known from all the hurt in the past! What am I going to do now? Who can I speak to? Who would possibly believe the things that have happened?"

Black thoughts now begin to cloud my normally clear mind and these same thoughts feel to be uncontrollable in the reactions from my emotions. I must try to remain focused and plan a route out of this nightmare as soon as possible just to maintain some level of sanity. I want to get away from here as fast as possible, from this place and this life. 'What a mess' fills my thoughts, but also I know that running away is never the answer to solving any problems. Then the next wave tumbles over the sea wall as the sirens remind me of all those people I single-handed killed today with not even another thought.

'Should I go to the police and confess?' races through my mind, but the answer of life imprisonment soon rules that option out.

"Having killed all those people maybe I should confess and go to prison, but no one forced me to join Nick's crew and exploding the chopper was all my choice and now the burden to carry."

"How about going to Wagstaff and giving up Nick? But that door is now firmly closed after today's events."

"Make a run for it with some of the cash. But Nick will just hunt me down and kill me in cold blood like he did to Greg."

"Maybe kill Nick? A person like him, the authorities may welcome the idea and the weight of guilt will not be hard, but he is a trained solider. There is no way I could achieve this and, after all, I volunteered."

The only answer is to live with my actions and this is the strangest part to the whole set of event, it feels as though I have been in this situation before. It keeps replaying in my mind over and over again. Leaning back on the sofa, I close my eyes and keep replaying the day's events.

7

On ground zero the examination teams can be seen picking their way around the bodies that are covered with white sheets in an attempt to show some dignity at this time of great sadness. A team of eight experts clothed in white paper suits can be seen exploring through the charred helicopter remains, trying to piece together any parts of the missile that struck the main body with such accuracy, sending the burning fragments to the ground. The line of black hearses escorted by two groups of police motorcycles finally stop next to the crash site at Stockwell Road after meandering their way through the traffic filled streets of London. The look of horror on the faces of the undertakers can be seen as they gaze across to the still smouldering devastation in front of them. Climbing out, the men and women, all dressed in black suits and white shirts, make their way to the rear of the vehicles to unload the body stretchers as police officers begin to gather. The air is silent as the police start to escort the undertakers slowly walking towards the bodies. After taking photographs they begin to lift the charred bodies onto the stretchers, leaving black outlines on the ground from the fire that engulfed everything. The undertaker teams working in silence, gently lift the bodies, lower them onto stretches and transport them back to the vehicles for departure to the mortuary where any post mortems will take place. A familiar black Mercedes suddenly arrives at the scene and Wagstaff can be seen climbing out, limping. Wagstaff stands next to his Mercedes, staring across at the crowds of film crews and the general public who watch the complete events as though they are not really happening.

Wagstaff looks across to a young police officer and asks, "Officer, where's the commander in charge?"

"Who might you be?" he asks.

"Director Wagstaff." The warrant card is pushed into the young officer's face.

"Ohh right, sir, sorry. It's Commander Kingsbridge in charge, he is standing over there." The officer points to another group of police walking around the devastation.

"Contact him immediately and inform him of my presence."

Just then the group of high-ranking officers make their way in the direction of Wagstaff as the young officer lifts his radio.

"The commander is here, sir." The officer indicates to the right.

In a quick move, Wagstaff stamps on the part smoked cigarette and limps his way over to the commander. Reaching the group of officers, Wagstaff stands for a few seconds listening to the conversation.

"Okay, men, it's such a mess here. Let us begin to collect the debris and start the clean-up process. The mayor is going mad that the street is closed."

"Nothing is moving from this site until I give clearance and the mayor can wait." Wagstaff's voice breaks up the group as they all turn around.

"I'm sorry, sir, but who are you to speak over this police operation?" Commander Kingsbridge asks.

"The man now in charge! Do we have a problem?"

The commander, with a look of shock on his face, replies, "No, Director Wagstaff, sir, that's fine."

Wagstaff gestures with his left hand. "May I have a word in private, Commander?"

"Yes, of course, sir." The two men walk to the left for a few metres.

"What fucking game are you playing here? These crowds are too close, there is hardly any security and don't these dead people deserve a little respect, not being on show for every TV news channel for the world to see?"

"But, but—"

"No fuckin' buts now, Kingsbridge, and if the mayor wants know why this street is still closed you tell him to speak to my boss the home secretary, who has placed me in charge."

Kingsbridge, looking pissed off, signals for the chief superintendent to join the discussion. "Chief Superintendent Redding, Director Wagstaff is taking charge of the site, please extend him all the courtesy of the Met Police."

"Hello, Charles, how are things going?" Wagstaff asks

"We've had better days John, how are things with you?"

"Excuse me, do you know each other?" Kingsbridge asks.

"Yes, sir, I served with Director Wagstaff in Northern Ireland for a few tours."

"Hmm, typical." The Commander walks away with his entourage, trying to look important.

"What's his problem?" Wagstaff asks.

"He's punching way above his pay scale, John, but it's great to have some common sense on the scene. It's so terrible. What do you need, John?"

"Get these crowds back, Charles. Let's get some examination tents up and also some perimeter screening to reduce these camera crews."

"Will be done immediately," Redding replies

"No problem. What a mess, hey Charles?" Wagstaff lights another cigarette.

"Yes, John, a real mess. Do you have any clues?"

"I have a few leads and may need your help in a couple of days if that's okay."

"Yes, anything for you," Redding replies to Wagstaff.

Chief Superintendent Redding immediately starts to instruct officers in arranging for the crowd barriers to be pushed back as examination tents begin to be erected over the areas where the bodies lie. Wagstaff walks back to the team of agents and then, picking their way through the wreckage, he begins to look at the damaged remains in an attempt to look for answers.

Wagstaff beckons for an agent to join him and then requests, "Hughes, arrange for a command centre on site and ensure all evidence is collected, bagged and tagged. I want a full map of the city from the Pearson money deposit warehouse all the way to the area where the burnt out getaway cars were dumped. Then set up surveillance teams at every airport, railway and tube station in a fifty mile radius."

"Yes, sir, understood," Agent Hughes replies.

Wagstaff beckons over another agent. "Williams, what about the explosive used on the wall of the warehouse?"

"Forensics working on it now, sir, but from the blast scorching, it looks like low grade C4 seems to be the best guess. We should have the age and batch details in the next hour."

"Okay, so the shaped charge shows they are technically proficient so use our usual contacts to see who imported this material into the country," Wagstaff instructs.

"Yes, sir," replies the agent.

Wagstaff, looking around the street, points at the surveillance cameras. "We need all information from the cameras along with the last transmissions from the helicopter videos."

"On it now, sir," Agent Hughes replies.

"Okay, I want all information collected, contained and to be operational in the next two hours." Wagstaff turns and looks across the devastation.

"All these people had family and loved ones and with all this press we need to make sure all is done correctly with no stone left unturned in this investigation." All the agents nod in agreement and watch Wagstaff making his way back to the car.

"Where to, sir?" the driver asks.

"To Whitehall. I need to brief the PM and home secretary at Cobra." Wagstaff takes a deep sigh as the car instantly is driven away at high speed with the blue grill lights flashing.

Wagstaff's cell begins to ring and, taking it out of his jacket pocket, he pushes the answer button. "Yes, Briggs, what's the status at the warehouse?"

"Sir, confirmed one security guard killed along with one of the gang. We are running forensics on what's left of the body but the acid damage is extensive."

"What about the other hostages?" Wagstaff asks.

"Apart from being shaken up, along with a few cuts and bruises, nothing major. We are taking statements from them all now."

"Okay, Briggs, thank you; keep me posted of any updates." Wagstaff rings off.

Finally reaching the cabinet building at Whitehall, there are police and military personnel everywhere as the driver stops by the main entrance gate. The car is waved through and Preston can be seen standing next to the main entrance.

Reaching the entrance, the car stops and Agent Preston reaches for the handle and opens the rear door for Wagstaff to climb out, saying, "Good luck, sir." He hands him the latest report file.

"Thanks, Preston, I will need it for this damn mess," He limps towards the main entrance where two heavily armed officers salute as he reaches the doors.

Walking past the open door, Wagstaff makes his way towards the war room along the brightly lit corridor and is greeted by another agent standing just outside the large wooden oak doors.

"Okay, Atkins, let's get this over with." Atkins opens the door for Wagstaff.

The room is filled with raised voices and people attempting to pull together any reason behind the attack. The PM is listening to all the conversations with limited success and with the arrival of Wagstaff he jumps to his feet.

"Ah, John, at last some common sense in the room. What do you have to report?"

Wagstaff, standing opposite the PM, opens the red A4 folder. "Prime Minister, Home Secretary, ladies and gentlemen. MI6 received reports Saturday morning over a possible terrorist threat planned over UK soil in the next four weeks and, as reported Saturday, we had no clear evidence which organisation was behind this threat. The source of information came from our colleagues at Langley and I believe was accurate. The attack that occurred on Stockwell Road at 9.01 a.m. today is what we believe to be part of a robbery against the Pearson money warehouse that was targeted at 8.30 a.m. We have information that the robbery could have been planned through an ex special forces team now working for their own gains." Wagstaff pauses.

"This has not been confirmed, but the first indications are that the Pearson's money warehouse is used to launder drug money and the outer wall was breached by the use of low grade C4 explosive. The muffled blast zones indicate to a professional ex-military hit. The helicopter was targeted by what appears to be a rocket-propelled missile with heat seeker guidance, available through many of the ex-eastern block countries, again showing military personnel involvement of some kind." Wagstaff, still standing, takes a drink of water and coughs to clear his throat. Then, turning over another page, he continues to read from the file.

"In brief summary, this robbery appears to have been planned and organised by ex-military personnel. The amount of money taken is not clear at this stage but is estimated to be in excess of fifteen million pounds."

"Thank you, John, and what about the terrorist attack?" the PM asks.

"Sir, at this time we have all airports and border patrols on high alert, but it is clear this threat is still active. It is not clear whether the two are related in any way but we have some strong leads that are being explored and investigated at this time."

"Again, thank you, John. So around the table, any questions?"

"How can you be sure that the exploding of the helicopter was not a terrorist act? It looks very much like one to me." one cabinet minister asks.

"Your wealth of field experience leads you to that conclusion, does it?" Wagstaff snaps back.

The minister slumps back in the chair as Wagstaff begins to speak. "As stated before, a missile was fired at the helicopter and initial indications from the scorching around the entry puncture point confirm a firing distance of less than two hundred metres. I doubt that terrorists would be carrying a one and half meter long missile launcher in downtown London just in case a police helicopter files past. Plus the first video images confirm one of the robbers was seen standing holding what appeared to be the launcher." Wagstaff smiles.

"When will the street be reopened?" asks the mayor.

"The street will reopen as soon as possible, but firstly all the bodies, helicopter and any evidence needs to be collected.

It could take a couple of days due to the blast radius and size of the evidence we are trying to collect."

"A COUPLE OF DAYS? Are you serious? This road needs to be opened as soon as possible for business to resume. Can it not be hurried up with some more people and cleaning teams?" the mayor asks.

"Mayor, with all due respect, there are over a hundred dead bodies lying on the street with some of them burnt and charred beyond recognition and the only way to identify them could be the last ground where they lay with fragments from their clothing. Besides, do we want to be seen simply sweeping away their memories so the road can be reopened for business as usual?" Wagstaff stares at the mayor.

"John, is any more help required in supporting the intelligence department with investigations connected to the terrorist threat?" General Jenkins asks.

"General, I have all lines of communication open at the moment, but any assistance is always welcome."

"John, I will arrange for fifteen staff from intel to join your team within the hour."

"Thank you, General, that help would be much appreciated." Wagstaff takes a sip of water.

"John, many thanks for the update and please keep me informed at all times."

The PM continues, "Okay, we have a mess in the centre of London that needs to be tidied up with some compassion. I will make a statement shortly to the press from Downing Street confirming our loyalty to the families that have been affected." The PM stands and everyone else follows suit.

"That will be all for now. If the situation changes, we will of course need to reconvene. John and Home Secretary please walk with me."

The three men begin to walk out of the cabinet meeting room and begin a separate conversation. "John, this terrorist threat. Do we have any true leads?" the PM asks.

"Prime Minister, presently not and I can't find out any more information as of yet."

"Do you have a hunch, John?" the PM asks.

"Yes, sir, but it's a long shot and has no hard evidence at this time."

"What does your hunch tell you, John?"

"Well, it's not Middle or Far Eastern since all these bases are covered and it's not South American so it could be European or African."

"Why do you say European?" the home secretary asks.

"Well, the explosives used have been traced to a factory in Poland and only supplied European markets, but some could have made their way to north Africa and following the agent snatch back in Algeria a few months ago this could be a possibility."

"We have no major threats in Europe, other than the Middle Eastern factions, do we?" The PM asks with all three men looking at each other.

"Or do we?" the PM stares at the home secretary.

"Well, sir, the undercover operation carried out in Syria three months ago hasn't done any favours with some of our European colleagues." Wagstaff stops by the main entrance.

"Hmm, we had to get our men out and it was unfortunate about the others but our European colleagues were not willing to support," the home secretary replies.

"I assume you are both referring to operation Damascus. Hired help was the only option and I don't want it mentioned again." The PM points at them both and then walks away to the waiting car.

"Do you really think it's a European threat, Wagstaff?" Home Secretary Allen snarls as the two of them watch the PM drive away.

"Sir, it could be within the UK itself. We have that many immigrants and inner circle religious factions working outside Middle Eastern beliefs, we just don't know at this time."

"Okay, Wagstaff, look, that black op was a dirty word in Whitehall and we would never have been given clearance to use official means so keep up the good work, old boy, and pass any information to me before the PM sees it, okay? And don't mention your Damascus hunch again."

"Yes, Home Secretary, understood." Allen walks back in the direction of the cabinet offices.

Wagstaff walks outside and, lighting a cigarette, watches the Prime Minister's car disappear with the police escorts, blue lights and sirens clearing the roads back towards Downing Street. Wagstaff, now deep in thought over his instructions from the home secretary, takes a deep inhale of his cigarette as agent Preston arrives.

"Is everything okay, sir?" he asks.

"Not sure at the moment, Preston, ask me again in a few days."

"Is there a problem with the PM or home secretary?"

"Nothing I can't handle. Come, let's get some lunch. My treat." Wagstaff shows a concerned side.

"How about some good old fashioned fish and chips?" Wagstaff asks as they reach the car, with Wilson leaning against the driver's door.

"Sounds good to me, sir," Preston replies.

"Okay, let's go, I know a good place."

They all climb into the car and speed off with the blue lights flashing as they drive away from the direction of

Whitehall with Wagstaff deep in thought, looking through the side window trying to evaluate the statement from Allen and the request to intercept information from the PM and the possible reasons behind it.

Hours pass by as I try to think of options to escape and break the feelings soaking through my body, only for the silence to be broken by my cell ringing and vibrating. Taking it from my pocket, a familiar number can be seen flashing across the screen and, pressing the answer button, it is lifted to my ear.

"Fuckin' hell, mate, have you seen this shite? What a fuckin' mess," Shaun's voice shouts down the cell. "What are your plans tonight, fella, fancy beer and pizza at mine?" he asks.

"Yeah, that sounds great, Shaun. What time are you thinking?"

"Well its six now, mate, so any later and it will be breakfast, so move your ass over here."

Looking at my watch in shock, I reply, "Will be over in twenty mins." Shaun rings off.

Quickly walking into the bedroom, I undress and take a shower then, selecting some more jeans and a fresh polo shirt, I dress. Finally applying some aftershave to my face, I stroll back into the living room. Lifting my phone, keys and wallet from the glass coffee table, I make my way out of the apartment, closing the door behind. Reaching Shaun's apartment, a sudden feeling of security engulfs my emotions with the shock over the fact that Sophie was in my apartment earlier and furthermore what was she doing there. The TV can be heard blasting out and knocking on the door with very hard actions. Shaun is heard moving around inside the room. The door flings open and he stands wearing shorts and a T-shirt with a worried look on his face.

"Are you okay, Gezza?" I ask him with a raised voice over the TV noise.

"Mate, come in. I have tried to contact Chloe but can't get in touch with her after that shite today I'm getting a little worried." I take a deep breath and walk into his flat, closing the door behind me and following him in to the room.

"Mate, I'm sure she is fine, maybe just some family stuff today."

Shaun, lifting the TV remote, lowers the volume and then, throwing it onto the sofa, smiles and claps his hands together saying, "Okay, what about biker night watching Moto GP from yesterday and this year's TT races with a few beers and pizza?"

"Sounds good to me, do you ever fuckin' tidy up?" I start to lift some of his stuff from the chair, placing it on the floor, making some space.

"Fuck it, mate. Today, maybe her husband will come arrive and kick off again so not much point in tidying up, hey. What drink do you want?"

"Beer sounds good, Shaun," I reply, lifting the TV remote and starting to click through the channels, but all that can be found are live broadcasts from near the incident with the helicopter.

"First reports are over a hundred and twenty dead from this terrible act and the perpetrators are still at large with police confirming that they have no positive leads," a news reporter announces.

Taking a small sigh of relief, Shaun returns with two bottles of Budweiser and continues to speak. "Over a hundred and twenty dead. Fuckin' hell, it must have been some serious shite when the chopper fell."

Taking a quick swallow of beer to moisten the back of my throat, I reply by saying, "Yeah, fuck, must have been awful."

"What pizza do you fancy?" Shaun asks as I pass him the TV remote. He clicks onto the playback and starts to load the GP race from Sunday.

"Meat lovers feast is good for me, but only a small one, not that hungry today." I take a big swallow of beer.

"What you been up to today?" Shaun asks.

Almost choking on the beer, I quickly swallow the mouthful and the gassy bubbles make me cough slightly. "I had lunch with Sophie." I know full well he won't check up.

"Oh right, anywhere nice that I could take Chloe?" he replies.

"We went to that bar Castro's from Friday night. They do lunchtime menus." I take another swig of beer.

"Fuckin' hell, Deano, you must love both that bird and the place, going there night and day." Shaun starts to laugh.

"Yeah, mate, mad in love. So you want another beer?" I realise mine is empty.

"You on a mission, pal? There are plenty in the fridge. Grab two more and I will ring the pizza order in."

Walking into the kitchen, I notice a pile of smashed furniture and ripped clothes dumped by the dining table.

"Don't look at the mess!" Shaun shouts as the noise of motorbike engines can be heard coming from the television in the living room.

"Okay, not seen that pile of shite," I reply laughing.

Spending time with Shaun is quite relaxing after today's events, but deep down the feeling of guilt in killing those people keeps washing back into my mind. Walking back into living room, Shaun has spread himself over the large corner sofa and is beginning to dial the pizza house to place the order.

Handing him a bottle and walking back to the armchair that was cleared earlier, I sit into the chair and take another big gulp of beer, hoping that a drink will drown out the pain of the people's screams echoing through my head. Shaun can be heard placing the order as I stare at the race start from the

Sunday Moto GP. My eyes watch the screen but my mind continues to play back the events of today with Lloyd, Nick killing Greg, Vernon dying but mostly the sound and smell of people burning from the chopper aviation fuel. I begin to remember how good it felt to use the machine guns and the missile launcher, but all of this adrenalin rush now appears to be washed away with fear and guilt.

Shaun rings off the cell and says, "Delivered in thirty minutes or it's free so let's fuckin' see, hey!"

We both start to watch the GP race with Rossi doing battle with Lorenzo and Stoner. Shaun fetches another set of beers as the front door bell rings.

"Get the door, Deano."

Lifting myself from the chair, I walk to the door and, quickly looking on the intercom system, I see Rahul and a pizza delivery man standing on the other side of the door.

Reaching for the handle, I pull the door inwards and Rahul asks. "Hello, Mr Dean, did you order pizza?"

"Yes, Rahul, and it's under thirty minutes." I check my watch.

The man takes out two pizzas from the hot bag and hands them over.

"That's eighteen seventy-five, sir," he requests, handing me the bill.

The bill shows the name Roberto's Italian Restaurant, as does the name on his shirt. I look the young man over to see if he has any wires or acts strangely but all seems well.

"Hmm, the pizza smells good, Mr Dean," Rahul replies, almost slobbering in an attempt to have a few slices.

Taking some money from my pocket, I pass a twenty-pound note to the delivery man.

"No dinner, Rahul?" I ask.

"Sir, the wife has Rahul on strict diet so no pizza."

"Oh, that's a shame. I was going to offer you some." I smile as the delivery man starts to hand me the change.

"Keep it, Gezza, think of it as compensation for meeting Rahul." Both the pizza man and I laugh as Rahul looks at me, then he begins to also laugh.

"Thank you, sir, have a nice evening," the delivery man replies.

"Have a good evening, Mr Dean." Rahul turns and walks away with the man following.

Closing the door, Shaun has made his way to the door and, grabbing at the bigger box, says, "Fuck, Deano, yours must be for children."

"Well, maybe so, but I won't need four hours in the gym to burn mine off like you!"

"Hmm." Shaun hands me another beer and then slumps back on the sofa, opening the box. Walking back to the chair, I place the pizza box on my knee and the beer bottles by the side of the chair. Lifting the pizza box lid, my nose is filled with the smell of fresh dough, salami, onion, peppers and cheese from the pizza.

The night continues with Shaun and me watching the motorbike racing and reliving events out on our bikes and our adventures. After several beers and pizza, we both begin to feel sleepy and the next thing I remember is waking up in Shaun's armchair with a throbbing headache from all the beers and the taste of aniseed from the Sambuca shots hanging in my mouth. Standing quickly, my head feels heavy and at that moment, realising I still feel slightly drunk, the time on my watch is checked. Seeing the time is 6.05 a.m., I look across to Shaun who is still fast asleep and walk over to him to give him a shake.

"Shaun, it's 6 a.m., time to get up."

He replies with, "Hmm."

Acknowledging he is awake, I begin to make my way to his front door, leaving the flat and closing the door behind, with every footstep echoing through my head like a sledgehammer hitting the side of my skull. Today is going to be a bad day anyway with a fuckin' hangover to complement it, making it worse. Deciding in my delicate situation not to take the lift, the stairs seen the better option so after slowly walking up the two flights of steps, I finally reach my apartment. The keys are taken out and the door unlocked with my head throbbing even heavier. Looking at the time, it's 6.15 a.m. so taking a quick shower and shave, I clean my teeth and then swallow a couple of tablets for the now well advanced hangover and dress in front of the mirror, wearing a blue checked shirt and light grey boss suit.

Walking into the kitchen, I make some toast and a large mug of tea in attempt to kill the hangover but I know it will be part of my long, dreadful day. Collecting my wallet, cell and keys, I make my way down the stairs to the main entrance doors and out into the dull, grey morning. It appears that the world is in mourning after yesterday and the clouds reflect the sadness felt in the city. Looking back into the reception, Rahul isn't seen at the main desk. Maybe he is on break. And then the long painful walk to the tube station. The streets are unusually quiet for this time of the day and, seeing the train station of Imperial Wharf in the distance, I understand why.

The police have erected large blockades across all main roads into the city and have more police officers standing at the lower section of the stairs as the train station entrance is reached. The air has an eerie silence with all the televisions switched off and no hustle of people running for the metros. The police stare at every person that walks past in an attempt to worry any possible terrorists after yesterday, but I simply walk by, trying to act calm. Making my way through to the platform, all that can be heard is people talking about the events of yesterday and I look across to a newspaper stand that shows a child standing near the crashed burning helicopter crying, with blackened face and hands and his clothes all burnt and charred. Behind the boy, people can be seen in the photograph that looks like it was taken in a war zone and not downtown London city with all the emergency services trying to help. "120 dead with 200 injured. Murdering bastards," is the headline from one of the tabloid newspapers with the well-known broadsheet showing a similar picture and the headlines, "Destruction in London City. Country in mourning." I hear a person say that the police are trying to lock down the entire city, but this is impossible to complete with all the offices and people that work and trade in London city.

Standing on the train platform amongst all the other commuters, I begin to imagine what would happen if they knew that I launched the missile that blew the chopper from the sky. Taking a deep breath, the noise of the train carriage thundering along the tracks can be heard breaking the silence. I try to avoid any eye contact with anyone, staring at the opposite platform. The doors slide open and a few people exit and then, walking into the carriage, I instantly realise how empty the train is today. None of the usual people that I notice on the route to work can be seen in the carriage and, taking a seat, people can be seen carrying bunches of flowers and wreaths. Some people can be seen wearing all black clothing with the noise of crying echoing through the metallic structure. People stare across into the openness of space, trying to understand who would do such a thing and cause so much loss on a sunny bank holiday weekend. The weight of all this guilt hangs firmly on my shoulders and the pain felt from all this suffering suddenly becomes more evident as the train stops at West Brompton. Waiting in the carriage, even more people climb inside, carrying flowers, heading for the crash site. My attention is drawn to a TV screen on the tube platform which shows live coverage of police and military personnel guarding the scene of the accident. Forensic experts wearing white overalls can be seen collecting pieces of evidence from different sections of the site.

TV camera crews can be seen filming the whole event as helicopters circle overhead. It is a scene of utter destruction with burnt out cars and large white tents covering the remains of charred bodies. At the edge of the police blockades people can be seen placing flowers into the ever-increasing sea of colours as respects are made. The tube stops at Victoria Station where most of the people from the carriage walk out and must be heading for Stockwell Station. A few people enter the carriage and from the expressions on their faces they have already been to see the large floral tribute. Sitting in the carriage the emotions felt from the entire city can be sensed with the quietness and atmosphere hanging heavy in the air and I feel suffocated from the guilt caused by my actions. The emotions of guilt begin to churn deep inside and tears can be felt welling in my eyes as the tube stops at St James Park Station. Standing quickly, combined with the hangover and guilt, I suddenly become giddy and nauseous and race for the nearest toilets to be sick.

Rushing into the toilet block, I reach the sink and regurgitate the tea and toast from breakfast and switch on the taps and wash the sick down the plughole. I throw some water on my face and, composing myself, continue back out of the toilets and into the station main area. The silence felt in the tube hangs everywhere like a heavy weight across my shoulders as I make my way towards Westminster Station and back down onto the tube and for the first time I feel claustrophobic and dizzy. Standing in the partly filled tube, my mind is overwhelmed with the feeling of sickness and, finally reaching Canary Wharf Station, I somehow manage to make it through the station and towards the direction of the main office building reception. My legs and brain must be pre-programmed for this journey today as people are seen in small huddles just standing and hugging each other, crying. My mind drifts back to the journey on the tube where people were carrying bunches of flowers along with the noise of the police helicopter blades cutting through the sky with the pilots and cameras scanning for any intelligence as I walked from the station. It will only be a matter of time before we get caught and this Tuesday morning commute to work feels like a complete blur and I don't even remember how I reached the office or what the time is.

Beginning to collect my thoughts, I look past the glass partitions into the open plan area, watching the people gradually making their way to the desks, sitting down and still crying. Turning on my swivel chair, I push the vertical blinds towards the left side of the window to look into the outside world, watching the now constant hammering of the rain bouncing against the office glass. As I look through the window, my breath hits the glass, causing condensation to form on the surface like a dull mist blanketing out the raindrops. Continuing to stare through the window, I observe the daily commuters making their way in to the offices of Harpers and Harpers. The people are using umbrellas to shelter from the driving rain, but, occasionally, the wind catches the canopy, turning them inside out. The owners then try to do battle against the weather in an attempt to correct the twisted material. I look at the people entering the building and can tell that they are thinking nothing about their surroundings and what could be waiting for them. My head is so dizzy over what has happened and what I have done.

"Morning, Dean you look deep in thought," a familiar cockney voice asks.

Still looking through the window, without even turning my head, I reply, "Well, it looks to be another depressing day here."

Releasing the window blind with my left hand, I turn back quickly in my chair, looking straight at Peter. Behind his body, I look back into the office, wondering if people here realise what I have done.

"Christ Gezza, that was some bad shit yesterday, hey. Guns, helicopters, police. Fuck, I thought that type of thing only happened in movies, not on our back doorstep."

I turn my head towards him and say, taking a deep sigh, "Yeah, Pete, I see it's all over the news today and the police haven't got a clue who could have done it or why. Serious shite, Pete, have you heard how many people were killed?"

"No official figures yet, but when the chopper fell and blew up onto the crowds of people who were making their way towards Notting Hill Carnival, they are saying hundreds."

I feel so sick from the lower pit of my stomach over what I have done and what made me do it, but during the escape the police were following us that close and we could hear on our radio scanners that they had arranged for stingers and roadblocks preventing our escape and the chopper was getting ready to track our every move. It caused enough of a distraction to get away and fuck, it certainly did that. Inside, though, I'm smiling to myself that we managed to escape, but equally I feel sorry for the people that got killed in the wrong place at the wrong time. If only that fuckin' manager had not pressed the silent alarm off when he did it and it would have been clean, tidy, almost perfect.

"Dean, are you all right? You look ill," Pete asks.

Lowering my head, I shake it, saying, "Yes, mate I am fine. Just had bit of bad news last night that has knocked the wind out of my sails."

"Anything you want to talk about, Dean?" Pete replies.

I'm sitting there thinking about where to possibly start telling him what I have done and at which point of it he would believe and where he would think that I've lost the plot. Last night's sleep was full of my mind imagining the faces of the people I had killed and I don't think this is what Pete the office oracle wants to hear and besides, the last words from Nick yesterday are still haunting my thoughts.

"Dean, this is what you were born for and besides, they were in our way, it's only natural to have the survival of the fittest." I still remember Nick's mouth moving as he spoke.

I still can't believe that he could be so cool and calm after what had happened. The past week has been a railroad of emotions, from joy and happiness to utter sadness and disgust. Even now sitting in this chair, the people in this building will never understand what was done and why it was me who has done it. I know deep down that one day I will be judged and take the consequences for my actions.

"No, Pete, I'm fine. Let's just get today over, hey."

Sitting back in my chair, Pete leaves my office and my thoughts start to drift back just a few days ago when I was a nobody called Dean Nash working as a manager in an office of an accounting firm. Thoughts of my family and friends fill my mind and enjoying life and finally getting back to normal, but now I begin to realise the harsh truth that I am truly a monster that will never be forgiven and the feeling of being alone washes over my emotions. Witnessing the world though my troubled eyes, I can see the look of danger on so many people's faces following my actions. A black cloud now hangs over my emotions with an aching of sadness and hurt tearing away inside.

These black emotions are overcome by a colossal fire burning inside that really enjoyed it and the adrenaline rush was massive, better than any scary time on the motorbike, carrying out a bungee or a parachute jump and I fear that nothing will match that level of excitement again. The simple instruction from Nick will always be deep in my thoughts but equally I seem to have released me from this non-existent life.

"Dean, just fetch the sidewinder missile launcher from the back of the Range Rover and kindly blow that fuckin' police chopper from the sky. It's affecting my escape plans and my thoughts."

How can someone be so cool in such a critical moment and not even seem to think about anything else? This guy is so calm and calculated and he knew that blowing up the chopper would have caused absolute mayhem in the city that helped us to escape. In fact I could almost sense that deep down that this was part of the plan, but not many of the team knew about it. A flashback filters into my mind. I remember the devastation at the police roadblock where the barrage of bullets and gunfire hitting the police cars was deafening. The sound from each bullet hitting the car windows as the glass shattered into tiny fragments and the rounds punching holes in the car bodywork, peeling the exit holes open like a can opener and the deafening echoes from the guns being fired in the narrow street. The police officers fall to the ground like lumps of dead meat from the firepower that was hitting them with six MP5s on full auto with Teflon coated rounds plus two Barrett 50 calibre sniper rifles taking them out from over six hundred metres away. They stood no chance armed with a few basic Beretta handguns and a couple of MP5 sub machine guns. The noise from the gunfire still echoes in my head along with the smell of blood in the air as the bullets hit the officers' bodies.

On the road surface underneath the police cars pools of blood were beginning to form from the dead and dying police officers as though they had been involved in a battle. The air was filled with a mist cloud of blood as the Barrett 50 calibre rounds hit the policemen's bodies through the cars and seeing the reaction on their faces, along with the noise of their screams, brings back such vivid memories in the back of my mind, but I can't remember from where. The strangest thing with all of the events was that with all the pain and gunfire noise nothing seemed to bother me at all and this seems to be the scariest part of the whole day. Why didn't this affect me? Looking back, it almost felt as though it made me sharper and keener with every single bullet strike.

Ring ring. My office desk telephone starts to illuminate with an incoming call.

Snapping out of my daydream, I reach over with my right hand towards the receiver and lifting the receiver a familiar voice is heard. "Hi, Dean, I just wanted to apologise for what I said yesterday and hope you can forgive me. I hope you are well, I was so worried after yesterday."

Waiting for a few seconds, I reply, "Hi, Sophie. Look, I don't know what games you're playing, but yesterday you told me to back off and today all nice again."

"Dean, what happened yesterday? I was so confused after the things you said and sometimes I snap," Sophie answers with nervousness in her voice.

"As I said yesterday, it's a bad time at the minute and dealing with your emotional tidal waves is more than I can stomach," I reply sharply.

"Dean, please can we speak later? I need to talk with you over a something," she answers back, with quivering in her voice.

"Not at the moment, please leave me alone for a few days and think about what you're doing first." The phone hangs up.

I place the receiver back onto the phone and continue to stare out into the office. My cell is sitting on the top of my desk and starts to vibrate with an incoming message and I lower my eyes to watch the cell dancing across the desk. Lifting the cell, I press the screen unlock button to access the resent messages. There is one from Sophie, with another message from an unknown number. Another flashback appears in my mind of a person being killed and I remember holding a man as he tried to fight back against me as I slit his throat with a knife. As I lower the body to the ground, the colour and emotions drain from the young man's face as the blood pool collects on the white mottled marble flooring with a voice echoing through my brain of an older man saying, "This man is a traitor to queen and country and must be silenced."

Feeling sick, I rush towards the toilets in the office block and, almost kicking the door open, rush into the washroom to lean over one of the white sink bowls. The vomit hits the sink basin and my body shakes with emotion and adrenaline as the smell of vomit begins to fill my nostrils. I turn on the taps to rinse the watery vomit away down the plughole and, throwing some water on my face, place my hands gripping each side of the basin. Another flashback returns with the same mature voice saying, "This is always a normal reaction to the first death." Lifting my head, I look into the mirror hanging over the sink and the reflection of an old man with grey longish hair and dark grey suit is standing behind me.

Quickly turning around to look behind me, I realise that the person is a figment of my imagination, but then a conversation begins to fill my brain with me saying, "This man has done nothing to me."

"Anything against this country is something against you and do not question my authority, you are here to follow instructions!"

"Yes, sir, I understand."

The toilet door opens and Pete enters. He looks across and says, "I thought you didn't look well, Dean. What is it, food poisoning?"

"Yeah, must be the pizza I had last night from a new place."

"I have just heard from one of the directors that due to the accident they are going to close the office as a mark of respect for the rest of the day." Pete still stands near the door.

Another wave of stomach cramps begin to take hold and, leaning over the basin again, I begin to retch with sick beginning to form in my mouth.

"I will leave you with it, Dean." Pete quickly leaves, closing the door.

After being sick again and throwing more cold water on my face, I begin to compose myself and walk back into the office. Opening the toilet door, the few people that have made it to the office today are already starting to close down the computers and collect their personal effects. Making my way back to my office, the director's assistant Rachael appears.

"Hi, Dean, have you heard that Mr Harper has declared that the office will be closed today as a mark of respect?"

Nodding back I reply, "Yes, Peter has just informed me."

"Are you okay, Dean? You don't look well," Rachael asks.

"I think I have some food poisoning from a pizza last night, but will try to be here tomorrow."

"Take some rest, Dean, and hopefully it will be better tomorrow. Wasn't yesterday terrible?" I can see her eyes are slightly reddened.

"Yes, Rachael, what a disaster with so many people injured."

"What is the world coming to, Dean, for people to do things like that?"

Feeling nauseous again I reply, "Desperate times mean people do bad things."

"Okay, Dean, take care and see you soon." She turns and begins to walk away.

"Goodbye Rachael."

Walking out of the building and towards the direction of the tube station and feeling so ill, I decide to hail for a cab and, although it will cost more money, I don't really care. A black cab pulls over and the driver asks, "Where to fella?"

"Apartment building Chelsea Crescent, Chelsea Harbour. Thanks." I reach for door handle and climb inside.

As the driver starts, the conversation falls straight to the explosion. "Christ, guvner, that was some bad news yesterday, hey half of London is still shut. All those people, lucky I was off duty or that would be my usual run."

"Yeah, it was terrible," I reply.

The driver looks into his rear view mirror and continues in his strong cockney accent, "I hope they catch those guys, they are saying it was part of that robbery of the money sorting house. Its rumoured those guys got away with over ten million."

Trying to be polite and stop myself from being ill in his cab, I answer, "Oh really? Look, mate, I don't mean to be rude but I've really had a bad day so far, would you mind if we just get there as soon as possible?"

"Yes, governor, no problems. I noticed you didn't look at your best."

After being bumped around the cab and fighting against being sick, we finally reach the apartment block and, looking at the meter, see the bill is thirty-five quid.

"That's three and five guvnor, thanks," he asks.

Reaching into my wallet, I hand him over two twenty pound notes and reply with, "Keep the change," as I begin to open the rear door.

"Thanks, governor, and hope you feel better soon."

Continuing to walk towards the main entrance of the apartment building, I pass through the swing doors and onwards to the lifts. Thankfully Rahul is nowhere to be seen on the reception since I'm not in a talkative mood, but as with so many times recently the sensation of being watched fills my every footstep. The lift journey, although short, makes me feel as sick as ever and rushing for the apartment door the keys are dropped in the corridor. As I bend down to pick up the keys, I almost pass out from the lack of food in my stomach and, with my hands shaking, I finally manage to open the door and, closing it behind, I quickly make my way to the bathroom to be sick again. After taking a few sips of water to clear the back of my throat, I lie on the bed still fully clothed, trying to fall asleep, but my mind is filled with different scenes of the robbery and vivid parts keep playing. Quickly looking at my watch with a raging hangover, the time reads 2.45 p.m. Drifting off asleep, I try to forget the terrible events.

Later in the day Nick sits in the darkness of Lloyd's living room with the curtains drawn, playing back the events of the robbery along with where things went wrong. Talking to himself, he says, "All the security systems should have been deactivated so how did the manager trigger the silent alarm?" Suddenly he clicks on a side lamp, illuminating a corner of the room, and lifts an old thin, black leather briefcase from the side of the armchair. Taking out various papers, he places them onto the coffee table and begins to study the architectural schematics of the electrical and security systems, tracing through the various circuit drawings with his fingers. Finally stopping at a point on the plans, he focuses in more and sees that a small detail had been missed with a remote activated push button alarm fob. Immediately sensing that something was missed, he quickly stands and leaves Lloyd's house, climbing into the Passat. Nick, with a look of anger on his face, starts the engine and, engaging first gear, drives away from the house at speed as the darkness of the night consumes the last rays of light from the day.

8

Suddenly awakening Wednesday morning, I quickly look at my hands, imagining that they are covered with wet blood from Lloyd as my brain still replays the events with me wearing black overalls. Trying to wipe the blood off with the bed sheets, I look again at my hands only to see nothing. My brain has suffered a massive trauma combined with only cat naps of sleep and my body is still in complete shock over the actions from Monday with my mind still trying to picture together all the events. I see Lloyd lying in my arms with the look of fear in his eyes, knowing that his life was coming to an end. This thought haunts my every moment along with his final breath when he gripped on my right hand so intensely as the last part of his life drained away. This was not what I expected from the robbery and losing a guy like Lloyd shows how even a professional can be killed in this type of work. Getting out of bed and then taking a shower, I dress and prepare for another day at the office trying to continue with my normal life as Nick instructed. But how can life be normal after the death of all these people by my hands?

Walking into the kitchen, the coffee machine is switched on and, operating the remote for the TV, I try to hide my loneliness with some background noise filling the quietness of the apartment. All the main channels are still filled with the public's outrage of the events and the lack of police answers. The death toll now stands at over two hundred and apart from a few people at work, not a single message or phone call from anyone has been received to see if I'm alive. Am I such a bad person? And now feeling so alone my emotions begin to well deep inside, causing me to start crying. The darkness of my situation clings deep into my soul and after all my past mistakes this is the time that I'm being judged for all the wrongs done in my life and have brought all this to myself and I only have myself to blame. The only way to get through this situation is to gain an inner strength; otherwise the darkness of my past will eat away at my insides until there is nothing left, sending me deeper into the pit of darkness. Sitting in the living room and taking a sip of the fresh coffee, I begin to reflect on a life that from the outside looks quite normal, but on the inside these flashbacks lead me to think about another life that I don't seem to know and this is what I need to understand. Nick is the only person that can show me this. After finishing my coffee and feeling completely drained, I decide at that moment that fighting this blackness is the only option otherwise it will eat me alive. Looking at the time, I see the travel journey to work is calling.

Now trying to remain more focused and determined, I confidently leave the apartment building and make my way to the train station. Ignoring all the news channels bellowing out the names of the victims, I catch the usual carriage that will shuttle me through the dark tunnels of London and finally to the station closest to Harpers and Harpers offices near to Canary Wharf. Entering the building past the security guards and continuing in the direction of my office, I walk into the room switching on the light, then open the laptop to check my calendar for today. I begin to check my number of holidays left and decide maybe a few days away from work is the best option. The last few days have been an absolute hell with my emotions rising and falling like a ship on a stormy sea. One minute my confidence is riding so high that I feel anything can be accomplished and in the next minute it feels like I'm falling into a black hole, out of control and my senses are becoming super sensitive and a person's body language stands out long before any words are said. The feeling of depression after killing all those people keeps rolling over me like a wave of emotion, drowning me at the same time, but my thoughts then begin to shift over to Nick and what answers he has over my past.

My cell begins to ring, displaying a withheld number. Deciding to answer the call, a familiar voice can be heard. "Dean, how are you doing? I was trying to contact you."

"Hi, Nick, it's been tough these last few days," I reply with a submissive voice, but the real truth is that I want to speak with him.

"Dean, can we meet later at Gaucho's steak house? I need to speak with you over a few things," Nick asks in a persuasive manner.

Wanting to try and learn more about my past, I agree quickly. "Yes, Nick, what time?"

"How about 8 p.m., okay? The table will be booked under the name Smith!" Nick answers.

"Yes, no problems, Nick. See you later," I reply.

With thoughts more collected already, I complete the holiday form for a couple of weeks' leave and walk towards Rachael's desk with a new level of inner confidence.

"Hi, Dean, how are you doing, are you feeling any better?" Rachael asks.

"A little better thanks, Rachael. Can you ask the big boss if he will sign this holiday form? I have had some bad news and need a few days off for personal reasons and my calendar shows a few days owing," I reply back.

"Haven't we all, Dean. Mr Winters is out of office until Monday, but most businesses are almost closed this week anyway so I don't think there will be a problem." Rachael now stands looking at me with a tear in her eyes.

"Have you heard who was killed on Monday?"

I answer back, "No, Rachael. Who?"

"Chloe from sales and her husband Ben who were just out shopping when the helicopter crashed. Chloe had just found out she was pregnant." A tear drops onto her cheek as she tells me.

"Oh my, that's terrible. I was only having a drink with her and a few friends on the Friday." The news feels like a knife stuck in my side.

"Dean, are you okay? You have gone two shades of grey," Rachael asks, touching my left arm.

"No, Rachael, it's a bad time for everyone."

"Dean, please go take some time off. I will clear it with Mr Winters, just look after yourself, okay?" Rachael answers in a concerned voiced.

Turning away, I make my way to the washroom to freshen up after hearing about Chloe being killed. That was a little bit too close for comfort. Reaching the basin, my body starts to shake from the adrenaline. Being exhausted and switching on the cold tap, a voice echoes from one of the toilet cubicles behind me.

"Deano, is that you, mate?" Shaun's familiar voice bellows.

Turning and looking in the direction of the voice I reply, "Hey, Shaun. Yes, mate. I'm not going to ask what you're up to in there. Have just booked a few days holiday so will be heading home shortly."

The toilet is flushed and the cubicle door opens as Shaun walks out, still fastening his belt. It's good to see his friendly face. "Mate, you look like shite, do you need any help?"

"Cheers, Shaun, you don't look much better yourself." We smile at each other.

"Chloe and that arsehole husband were killed on Monday." Shaun reaches the next basin and looks at me in the mirror with redness in his eyes after crying as he starts to wash his hands.

"Yeah, Rachael just told me. Are you okay?" I answer back, standing.

"She was pregnant, Dean," Shaun looks across with sadness on his face.

"No way! Well, was it yours?" I reply with a level of shock in my voice.

"Mate, we had been seeing each other for about two months and she was planning to leave him as it was starting to get serious!" Shaun looks at me again as though he knows something. I can see the hurt in his eyes.

"Fuckin' hell, Shaun I'm really sorry to hear that. So it could have been yours?" I ask, surprised.

"Mate, if I ever find out who those guys were, I will fuckin' kill all of them," Shaun replies with aggression in his voice.

Taking a deep sigh, trying to hide my guilt, I try to think of an answer. "Mate, I'm so sorry, the guys sure have ruined a lot of families and killed many people. Let's hope the police can catch them. Is there anything I can do?"

Shaun then asks the question that I was expecting and dreading. "What would you do if you knew any of the robbers?"

Staring into the mirror, I look across to Shaun, saying, "I wouldn't know where to start."

Leaning over the basin, Shaun says, "Yeah, I know what you mean, Deano. Take care and speak soon, okay?" He stands up straight, slaps me on the back, turns and begins to walk towards the door.

Shaun continues to walk out of the washroom and, as the door closes behind, my eyes begin to fill with a tear knowing that I may have killed Shaun's baby and possibly a new life for him and Chloe and he is putting on a brave face but is hurting inside. It fills me with pain. Splashing some water on my face and trying to feel better, I know deep down what has been done feels so wrong and my mind begins to imagine what Nick wants from me and how tonight's conversation may go. Finally walking out of the washroom back towards my office, I look around to see the shock and despair on the people's faces as they sit around in groups in the open plan areas. With being wrapped up in my own self-pity, I had not realised how much pain and suffering lingers in the office with the low humming sound of people talking, hugging and crying together until the air is filled with the solitary ringing of a cell in someone's desk.

"That's the eighth time already this morning Richard's cell has rung, has anybody heard anything from him?" a lady's voice announces.

Reaching my office, I close down the laptop and, looking through the window, see the streets full with police officers and television vans parked up with film crews, interviewing people who are trying to continue with their normal lives. Walking out of the office and switching off the light, I close the door and make my way out through the open plan area. As I glance across, Shaun can be seen slumped in his chair, with his head in his hands in total shock and despair. This must be one of the worst days for Shaun and this guilt bites inside me and I wonder what would happen if he knew that it was me who blew up the helicopter. Leaving the office and finally in the crowded streets outside, film crew helicopters fill the sky, still showing the destruction. As I pass through the crowds of people, the police stand wearing full-body armour, holding machine guns. The tension hangs thick in the air from their body language showing that they could erupt at any time following the death of many colleagues after Monday's tragic events.

All the news headlines seen on every newspaper, TV channel and radio station, only talking about the events and what occurred around who was behind it, overload my senses again. Reaching the tube station, I walk down the staircase and stand on the platform amongst all the other passengers waiting for the train to arrive. Police officers continue to mingle and walk through the crowds, trying to look for any type of person that could be suspects. The tannoy system announces the tube for my area is reaching platform three and moving forward slightly, I see the headlights illuminating the tunnel. Even in the crowded area of the platform, my senses pick up that someone is watching and my heart begins to beat a little faster as the train stops next to the platform. Looking in the glass, the reflections of two police officers dressed in black combat clothing and carrying machine guns loom over from behind. The tube doors open and people begin to flood into the empty carriage as the police continue to follow. Entering the carriage, I quickly stand at the far side and turn slightly to see the officers' reflections in the glass as the train lunges into action. I try to blend into the crowded people that are already inside.

I try to keep a safe distance away from the officers, but can see them scanning every person in the carriage, just looking for any possible suspects. A commanding voice then echoes an instruction and my stomach turns over with fear. "Excuse me, sir, want to pass?" A police officer stands behind me and brushes his way through, moving towards the next carriage. The tension in the carriage is so heavy, even more with the attitude of the police and the deadly silence from nobody speaking. Shuffling closer to the side of the carriage and allowing the two officers to pass, I turn slightly and watch their reflections in the glass for any reaction. The redness in their eyes tells me that they have been on duty for a long time trying to find suspects as my heart beat starts to stabilise. Remaining composed and trying to bury my emotions deep, I think about the meeting with Nick tonight and if he can tell me more about my past. The journey feels like an eternity as each station gets ever closer to my stop and then a few people start a conversation in the carriage, talking about the robbery and all the numbers of people who were killed, with their voices suffocating my every breath.

Finally my station, and as the train rattles to a complete stop the doors open and freedom from the pain and suffering overwhelms my emotions. I'm not sure how much more I can take at the moment, but for sure, the meeting with Nick and the answers I seek ring in my head like a bell before a church service. I walk quickly through the train station and make my way up the stairs and outside away from the suffocation felt inside the carriage, with a feeling of nausea making my stomach churn over, but the freshness and freedom of beginning to walk along the street back to my apartment is suddenly killed short as the sight of a black Mercedes car waiting in the train station parking lot confirms my worst fears. "What could possibly be any worse than this?" fills my thoughts and as before the man and lady agents are sitting in the front of the car, but this time Wagstaff stands outside, leaning against the side of the car, having a cigarette, staring at me. My heart sinks to even lower level of depression, knowing that he will want to speak with me. I scan across the car park and see another familiar car fifty metres away from the black Mercedes; it's the white VW Passat from the Gatwick run.

Quickly glancing across, Nick is seen sitting inside with the window slightly open, smoking a cigar and trying to read a newspaper, but it's quite evident he is staring at the two of us. My brain now has the worst possible decision to make. Speak with Wagstaff, walk across to Nick or try to ignore them both and disappear into the ever-darkening black hole that is becoming part of my new life. Wagstaff drops the cigarette and stamps on it, sending a shower of sparks into the air, and signals me to join him at the car. Looking across at him, my throat suddenly becomes very dry and I try to cough to clear it but to no avail. I turn slightly and begin to make my way over towards him, still leaning against the black car with all manner of questions and answers running through my mind. Even from this distance Wagstaff must see the guilt across my face and with every step closer to him I feel like a man walking to death row. What will he say? How will I answer? What must Nick think? These thoughts keep playing over and over in my mind with no clear right or wrong decision. The distance is only fifty metres but it feels like an eternity with my legs getting heavier with every single footstep. I start to feel dizzy and faint again with the lack of food and dehydration from the last few days.

Finally at less than five metres away from Wagstaff he looks at me and asks, "Christ, Dean, you look terrible, as though you have the weight of the world on your shoulders?"

I replying back, "Mr Wagstaff, no, I have stomach flu and left work for a few days' rest."

"Really? You look like hell, as though you have killed a man." Wagstaff's voice confirms my worst thoughts.

Looking back at him with sunken eyes, I wish I could open up and explain everything to him, but I also know that after the police were killed he can't save me anymore. "The only man that feels killed is me at the moment!" I reply, trying to humour him, but he isn't impressed.

"Do you have anything to tell me, Dean, following the events from Monday? Were you and Nick involved?" Wagstaff asks calmly.

He continues, "If you were involved and you give up, Burns, I could strike a deal with the CPS and maybe save you from some nasty time in prison."

I lie through my back teeth and try to look even more ill. "Mr Wagstaff, I'm not sure what you mean. I haven't seen Nick since we last spoke on Sunday. What happened on Monday was terrible and I hope the authorities catch who was involved."

"The police have concrete evidence over the team who carried out the raid and know the gang members who died." Wagstaff takes out another cigarette and begins to light it.

"Really, Mr Wagstaff? I have been ill and now want to go home to rest," I reply submissively.

"Where were you on Monday, Dean?" Wagstaff looks past me towards the railway station entrance.

"I can't see that's any of your business, but if you must know I took a friend to Gatwick airport, drove back to my flat and went back to bed. After waking later in the day, I went round to my mate Shaun's flat where we drank some beers and ordered a pizza. This was when I also heard about the robbery." Technically the second part of my day was true, answering with more confidence.

"Hmm, so you have nothing to tell me over what happened Monday morning after the airport?" Wagstaff finishes his cigarette and, as before, drops it on the ground and stamps on it, sending out sparks.

"Yes, I got in the car and drove back to my flat," I reply sharply.

"What type of car was it, Dean, since I know you don't own one. And who was your friend?" Wagstaff still looks unconvinced with my story.

"The car was a blue Ford Fiesta and the reg was NL54, but I can't remember the last part and my friend Peter, his girlfriend owns it. Peter was travelling to Prague for a stag do with about six of his football mates. They asked me to join, but I didn't want to go, okay?" I snap at Wagstaff and remember the blue Fiesta when we left the airport in the Passat.

Wagstaff taps on the car and the front driver's window opens slightly. Wagstaff instructs an agent inside. "Preston asks the team to check a blue Ford Fiesta with reg plate NL54 on the security tapes for Monday morning to confirm his story."

After a few seconds Preston's voice can be heard. "Confirmed, sir. A blue Ford Fiesta with registration plate NL54 ZFD did leave the airport parking at 6.38 a.m. with one male occupant."

"Shaun who? From Monday evening?"

"Shaun Neal. Do you want his mobile number to confirm?" I reply.

"I will talk with Mr Neal in good time, Dean, don't worry, but I already know that fact is true. It's the rest of the morning I want an answer for!"

The window closes again and Wagstaff continues with his lecture. "Mr Nash, I think you're playing a dangerous game and when you get caught out, I won't be able to save you, but that's your choice now!"

"Is that all?" I ask.

"Yes, for now, Mr Nash," he replies.

Returning back along the footpath that leads in the direction of the main road to my apartment, I look back and see Wagstaff starting to climb into the back of the Mercedes as the engine starts. Nick is still sitting in the Passat further down the parking area and continues to stare at every movement.

Inside the Mercedes Preston asks Wagstaff a question. "Sir, do you want me to trace the blue Fiesta owner?"

Wagstaff replies quickly, "No, it's a red herring, he was lucky when he noticed that car. He was thinking on his feet, but his body language reads as though it was the truth. Is this man something or what?"

Preston looks back into the rear view mirror at Wagstaff and asks, "What do you mean, sir?"

"I mean he knows we are onto him and Burns' team, but he still had the balls to stand there and lie to a government agent director without even flinching. Anyone would think he was government trained." Wagstaff laughs.

Agent Preston looks at the other front seat passenger, Agent Wilson, with a look as though they know more than Wagstaff on this matter. I continue to walk along the main road as the black Mercedes drives past at quite high speed with small blue lights flashing in the radiator grill and back windscreen. After a few more minutes the white Passat drives past more slowly, but the driver never makes any contact and several seconds later a silver Ford Mondeo drives past with two men dressed in suits. The passenger looks across at me for a few seconds, and then turns his head to continue watching the road in front. His face details of nose, chin and haircut flash back in my mind, but I can't remember from where and as the car gradually begins to speed away into the distance, it appears to be following Nick. Reaching the main entrance of the apartment block, the doors open automatically and I walk through towards the direction of the lifts. My brain feels like it will explode with everything that is happening around me and hopefully I can try and get some rest before the onslaught of tonight's events with Nick.

Entering the lift and standing slightly to the left, the twelfth floor button is pressed and as the movement starts I begin to feel a little giddy. Having never suffered from motion sickness before, it must be down to the lack of food, water and sleep deprivation. My body feels completely delirious. The lift doors open on the twelfth floor and I gradually make my way towards the apartment and hopefully some level of security, but after the pictures were left in there even this safe place seems compromised. Placing the key in the lock, the door is opened and I walk into the brightly lit lounge area. Scanning around the apartment it's quickly noticed that nothing has been moved or changed and this time the room feels safe and secure. Reaching the settee, I collapse onto the soft, cool, dark brown leather cushions and quickly fall asleep as the time on the large wall clock clicks over to 11 a.m.

Meanwhile, Wagstaff reaches the counter terrorist branch of MI6 and makes his way to the office that people call his second home. Opening the door of his office, he walks inside and looks across to the pictures of his wife and family neatly placed on the green leather covered heavy oak desk. He is deep in thought, thinking about how to capture Burns and the rest of the gang as he sits in his dark green leather swivel chair, leaning backwards slightly. Nick continues to follow Wagstaff and watches him walk into the MI6 offices and then heads over Tower Bridge with the silver Mondeo following him at a distance. Nick is fully aware they are following and gradually keeps checking his rear view mirror to try and determine who they are and now decides to spend the next few hours driving around the outskirts of London to see how long the two men in the Mondeo will follow him. He quickly notices their facial details being around thirty years old, wearing heavy cut suits and senses from their actions that they are professionals with excellent trailing abilities, just keeping the right distance to try and look normal. Nick is more than happy to drive around for a few hours but gradually reaches over to the passenger glove box, lifting a Glock handgun placing it onto the seat, checking the safety button is clicked ready just in case.

Shaun still sits at his desk with a look of shock on his face as his mobile begins to ring. Picking up the cell, he notices that the number is withheld and decides not to answer it. After a few minutes the cell rings again so this time he presses the 'receive call' button and lifts it to his right ear.

The call is silent for a couple of seconds and then a strong, frail English voice can be heard. "Is this Shaun Neal?"

"So what if it is? Who is this?" Shaun asks.

"That's not important, Shaun, but I can give you some information you have been waiting for."

The voice continues, "I know the names of some people that killed your girlfriend Chloe on Monday. Do you what to meet up?"

Shaun shakes with both fear and aggression as a tear starts to roll down his right cheek and with a nervous voice he replies, "Okay, where and when?"

"Do you know O'Neill's on Muswell Hill, Broadway? We can meet at 8 p.m. Sunday," The old frail voice replies. "Yes, I know the place. What do you look like?" Shaun asks.

"Don't worry, Neal, we know what you look like," the voice answers smugly.

The cell rings off, then Shaun places the cell back on his desk and looks into the distance, thinking about what to do and who the old person could be. This information makes him feel better knowing that he may finally place a name to the people that killed Chloe and revenge starts to flow through his veins. Maybe this information could make him do anything to revenge her death.

My eyes open to the late afternoon sunshine warming the lounge room of the apartment and now, feeling a little better, I decide to take a shower and try to eat some food.

The warm shower is so refreshing and the thought of some light food in my stomach makes me hungry, just enough for some scrambled eggs on toast. After making the food, I walk back into the lounge from the kitchen and sit on settee with the plate of food on my lap. Starting to eat the eggs and toast, I feel every mouthful hit my empty stomach and hopefully try to keep it down without being sick again. Finishing the food, I slide the plate onto the glass coffee table as my mind starts to think about the pictures and why I have them. Standing, I walk over to the drawer unit and take out the envelope from the centre draw and place it onto the glass table next to the empty plate. Lifting the plate, I walk into the kitchen and place it, along with the dirty saucepan and cutlery, into the dishwasher.

The cold water tap is switched on and a glass beaker filled with cool, fresh water. Returning to the living room, the beaker is placed on the coffee table next to the envelope and the pictures are then tipped out. Lifting the pictures. I begin to sort them into what appear to be three main categories: military, family and others. After sorting the pictures I begin to flick through each one, trying to study the person's facial details and any information from the background. As before, each face looks familiar, but not remembering from where is so frustrating, until suddenly in the back row of one old black and white group picture is the face of the man I imagined in my mind a few days earlier. The face of the man is much younger, with short black wiry hair, standing almost hidden behind several ladies holding newborn babies. Looking across the faces of the women and other men in the picture, no one else looks familiar, but this detail must be information for me to start with. I turn the picture around and see a small ink print address, which appears to be in German writing.

After taking a sip of water from the glass beaker, I start to look through the military pictures with none of the faces appearing familiar, but then another detail stands out in the background of another group photo with a company flag in the distance, slightly floating on the wind. The unique colours and pattern on the flag might be traceable to the garrison and, quickly fetching my laptop, I begin to investigate through search engines different colours and patterns of military units. Scrolling through the military flag pages, a similar pattern is found, but not the actual one on the picture.

The internet page reads 'Company 1264 ops'.

I try to trace the photo processing address in Germany, but nothing can be found as the time clicks over to 6.45 p.m. I begin to flick through the last pile of pictures with many being the most recent, including Sophie, Shaun and me. I study each picture for any details in the background but nothing immediate is seen and finally, after what appears to be hours, the piles of pictures are placed onto the glass table and I walk to fetch some elastic bands to bunch them together. After segregating the pictures and placing them back into the envelope, I return them to the draw and head towards the bedroom to prepare for tonight's events. Gaucho's is a very popular designer restaurant that once held a Michelin star so the food at least should be good. With my dizziness and sickness now subsided, I begin to look forward to eating some quality food but I worry over what Nick wants deep down.

Deciding to dress in a casual suit seems to be the best option and as the hands of the large clock hanging solemnly on the white wall in my living room click over to seven fifteen, I walk towards the front door, knowing it's time to leave for the dinner with Nick and everything he will be wanting from me. Taking a lightweight overcoat, the front door is closed and I begin to make my way along the corridor and then down the lift. Crossing the lobby, I walk out of the apartment building and continue towards the Fulham Broadway tube station with my mind wanting to collect information. Nick may be the key and may know someone who could help with trying to find out about the pictures and the company 1264 ops, assuming he has a military background. The tube journey, stopping at Tower Hill underground, is a complete blur as I walk almost in remote control, not noticing anything that's happening around me until I reach the entrance doors outside Gaucho's. Stopping by the main door, I turn and look across the River Thames and Tower Bridge. Then my heart, once prepared and looking forward to the night, now sinks into dread over the conversation that will happen as a knot twists deep down in my stomach, confirming that this is a bad idea.

The activity in my brain overtakes my negative feelings and wanting to know more about the pictures is so overwhelming and draws me closer to the door handle. Slightly open vertical blinds hang behind the windows and my thoughts turn to what Nick will say about the conversation earlier at the tube station with Wagstaff and my reply can only be truthful since he will smell any lie instantly. Wagstaff knows I was involved in the robbery even if he didn't say it and ultimately knows that Nick is behind the whole plan. Taking a deep sigh I push one of the main doors open and instantly my ears are filled with the noise of people talking and at that point I realise why Nick has chosen this place. No police or agents would risk trying to take Nick or me in this restaurant without lots of casualties so our protection is almost guaranteed. The restaurant is a large open plan layout with simple lighting and classical music floating in the air. All the tables are full, even on a Wednesday night, showing how popular the venue is with the white walls and ceilings illuminated by the subdued lighting. Candles flicker, held in brightly polished holders sitting on the heavy oak dining table tops.

Standing at the front of the room, the maître d' makes his way over, wearing a black suit, white shirt and black dickey bow. "Good evening Mr Nash, Mr Smith is waiting for you, please follow me," he speaks in a strong French accent, giving me a wink.

"Thank you," I reply with a fake smile and quickly register his facial details, a pointed black beard and combed back dark brown hair tied into a ponytail.

The restaurant's atmosphere is alive with people laughing and talking as the maître d' threads his way past the neat rows of tables and chairs with the smell of fresh food and drink filling my nostrils. Wine, beef, fish and strong herbs all hang in the air like an invisible mist and then at the far left side of the restaurant Nick sits on a table staring into the unknown. Realising I am close, he looks across and then stands to greet me with a large smile on his face.

"Dean, my old friend, how the devil are you?" he asks confidently.

We shake hands and I reply by saying, "Hi, Nick, I'm well. How about you?"

The maître d' asks, "Shall I take your coat, sir?"

"Thank you," I reply.

Taking off my coat and handing it to him, the maître d' pulls out my chair then, as I reach my place, pushes it gradually underneath, supporting me. Nick re-sits and the maître d' ensures his chair is correct. "Would Mr Nash care for a drink, sir?"

"I will have a glass of water along with a double gin and tonic, thanks."

"Very good, sir. Any preference of gin?" the maître d' asks.

"Bombay Sapphire, please," I reply with a smile on my face.

"Your table waiter, Marcus, will bring your drink over, sir and I wish you a pleasant evening." The maître d' walks away.

I look around the restaurant and notice Nick has picked a table within fifteen metres of both the emergency and kitchen exit doors. Any police or agents would need to either enter from the front, making their way through the crowded room, or from the rear exits, but where he sits he can observe the complete room.

"So, Dean, how's tricks?" Nick asks with a level of excitement in his voice.

"Pretty shite at the minute, Nick, and as you know Wagstaff collared me again today!" I reply with some nervousness.

"Yes, old boy, I observed it and am glad you noticed me too, so your senses are beginning to sharpen?" Nick takes a sip of his gin and tonic.

"Senses sharpening! I think they are on overload at the minute," I say as the table waiter brings over my drinks.

"Gentleman, good evening. My name is Marcus and I will be serving tonight. Would you like to see the menus?" he asks, standing by the table.

"Could you give us five minutes please?" Nick instructs the waiter and he smiles and walks away.

"Dean, that's excellent news. So we can prepare for what happens next." This was the conversation I was dreading.

Nick continues, "Dean, I imagine you have been feeling quite ill these past few days. It's only natural to feel that way."

"Back in your mind though, I bet you remember feeling this way before?" He takes another sip of his drink.

Looking across at him, I lift my glass of water and take a big sip and answer, "Nick, I've had what I can only think are flashbacks or thoughts in my mind."

"Dean, that would have been the first few days of training. Was there an old man in your imagines?" I nod back at him, agreeing.

"Dean, there is a side to you that you have forgotten or, let me say, has been hidden." The waiter returns to the table with the menus.

I stare at Nick, realising what he is saying seems real, but also far from any truth my brain can connect together. The waiter passes out the menus and says, "The soup of the day is roasted oxtail and herb dumping."

"Thank you," Nick replies. The waiter walks away.

"I couldn't tell you before because of the robbery, but now things have changed and now everyone will be after you, both friends and enemies." Nick opens his menu.

"So what are you, Nick?" I ask, opening the menu cover.

"I'm glad you asked, Dean. What do you think?" Nick lifts his eyes to look at me.

"I think you are either ex-military or an ex government agent!"

"Your thoughts are not far away Dean."

"Let us select food and we can continue to talk, what do you want to eat friend?" Nick asks.

"What do you recommend, if you're a friend?" I take a sip of gin and tonic.

"The filet mignon is fabulous along with the salmon soufflé," Nick answers.

"After Monday, I haven't eaten at all and don't have much of an appetite," I reply back and close the menu cover.

"Dean, the past is the past and unless you let it go it will always haunt you." Nick calms his voice.

"I am here to help you find out who you truly are and help support you in this time, but our enemies will find us and kill us if we don't work together." I sense nervousness in his voice.

The waiter arrives back at the table. "Gentleman, are you ready to order?"

Nick, speaking clearly and calmly, says, "We will both have a salmon soufflé for starters followed by the filet mignon."

"Very good, sir, the filet as usual?" asks the waiter.

"Yes please, with a little black peppercorn and truffle on the side," Nick replies.

"What about the wine, sir?"

"Argh yes." Nick opens the list.

"Bollinger rosé for the starters and Vina Cobos Corte Malbec for the mains."

"Excellent choices, sir." The waiter smiles and walks away.

The conversation continues with Nick constantly talking about how glad he is we are working together and how impressed he is with my skills seen during the robbery and the escape afterwards, along with how good I kept cool even under fire and threat from the police.

"Many other men would have cracked under that pressure, causing probably the death of us all." Nick takes a sip of the gin and tonic.

Thinking back as Nick talks, deep down it just felt normal with taking gunfire and police chasing us. That is a big difference to how I felt earlier in the week. Making such a good impression to him feels as though I have finally gained his trust and proved to myself that maybe I am cut out for this type of life, but buried in my subconscious is the feeling that my actions will one day come back to haunt me. The guilt from Monday disappears with every passing hour and the confidence being offered by Nick's powerful words helps me to forget all the pain I have caused.

"We can achieve anything together," Nick continues, with his confidence flowing as though on the top of a wave.

The waiter brings over the bottle of Bollinger, along with the flutes, and after opening the champagne, a small amount is poured into Nick's glass. He takes a sip and after nodding in approval, both the flutes are filled. The waiter returns with the salmon soufflés and, after lowering them onto the placemats, we continue with our conversation.

"So what happens next, Nick?" I ask.

"Well, Dean, Wagstaff will probably arrest you in the next couple of days in an attempt to try and crack you, leading to me."

"So what should I do?"

"Well first we have a drink. Cheers." We raise our glasses and take a sip of the Bollinger.

We lower the glasses and starting to eat the soufflé. "There is no point fighting it, just go with him and sit through the questions and ask for my solicitor, Archibald."

Nick passes over a piece of paper with the solicitor's name, office address and telephone number.

"Just say 'Archibald' at the right time and Wagstaff's heart will sink anyway." Nick looks around the restaurant, checking for any possible threats and with a lowered voice continues.

"Well, what does Archibald look like so I don't get set up?"

"He is early sixties and has as a poor comb over with a few strands of white hair trying to cover his large bald head. He will always wear glasses on the end of his nose and has a round face and potbelly. You won't miss him."

"Once Wagstaff's belly is full he will release you after a few hours. Watch out 'cause he will place a tail on you, so go back to your apartment."

The maître d' walks over and asks, "How is the salmon, gentleman?"

"Excellent, thank you," Nick replies.

"Very good," I reply and the maître d' walks away.

Nick lowers his knife and fork, then takes out a cell from his pocket and passes it across to me, saying, "Use this cell and send a message to the pre-programmed number for Collins. Your current cell will be tapped anyway so just leave it active."

Nodding in agreement, I take the cell and slip it into my trouser pocket. "What happens then, Nick?"

"Well, let's deal with Wagstaff later and clear him off the scent." I know Nick won't tell me what we are doing next in case I let it slip in front of Wagstaff.

"Enjoy your meal, Dean, and don't worry. Everything will be fine." Nick smiles across and lifts up his cutlery again.

We both finish our starters and the waiter walks over to collect the empty plates.

"What do you see in this restaurant, Dean, apart from the obvious diners?"

Lifting my head, I begin to scan around the tables of people and reply, "Well, there are twenty-eight men and thirty-three women, but no children. The people age from early twenties to late fifties. There are two exits with one near the kitchen and the other on the far right side of the restaurant. In total there are six waiters and possibly up to six people in the kitchen with how fast the food is being presented."

"Okay, Dean, so that is the basic stuff. So what else? Do you see any threats?"

"Threats could be anywhere. What should I be looking for?"

"Well, at the tables which people don't seem to fit in or where they are hardly talking to each other or maybe look out of place. We are in a top restaurant so which people are not here for food?"

Gradually I begin to look around the tables again, quickly reading people's body language and two groups start to stand out. "Okay I see two different tables."

"Good, Dean, so which one is a possible threat?"

"The woman on the table near the right exit door dressed in black with the three men keeps gradually looking across and none of them seem to be enjoying the meal, maybe them?"

"The other table could be with two men who are sitting near the entrance. The man with the balding head looks uncomfortable and keeps looking around the restaurant."

"Maybe that table of four is from work and had a bad day and the bald man may be playing away?"

"Okay, what about the table with three women to our left? Do you not see them as a threat?"

Lifting my glass and taking a drink of Champagne, I look across but don't sense any threat. "No, Nick, I don't sense anything with that table."

"Well, that's good. Even when challenged your decision is made, but there is one more possible risk."

"What is that?"

"The exits! Always remember the exits; these could be your best friend and worst enemy. Always make sure these points are close enough, but not too close, and check they are not locked. Your observation skills are improving."

"Thank you, it must be a good teacher."

The waiter brings over the bottle of red wine and opens it by the table as I continue to gradually look around the restaurant. The cork pops and the waiter begins to pour a small amount of red wine into Nick's glass. After taking a quick drink of water, Nick lifts the glass, gradually spinning the red liquid against the sides of the glass. Nick looks through the glass to check for the colour and teardrop run before he lifts the wine to just below his nose. After inhaling the scent of the wine, he lifts the glass to his lips and takes a sip. "Perfect," he answers, and the waiter continues to pour the wine, leaving the red wine bottle and taking away the empty Bollinger and champagne flutes.

"Remember, though, some people always appear to look guilty even when they are not and you don't want to cap them by mistake! Okay, there is one last table and I think that they could be agents sent by Wagstaff." Nick gradually gestures with his head.

Feeling a little bit panicked, I stare across at Nick, saying, "Are you sure?"

"Possibly, it's that table behind you in the right with a man and woman sitting trying to blend in," he replies.

Knowing if I turn around they could clock me, the highly polished wine glass is lifted as though I'm looking into the liquid but staring at the reflection I can see the two people attempting to talk. The couple appear to be observing everyone in the restaurant, smartly dressed and around forty years old.

Lowing my wine glass, Nick places his serviette on the table and says, "Let's see what happens if I use the restroom." Nick places his white napkin onto the table, stands and gradually walks in the direction of the toilets.

I don't know whether it's just hearing what Nick said, but I sense that one of the people is moving behind. That is confirmed when I hear the familiar sound of a chair moving and by the action sense it is the woman. After three footsteps on the light oak laminate flooring, she passes by in the direction of the restrooms. Nick must have been right with his observations and surely these must be the agents that are now following the both of us. Nick returns from the restrooms and instantly notices that the woman is missing and the expression on his face almost confirms his worst fears.

"Dean, I knew we were being followed, but if we make any sudden movements or actions then this will draw more attention. Let's finish our meals and act as though it's just a normal evening."

"Well, that's going to be pretty difficult knowing that agents are here watching us," The woman returns from the restroom and the waiter walks to the table carrying the two filet mignon main courses.

Placing one plate in front of Nick first, followed by myself, the waiter smiles and gestures to the food, saying, "Please, gentlemen, enjoy your filet mignon."

The steak is cooked perfectly and, cutting the tender meat with the knife, it slices smoothly and cleanly. Taking a piece to my mouth with the fork the meat is so tender it melts with hardly any chewing. "I think that's the best steak I have ever had, Nick, thank you."

"I know another place, but it's a bit further to travel," he replies.

The maître d' returns, asking, "Gentlemen, are the filet mignons to your liking?"

"Wonderful, thank you Peer," Nick replies.

The maître d' smiles and, as he walks away, we continue with the main course, enjoying the quality of the food and trying to avoid any contact with the agents sitting close by. Knowing that the net is gradually becoming tighter around me, I feel constricted with every breath. I try to hide my fears behind a fake smile using the last of my fading confidence. My thoughts then return to the main reason for being here tonight, wanting to know more about myself and the pictures. My uncontained curiosity is overwhelming as I start to ask more questions. "So how long were you in the military, Nick?"

"How long was I in? I have never left. When you sign up for a military career you never leave, all your life is taken over by it with all your friends part of it."

"What regiment did you serve in?" I ask in a nervous voice, not knowing what the answer will be.

"I never really served in one regiment but many different operational countries. All basic training is the same, but once you specialise in certain core skills you are sent all over the world," he replies.

"So which countries have you worked in?"

"My, you are full of many questions tonight, hey? Well, let's just says wherever the crown had disputes, guys like me went for negotiations."

"Negotiations, I would hardly call it that, Nick!"

"Dean, although I no longer serve in the military I still have honour and can't really say the places where the job took me, but one thing is true and I'm sure nearly every country in the world has a part of me left behind."

Still trying to get more information, I can tell he will not open up more yet so I try to change subject slightly. "Did you like the travelling?"

"Well, being thrown out of an aircraft at ten thousand feet or being driven over country borders smuggled inside animal wagons certainly beat airport arrival halls. I bet you're curious to know more about yourself, hey?" I nod in agreement.

"All in time, Dean, all in time. Now forget about these agents and Wagstaff, they are nothing and you are far cleverer. Just sit through his questioning saying the bare minimum, but remember this guy will stop at nothing until he gets me."

I can sense from his answers that tonight is possibly the wrong time to ask about these pictures and, with my inquisitive feelings burning deep inside, I decide to leave it for another time and turn towards Wagstaff. "What is it with you and Wagstaff?" I ask, finishing my meal and placing the cutlery across the plate.

"Let's just say we have some old history together and we both felt betrayed and double crossed." Nick also finishes, placing his knife and fork on the plate.

I sense Nick will not tell me any more as he continues. "Dean, you are the only man I trust my life to and we need to clean up the mess left behind. Once Wagstaff has finished with you we can decide what to do next, okay?"

Nodding, I reply, "Okay."

"Your loyalty means everything to me, Dean, and I need your help. Knowing how strong you are, the interrogation with Wagstaff will be like a walk in the park for a guy like you."

Sensing for the first time in my life that I actually have a value to somebody, an inner strength and calmness, along

227

with a feeling of warmth, flows through my body and with a smile I reply, "Thank you, Nick, that means a lot."

The waiter arrives at the table. "Are we finished, gentlemen?"

"Yes, that was excellent, Marcus. Please give our compliments to the Chef," Nick replies, smiling.

"Can I get anything else, sir?" Marcus asks.

"Just the bill, please," Nick answers.

"Very good, sir." The waiter walks away.

We finish our wine as the waiter brings over the bill along with a couple of complimentary grappas. Nick, paying for the meal with his credit card, looks gradually over towards the couple he thinks are agents and then, taking out a twenty ten pound note, gives the waiter a tip.

"Thank you for your service tonight, it was excellent."

Marcus replies, "Thank you, sir, and I hope to see you again."

Both standing, Peer the maître d' appears, bringing my over coat and asking, "Mr Smith, how was the meal?"

"Excellent, thank you, Peer. How is the family? I didn't ask earlier." Nick hands him a fifty-pound note in a cupped hand.

"Mr Smith, yes, they are all fine. Thank you for asking," he replies with his French accent.

Turning to me, Peer opens the coat for me to place my arms into the sleeves and asks, "Mr Nash, did you enjoy the evening? Will we be seeing you again?"

"Yes, the food was excellent, thank you, and hopefully if Mr Smith wants to treat me again I will be here."

We all laugh, after shaking hands with Peer, Nick and I begin to walk through the still filled restaurant towards the direction of the main exit doors. Nick, in front, opens the door and, stepping outside, the dampness from the early autumn evening air touches my face and I look at Nick and gesture with my right arm. "Well, I am this way as you know."

"I am the other way, Dean."

"Thank you, Nick, for a lovely evening. I really enjoyed it."

"It's my pleasure, Dean. Now just be prepared for Wagstaff and keep calm, okay? Now there may be agents watching us right now so don't react in any way."

"Okay, I'll try to keep calm and wait to hear from you."

"Excellent, Dean. I will make contact with you soon." We both shake hands.

Nick then turns and as we go our separate ways, I walk towards the tube station and reflect on the evening's conversation. I wanted to ask Nick about the pictures, but this never happened. I did, however, find out he was at least in the military, that was a good start. The main thoughts filling my mind are that of Wagstaff and what may happen. Walking along the pavement back towards the bridge and Tower Hill tube station, my senses know I am being followed. Having a dinner with Nick in one of London's most prestigious restaurants certainly sends out a clear message stating that he needs me to help him, and the confidence he offers feels so rewarding after years of just being a somebody in an office. Showing me how much he needs me glows deep down inside with a warming sense of achievement. Stepping inside the half empty tube carriage, I look around for any possible threats and notice several men with clear distance between themselves. All my senses know that I'm being followed and, as Nick instructed, I remain calm and collected showing these people that I will not be intimidated.

Still swimming with the confidence that Nick has poured over me during the night makes me feel almost bulletproof against any possible threats from government agents or police. Standing in the tube carriage I smile to myself, knowing that no one could hurt me. The tube gradually grinds to a halt and, as I walk along the platform, then up the staircase through the exit, two men are standing by the large glass doors clearly waiting for someone, but with my inner confidence still overflowing I simply walk past them, not even looking back to see if they are following. Walking past a parked car, I take a quick glimpse at the door mirror, noticing that both men are slowly walking behind me. As I cross the road, a casual glance to check for any traffic confirms they are definitely quite close behind and, with my confidence at boiling point, I stop on the pavement and turn around to stare at them beginning to cross the road towards my direction.

Not having any type of fear running through my body, I simply stand and wait for the two men, but at the last moment both men quickly realise that they have been caught following me and, as they reach the pavement, they walk in opposite directions with one crossing to my left and the other to my right. Memorising their facial details, both men register from Monday morning at the airport. They were at the drop off point and were being given a telling off from Wagstaff. Knowing that Wagstaff will be shadowing my every move confirms that it won't be long before I am taken in for questioning and having a meal with Nick tonight may have sent the wrong signal, but now I don't really care, and deep down want a standoff with Wagstaff to see how strong he is against me. Watching the two men disappear along the pavements, speaking into their radios, I continue to make my way back to the apartment with a sense of happiness, knowing that I have beaten them. Finally reaching the entrance of building, the entrance door is pushed open. Walking through the lobby, I continue to the lifts and then the apartment with no negative thoughts of fear or being afraid for the first time in more than a week. Reaching the front door I walk inside, take off my coat, place it across one of the armchairs and, after another hectic day, retire to bed.

9

Awakening on the Thursday morning, I lie in bed, reflecting over how my mind now feels more focused and relaxed after speaking with Nick. The guilt felt from the last few days has gone but there is still a lingering thought, more like a toothache than open-heart surgery, as to what will happen next. My concentration is broken by a large knocking noise heard on the apartment door and instruction being barked out from the corridor.

"Mr Nash, we know you're in the apartment, the main reception confirmed. Open the door now," Wagstaff's voice echoes.

With the panic of Wagstaff standing outside I freeze, trying to ignore the instruction, but the next order comes.

"Nash, if you don't open the door we will smash it down, we have a warrant for your arrest."

Warrant for my arrest for what charge? The thought rushes through my mind. Knowing I can't escape from the top floor spooks me into a reaction, "Okay, just give me a minute."

Jumping out of bed, I grab some clothes, get dressed then, quickly grabbing my toothbrush, begin to clean my teeth as I make my way to the door. Looking through the peephole, I can see Wagstaff, the man and woman agents from yesterday by the car and at least three other men.

"We don't want any trouble, Nash. Remain calm. Are you on your own?" Wagstaff asks with a nervous tone in his voice.

Beginning to unlock the door and still using the toothbrush, I pull the door inwards and Wagstaff walks in first, holding some papers. The other agents follow apart from one man who can be heard talking to one of my neighbours, reassuring them not to worry.

"Mr Nash, I am arresting you on suspicion of being involved in the robbery of the Pearson's money warehouse on Monday, the thirtieth of August, 2010. You don't have to say anything but it may harm your defence if you do not mention, when questioned, something you later rely on in court. Anything you do say may be taken down and given in evidence." The agent then takes out a pair of handcuffs.

Remembering that Nick said this would probably happen, I stand opposite him and say, "On what proof? I am saying nothing until I speak with my lawyer."

"Fine, Nash not a problem. Come with us to the station. We also have permission to examine your flat and take anything we see as evidence." Wagstaff smiles.

Shrugging my shoulders, I finish cleaning my teeth then place the toothbrush on the coffee table refusing to say anything as the search begins. The agents start to look through the apartment, banging doors as they check through cupboards. Nick had already ensured everything was clean so, other than my cell with a few messages and calls, there is nothing linking me to the robbery. The words float through my brain and suddenly my actions from Monday finally become true as the handcuffs click shut around my wrists as Wagstaff leads me out of the apartment and towards the lifts. My heart begins to sink lower, knowing that this day would come, but I also remember the telephone number Nick asked me to memorise. Wagstaff walks slowly and difficultly due the artificial leg, but also has a type of swagger where he tries to prove he is still the best. My worst fears have happened, but inside there is a warm glow of the thought when there is no evidence, they will have to release me.

"Nash, I normally don't get involved with fetching in suspects but I couldn't miss this opportunity." Wagstaff looks across as the lift doors close.

He continues, "Your silence is a sign of guilt, Nash. Better to be open and talk, maybe I could still get you a deal to save your worthless ass."

"I will wait for my lawyer," I reply, trying to remain calm and composed.

"What's your lawyer's name, Nash, Harry Houdini? Because that's who you will need to save you," one of the agents asks and begins to laugh.

Looking across at him with 'fuck off' written in my eyes, he quickly stops laughing and lowers his head as my confidence in this situation begins to grow, whereas earlier in the week I felt very weak, afraid and emotional. Nick's words have given me something, but there is more inside and actually feeling comfortable in this situation seems really strange. Finally I am beginning to live with my actions and a new inner strength starts to grow, conquering my fears of doubt and insecurity. Even with the handcuffs tightly bound around my wrists, I can see in my mind how to disarm the agents and escape from this situation. It feels as though a trigger has been clicked in my subconscious that now awakens actions, thoughts and movements that I have only ever dreamed of in the past.

Maybe my mind is acting through a game from a PlayStation or an action movie, but either way it doesn't seem to be a threat and more an opportunity for using a new set of skills. Looking around the agents, I can see their guns holstered and canisters of pepper spray hanging from their belts and the small communication earpiece, as my senses feel sharper and more alive. I can almost smell the fear coming from one of the agents as he tries to avoid eye contact with me. *'What are they so worried about?'* runs through my mind as I begin to size up the agents, ranking them from the highest to the lowest threat against me as the whole situation seems too relaxed to be a serious arrest. The lift stops at the lobby floor and the doors open as Wagstaff continues to be at the front, walking towards the four, parked cars by the main entrance. As we reach the outside, there are four police motorcycles holding up the traffic and the agents' cars are quickly recognised from the airport journey on Monday, including a black BMW and silver Mondeo.

The female agent I have seen before opens the rear door of the Mercedes and Wagstaff climbs inside. She looks back at me and points at the black BMW just as a male agent opens the rear door, beckoning me over. Reaching the car, a third agent opens the opposite rear door and climbs into the back and as I am aided into the car by the second agent with the handcuffs pinching my wrists. Beginning to scoot along the rear seat, I look through the windscreen to see the black Mercedes beginning to move away from the pavement as two police motorcycles take the lead. The car engine is started and my next journey begins with thoughts racing through the mind over what will happen, but it feels that this is just a stunt from Wagstaff, trying to scare me into telling him everything. The third and fourth agency cars follow behind us as we begin to speed away with the other two motorcycles behind holding the traffic back. The nervousness from the agent sitting alongside me in the back of the car is overpowering and casually I look across to see small beads of sweat forming on his forehead just below his crew-cut hairline with the smell of fresh sweat oozing from his body.

Lifting his right hand to wipe the sweat from his head, his hand tremors slightly and as he tries to avoid eye contact, looking through the side window as I notice the agent who is driving keeps looking at me in the rear view mirror. The words from Nick last night are lodged firmly in my mind as we continue at high speed in the direction of Kensington, then suddenly the two front motorbikes make a sharp left turn opposite the Butchers Hook pub and continue along Finborough Road and the precession of cars travels down a small back street until we reach a pair of large black steel gates to the back of Kensington police station. Two armed police officers can be seen each side of the gates and one man lifts his personal radio as the convoy stops ten metres away. After a few seconds, the gates begin to open, allowing us to pass. Inside the compound rows of cars and minibus vans stand out against the shining brick walls of the police station, covered by fresh rain. Police officers can be seen walking around, but all stop and stare as the agents' cars park next to the main doors. As Wagstaff begins to climb out of the car along with the two agents seen with him in the past, they all walk in the direction of the rear entrance of the station.

Wagstaff, reaching the duty sergeant's, desk calmly asks, "Please inform Chief Superintendent Charles Redding that John Wagstaff is here with the suspect."

The mid-fifties desk sergeant looks over his half round glasses hanging off the end of his nose and replies, "Yes, sir. Do you have any ID, Mr Wagstaff?"

Wagstaff reaches into his jacket breast pocket and shows the sergeant his warrant card with 'director' and the officer, without even pausing to take a breath, instantly lifts the receiver to ring through the instructions. A voice can be heard on the line then, with a look of fear in his eyes, the sergeant points at four officers fully armed and waves them outside with a clear instruction. "Do whatever Mr Wagstaff requires. No discussions."

Meanwhile the two agents sitting in the car with me twitch and move around uncomfortably as the dark blue door of the building opens, with four armed officers running in the direction of the waiting cars. The agents sigh with relief, releasing them from this fear. Looking forward, I take in the excitement, laughing to myself. The four police surround the black BMW as the agent who was driving jumps out and quickly opens the rear door, allowing me to move.

"Are we going to have any problems?" one of the officers asks.

"Not from my side!" I reply as I wiggle along the seat.

Beginning to stand, it is instantly noticeable that every police officer in the car park stops and stares across at me almost burning holes into my skin with their eyes. I return the complementary stare with 'fuck off' written in mine. Nick's words have already taught me to shrug off this small inconvenience and concentrate on the bigger picture of being loyal to him and with my inner strength feeding from all this negative energy. Nothing that Wagstaff could push at me will break my willpower. Walking towards the blue door, the rain begins to fall as though it's a final walk. Taking it all in my stride, I continue to head for the unknown and my head is filled with the thoughts of what Wagstaff is truly after. Reaching the inside of the police station, the off white walls are covered in notice boards showing officer rotas, arrest charts and statements concerning suspects rights and official police policies, but I am here with a government agency where normal laws are not followed. The matt black tiled floors echo with every footstep as the desk sergeant fills in some basic paperwork with Wagstaff giving all my details as though he is reading it from a book. From what he is saying, I can now tell he knows a lot more about me than he mentioned before.

"Take him to cell four," the ageing sergeant growls and points down the corridor.

As the hand of one agent touches my right shoulder, a young officer begins to lead the way. He slows slightly and tries to make conversation with one of the agents that is walking in front of me. "So who is this guy? I've never seen the Sarg so nervous before."

"All I know is he is connected to the Pearson robbery from Monday and needs to answer some questions for now," the agent replies.

"What, this fuckin' guy? He's not exactly gangland material is he?"

"Gangland? What do you mean?" the agent asks, looking at the officer.

"Well, word on the street is that it was gangland style turf war." The young officer talks with his strong cockney accent.

"Well, maybe this guy can explain a little bit more about the events." The agent turns around slightly to look at me.

We continue to walk along the brightly lit corridor, past the large green metal cell doors, with our footsteps echoing with every step until we reach the last door. The black chalkboard has the faint outline of the last prisoner's name still evident and the young officer takes out a large bunch of keys from his blue trouser pocket and pushes the long thin key in to the mechanism. With a strong mechanical click the door unlocks. The officer, turning the handle, pushes the door inwards to reveal a small cell with a raised concrete platform along the left side of the wall and a white toilet with hand basin to the right.

"Inside, Nash," the agent instructs.

"Sir, you need to remove his handcuffs," the officer requests.

The agent takes the keys from his jacket and begins to lock the cuffs that have been binding my wrists. An overpowering emotion of freedom fills my mind. The officer slides over a wooden tray and instructs, "Okay, take off your shoes, belt and watch, we don't want you accidentally hanging yourself do we?" with a smug grin on his face.

Bending down to remove my shoes, my fingers have pins and needles stabbing inside my skin as the nerves recover from the blood loss of the cuffs. As I place the shoes in the tray, I click the watchstrap open and place my omega into one of the shoes. Removing my belt and lowering it into the tray,

I take out my cell and wallet from my pockets and align them next to the shoes. The officer lifts the tray and stares at me.

"Take a seat, Nash. We will be with you shortly," the agent replies as they both turn and walk through the doorway and with a heavy metallic bang the large metal door is closed shut, sealing me inside. I hear chalk scraping on the board as my name joins the list of the previously imprisoned.

Looking around the cell, I filter out all the detail of the graffiti with people's names across the walls and then my senses pick up the familiar smell from the toilet and the dampness from the concrete walls. Walking to the concrete slab, I sit on the edge and stare across the cell with thoughts of what will be said and, beginning to daydream, my mind begins to remember a similar situation, along with the other flashbacks I have experienced this week and with more inner confidence flowing through my body. Sensing that this is just a sweat test shake down from Wagstaff to see if I crack, I sit further back onto the slab, remaining calm and collected with the dampness of the wall being felt through my clothes, waiting for what will happen next. Wagstaff has made his way to the chief super's office and both men sit and talk over me.

"What's his background, John?" Redding asks.

"Well, Charles, at this stage it's classified, but what I can say is he has very dangerous friends who I know carried out the robbery. I don't fully know what part Nash played in the heist, but there is a lot of blood still on the street that has covered his hands," Wagstaff replies.

"So today is just a scare tactic or are you looking for something more?"

"I don't think any scare tactics would work on this guy, but I want to send a signal to the others in the team that we know about them."

"Surely they must know that already, don't they?" Redding replies.

"Do you remember Burns?" John asks.

"How can you forget that guy? Why do you think he is involved?"

"It's his type of job and handy work, but I just need to know why."

"Burns, I remember he was the contact for the San Paulo contract, yes?"

Wagstaff, nodding, then stands and starts to walk towards the office door and answers with, "Thanks for allowing me to use your station today, Charles, it means a lot."

"Not a problem, John. How's the family, by the way?"

"They are all fine, thanks. I love spending time with my grandson and look forward to every day with him. How are Vivienne and the girls?"

Charles, now standing from behind his desk, replies with, "All is good, thanks. You're more than welcome to visit any time and please bring your grandson. Vivienne would love to meet him."

Wagstaff, nodding, smiles and walks away down the corridor. As Charles sits back down, he looks at the pictures of his family on the desk and, taking a deep sigh, looks around his office at the various awards and certificates that cover one side of his office.

After what feels to be an hour of waiting, the jingling sound of keys is heard as the door is unlocked and pushed open by the young officer. "Okay, Mr Nash, they are ready for you."

As I begin to stand, the young officer continues to stare at me with one hand next to the pepper spray canister hanging on his belt and the other holding the big bunch of keys.

"Don't worry, Officer, you won't need the pepper spray with me, it's the agents you need that for," I reply.

"The agents have warned me differently, Mr Nash."

"Do I get my shoes back or is it walking in socks only?"

"Socks only I'm afraid, Mr Nash."

Nodding in agreement, I begin to walk in the direction of the door and as I pass the officer I see two agents standing in the corridor just outside the cell.

"This way, Nash, towards the right." One of the agents points down a short corridor.

Walking towards the interview room, my mind begins to replay answers over and over again, but also I know Wagstaff will be asking lots of different questions. One of the agents opens the dark wood door of the interview room and walks inside. The second agent follows a few steps behind me and, reaching the room, I notice the simple wooden desk with chairs opposite to each other and a tape recorder sitting on the tabletop. The first agent drags one of the chairs along the quarry tiled floor from under the desk and gestures for me to sit. Reaching the chair, I turn slightly to hear a familiar voice in the corridor outside and as I sit down Wagstaff appears through the doorway.

"Tea or coffee, Nash?" Wagstaff asks.

"Tea, white with one sugar, thanks," I reply.

"Hopkins, sort the drinks. Same for me," Wagstaff instructs the agent then drags the other chair out to sit on it.

"That will be all Briggs. Help Hopkins with the drinks, please." Wagstaff looks across to me as I watch the two agents leave the room.

Briggs reaches the door and, then closes the door behind himself; Wagstaff then takes some papers from his jacket pocket.

"You're playing a dangerous game, Nash."

"Don't I get a phone call and right to remain silent?" I ask.

"Of course you do, Nash, but that is for guilty suspects and not you."

Staring across at him, confused, I reply, "So why have I been arrested?"

Wagstaff's answer is stopped by a *knock* on the door, as Briggs pushes it open, Hopkins can be seen carrying two polystyrene cups.

"Nothing but the best for you, Nash," Wagstaff laughs as Hopkins places the drinks on the table.

The agents leave again and close the door as Wagstaff continues. "I had to arrest you so it looked real, Nash, surely you must know I'm here to protect you from Burns?"

"I am saying nothing without my solicitor present."

"Mr Nash, please, not co-operating is a sign of guilt and we know that is not true."

Just staring across at him, I give no answer. Wagstaff takes a sip of his drink and continues, "Dean, please at least let us talk."

"I have nothing to say without the solicitor present."

"All right, Nash, if this is how you want it to be, fine. I have tried to be reasonable." Wagstaff gradually looks to the right side of the room to where the mirrored window I noticed earlier is placed.

Looking across, I ask, "So who is watching us then, Mr Wagstaff?"

Wagstaff, seeing an opportunity, quickly answers, "I'm not sure what you're talking about, Nash."

"Mr Wagstaff, I will tell the people behind the glass in the cheap seats the same as you. Call my solicitor before I talk." I take a sip of tea.

"So you have nothing to say, Mr Nash."

"Yes, Mr Wagstaff, I have something to say." Wagstaff leans forward.

"Your tea is shite so call my solicitor before you poison me." I lean back in the chair.

Wagstaff, taking a deep sigh, looks at the glass and instructs, "Okay, call his solicitor. Who is it, Nash?"

"Mr Archibald. Do you want his number?"

Wagstaff takes another sigh and then, rubbing his forehead, gently says, "No we have his number, thank you."

Wagstaff tries another approach. "Dean, I know it must be difficult for you and your loyalty to Burns, but imagine the pain all those families are going through after this great loss. That weight must be hanging on your shoulders like carrying around a house."

"I was saddened to hear about the accident," I reply.

"Dean, please let me help you spread the weight of guilt, if you confirm Burns was involved in the robbery."

"Mr Wagstaff, has my solicitor been contacted yet?" I ask, trying to keep my emotions under control.

"Yes, Dean, he is now on the way. Do you really think that Nick Burns cares about you? He has never cared for anyone before so what makes you think you are so different? When he can he will ditch you without thinking and be gone!"

I sit there trying to act as though I have no emotional contact to what he is saying, but Wagstaff's words burn deep inside even after all the positive words from Nick. Wagstaff must smell my weakness and then, thinking he has found an opportunity, he continues with his questioning.

"Dean, I know it must be hard with split loyalties, but remember the first loyalty is to yourself and I am the only person who can offer you a way out from this torture you must be feeling."

My mind starts to fill with what could be a protection programme, new identity, and new life with one of the country's most wanted after me. I can't possibly imagine that even if they caught Nick, he wouldn't know who grassed on him and I would be killed in an instant even if Nick was behind bars.

Wagstaff stands and takes out his cigarette packet saying, "I'm going outside for my nicotine fix and when I return, I hope you will be more cooperative!" As he removes one of his cigarettes, placing it to the side of his mouth.

Wagstaff taps on the questioning room door and the young officer rattles his keys as he starts to open it then Wagstaff walks out. He turns to me saying, "I hope you're getting prepared for round two. Take him back to the cell for a few hours to cool off," Wagstaff sniggers.

The young officer walks into the questioning room and drops a pair of thin grey paper slippers by my feet. Placing my feet into them, the immediate warmth away from the cold floor is instantaneous. We continue back along the corridor towards the direction of the cell. Walking into the cell, the coldness of the floor quickly gets absorbed into the thin paper slippers, and as I stare at the concrete plinth, the cell door closes with a strong thud behind me. My rest is constantly disturbed by the ticking of the red second hand passing by the black numbers on the large white-faced wall clock. The clock face glass is partly shattered from where other prisoners have damaged the black metal cage that covers the front in an attempt to stop the ticking. I lie on the concrete surface with my eyes closed, counting every sound and imagining the red hand moving around the face as my thoughts drift to a similar experience from the past but my mind tries to scramble from any information as from where. After five thousand four hundred ticks the sound of the metal slide that covers the glass peephole in the door can be heard being moved, followed by the rustling of keys entering the lock. As the keys rotate, the lock mechanism can be heard clicking and creaking until the handle is turned and then the door opened gradually. Opening my eyes and turning my head, I stare at the young officer who is standing in the open doorway as my eyes refocus.

"They say a guilty man rests in the cell because he knows he has been caught," the young officer announces.

"Yes, Officer, but what about the prisoner who didn't have much sleep and is resting because of his innocence!" I reply.

"Hmm, maybe you have a point, Mr Nash," he replies as the two agents arrive.

"Okay, Nash, are you ready for round two?" Agent Hopkins asks.

"Well, if it's going to be as thrilling as the last time, I can't wait." I stand quickly and walk towards the door.

"Easy, Mr Nash, no sudden movements. We wouldn't want any accidents." The younger agent Briggs announces.

"Is that a threat, Agent Briggs?" I sarcastically smile at him.

Briggs looks at me in complete shock that I know his name, trying to think of a reply.

"Just walk, Nash, and no talking."

"Well, that's funny, your boss is not happy I'm not talking, now you're telling me to shut up."

"Your solicitor is here now, so I'm sure you will have more to say now," Hopkins, replies in a strong voice.

We reach another interrogation room and the young officer opens the door. Beginning to walk into the room, an elderly man sits behind a rectangular table with four chairs placed two on each side. He turns quickly and stands, looking at me wearing a dark pin stripe three piece suit and bright red tie against his white shirt and red handkerchief in his jacket top pocket.

He is very smartly dressed with highly polished black Oxford shoes and, as he places the half round glasses on top of the pile of documents, he reaches out with his right hand, saying, "Dean, how are you? Have these people tried to harm you in any way?"

Remembering what Nick said Archibald looked like, I raise my right hand and with a firm shake reply, "Hello, Mr Archibald. No, everything is fine, thank you."

The officer and agents do not enter the room, as the door can be heard starting to close. Archibald shouts out, "Any chance of a few drinks in here, old boy?"

He then gestures for me to sit next to him at the table and pulls out the chair. "Sit, Dean, next to me," he instructs.

Sitting next to him, he lifts the glasses and replaces them onto his nose. "Now, Dean, Mr Burns has given some details of the events, but the first thing I need to ask is if you have said anything."

"No, Mr Archibald, I haven't said a word. I have been waiting for you to arrive."

"Okay, Dean, that's good. Now technically these muppets have nothing on you, or anyone else for that matter, and are fishing for information." He coughs to clear his throat as the door can be heard opening with Agent Briggs bringing in two polystyrene cups of tea.

"No bone china then, old boy?" Archibald asks.

The agent simply shakes his head and walks out, slamming the door behind.

Archibald lifts the cup to his lips. "This smells like dishwater and probably tastes the same." I agree with a nod.

Lowering the cup after taking a quick sip, he speaks. "Now, Dean, I have meet this Wagstaff before and he won't like that I am here so will probably take out certain evidence such as phone calls, text messages and maybe some video footage with you. The best way to handle this is not to react and remain calm. He may try the 'nice guy I can help' or the 'nasty you're going to prison' but at this time they have nothing, okay." He coughs again.

"Okay, Mr Archibald. How is Nick and what has he said?" I ask.

"Well, old boy, he is fine and knows you are here and says there is no problem. The main thing is to say nothing that could give Wagstaff any leverage and you should be home by teatime." He clears his throat.

"Now, Dean, am I correct that Wagstaff knows you were at Gatwick airport on Monday the thirtieth of August, and you told him that you had dropped off a friend?"

"Yes, that's correct, but what happens when they see me at the counter checking in?"

"Well, we can say you were asking about your friend's flight and walked away."

"What about the meal at the restaurant with Nick last night? We were certain agents were watching us."

"Old boy, two people having a meal in a restaurant is hardly evidence of a crime, only that you spent time together. If they ask it's none of their business, but you could say Nick offered to buy you dinner and you wanted some business advice." He takes another sip of tea.

"God, that stuff is awful. Now, remember, you are innocent until proved guilty. These clowns will think something is not right but they want you to talk against Mr Burns and that's very important." Archibald twitches in his chair.

"What do you mean, Mr Archibald?"

"Archie, please call me Archie. Well, what I'm trying to say is how much do you want to protect Mr Burns? Would you risk your life for him and your freedom?" He coughs again.

"What are you trying to say, Archie, give up Nick to save my own skin?" I ask, looking at him puzzled.

"Well, old boy, those thoughts must have crossed your mind," Archie replies.

Is this another trap from Nick to test my loyalty? Or maybe, is it Wagstaff trying to strike a deal? These thoughts rush through my mind but after a few seconds I give my reply. "Mr Archibald, I have only just met you, and already you seem to be testing my loyalty and commitment to Nick. I don't find this conversation very positive for his solicitor."

"No, Dean, you have taken it the wrong way. What I'm trying to say is that you need to be sure over what your feelings and emotions tell you, otherwise Wagstaff will sniff it out and use it against you."

"You seem to know a lot about Wagstaff, you keep mentioning him."

"I have been doing this type of work for a long time and paths always cross. Yes, I have also worked with the agency in the past so know their tactics."

Still not fully sure where Archie stands, I reply, "Oh right. Okay, so what I can tell you, Archie, is that some events over the past few days have been very difficult but my loyalty for Nick remains strong."

"That's good news, Dean, and shows your actions are true, but people do sometimes change in a stressful situation and that is what I am doing. I have a lot of friends that would like to meet you."

"Friends? What type of friends?" I ask

"Let's just say friends that help grease wheels and a man with your talents always has a few followers of your work."

"My work? I'm sorry, I don't know what you mean," I reply, a little shocked.

"The helicopter incident. Don't worry, Nick told me what happened after Lloyd got killed. Such a waste. Lloyd was a good guy, but covering the escape with using a missile was a great idea and certainly won some admirers."

"I'm sorry, Archie, I don't know what you mean. We have only just met and you talk as though I am an artist with people admiring my work. What I can tell you is that this conversation seems to lead to a set up for something and frankly I don't know if you work for the same agency that is trying to blame me for the robbery."

"Dean, I have many clients from both sides of the chess board and all that is being said is that yes, I represent Mr Burns, but I also represent people who in certain cases can help."

"This help I assume has a repayment in the future, am I right?" I stare at his old crinkly face as he starts to try combing the last few strands of hair over his baldhead.

"Dean, please allow me to explain." The cell door opens and Wagstaff limps his way into the room.

"Mr Archibald, I smelt your odour from half way down the corridor. Are you and Nash now acquainted, since you both never met before?"

"Mr Wagstaff, I know my client very well and yes, we also know all about you," Archie replies.

"Hmm. Are you ready to continue with the interview, Nash, now your SOLICITOR is here?" Wagstaff speaks in a sarcastic voice, looking at me.

Looking at Wagstaff, I reply, "Well, I am ready to listen to what you have to say if that's what you mean." Archie looks at me with a smile.

Wagstaff turns and, with a slight raised voice, barks out an instruction. "Take Nash and Mr Archibald to interview room four." Two agents appear at the door.

Both standing, Archie collects all his papers together and, after lifting his old brown battered briefcase onto the table. He pushes them inside.

We turn and walk out of the room in the direction of the door, following behind the faint footsteps of Wagstaff down the corridor. The two agents, one in front and one behind, escort Archie and myself back to the original room where I was interviewed earlier. I notice a digital clock on the wall with the red numbers illuminating 15.45 and Archie whispers, "Should be out by 4.30 pm, old boy." We reach the open door to the interview room with Wagstaff standing staring at us.

"Sit down, gentlemen, and now hopefully you can enlighten me." Wagstaff smiles.

Archie and I sit side by side and Wagstaff then limps from the corner of the room, sitting opposite us, and immediately starts to drum his fingers on the table top in a continuous action.

"Well, Nash, have you come to your senses?" Wagstaff snaps.

Trying to think how to answer this question is one of the most difficult decisions I have made. Save my skin and tell about Nick, or say nothing with possible prison time? Still not knowing on which side Archie sits, rips at my insides. After a few seconds I lift my head and, looking straight at Wagstaff, begin to open my mouth. "Mr Wagstaff, as I have said before, there is nothing to say."

"Okay, Nash, if you want to play it that way." He turns and beckons over agent Briggs who hands him an A4 brown envelope. Wagstaff holds the envelope with his left hand and reaches inside, taking out some pictures.

He passes over a photograph of me at the EasyJet check in.

"Can you confirm if this is you at the EasyJet counter on Monday, the thirtieth of August?"

Archie looks at it and whispers, "You can deny it if you want, it's your choice, but the face is clear."

Looking at the picture I stare at Wagstaff, replying, "Well it's someone that certainly looks like me."

"You confirmed yesterday afternoon when we spoke that you were at Gatwick airport to drop off a friend in car registration NL54 ZFD. The security camera from this exit gate shows this man." He hands over another picture.

"No that statement is incorrect, I stated the registration number started with NL54 and couldn't remember the remaining letters. So what is the question Mr Wagstaff?"

"Okay to be accurate, you did only state NL54, but the camera footage confirms the last remaining 3 letters of NL54 ZFD, therefore my question is why is the person in the car wearing different clothes to you at the check in counter?"

Archie whispers, "You don't have to answer."

"Well since I wasn't at the check-in counter we wouldn't be wearing the same clothes anyway would we?" I reply

"Don't try to get smart, Nash, because this same person at the check-in counter was also checked into a flight for Prague, but never reached the departure gate."

"All I can tell you is that yesterday, I dropped a friend off at Gatwick airport, then went back to my flat. I also told you to speak with Shaun Neal who would confirm we spent Monday night enjoying a pizza." The chair creaks as I lean back in it.

"I've spoken with Mr Neal who confirms Monday night's events and we will get to this shortly, but what I'm interested in at the moment is the twelve hours prior to your pizza night.

These two pictures show what I believe is you at the check-in counter and then a person resembling your appearance leaving in the aforementioned car." Wagstaff taps his finger at the picture of the car at the airport, sending a small vibration through the table.

"As I explained yesterday, Mr Wagstaff, I dropped off a friend and then I returned back to my flat and went to sleep. I awoke later in the morning and watched some television."

"Oh really?" Wagstaff takes out another picture of me entering the apartment building with the time and date displayed at 17.58.

"Can you explain this?" Wagstaff asks.

"Well, it's a picture of me entering the building heading for my apartment on Monday evening. I was returning from a walk."

"You never mentioned that yesterday. Why not?" Wagstaff snarls.

"I didn't think going for a walk was a crime!"

"Well, Nash, what's more relevant is that your apartment's surveillance system shows you never left the building all day. In fact, it appears you haven't been in the apartment since Sunday evening. Do you have an answer for that?"

Archibald coughs and speaks. "What you are trying to say, Mr Wagstaff, is that because my client wasn't seen on a surveillance camera, he has been arrested?"

"No, Mr Archibald, what I am saying is that your client left his flat on Sunday evening and did not return until Monday evening and during this time he was seen at an airport check in for a flight to Prague and never made the flight, and was absent from his apartment."

"This is the only evidence you have." Archibald looks at Wagstaff with the glasses on the end of his nose.

Wagstaff reaches into the envelope and takes out another picture, handing it over. "This man was found dead on Stockwell Road Monday morning after being shot by police and his name is Lloyd Farrell and this man is on Interpol most wanted criminals list."

"Yes, Mr Wagstaff, your point?" Archie coughs after speaking.

"My point, Mr Archibald, is that this man was also booked onto the same flight for Prague and never showed at the boarding gate along with this man." Wagstaff slides over a picture showing Nick Burns.

"Do you know this man, Mr Nash? Well, you should since you were having dinner with him last night at Gaucho's." Wagstaff hands over another picture.

"So my client was having dinner with a person. There is no crime being committed so what, Mr Wagstaff, is this grounds for arrest of my client?" Archibald replies.

"All three men that checked into the EasyJet flight for Prague had false passports, and all three men were at Gatwick airport at the same time. What I am saying is that your client was seen with two of Interpol's most wanted criminals who were at the same airport, isn't that a coincidence?" Wagstaff takes out another picture and slides it across the table.

"Your client has also been seen spending time with both men over the last few days and, by association, I believe that Mr Nash was involved in the Pearson money warehouse robbery that took place on Monday, the thirtieth of August, 2010, that also included the missile attack on the police helicopter above Stockwell Road. Do you have anything to say, Mr Nash?"

Archie whispers, "There is still no actual evidence."

"I spoke with you on Sunday and I am certain you followed me from my apartment whilst I was on my motorbike, so yes I did leave my apartment on Sunday."

My heart is racing faster with every beat and the confidence from last night is beginning to disappear. Wagstaff must smell the guilt coming from the sweat starting to form in my armpits. I look across at Wagstaff with the image of Nick filling my thoughts, along with Lloyd dying in my arms. I sit thinking about how I'm going to answer these questions from the pictures taken. Wagstaff pulls out another picture and slides it across the table, showing Sophie and me dancing at Castro's on Friday night, identical to the one left at my apartment.

"What about Miss Sophie Roberts, hey Nash? What do you know of this fragile sad English rose?"

I lift the picture and stare at it, clearly seeing Nick and Lloyd in the background. My stomach churns over and over as my excuses seem to be too thin to escape. "We work together at Harpers and Harpers, is there any crime in having a dance together?" I reply to Wagstaff.

"Maybe not a dance, but this woman is of interest to Interpol with her close friendship to Mr Burns. You have made some very dangerous friends over the last few days and with this robbery the net has been cast and is getting tighter by the day and you, Mr Nash, are right in the middle."

Archie whispers, "Say nothing, there is no actual evidence."

"I could still see if there is a deal with Interpol, but you would need to tell me everything from the last few days and confirm that Nick Burns was involved." Wagstaff stands.

"I will leave you gentlemen alone for a few minutes to discuss your options." Wagstaff gestures to the agent, standing, and both walk out, closing the door.

"Dean, they can't charge you for being guilty by association to known criminals. It's all a tactic to surrender Burns. Like I said before, it's your choice, but I could protect you if you decide to give him up."

My head feels like it has been hit from one side of the room to the other and giving up Burns could save my skin, but I also know Burns has more answers over my past and this is what I need at this time. Surrendering Burns now will leave much unfinished answers for me and, besides, I chose to join his crew for the robbery. Prison time would happen even if I gave up Nick now so why not enjoy the freedom for some more time and see where it leads? I'm interested in what Archie is offering but I could use him in the future, so for now I need to get out of this place.

The door opens and Wagstaff limps back into the room. "So have you thought things over, Nash?"

The words begin to form in my brain and, as I lean forward in the chair, the answer starts to leave my lips. "Mr Wagstaff, what can I say other than it appears I am guilty of a crime just by having dinner with a person or by taking another friend to the airport? So unless you can charge me with something, I think it's time I was released. I have been here several hours and seen pictures of me dancing with a work colleague in a nightclub so I don't see that as a crime."

Wagstaff limps across and places his hands on the table top in an aggressive stance and in a nasty voice says, "Okay, Nash, you can go, but remember I have given you every chance to tell the truth and once more evidence is uncovered you will be rearrested and this time no solicitor will be able to save you."

Wagstaff leans away from the table and instructs the agent. "Briggs, prep Mr Nash for release with the sergeant in charge."

He continues, "I truly hope that we don't meet again, Mr Nash, but one thing to remember is that no matter how much washing has taken place some certain accelerants used in missiles, gunpowder and plastic explosives leave trace elements on any surface they come into contact with for several days. So once the forensic laboratory find these trace elements on the hair samples taken from your apartment, along with some underwear found in your bins, I'm sure our next meeting will be very different so please don't leave the country in the next few weeks."

Wagstaff turns and limps out of the room with a serious smile across his face, leaving agent Hopkins to deal with the release documents. "Ready, Mr Nash?"

"I will wait for you by the main reception, Dean, and if you like I can give you a lift back to your apartment." Archie stands.

"Okay, thank you Mr Archibald."

Following Archie, I stand and walk towards the agent and we both continue down the corridor in the direction of the desk sergeant to complete all the release papers. Reaching the glass-fronted desk, the agent briefly speaks with the sergeant who has already completed the papers for release. Attaching the papers to a clipboard, the sergeant passes the board over to the agent and me for signing. He turns around and takes a clear plastic bag containing my shoes, belt, watch and keys from a secure cupboard with the words 'prisoner belongings DEAN NASH' written on a sheet of laminated paper and begins to opens the sealed bag, removing the contents.

Hopkins takes the clipboard and flicks through the two attached documents and, taking a pen from his jacket inner pocket, signs both papers and hands it to myself along with his pen, saying, "Sign here," pointing at the two lines with 'prisoner release signature' below. I sign the papers and hand the clipboard back to the sergeant who passes me the plastic bag of belongings.

The agent stares at me with 'fuck you eyes', knowing that I am guilty but can't prove it yet. He says, "We will catch you soon enough, Nash, and when we do nothing will save you after killing those police officers."

Lifting the watch first, I slide it onto my wrist and click the clasp shut then takings the shoes, I bend down and place them on the floor sliding my feet into them.

As I fasten the laces, the sergeant whispers to Hopkins, "Are you letting that bastard go?"

"We don't have enough evidence yet," Hopkins replies. As I stand up, I start to push the belt through my trouser loops with the fat desk sergeant staring at me.

"Okay, Mr Nash, you are free to go but if any evidence is found that links you to this case you will be rearrested." The agent points down the corridor in the direction of the main reception door.

Nodding my head in agreement, I start to walk down the corridor holding the wallet, keys and mobile in my right hand in a complete blur as police officers begin to appear from doorways, staring at me. As I pass by, their eyes burn even more holes into my skin making me feel very uncomfortable. Reaching the front door, Archie can be seen standing in the reception waiting for me and his face changes from a frowned look to that of gladness.

"Okay, old boy, that didn't take long, is everything alright?" he asks.

"Fine, Archie, just get me the hell away from here." A sensation of being stabbed in my back is felt and, slightly turning around, a group of at least ten officers all standing in uniform can be seen staring at me with piercing eyes clearly wanting a piece of me.

Archie and I walk out of the police station and taking a deep breath of air, even if it's bad London city air, is better than the musty, stale air being breathed for the last few hours in the cells. As I walk out of the reception, the digital clock clicks over to 16.30 and Archie, looking at his wristwatch to confirm, says, "You see, old boy, I told you four thirty. Your answers in there were excellent but these accelerant trace elements could be an issue."

Walking into the car park I look across, replying, "I don't think so, Archie, they will find nothing other than the latest Persil washing liquid along with Head and Shoulders shampoo. You don't catch old birds with chaff."

Archie smiles. "I never doubted you, Dean, as expected. So what now?" He walks to a large, dark green jaguar car.

"Now, back to my apartment and you contact Nick over what to do next."

The doors unlock and, as I climb into the passenger front seat, the smell of fresh leather fills my nostrils. Archie opens the driver's door, placing the keys on the seat then, walking behind, opens the boot, placing his old briefcase inside. Returning to the driver's side, he takes the keys from the seat and slides inside, closing his door and then, starting the engine, looks across to me, smiling.

"Your old friend Wagstaff is standing on the top step of the main entrance watching us, old boy." Archie speaks with a sarcastic deep voice.

"Yes, I sensed it and then looked across to confirm." I wonder what must be racing through Wagstaff's mind.

"He won't be happy about today and I'm sure that he will stop at nothing until he gets what he wants from you."

"Yes, Archie, no doubt on that fact." My mind already drifts to what Archibald was talking about in the room and accepting a lift from him may shed more light on the conversation.

Driving away from the police station, one of the agents stands next to Wagstaff and asks, "What now, sir."

"Now we wait, he will make contact with Burns immediately, maybe even in the car as we speak so we have him running scared now. He will be ours soon enough and I think he will hand himself over before the week is over."

"The forensic lab has made contact. Not good news I'm afraid, sir. They confirm no trace elements found on the clothing or hair samples that were taken from Nash's apartment." Agent Briggs shares the bad news.

"Dammit, I was depending on that being positive." Wagstaff throws his part-finished cigarette to the floor and walks back inside with the agent following close by. Wagstaff walks back towards Charles' office and knocks on the door.

"Enter," is heard.

Wagstaff opens the door and walks inside.

"Is everything all right John? I've heard that Nash has been released?"

"Dammit, Charles, I know this guy is guilty but the forensic lab has confirmed no trace elements from the samples we took."

"Maybe it's better to lose the battle but win the war and I'm sure you will catch him eventually. Guilty people always slip up, you know this."

"True, Charles, but just letting him go after all those people were killed even today just doesn't seem right."

"I fully understand, but his time will come. Just wait for that look on his face when you finally catch him."

"There is something different with this guy. He shows no signs that I can read."

"What do you mean?" Redding asks with a puzzled look.

"Well, I told Nash that hair and clothing samples were at the forensic lab for testing and he didn't even twitch."

"Maybe he knew you were going to take samples so placed things for you to find."

"Possibly, but to give no reaction, it felt like he had been trained not to react."

"What's in his past?"

"Nothing special, Charles, that I can find. He grew up in a normal family near Knutsford, Cheshire, and after university moved to London for the work."

"If your senses are telling you more, maybe a trip down his memory lane could work. After all, that was one of your favourites back in Northern Ireland."

"Yes, that could be an idea, and see what can be uncovered, but with this investigation it will take a few days so I could drop an agent onto it."

"So what's next, John?"

"Hopefully if I can tidy up some more of this mess by Saturday I should be having Adam around with Helen this Saturday and staying over for Sunday dinner."

"That's good, family time it's very important."

"I know, Charles, but it was too late before I realised. Anyway, many thanks for your help and use of the cell, I must get on with the PM and home secretary on my back. I have a lot of tidying up."

"No problem, and if you ever need any help or just someone to talk I am always here. After all your help in Northern Ireland it's the least I can offer."

Wagstaff stands and, with a raised arm, shakes hands with Charles, replying, "Many thanks, old friend, see you soon." Then he turns and limps out of the office towards his car waiting in the car park.

As Wagstaff leaves Redding's office, Charles pauses for a second to watch his old friend disappear with a slight look of worry on his face, concerned about Wagstaff and the investigation. After a few seconds, he takes a deep sigh and continues with his paperwork.

Wagstaff is driven away from the parking space and starts back towards Whitehall for another cabinet session with the investigation status and as he stares through the side window of his car looking for any inspiration needed for this case. His mind plays over the conversation with Redding and the thoughts of tracing Nash's past begin to fester. After several minutes of thinking, Wagstaff agrees with himself and, taking out his cell, looks for an agent he can trust to be discrete but also find out the truth. Agent Briggs quickly fills his thoughts and, scrolling through the phone contacts, his number is found. Briggs was found by Wagstaff, thrown onto the scrap heap and placed into a back room of counter intelligence in the met police, five years ago. Since his transfer to MI6, Briggs has excelled and with such a strong role model on his side, Briggs is now well respected, owing his career to Wagstaff. Pressing the call button, Wagstaff lifts the cell to his ear and, as it starts to ring, his prodigy is seen standing talking to a few colleagues after the police station interview of Nash earlier.

Briggs takes his cell out of his pocket. "Chris Briggs. Yes, sir, how can I help?"

"Argh, Briggs, is it safe to talk? I need you to do something for me."

"Anything, sir, how can I help?" Briggs replies as he walks away from his colleagues.

"I need you to investigate Nash's past for me and confirm a few points."

"Yes, sir. What information are you looking for?"

"Do you have something to take notes? It's a big list," Wagstaff asks.

"Yes, sir, all ready." Briggs walks towards his desk.

Wagstaff starts his list. "Okay, start with his birth certificate, parents then work forward including his schools, colleges, places of work and addresses. There must be something in his past and we need to find it."

"Yes, sir, I will do a full character profile. I will cover friends and family and any previous work colleagues."

"Excellent, Briggs, thank you. And one more thing?"

"Anything, sir."

"I need the info ASAP, okay? So send me regular updates over what you find" Wagstaff instructs.

"Yes, sir, will start right away. What about if I require any top level security clearance?"

"Speak with Amanda and I will grant any approval. One more thing Chris?" Wagstaff says with compassion in his voice.

"Watch this guy and any stones that you turn over, he could be hiding anywhere now he knows we are onto him."

"Yes, sir, I will be careful and hope we can catch this guy soon. I have a feeling that eventually Nash will slip up and we will have him."

"I hope so, Chris. Keep in touch, yes?" Wagstaff rings off and places the cell into his pocket.

Briggs, lowering his cell immediately, begins to access records and documents of the MI6 secret server in the chase to unearth Nash's past.

Archie drives calmly and quietly, hardly saying a word other than how impressed I acted during the interrogation with Wagstaff.

After listening to this for some time, my mind is keen to learn more about what he could offer so, turning my head gradually, I ask, "Archie, what is the deal with Nick?"

"Deal, old boy? What do you mean, deal? There is no deal, I am just his solicitor like for many other clients."

"In the room it felt as though you were testing my loyalty towards Nick as if he had asked you to question it."

"Dean, that's not true. Nick is my client so yes I needed to know if there was a risk to him, but clearly you are a free thinking person as Nick said you were and that is what some of my other clients admire. Loyalty, trust and honesty go a long way in this world and some of the parties I represent see these values as critical to success. Being disposable and having integrity are commodities not found very often on the open market and some of my clients are keen to understand who owns these values since much of what Nick has said involved training and these people want to know by whom."

Archie coughs and continues. "If you like I could maybe do a little digging around to see what I can uncover if you want me to, because I may be able to gather more information than Nick on your past, and for sure Wagstaff will be planning to investigate you further for another weakness to exploit."

Reaching my apartment building on Chelsea Harbour, Archie stops the car and, turning to him, I say, "Thank you, yes, it would be good to know more about my past so you know how to get in touch. And thanks for the lift."

"My pleasure, old boy, and try to keep a low profile for a few days and I will be in touch once I have more information." I open the door and climb out of the lush leather seats.

Closing the car door, I watch Archie drive slowly away then turn and begin the walk towards the main building entrance. Rahul can be seen staring through the front window, waiting for me to enter so he can ask questions, but after being stuck in a cell I just want some fresh air and decide to take a stroll around the harbour quay. Waving at Rahul, I turn and walk away past the rows of moored yachts. Continuing past all the coffee shops and restaurants along the front, I walk in a complete loop with my mind in a blur over the last few hours and the conversation with Archie who could find out more about my past. I know Nick is the main key but another card in the game is always a good idea. Each day of my new life is getting more and more complicated and not the type of freedom I was looking for, but helping Nick to clean the mess and collecting my share of the money is the only thing on my mind now. Walking around the waterfront, my mind starts to imagine living next to water with the noise from the waves acting as a calming effect away from all this negative energy and having that money from Nick is critical to achieving this dream. The words of Archie still hanging heavy in my thoughts as I reach the main entrance doors of the apartment building, my feet instantly walk inside almost on autopilot.

Rahul jumps from behind the main reception desk and almost, running across with a look of shock on his face, says, "Mr Dean, is all okay? I was worried when the police arrive this day?"

"All is fine Rahul; they just wanted to ask me some questions over an unpaid speeding ticket."

"It looks very serious with all the cars and men?"

"Well, I was travelling fast. Rahul, the police in this country have to try and scare any confession due to human rights, but I guess it's very different in Brazil."

"Yes, very different Mr Dean, you never want problem in Brazil."

"Okay, well that's a good start to my two weeks holidays, hey? Anyway, speak to you soon."

"Yes, Mr Dean, we speak later." I walk towards the lifts.

Removing the keys from my trousers after using the lift and reaching my apartment door, the key is slid into the lock and the mechanism turned along with the handle to open the door. My senses pick up something and, walking into the apartment and closing the door behind, this is confirmed with Nick sitting in one of armchairs holding a glass of water and his black outer jacket neatly placed across the coffee table.

"So, Dean, how was it?" he asks.

"I've had better days if that is what you mean! Spending several hours in a police cell is certainly an experience." I say, walking past him and collapsing into another armchair.

"How was Wagstaff?"

"Relentless about trying to get information." I lean my head back against the armchair.

"What about Archie? Was he ok?"

"He was fine, Nick, and nothing was said to Wagstaff about you or the robbery in case you are thinking I grassed."

"I never doubted you, Dean. Maybe it's best if we disappear for a few days."

"Wagstaff would suspect something. By the way, did you know he has camera footage of this apartment building?" I ask.

"Yes, of course. It's all part of my plan."

"Your plan? Well things don't seem to have gone right so far have they, with people dying and every fuckin' copper in London on the warpath?"

"Dean, I understand your frustration and I told you last night it will get worse before it gets better. Please, we have come this far, let's tidy up then we can move on."

"Move on to what, Nick? I'm a marked man and can't go anywhere or do anything."

"Let us change it together. It's only people that do things who survive. If the rules of society take grip we choke and die."

"What are you saying, Nick?"

"Look, Dean, we both need a few days away so grab some stuff and let's get away from here. We can stop at Lloyd's place tonight then move somewhere to plan how to get these bastards once and for all."

"Then what, Nick?" I ask, feeling exhausted.

"We split the money and that way you can start your new life like I promised, but I need your help first. What needs to be done – I can't do it on my own."

"Okay, Nick, let's get away from here for a few days. I'm sorry to be a little negative."

"Christ, Dean, after several hours in a police cell, I would be too, but don't let these bastards grind you down. You're much stronger than that."

Standing, I walk into the bedroom and grab some clothes and place them into a small holdall bag along with a wet bag containing a toothbrush, deodorant, aftershave and toothpaste. Making my way back into the living room, Nick takes the last sips of water from the glass then he stands and walks into the kitchen where I hear him place the glass onto the granite surface next to the tap. His footsteps can be heard returning from the kitchen and we both make our way towards the front door. With one quick action Nick opens the door and walks confidently into the corridor, not worried about the surveillance cameras at all.

Following him, I close the door and we continue towards the stairwell where Nick then informs me, "I have a signal scrambler so any cameras will not be able to send any signals as we pass by them within two hundred metres."

Walking down the staircase, we continue all the way to the basement where we then make our way through the doorway and towards the VW Passat car. Opening the doors, we climb inside and Nick starts the engine, beginning to drive slowly through the basement to see if any cars are following us. Reaching the exit ramp, it's clear no one is following and we continue in the direction of Crawley and Lloyd's house for the evening. After a short journey we arrive at Lloyd's house and Nick parks on the driveway. Taking out my overnight bag from the car, we walk into the house. As the door opens there is an eerie silence and, knowing Lloyd is gone, it feels very strange being here as we continue down the hallway and through into the living room.

"I have contacted the letting agent and they will be having the keys back next week. There is a waiting list for houses in this area so it will move quickly and with it being rented not many of the neighbours take much notice,"

Burns continues, "Okay, you know where the bedrooms are. Pick one and let's rest here tonight before moving elsewhere tomorrow. I have another safe place where we can wait out and plan our next course of action. I will make a drink, do you want a coffee?"

"Yes, Nick, that's fine, thanks." I walk up the stairs and, using the same spare room as before, I place the bag on the bed.

Walking back into the kitchen, Nick is standing looking out of the large glass doors at the garden. "What a fuckin' shithole garden, the agent will go mad but hey, that's life."

"Okay, Dean, we need to drive to Germany, capture Josef and Thomas and interrogate them to see how much they know and how much they have told." Nick's voice has a level of excitement.

"Where are we going to interrogate them?" I am being inquisitive.

"My, Dean, you're full of questions today, hey? I can soon locate a place where we won't be disturbed during their questioning," Nick answers with a serious reply.

I decide not to ask any questions about what the interrogation techniques will cover, but I know deep down Nick will enjoy every minute of it. The time on my wristwatch reads 6 p.m.

"Do you want a little dinner? I can go fetch some Chinese because I know Lloyd never cooked anything."

"Yeah, that would great after the fun from today," I reply.

"I won't be long. So is Peking duck okay."

"Yes, fine, Nick." He walks out of the house, closing the door and driving away.

I sit in the empty house thinking about Lloyd and the events from Monday and then the interrogation from Wagstaff today. It's clear that I'm way out of my depth, but Nick clearly knows more than he wants to tell me at this time and finding out about who I am feels like an open book. Not having closure on these critical facts aches inside and for sure will stop me from moving forward in my life. The eerie quietness of Lloyd's house feels strange after the last time I was here, but there is one underlying sensation as though he is still here and watching. I remember our last time in the house and have flashbacks of him dying in my arms as I watched his life drain away. A tear begins to form in my eyes and coldness overcomes my body with these thoughts that are broken by Burns returning into the house with the takeaway. His footsteps echo along the corridor with the smell of the food floating in the air behind him into the kitchen. The sound of cupboard doors opening and the clinking of plates can be heard as they are placed onto the worktops. Standing, I follow him to the back of the house as Burns starts to prepare the food by placing it neatly onto the two plates and then he lifts the food and takes it over to the dining table.

"I could have made better, but not tonight. Do you want a drink?" Burns asks.

"Yes, just some water is fine, I will fetch it." Reaching into a cupboard for a pair of drinking glasses, they are filled with tap water.

Burns sits at the table, waiting for me to join him with his knife and fork being held waiting to start. Reaching him, I place the glasses on the table and sit opposite him as we begin to eat the takeaway. Nick is completely focused on the next stage of the operation and preparation is the key to success so he knows that my help and support is critical for a quick sweeping up of the loose ends. My feelings are mixed with excitement of what will happen next but also sadness over Lloyd. I only knew him a few days but his actions and loyalty seen in those days is difficult to forget so I can imagine the pain Nick must be hiding. After our meal we wash and clean the plates then continue through into the living room to decide our next course of action. I'm not sure where Nick wants to go next but for sure it will be safer than here. This house has memories and closing the door on this stage of my life needs to happen before moving on. Finally I decide it's time for bed and retire to the bedroom.

10

Friday starts with breakfast at a small roadside greasy spoon out in the countryside away from the city streets of London near Horsham with thoughts filling my mind on how Nick plans to capture Thomas and Josef. My body shakes with both fear and in trepidation of what we are going to carry out. The confidence given by Nick makes me feel that I can accomplish anything and now, with a few days away from work, this is the start to my new life. It's a strange emotion knowing that I need to kill a few more people to feel contented in my new life, but Nick's words build such loyalty and trust. Knowing that he will be able to help, giving me support at this time gives me a layer of hope in these changing times. Nick starts the car engine and begins to drive back in the direction of the city.

I look across at him and ask another question. "Wednesday morning at the railway station, when you drove past me, I think there was a car following you, did you notice it?"

Nick replies quickly and sharply, "Yes, Dean saw them and I'm just trying to establish who they are."

Feeling a little shocked, I turn to stare through the windscreen as we drive along the A23, heading back towards Gatwick. Nick then asks, "If we are going to kill these German traitors we need to make sure you are ready."

Nodding my head in agreement, a huge smile starts to appear on his face and then he turns sharp left down a small road heading back out into the countryside. We continue to drive along twisty high-hedged country lanes until we reach a small village called Nuthurst. From here we turn left at the church and continue along a narrow single car track just barely covered in tarmac until an old farmhouse can be seen hiding behind a row of tall black poplars that line the lane. The house is protected by high brick walls and rusty old wrought iron gates. Nick stops the car in front of the gates and gestures for me to open them so he can drive through.

Opening the car door and making my way to the gates, I suddenly have the feeling of *déjà vu* and that it looks familiar as though I have been here before. Walking along the gravel driveway, the local male blackbird shouts out the distinctive alarm call, ensuring our presence is not missed as I start to slide the heavy bolt open. The heavy metal gates are difficult to push open because the hinges have broken, but finally there is enough space for Nick to drive the car through towards the small building at the side of the farmhouse. Small pebbles can be heard hitting the underside of the car, breaking the silence of the birds singing in this green and peaceful place. Pushing the gates closed, I walk along the gravel drive in the direction of the house with the small stones crunching under my feet as birds sing and fly from the high trees and hedges. Each side of the gravel driveway is a sea of long uncut grass, broken up by fruit trees placed in neat lines with branches full of this year's harvest of apples, damsons and pears. The driveway is around a hundred and fifty metres long and encircles a central area of grass.

Reaching Nick where he had parked the car, I notice he has opened the boot and is starting to lift out a medium sized cardboard box. Taking my bag from the back seat, Nick asks, "Dean, can you give me a lift with this box?" He hands it to me.

"Sure, no problem. What's in here, the crown jewels?" I reply back as I take the load in my arms, feeling the coolness from the cardboard against my hands.

"Make your way to the front door and I will join you," he replies, lifting out two large black holdall bags.

The old farm has walls built from sandstone and the window holes are encased in white stone blockwork with dark grey windows inset. The front door is clearly made from thick oak with heavy black metal furniture complementing the defined honey coloured wood grain surface with the brass nameplate reading 'Grebe Farm'. Nick reaches the front step and takes a long black hammered key from his pocket. He pushes the key into the lock and the levers can be heard clicking as the mystery begins to unfold.

"Is this your place, Nick?" I ask curiously.

"Dean, you are only the second person that has been here, Lloyd was the first."

Nick continues, "This place has been in my family for a couple of hundred years, but it is in my mother's family name so it's clean."

Nick begins to push the heavy door open, revealing the large entrance hallway with a grand central staircase and oak flooring running each side to the back of the hallway and a set of French doors that overlook the rear garden. As my nostrils are filled with the smell of damp musty air, I look at the walls of the hallway that are plain white with heavy door casing and wall beams criss-crossing. Large exposed oak beams support the first floor and also the large slate grey roof that I noticed from the driveway. Following Nick into the house, we make our way towards the base of the staircase and he places the two holdall bags on the floor, closing the front door with a firm thud. I look around and notice two doors, one to the left and another to the right of the staircase as he walks past me. Then we start to climb the light oak stairs that lead into an open plan kitchen / dining room on the first floor. My eyes are instantly filled with the sight of a large lake with the morning sunshine burning the last of the mist away.

"Wow, what a fabulous view! That is so impressive." I stand shocked as I look through the large floor to ceiling windows and doors.

Looking around, the kitchen is plain white with black granite work surfaces and a large AGA cooker inset into an island, separating the dining area from the kitchen. The large glass topped dining table has a very modern design mounted to a wooden plinth and is enclosed with six high backed chairs, again with a white design.

"Yeah, it's sure a nice place to have breakfast. Just place the box on the work surface by the kettle," he replies.

Lowering the box onto the cold black granite, I place my bag on the floor by the unit and make my way over to the windows. The view is so impressive with a lake covered with ducks, geese and a few swans swimming, breaking the surface of the water. A trout jumps from the water to catch a fly as a great crested grebe appears from underneath the water surface, shouting its distinctive territorial call.

"Dean, slide the bi fold doors open and we will sit on the balcony," Nick replies.

So turning the handle, the doors are slid to the left and instantly my ears are filled with the sound of the birds singing and observe them flying around the lake. The doors reveal a wooden balcony that hangs the full length of the house with black wrought iron framework and glass panelling. Walking out onto the creaky wooden decking, I lean on the metal framework and look across the lake and to the land beyond. There is a large wood on the left side of the lake and another large wood two fields on the right. The majority of the land appears to be farmed with the arable crop roots left from the recent harvest.

"It's all mine, Dean." Nick's voice rings in my ears as he joins me on the balcony.

"Five hundred acres in total and the closest neighbour lives in that cottage three miles away." He points to a small line of smoke rising in to the sky.

"Mrs Vaughan is stone deaf and won't bother us here." He turns and walks back in the kitchen.

"How long are we planning to stop here?" I ask, joining Nick in the kitchen as he begins to unpack the box that is full of food.

"I was thinking we could stay a few days and complete some refresher training." He looks across at me.

He points downwards and says, "Your room is back downstairs, take the left door into the hallway and use the first bedroom, it has its own en suite bathroom. There are some combat clothes in the wardrobe, put them on."

Walking back into the kitchen I collect my bag and begin to walk down the huge staircase in the direction of the bedroom. Following Nick's instructions, I open the left door and see a small corridor with large windows running along the right side and two doorways positioned to the left. Reaching the first bedroom, I open the door and am confronted with a large king size bed against the right wall which is painted a light grey with a set of modern white bedside cabinets each side. The rest of the room has bright white walls and ceiling with more modern furniture. In the far left corner is a door that leads to the bathroom and to the side of the bathroom wall is a set of large double French doors that open out onto the lower decking beneath the balcony. Opposite the bed, against the left wall before the bathroom, is a double wardrobe and a simple chair where I lower my bag. Opening the wardrobe, the black trousers and green shirt are hanging along with a green combat jacket, so after changing my clothes I return back upstairs.

Nicks continues his conversation. "We have to clean up some rubbish and this place is a good base to work from." He closes the fridge door after placing the food inside.

"Is the room okay?"

"Yes, Nick, it's great, thanks."

"We shall carry out some additional training for you to refresh your memory, but first we need to talk about your feeling because I can sense they are affecting your reactions."

Nick collects some mugs from a cupboard and switches on the kettle for a drink.

He continues, "I imagine that the sickness you have been feeling is due to what happened with the helicopter and the police, yes?"

I reply with a feeling of total guilt, "Yes, Nick, I feel so guilty for killing all those innocent people and the police."

"Let me ask you a question, Dean. Would you rather be the person dead now lying in the morgue? Coffee, white with sugar?" Nick starts to make the drinks without even changing the look on his face, showing no signs of remorse.

"Nick, the guilt keeps playing through my mind over and over again, but you are right, I'm glad not to be dead but it feels like something has died inside me," I say, turning to walk back onto the balcony.

"Dean, it's only natural what you're feeling, but you need to cut that shit out from your thoughts and remain focused. Remember, it was either them or you and even if you weren't there Monday things would have happened in the same way." Nick finishes making the drinks then joins me on the balcony.

"Dean, I kept you out of the money room to protect you so no one would recognise you. Do you know why I did that and why I wanted you there so much?" The smell of coffee drifts across in the morning breeze.

My mind keeps playing over and over my importance to Nick so, taking a deep sigh, I ask the question hanging from my lips. "No, Nick. What was the main reason you wanted me there so much?"

"Because I know that I could trust you, not like some of the other guys there."

"What do you mean, Nick?"

"There were a few new guys on this job and although they came highly recommended, they were not my usual type of team. Those Germans were not loyal and these guys must be the starting point!"

"What about Wagstaff? He will be tracking everything we are doing and where we are travelling."

Nick replies, "Don't worry about that bastard, his time will come soon enough. We need to keep Wagstaff guessing."

"That interrogation yesterday was really soft, I was expecting more from him." I reply.

"Dean, don't let it fool you, he's a real bastard and just wanted to try and shake you to see how strong you are," Nick replies.

"What he will have done, Dean, was watch your reactions. He knows we are in this together and is just waiting for a mistake, but with sweeping up behind he will be completely lost until it's too late."

"Too late? What do you mean, Nick?" I ask.

"Dean, Wagstaff is a clever guy, but also blinded from things around him. Just wait and you will see."

Continuing to drink the fresh coffee with the late morning sunshine now warming our skin, we sit just enjoying the day as though nothing over the last few days has even happened. Nick seems to be completely relaxed and at ease, watching the birds on the lake diving and swimming around with a contented look across his face. The sensation of feeling comfortable washes over my turbulent emotions after these last few days and even a sense of belonging begins to warm my insides to battle against the cold darkness of what lies ahead.

Finishing our drinks, Nick stands and makes his way into the kitchen and, beginning to tidy up, shouts through to me, "We are not on fuckin' holiday, you know. Come on; get your ass moving. I'm going to change my clothes." He walks in the direction of a door that is at the end of the living room.

Smiling back I reply with, "Bollocks."

Helping to finish clear away the drinks, he quickly returns in similar black and green clothing and I follow him down the stairs where we stop next to the black bags. He bends and unzips one bag, taking out two pairs of combat boots and passing one pair to me. Both sitting on the lower step of the stairs, we slide our feet into the boots and, after lacing them up; we walk along the hallway in the direction of the front door and continue outside towards the smaller hay barn with Nick carrying the other black bag. The barn has been converted to a garage with two metal electric garage doors painted light grey blending into the brickwork. A dark wooden door sits nestled between the cold steel grey doors and, taking a key from his pocket, Nick unlocks the door and with a small kick at the bottom pushes it open. He reaches to the right and clicks on the internal light, illuminating the inside space. Following him inside the barn, a car and motorbike covered by dustsheets stand on the left side along with a ride on tractor mower partially covered by another grey sheet.

Rows of garden tools hang on the wall to the right above a large bench with different power tools neatly arranged close to a dark metal door. The musty dampness hangs in the air as though the place has been sealed for years as Nick walks over to the door, unlocking it then pulling it open. He switches on another light that casts a beam of light into the shadows of the building corner. Beckoning me across to join him, I reach the door and notice a wooden staircase leading down to what appears to be a cellar. We walk down the creaky stairs to the basement of the barn and Nick, placing the black bag on the floor, unlocks a pair of steel doors, sliding them open and revealing rows of weapons sub divided into different types: pistols, sub machine guns, sniper rifles and various other knives, swords and spears and grenades.

"Christ, Nick, are you expecting World War Three?"

"Be prepared, Dean, always be prepared," he replies.

He begins to unlock a padlock then unthreads chains from inside the trigger guards. He takes out a familiar gun, the AK47, and, pulling open a drawer, lifts out two machine gun magazines. Handing the gun and mags to me, he continues to walk along the firearms, taking out different weapons and other equipment and gradually passing some to me, hanging it on the strap across his shoulder. Finally he takes out several pistols, both automatic and revolvers, then, lifting a large black bag from the end of the gun rack, we load all the weapons inside. He lifts the bag and slides the doors closed, then gestures with his head for us to walk towards the steps. Reaching the ground floor of the barn, we continue to walk out into the warm morning sunshine and, closing the access door, we head off in the direction of the forest to the side of the large lake. We continue along a narrow winding path into the pine forest with the armour of pine and sound of bird song filling the air. The forest gets gradually darker and cooler until in the distance a small pocket of light illuminates a clearing and, continuing to walk along the soft pine needle carpet, we finally reach some warmth and daylight. The clearing is around forty metres long and twenty wide with long grass covering the ground where trees have fallen over, exposing the tree root bases now standing like a vertical modern art sculptures.

Nick places the black bag onto the damp grass and begins to take out the weapons, laying them carefully on top. With all the guns placed, Nick reaches into the end pocket of the bag and takes out some large paper targets and a box of paper pins then, with a smile back towards me, he starts to walk in the long wet grass towards the tree roots that can be used as backstops for firing bullets into. As I stand watching Nick, he gradually makes his way through the undulating ground, occasionally stumbling until finally he reaches the fallen trees and begins to place the half metre square targets onto the root bases. At forty metres away the six placed targets look quite small as I watch Nick walking back in my direction, noticing swallows gracefully flying in front of him, trying to catch flies ready for their migration to Africa.

He reaches into the bag and takes out two sets of ear defenders. "It might get a little noisy in a bit, but these electric defenders blank out all gunshot, apart from our voices."

So placing the defenders over my ears the soft cups instantly blank out all noise apart from his voice as he continues with the lesson.

"Okay, Dean, let's have the AK first. This weapon is very reliable and easily available anywhere in the world capable of firing 7.62mm rounds in any climate or conditions." I hand him the machine gun.

"As before, the loading and cocking of the gun is simple." He pushes a mag into the slot and clicks back the action then, pushing on the safety catch, lifts the gun to his shoulder standing around thirty metres away from the targets.

"This gun can be short, folding and fixed stock, but also with scopes can make a deadly sniper rifle in the right hands." Standing closer to him, I can see him leaning slightly forward and, pushing the gun into his shoulder, he clicks off the safety and, lining up against a target, squeezes the trigger.

'BURR, BURR, BURR.'

My ears echo, even wearing defenders, from the familiar hammer recoil from the gun and Nick's body can be seen vibrating as he absorbs the shocks. He clicks back on the safety, lowers the guns and, as the smoke clears, he hands the gun over to me. "Now you try, it's a bit more violent than the MP5 but you will handle it."

Taking the warm gun from his hands, I walk forward and look at the second target then lifting the gun to my shoulder align the front and rear open sights. Clicking off the safety then gradually pulling the trigger, *'BURR BURR BURR' echoes through the forest, as* the instant recoil from the bullets hammer the stock into my shoulder, feeling as though a horse has kicked me. The violence felt from the recoil is much harder than from the MP5 combined with the weight of the gun and at the tree root dirt clouds are flung into the air from the bullets missing the target. Lowering the gun with my ears still ringing and feeling slightly disheartened, I click the safety back on.

"Ha–ha–ha!" Nick laughs out loud. "Told you it was more violent."

Smiling back, I reply, "Just a bit, but exciting."

"Try again, but this time hold it firmer but be more relaxed with the trigger you snatched on it." Nick simulates with his arms as though holding an imaginary gun.

So, lifting the gun again, I push it harder into my shoulder and click off the safety with my thumb. Looking down the barrel, the target can clearly be seen on the second tree and as instructed I gradually squeeze the trigger. This time I concentrate more on the target with the recoil being absorbed and watch the bullets hitting the target as I aim for the black circle. Suddenly the gun stops and, as the smoke rises, I realise it's out of bullets so lowering the gun the empty mag is removed and we exchange clips noticing the weight difference is considerable.

Copying what Nick did, the full mag is pushed into the receiver, but the action is already cocked and, clicking on the safety, Nick speaks. "Now in small bursts gradually squeeze the trigger, making each shot count."

I lift the gun back to my shoulder and in short bursts the second mag is emptied successfully with at least some rounds hitting the target.

"That's fine for now, Dean, good work. Now remove the clip and place on the safety and we can try another gun."

Nick walks over to the bag and takes out two different types of handgun as I remove the mag and make the AK safe with the warmth of the barrel still radiating. Reaching Nick, he takes out a box of nine mm bullets and a couple of metal clips and points to the bag where I place the AK-47. Then we walk back in the direction of the targets with not a word spoken. Standing around twenty-five metres away from the target trees, Nick hands me the Beretta automatic handgun then he opens the rotating cylinder of the Smith and Wesson revolver and begins to drop bullets into the cylinder. After the gun is loaded, he clicks the cover shut and then, lifting the gun in the direction of the fourth target, takes aim and squeezes off a round. The smoke rises from the end of the barrel as the target shudders from the bullet impact as a faint soil cloud erupt from the tree stump. Clicking over the safety, he gestures for me to exchange guns with a smile across his face as to say 'beat that, kid'. Taking the gun from his hand, the warmth from the spent round quickly disperses and, turning slightly to the right, I lift the gun and take aim against the same target.

Looking down the barrel, I align the back and bead sight but with the weight of the gun at full stretch my arm starts to shake slightly. Relaxing slightly, it feels as though preparing to take the shot is an instinctive action requiring almost no thought. As my breathing begins to be controlled I pull at the trigger, sending a bullet towards the direction of the target. Without even sighting I know that it was close to Nick's placed round, but the gun's recoil sends the pistol upwards slightly. Feeling completely at ease, I continue to pull the trigger with the four more bullets in an arc on the target and, as the gun smoke fills my nostrils, I smile to myself. Then after emptying the cylinder I lower the gun and turn around to see Nick staring at the target where the cluster of bullet holes have been punched into the target with a slight grin on his face.

"Hmm," Nick sighs, and, taking out a clip, offers me the Beretta.

Knowing he isn't impressed, I push the spindle and crack the gun open, dropping the warm bullet cases into my hand. Then placing the spent cases into the holdall front pocket.

"Try this gun, Clint?" he smiles as we exchange guns.

Taking the loaded clip, I push it into the slot inside the handle and pull back the top slide and with the gun loaded the safety catch is applied. Aiming at the fourth target and feeling relaxed, I depress the safety catch and gradually pull on the trigger once the sights are aligned. As the recoil causes the gun to lift slightly, the smoke clears and a bullet hole can be seen just to the left of the main centre circle. Nick turns and steps back ten metres as if to say 'try here'. So, pointing the gun at the ground, I walk back ten metres and repeat the shot with the result again 5mm to the left.

"You're compensating for the weight and recoil too much. Relax, you're thinking too much about the shot. Think of something else," Nick explains.

As instructed I try to relax more and think of something else, but my mind is still filled with the actions from the last few days and the revelations from Nick over our past, but the biggest thing filling my thoughts is our future that for the first time in my life is completely uncertain. As the trigger is pulled, it feels as though all this uncertainty suddenly begins to clear like the gun smoke drifting away in the air. Will all the problems now in my life disappear by simply pulling the trigger of a gun? The target clearly shows a direct hit in the bulls-eye and with repeated shots the grouping is around two centimetres. The last bullet case hits the ground and the sound of Nick clapping his hands and smiling proves my marksman skills.

Removing the empty clip, I pull the top slide and, ejecting the last case, then watch Nick tying a piece of red ribbon to a tree branch nearby. He then places the revolver onto the bag. He lifts the sniper rifle along with a box of bullets and what appears to be a telescope. Walking to the bag, the handgun is lowered and I continue to follow Nick as he makes his way back into the forest, occasionally glancing over his shoulder to check the distance from the targets. After several minutes we are back in cool darkness of the pine forest and finally Nick stops against a fallen tree. Lowering the rifle against the tree, he looks at the distance and, lifting the telescope to his eyes, sends a red laser light in the direction of the two remaining targets.

"Seven hundred and sixty metres and two miles per hour side wind." I stand watching as he begins to explain.

"Okay, this rangefinder measures seven hundred and sixty metres," he says as he points to the targets.

"What else do you notice?" he asks.

Looking back towards the targets, the sun's rays illuminate the clearing. I continue to scan around for any other signs but nothing is evident. "I don't see anything, Nick."

"Dean, in long range shooting, apart from distance what else do we need to know?"

"Hmm, wind strength and direction?"

"Good, and how do we find this? What else?"

"Err, I don't know?" I say, shaking my head.

"Okay, see the little red ribbon tied to the tree near where we stood? Is it moving?" he asks.

"Yes, just very faintly to the left," I reply.

"Can you feel the wind just touching the skin on your face as you look at the target in the same direction?"

"Yes, just about, Nick."

"Okay, well I can't show you everything today, but that faint wind would affect bullet travel at long distances. For this demonstration today it won't affect it too much."

"What about temperature, curvature of the earth, warmth thermals and air quality?"

"Okay, yes, so temperature is easy to find, but what about earth curvature, thermals and air quality?"

"Well, for air quality taking long distance shots in open land is okay since generally the air is cleaner and thinner so bullet resistance isn't too affected."

Nick continues, "For earth curvature charts are available, but it can also be measured using the range finder and a fixed point of focus. Finally, thermals are more difficult, but as we walked through the forest, did you notice if the air temperature changed?"

"Yes, as we came from the opening back into the forest."

"Right, well any standing object could create a thermal be it a tree or building. You always need to check your thermals before shooting at long distances since the bullet could lift or lower accordingly."

"Now open the bipod and make yourself comfortable resting the rifle on the fallen trunk and let's see if you still have that unmissable sniper's eye."

As instructed I lift the rifle and, opening the bipod, sit down on the ground with the feet of the bipod resting against the fallen trunk. Adjusting my position and making myself comfortable, I push the rifle deep into the shoulder and stare down the optics of the telescopic sight. As my cheek rests against the black synthetic stock the smell of fresh gun oil fills my nose as Nick opens the box of bullets. Handing the plastic bullet magazine to me, he gestures for me to load the gun. Lifting the operating handle with a positive click, the bolt is slid back to reveal the empty chamber and pushing in the magazine, the top bullet can be seen. Pushing the operating handle forward again, the first bullet is loaded into the chamber and with a firm click, the safety catch is operated. Resting my finger on the trigger guard, I begin to regulate my breathing as I begin to stare back down the telescopic sight.

"If you're comfortable, Dean, and there are no obstructions in your way, take a shot."

Looking back through the scope, I see no immediate problems but recheck by looking with my both my eyes. Feeling confident that all is good, I continue controlling my breathing and concentrating on target number five. I readjust my seating position to see the centre of the target through the scope and, after un-clicking the safety, gradually squeeze the trigger.

The bullet trail can be seen whizzing through the air as the vicious recoil hits hard into my shoulder. The smoke fills my nostrils and as I look through the scope the bullet hole can just be seen on the far high right of the target.

"Now, I think you maybe snatching at the trigger a little bit, Dean, so empty the chamber and send out another round."

Unlocking the operating handle, I retract the bolt and the spent round ejects onto the ground with a little smoke still rising from the empty case. Loading another bullet back into the chamber, the command is repeated. Another shot is fired and this time the round punches the target closer to the centre circle around one inch high and one point five inches to the left.

"Okay, better, Dean. Now every person shoots slightly different along with the actual shooting conditions and this gun scope needs to be adjusted, so empty the chamber and remember which way the bullet has hit the target."

Emptying the gun, I reply, "The last bullet was around half an inch to the left and half an inch high."

"Good, so on the top of the scope is the elevation and to the side is the windage adjustment screws that change the sighting plane. If you see the indications, they are marked with short and long lines. Most scopes have quarter inch markings at a hundred yards so each quarter will give you a quarter of an inch movement at 100 yards. We are at seven hundred and sixty yards so the number of clicks must be multiplied by seven to make it simple."

"I can see this, yes."

"There are two arrows opposite the markings that say up down for elevation and left and right for windage, okay. Now you have to move the opticals towards the misses and I think the slight wind is affecting the left, so how far out was it?"

"About half an inch to the left."

"Right, so the screw needs to be clicked how many times?" Nick asks.

"One click is quarter of inch at a hundred yards and we are at seven hundred and sixty yards so it's two clicks at one hundred multiplied by seven equals fourteen clicks," I reply. It's like being back at school.

"The elevation adjustment?"

"Err, two clicks at one hundred multiple seven equals fourteen clicks again."

"Okay, Dean, so make the adjustments and take another shot."

As mentored, the scope is adjusted for windage and elevation with the screws for the desired number of clicks and a bullet is reloaded back into the chamber. After readjusting and making myself comfortable, I stare back down the scope at the target and prepare to take another shot.

"Has anything changed before you take another shot, Dean?"

Clicking the safety catch on and looking with both eyes, I can see that the red ribbon has started to lift a little higher to the left. "Yes, the red ribbon has begun to lift a little higher."

"Good, I stopped you taking the shot then otherwise it would have affected your calculations. So what are you going to do?"

"Err, I can continue with my original shot and check that the elevation is correct then see how much the wind affects the bullet to the left."

"Okay, fine. Well, continue."

So taking a third shot and looking through the scope, the elevation has clearly been brought back to the centre of the target, but as expected the bullet is still too far left by around half an inch. So after emptying the gun Nick continues with his tutorial.

"So how far out is the last bullet, Dean?"

"The elevation looks good but is to the left again."

"Okay, so are we going to adjust the scope again or try something else?"

"Well, if the elevation is correct, I can move the shot further to the right to compensate."

"Correct, and this will be how much?"

"Well, the same as we adjusted the scope, yes."

"Okay, well try it."

Quickly calculating the adjustment value required to be around three and a half inches to the right, I load another bullet into the chamber and take a fourth shot with this round finally hitting the black circle closer to the centre. A feeling of both relief and excitement is felt; knowing that I have accomplished what appears to be a new skill for me but from what Nick was saying is probably just a conformation that I can still shoot.

With a pat on my right shoulder, Nick stands, saying, "Okay. Dean, that's enough for today. I'll go collect the stuff and we can walk back and have some well-earned dinner. It's nearly 5 p.m. already."

So, emptying the weapon and standing back up, I lift the rifle and place the gun sling over my right shoulder and then, reaching down, the small tray of bullets is placed in my pocket. After picking up the spent bullet cases, I watch Nick, who is already removing the targets from the tree roots. He walks over to the black bag and places the handguns inside before returning in my direction. We begin our walk out of the forest back along the small path just as a small rain shower begins with the rain drops hitting the foliage of the trees, sending small droplets of water everywhere. After a few minutes the rain stops and, as we emerge from the pine forest, the rain clouds can be seen moving over the next valley as the sun's rays try to puncture through the tail end of the grey clouds. Reaching the barn, we walk down the stairs and, after giving the rifle and AK a quick wipe with a gun rag, we place them into the rack along with the handguns. I give Nick the bullets used in the rifle. He places them into the black bag and then pushes the bags into one of the lower cupboards underneath the gun racks.

After closing and locking the doors, he announces, "We can clean them tomorrow, don't worry."

Nodding in agreement, we turn and walk back out of the barn towards the farmhouse and, making our way to the back of the house. We enter through the back door. Opening the door, I find myself in a drying room with different coats on hangers and boots stored in a boot rack. Removing the coats along with the wet muddy boots, we store them and continue through into the house.

"If you like take a shower then I will start some dinner, okay?"

"Okay, Nick."

So, walking into the bedroom, I close the door behind as I hear Nick's footsteps on the oak staircase going upstairs. Removing my outer clothes and taking the fresh clothes from my bag along with deodorant, I walk into the bathroom, which, as with much of the rest of the house, is white inside with Italian marble floor and wall tiles inside the shower.

After taking a shower and drying myself, I apply some deodorant, then walk back into the bedroom and pull on some fresh underwear and socks. Then, climbing into my jeans and pulling on a jumper, I walk back out of the bedroom and continue up the stairs to see Nick returning from his bedroom after changing.

"Okay, how about some salmon fillets, new potatoes and fresh vegetables?"

"Sounds good."

"You start preparing the vegetables and I will start on the salmon and sauce, ok?"

"Yeah, fine, just show me where everything is and I will get started."

After showing me where things are, I start to prepare the vegetables, by washing and cleaning them then, after slicing and dicing, place the potatoes in a saucepan of water on the hob.

After lowering the other vegetables into a steam, the pan is placed onto the induction hob as Nick finishes quickly, sealing the fish then wrapping them in foil with some herbs. He arranges them on a tray and slides them into the oven. He collects another pan and begins to make the sauce as I start to prepare the dining table that overlooks the lake. I open the doors slightly just to listen to the sound of the birds and peacefulness.

"There's a bottle of white wine in the fridge, so get some glasses. I'm almost done here."

Returning back to the kitchen, the smells from the fresh vegetables and salmon cooking instantly make me feel hungry and I collect the wine glasses and wine from the fridge, then place them onto the table. Nick takes the main course plates out and starts to drain the vegetables. I fill two large glasses of water and, returning to the table, place them next to the wine glasses and begin to open the wine bottle. He finishes preparing the food on the plates, starting with placing the salmon fillets from the oven, and then, after arranging the vegetables, he drizzles some dill sauce over the plates.

"Excellent." He walks to the table.

Lowering the plates onto the table, he has prepared the food like you could see in any top class restaurant and says, "Bon appetite."

"Looks fabulous, Nick."

He then pours the wine and, after saying 'cheers', we begin to enjoy the meal.

Half way through the meal, my incentive to learn more about where I came from is hard to control and I have to ask, "Nick, why did you want me to join you so much?"

Nick pauses for a few seconds and places his knife and fork on the plate and begins his answer. "Dean, you were part of an elite special unit developed and trained by the government for one main purpose: removal of enemies, foreign or domestic." Nick looks across at me.

"We worked in some of the most hazardous places of the world against friends and enemies of the British government on special ops tours with a primary function as assassins, but we also supported with intelligence gathering."

"You being there with me on Monday was so important because after your last contract, you disappeared and it has taken me years to find you again. Years of hoping that we would see each other again, and hoping that you would remember."

My mind can't even begin to register what he has said at first, but the feelings from deep inside seem to confirm the levels of death and destruction seem such a normal part of my life, but I still am shocked and ask, "Nick, that can't be possible, I would remember something like that. It's difficult to forget, but what do you want me to remember?"

"Dean, I know it's hard for you to digest right now, but place some of the parts of the puzzle together. The life you once lived, the feeling of freedom you love so much." Nick takes a sip of his wine and continues.

"I've received some intel info a few years ago over your whereabouts and have been tracking you ever since. Most government agencies thought you were dead after disappearing off the radar, but the cardinals monitor everything." Nick turns slightly, looking at the lake, and continues.

"You can tell me another time about how you escaped from them, but now back to business. I think we have a leak from the team and we need to find out who sold us out and I need your help now or we will both be caught."

Looking across at him, still shell-shocked and trying to digest this new knowledge, I ask, "Wait, cardinals? Who are the cardinals, a group of priests?"

Lowering his glass to the table, he looks across and says, "Well, they would like to think of themselves as a group of priests, but let's just say they were a brotherhood of senior agents and decision makers."

"What, a secret society of vicars? Well, I have heard of everything."

"Dean, following the Second World War and the Cold War of the 1950s, it was difficult times for England with a lot of countries being jealous of the previous size of the old British Empire and the government needing to protect British interests. The cardinal programme was started using the old school tie universities of Oxford and Cambridge as a cover. The cardinal programme was cleared through Churchill during the Second World War and was operational from the early 1940s through until the late 1970s with the main aim of keeping the faith of what is British real. It is said that the cardinals are still operational today, although the programme was disbanded.

"What, and you think the cardinals are still active and have been tracking me?" I stand and walk towards the edge of the balcony.

"Dean, even today the world is an unstable place and governments will always need agents and information. And yes, I think the cardinals are still active."

"You seem to know a lot about it, Nick, were you a cardinal?"

Nick begins to laugh. "Me, a cardinal? Hardly, but I did know some of the operatives. Dean, don't lose focus over the cardinals, let's deal with the now."

The last words from his mouth finally being to sink in as the favour is now called in and, knowing I don't have any option, I reply with, "What do we need from me, Nick?"

"We need to tidy up the loose lips from the robbery so let's finish our food and prepare for that first. Once that is done we can move forward knowing we are safe."

Returning back to the table, I lift my cutlery and continue to eat the food, but now with more and more information filtering into my mind I find it difficult to eat let alone concentrate on what is happening with secret government agencies. There are no more words said between Nick and myself and, after completing the dinner, I help him tidy the plates away then finish my wine.

Looking at the large clock in the kitchen, the time clicks over to 8 p.m. and I say, "I'm done for today, Nick. I think I will call it a night. It's been a busy day."

"No problems, Dean, I understand. You need your rest, we have a lot to do tomorrow." He walks across.

"I'm really glad you are here and it will be better soon, I promise."

I smile, turn and, walking down the stairs, retire to the bedroom for the night. I reach the room and lie on the bed, still fully clothed, thinking now about the cardinals and how they are maybe the same people Archibald was taking about. I wonder if Wagstaff could be a cardinal, watching what happens to me and trying to use me to kill Nick. After hours of thinking I finally drift off to sleep.

11

Awaking on the Saturday morning to the sound of birds singing in the stillness of the gardens around the farmhouse feels so comfortable and calming after the past few days and, as I lie in bed trying to imagine what more refresher training could include, the noise of Nick beginning to stir resonates through the old wooden structure of the house. Thinking back to last night and our other recent conversations, it is clear that Nick is very upset over the death of Lloyd and the betrayal of the two German guys. Noises can be heard from the kitchen, from the kettle being filled with water and the click from the electric switch. The sound of a radio then fills the air with the 7 a.m. world news and the first headline of the broadcaster is the police update from the robbery and that Monday will be a national day of mourning to remember the dead. The prime minster makes a statement confirming that with all his powers, he will ensure that the terrorists will be caught and that all the investigating teams have very strong leads. Rising from the bed, I make my way to the bathroom and, after a quick wash and cleaning my teeth, walk up the large staircase to the open plan kitchen dining room. Nick can be seen preparing some toast and has already set the table on the balcony for our breakfast outside. The radio volume is reduced as the broadcaster then moves onto the next main headline of fighting in the Gaza strip.

"That holy war will never be over in the Gaza strip." Nick takes a pot of coffee out onto the balcony.

"I hear we are still the main headlines for the news?" I join him outside.

"Dean, that will be Wagstaff keeping stirring up the news teams, telling them he has information. Don't worry, his time will come when he least expects it." Nick sits back down.

"Did you sleep well, Dean?"

"Not too bad thanks, I fell asleep in my clothes."

"Hard training does that to you. Today will be even harder."

The peacefulness felt sitting at the table in the late summer morning sunshine with the sound of ducks and geese shouting and splashing around on the lake, combined with the calls from great crested grebes through the thin blanket of the mist rising from the water, would warm even the most cold heart and I guess, deep down, even Nick, as I look across at him.

"I used to have breakfast here with my parents when I was a child. This place allows me to relax and refocus my thoughts," Nick proclaims.

"Nick, you are very lucky to have this magical place, but aren't you ever lonely?" I ask, smiling back.

"It can be a little lonely sometimes, but if you don't like your own company, then any other people have no chance." He takes a sip of coffee.

"Have you ever been married?" I ask.

"I was once, Dean, but the job made her leave. This job takes over your life if you want to be any good at it and, besides, trying to explain the work we do is a little difficult for anyone to understand." He looks at me, smiling.

"What about you, Dean? Has marriage ever crossed your mind?" he asks.

"There was a woman once that was marriage material, but there was a problem."

"Really? What problem, Dean?"

"She was already married and in the end wouldn't leave her husband, so the change of jobs at Harpers and Harpers came at the right time," I reply, smiling.

"What about Sophie?" Nick asks, buttering a slice of brown toast, laughing.

"Have you seen her again after the night in my club? You both looked very happy," Nick asks with a smile.

"With everything at the moment, Sophie is the last thing on my mind," I reply with a little disappointment in my voice.

"Sophie is nice, but I feel she has not been honest with me so it's better to walk away." I lean across the table to take a slice of toast.

"Not honest in what way, Dean?"

'Shall I tell him what she said?' flashes through my mind. "She mentioned that you knew her from long ago and you helped her friend with a problem guy."

"Argh, yes, the old boyfriend skeleton in the cupboard story, hey. My, that woman sometimes has a vivid imagination."

"So how long have you known Sophie, Nick?" I ask.

"A couple of years then I worked over seas and we lost touch."

"So it's not true then?"

"Dean, we are loners and our freedom gives us independence and most women find it difficult to understand that fact and the world has taught us to be that way, right?" he continues, changing subject quickly.

"I know a few guys who got married, but in the end with this type of work your partner can be your worst enemy if they get taken as a hostage. These government agencies can be as bad as the enemy you're trying to kill to loved ones."

Nodding in agreement, I know he won't tell me anything. I start to butter the toast as my mind runs back through the conversation we have just had and what could have been as an image of her fills my thoughts and as always I think about what she would be doing now. We continue breakfast with hardly any other conversation other than a few words as we both enjoy the morning atmosphere, listening to the stillness. Finishing our breakfasts, Nick stands and starts to collect all the plates and cups together.

"Okay, are you ready?" he asks.

"Ready for anything, I think," I reply.

"Hmm," he says as he walks into the kitchen.

After walking down the staircase and towards the drying room we wear the muddy boots from yesterday and my mind beings to replay the events. We continue to the barn and the autumn morning air feels so fresh touching our skin. The barn door is opened and stepping inside we walk towards the weapon storage area removing the dirty equipment. The weapons from yesterday's exercises are all cleaned; Nick takes a small fixed blade knife from one of the drawers in the main cabinet. "Now, Dean, in our profession guns are not always available, so hand to hand combat and the correct use of them are critical for staying alive."

"Okay, so what are we doing today, carving joints?"

"Well, before I show you how to use a knife correctly, the first thing to learn is how to disarm a person. It's quite simple really."

"It may be for you, but not for me."

Nick smiles. "Okay, lift that piece of blue rag and take it in your right hand."

So, as instructed, I reach for the rag with my right hand with Nick standing almost toe-to-toe, beginning to move the knife forward at me. "Now throw the rag over the top of my hand and, quickly grabbing it with the left, pull my hand in a downward action. This will cause me to lose my grip and drop the knife."

So, following his commands, I continue to pull against him and can sense he is beginning to loosen his grip.

"Now with the rag above my hand, I have to fight against your whole body weight." Releasing the rag, Nick lowers the knife.

"Another method is for you to grab hold of my wrists and complete the same action. This can be harder because you're closer to the blade and have more risk of being cut."

Again Nick lifts the knife and, after dropping the rag to the ground, I grab hold of his wrists. "Now, if you continue in a twisting action it becomes difficult to hold the slippery knife handle."

"Good, excellent, like you have done this before. Okay, so release your grip and take that newspaper from on top of the cabinet."

So, releasing my grip, I reach over and take the newspaper. "Now roll it into a tight tube."

The room is filled with the rustling of paper as I roll the tube and still standing opposite to Nick, awaiting his next command.

"Now, the human body is covered in pressure points that are used in massage and self-defence techniques. Some are pleasurable and others send intense pain into the nervous system. We want the pain pressure points."

Nick then begins to indicate where the pressure points are on the body with his fingers and also the methods to cause pain with gestures.

"The main points, starting from the top, are eyes and these can be damaged with a fist or fingers. Quite evident really. Ears are next and a slap from the inside flat of the hand sends a shock wave into the senses. Okay, a person can be rendered useless with a back of hand chop or fist to the bridge of nose or the base. The term 'glass jaw' could prove useful with a kick, fist or elbow.

"The side of the neck and a chop, kick or fist into the jugular vein could cause a shockwave into the heart and make the person drop to the ground. A fist, elbow or hand chop to the windpipe causes severe coughing and breathing problems. Now, as all men and women know, the groin region is very sensitive and a kick, knee or even fist will slow any possible attacker down. The knee is also very sensitive and a kick to the front, side, or even the back if you are defending from behind, will drop anybody. Finally, the last two and shins can be easily kicked and the instep stamp on the top of the foot."

Nick stands back and continues. "Now, a quick hit on any of these points will cause the attacker to drop any weapons and worst case fall to their knees in agonising pain, unless of course you have been trained in how to accept the pain. Okay, got it?"

I nod to agree with him. "Now when I move forward to attack you, hit the pressure point on my neck and if you're lucky I may drop the knife."

So Nick begins his slow attack and with a fast striking action the area on his neck is struck with a whack. He lowers the knife and stands back very slightly and can tell it was a good hit.

"I think you passed that exam, Dean. Boy,that came a little sharp."

"Sorry, Nick, but you did say hit you." We both laugh.

"Now anything can be used in self-defence and hitting the pressure points is critical. Pens, books, spoons, saucepans, whatever you can lay your hands on at the time. Now, a pen or pencil can also be stabbed into a pressure point that could be fatal, so remember someone could use it on you."

Nick places the knife back onto the cabinet and takes a sip of coffee from the mug he brought with him. "Now, hand to hand combat is the most difficult because of how close the attacker is to you."

He stands a little closer. "Queensbury rules don't really work anymore and with more agents being taught different styles of martial arts you can get in a mess quickly if you don't have your wits about you. Bare knuckle fighting is pretty hardcore but in any fight all the attacker wants to do is kill you so most people try the neck hold and if they can get under or over your arms you're knackered. Let me show you."

Nick then gives me some instructions. "Now, with my hands around your neck try to lift your arms to push me off."

Lifting my arms it's clear I can't overcome his upper body strength. "Okay, if I release my hands and we repeat with your arms above mine try again."

Not being in position for a good grip is very difficult and I can't apply any pressure to his arms.

"Okay, so let's repeat it again but this time try to kick me between the legs or even try to kick the pressure point on my knees or shins. This way you will start to throw me off balance and then it gives you the advantage."

So as instructed I begin to struggle and move around, attempting to kick Nick's legs. "Good, Dean. So can you sense how my grip has become softer on the neck as you move in an attacking action but sometimes the attacker may try to grip stronger due to frustration."

"Yes, Nick, I can feel that."

Now releasing his hands fully and standing away, he says, "Okay, so let's recap how to disarm with pressure points, a rag or cloth, and finally in an attack situation with my hands around your neck. Now there is no way you can pick up everything but what we can do now is carry out some stimulated actions over and over again until it becomes like second nature."

We both have a quick drink of coffee and start to repeat the moves over and over again for the next hour, using opposite hands and switching between me trying to attack Nick with the knife and vice versa. With each set of moves I can feel myself becoming faster and faster, not even thinking about the actions. Nick occasionally adds some more moves into the exercises in an attempt to show me other strong and weak points of attack. Many of the moves have a type of familiarity as though I have been taught some of them before. We continue with hand-to-hand combat techniques as I use sweeping actions to block his attacking movements in an attempt to overpower the aggressive advances. The strangest feeling is that it appears almost normal for Nick to try attacking me as it did when I fired the guns and helped with the robbery. It's clear this aggression felt inside must come from this part of my past and a history that still haunts my subconscious today.

We stop the combat training and return to the farmhouse for a well-earned lunch and I feel now it's the time to ask Nick about the envelope full of pictures as we sit around the dining table enjoying a fresh salad.

"Nick, in the pictures that were left for me one of the pictures had the name of an army training corp, 1264. Do you know anything about that regiment?"

"Hmm, which pictures were these?" He tries to avoid the conversation.

"The ones that appeared after we first met at Castro's."

"Argh, yes, *those* pictures. Hmm, that name doesn't sound familiar, Dean, but I could make a few discreet enquires if you like and see where it leads."

"Yes, Nick, thanks, that would be good. It seems strange that certain photos were left, almost as though it's a trail to follow."

"Dean, I wouldn't read too much thought into it, personally I think they were left by Wagstaff to try and confuse you."

Sensing that he doesn't want to talk about the photographs does annoy me slightly because deep down I know that these may be the only part of my life that is actually real and it still lingers inside over who left them and why. We continue our lunch, passing just small talk with Nick clearly deep in thought and, reading the body language from his facial expressions, I can tell he is deeply planning something else, but now isn't the best time to ask so better to wait for another opportunity to present itself. After the lunch we return to the garage and downstairs in the basement Nick begins to explain how to load, make safe, strip down, maintain and rebuild all the different types of weapons stored in the cabinet, naming critical components for me the remember. The weapons include various types of handguns, ranging from simple revolvers to automatic pistols with red dot sighting, and machine guns including UZI, M16, the MP5 as we used in the robbery, and the world famous AK 47 that has many different styles but is simple, reliable and easily available.

Finally we move to the sniper rifles that include various calibres ranging from .303 to the destructive 50 cals and the different types of telescopic sights used with them including night vision, fixed and variable designs. I look at my watch and 6 p.m. has already arrived before we move to the last subject matter of different grenades, timers and explosive materials. This is certainly a crash course in military hardware, but I feel completely in my element talking about and handling each weapon and I appear to be in my comfort zone. That is never what was felt in the old job as an accountant. It is clear that this is my background and wanting to learn more is starting to boarder on obsession and not a fantasy. Without an inner discipline I could quickly start to become out of control having all this power at my fingertips. After completing the world tour of military weapons, we close the cabinet doors at 8 p.m. and as we head back to the farmhouse with the coolness of the early evening air touching our faces and naked arms, causing the hairs to stand on end.

Looking across to Nick, I say, "Thanks for the last few days, it really makes me feel more comfortable knowing you have confidence in me."

Nick acknowledges my comments with a simple smile along with a head nod and it's evident that he enjoyed exchanging information for me to absorb. I could never have possibly imagined anything more exciting in a day of training before today, but deep down, though, the excitement felt probably comes as much from knowing it's wrong as the actual subject matter. Filled with confidence, I really don't care and look forward to putting the training into action and know that the day won't be very far away before Nick wants it to be used.

Reaching the farmhouse, the front door is opened and, as we walk up the stairs, the air is filled with the beef casserole that's bubbling away in the slow cooker just ready for us to enjoy that he prepared after lunch. Nick takes out a pair of bowls and matching side plates and, placing them on the dining table, gestures for me to fetch some wines glasses from the glass fronted cabinet. He walks back to the kitchen and the noise of a wine bottle being taken from the rack can be heard. He places the bottle on the granite surface and, opening a draw, takes out the opener. As it's opened Nick can be seen sniffing the cork with the look of pleasure on his face as he walks and places the bottle of burgundy in the centre of the table. The cutlery is fetched and as I begin to place it on the table Nick begins to cut some fresh bread, arranging it in a small wicker basket then bringing it to the set table.

"Take a seat, Dean. Let's eat, I'm starving." Nick unplugs the slow cooker and carries the warm casserole across to the table.

He dips a ladle into the steaming thick liquid and lifts out a serving, lowers it into my bowl, then, after filling his own dish, he then pours a glass of wine for each of us. We congratulate ourselves on a day well done, take a sip and start to enjoy the beef casserole. The meat simply melts in the mouth after simmering for many hours with the taste of the red wine complimenting the subtle herbs and, after spending hours in the basement of the barn, the warming food feels so rewarding. We continue to enjoy the dinner and our conversation starts to move to a subject I was expecting.

"Dean, one of my contacts has informed me that Thomas and Josef are near to Berlin, so I want to find out who set us up."

"Do you really think those guys could have done it?"

"I wouldn't put anything past those two bastards. I only employed them through Greg. That's why I killed him."

"Oh right, do you have any ideas who they could be working for?" I ask inquisitively.

"I have a few ideas, Dean, but I want it from the horse's mouth so to speak."

"So how are you planning we get to Berlin? Fly? I don't think that is possible with all the heat we have."

"No, Dean, I'm thinking of travelling up to Hull, catching the overnight ferry to the Netherlands then driving to Berlin. What do you think?"

"Travelling from Hull might be a safer bet than Calais because that will be swarming with agents."

"Yeah, that's what I thought so it's a good job that I have booked the ferry for tomorrow night, hey."

"Yes, Nick, I roll with you, no problems. These guys nearly got me caught so I have a score to settle too!"

"Good, then it's set. We leave tomorrow morning and catch the overnight ferry. It will take us about six hours to get there I reckon."

"We can share the driving, if you like?"

"Too bloody right, me going that far north I might get a nose bleed." We both laugh.

Finishing our dinner, we tidy up the plates, bowls and cutlery into the dishwasher and make our way to the living room. Nick begins to make a fire, and I fetch two glasses of water to drink with the wine as we both settle into an armchair, each watching the fire beginning to ignite the chopped logs. The silence is broken by the cracking of the wood and roaring of the heat starting to rise.

"The warm and sound of an open fire can't be beaten anywhere, hey, Dean."

"Very true. It helps cleanse the soul." I continue with a question: "What are you planning for Thomas and Josef, Nick?"

"What I'm planning is simple torture so we need to extract information and it will get messy. Dean, I have been meaning to ask you something."

"Okay, Nick, what?" Deep down I have a fear of what he is going to ask.

"I'm thinking of putting another job together and this one will make the money warehouse look like pocket change."

"We haven't tied up from the last one yet and you're talking about another job?"

"I know, and understand if you say no, but with the Lloyd being killed you're the only one to trust now."

"What job is it and where?"

"I don't have all the details yet, but it's based in the UK and involves extracting money from a large chemical company."

"Oh, and this company is just going to hand over millions in cash?"

"Well, not exactly. I will need to apply pressure in the right places."

"How are you proposing to apply the pressure?"

"I have a few ideas, Dean, and I'm sure they will be persuaded."

"There is no doubt on that."

I continue, "I only signed up for the money sorting warehouse job and I wanted to enjoy that money and freedom first before deciding on something else."

"I do understand, Dean, but this next job may be of a personal interest to you. But have a think about it and let me know in a few days, okay?"

"A personal interest? What do you mean?" I ask, slightly confused.

"Well, in a past life we both had some history with this company so it's time for a little payback."

It's so frustrating when he talks about our past and I can't remember. "A past I can't remember, Nick, so please enlighten me to some more facts."

"The company used to supply chemical hardware for military applications and a lot of the old reg boys used them." Nick is clearly starting to become drunk and opens a second bottle of red wine. I have never seen him like this before and clearly he is suffering in a way and it could be after the death of Lloyd.

"By reg, I assume you mean army reg or something else?"

"We liked to call ourselves that, yes, but really a group of us were brought together from different walks of life."

"So tell me more?" I ask inquisitively.

"We went through extensive training programmes and development so the cardinals could send us out on black ops."

"How many of us were there?" I have never heard Nick talking of the past before and I'm hungry to know more.

"In our reg there were twelve of us, but many guys didn't make it through the selection process."

"Selection process? So were we volunteered or nominated?" I ask Nick.

"Some guys were nominated, others selected and a few volunteered. It depended on your background really."

"What about me, did I volunteer?" I ask him, leaning forward on the seat.

"No one really knew your background and you never said, but all the other guys assumed you had volunteered."

"So the picture with training ops was our unit then?"

"No, our unit never had a name, it was just known as a date and number. Ours was 0471."

Still wanting to learn more, I try to ask more questions but also know he might start to close up again. "Did you volunteer, Nick?"

"No, Dean, I was nominated by a friend at university. Anyway, what do you think about the idea of the next job?" He changes subject quickly.

Looking back at him, smiling, I say, "It's not quite sold to me yet but I will think about it and let you know." Deep down I know that even if I say no he will kill me and take the money to front this next job so it might be the best option to say yes and maybe learn more about my past.

We continue our drinks and before long the second bottle of wine is gone, with Nick in an apparent self-destruct mode. Maybe even this man, who is normally so calm and composed, deep down battles against insecurity and loneliness like the rest of us and tonight he has certainly shown his more vulnerable side. As the fire begins to die out the time reaches close to midnight and, now yawning after another busy day, my brain and body now need sleep before the long journey to Hull and then onto the Netherlands. Being slightly anxious and excited over the journey ahead flows through my body, slowly picking away as my stomach muscles gradually keep clenching and relaxing, but I also know that this trip could give me more clues over my past life and confirm if Wagstaff's conversations about Nick are true or not. Both standing, we walk to the kitchen and place our glasses by the sink. It's clear he is quite drunk, but with his bedroom on the same floor it's only a few steps to reach his bed.

Saying, "Good night," I continue down the staircase and instantly notice the temperature drop from the lack of warmth from the fire in the living room and goosebumps show on my arms as the few hairs try to capture the last remaining heat. Reaching the bedroom, the door is opened and after undressing I prepare for bed quickly, falling asleep, probably from the wine we have drunk.

I awake the next morning with a slight fuzzy head but no real side effects from the wine and wonder how Nick feels today. It's no doubt that the drive to Hull will probably be me, but I don't mind. Looking through the French doors, it's evident how light it is outside, so checking my watch the time is almost 9.00 a.m. Climbing out of bed, I take a quick shower and then pack my bag for the trip to Germany. Leaving the bag by the side of the bed, I make my way upstairs and see Nick sitting on one of the chairs outside on the balcony, dressed in a jumper and jeans, just staring into the distance. Walking over towards him, the steam rises from the cup he holds between his hands and, as he stares into the beautiful autumn morning with the sound of waterfowl splashing and calling hidden by the low mist encapsulating the lake, the smell of his cup of coffee floats in the air.

"Good morning, Nick, how are you today?"

"Morning, Dean. A little tender in the head but otherwise okay, I have been worse. The kettle has recently boiled if you want a drink."

Walking back into the kitchen, a cup of tea is made and as he continues to stare into nothing it's clear he has much on the mind. Finishing making the drink, I join him on the balcony and sit on one of the other chairs as a little nip of coldness in the air can be felt and the warmth of the drink comforts me.

"A penny for them?" I ask him.

"Pardon? Oh, yes, right, Dean." He coughs and continues, "I'm just running through our route and what could happen on the way."

"Okay, and do you foresee many problems?"

"Well, if we can't get on the ferry we're certainty fucked but apart from that and a few border guards nothing I can't handle."

"What about me?"

"You'll be fine, don't worry." He finishes his coffee and stands up.

"Okay, a good fry up is in order. You set the table out here and I'll get started. One egg or two? Runny or hard?"

"One and sunny side up, soft."

"Good, good, that's what I like to hear."

He walks into the kitchen and starts to take food from the fridge along with placing several pans on the hob to start cook. I finish my drink, enjoying the peaceful surroundings as the smell of fresh cooking bacon begins to float from the kitchen. Standing and returning to the kitchen, the sound of bacon and eggs spitting as they get fried fills the room along with a haze of smoke engulfing the master chef busy preparing.

Placing some serving plates for him onto the worktop, I take the cutlery and glasses outside along with the bottle of fresh orange juice from the fridge. In no time Nick can be seen starting to serve the cooked food onto the plates and, fetching the rest of the thick cut loaf from last night, I join him at the table and the food as ever looks well-presented. He smiles across and we both sit down to enjoy our breakfast.

"We need to leave about ten hundred hours just to be sure we reach in time. Boarding normally starts about 16.30 hours."

"No problem, Nick, already packed and ready to go after this."

"Good."

We finish breakfast and, after placing the plates and pans into the dishwasher, Nick starts the wash cycle, then he takes the bag of rubbish out of the bin and wipes down all the surfaces. He looks into the fridge and takes out the last few bits of food and also places them in the bag.

"There is no refuge collection here so I will take this bag to the car and we can put it in a bin en route. Go around and check all the doors and windows are locked along with the barn while I get ready, okay, Dean? The car should be open but here are the keys." He hands them too me.

So as instructed I walk around the house, upstairs first, and check all the doors and windows for being locked, then I walk downstairs with the bag of rubbish. Fetching my bag from the bedroom, I continue outside and, reaching the car, I place my bag on the back seat and the rubbish bag in the boot. The barn is checked along with any lights and, after returning to the house, the back door is checked followed by the drying room and the other two bedrooms to make sure all is secure. I begin to walk back up the stairs to be greeted with Nick, already showered and changed, carrying a black bag. He starts down the wooden steps.

"It's all done up here, Dean, so let's go."

Looking at my watch, it's 9.58 a.m.

"Do you want me to drive?" I ask.

"Well, that is why I gave you the keys. I'll do the gates," he smiles.

Reaching the car, Nick can be heard in the background pressing the buttons on an alarm system keypad then he closes the large wooden front door with a solid thud. Climbing into the car, I start the engine as he begins to walk down the driveway, crunching with each footstep. I begin to drive out along the gravel with the heaters operated to clear the condensation already forming inside the vehicle. Stopping the other side of the gates where Nick is standing, he opens the passenger rear door and, placing the bag on the back seat, turns and walks back to close the gates. The metallic noise of a chain jingling through the centre frame of the gates can be heard followed by more crunching footsteps as he returns back to the car and shuts the rear door.

Pausing for a few seconds, he stares back at the house, gradually looking across every detail of the old farm. Then after opening the door, he climbs inside and gestures to go. I can sense that he really loves this place and doesn't like leaving, but work is work and we have a job to complete. The sat-nav that was programmed earlier starts to read out instructions on the long drive to Hull and, as we continue along even larger busier roads, I have a strange emotion that wishes deep down I was back at Grebe farm, enjoying the quietness and solitary life. Seeing all this traffic and people now feels quite strange after just a few days with Nick away from the hustle and bustle of my old life. A part of me seems to love the excitement, but a big part of me likes the quietness felt these last few days and the big question that is burning deep inside is can this change be one I could enjoy forever or is it just because it's different to my usual fast paced non-stop lifestyle? It remains to be seen. As we continue our journey north we reach the A1 and Nick has already been quietly asleep for most of the trip with almost no movement or even reaction. After three hours of driving, it's time for a quick break and now reading the motorway display boards for Peterborough service station. Trying to wake him up, I pull off the A1 and follow the car parking signs. Driving into an empty parking space close to the services, I stop the engine and Nick finally begins to wake from his deep sleep.

"Are we in Hull already?" he asks.

"Not yet, but I feel like a break and your snoring was becoming unbearable," I reply, laughing.

Opening the doors, my ears are instantly filled with the drumming noise of the motorway traffic rumbling past, we both climb out, then take a large stretch, Nick walks to the back of the car and takes out the rubbish bag. As we head towards the busy service station, he places the rubbish into a nearby bin. Walking in the red-tiled floors into the washroom, the off-white walls have the latest newspaper front pages displayed in glass fronted cabinets with the robbery still making the front pages of many tabloids even after almost a week. One newspaper shows a picture of Wagstaff standing by the wreckage of the helicopter slightly covered in a large white sheet as it is being loaded onto a lorry to be taken away. I finish in the washroom and walk out towards Burns who is now standing in the long queue for a drink.

Joining him, he asks, "I'm buying. What would you like, Dean?"

"Just a large coffee and a sandwich are fine, thanks, Nick. I'll go find a seat." He nods in agreement.

Turning, I walk towards the large seating area and notice a table with two chairs near the window. Reaching the table. I clear off the empty cups and place them onto another table close by that other people have left and sit looking through the window waiting for Nick. I watch the cars arriving and leaving to see if any of Wagstaff's agents are following us but no familiar vehicles are seen. Nick joins and, placing the tray onto the table, he sits as I start to remove one of the coffee drinks and the sandwich.

"How do you know they are yours?" Nick asks.

"A lucky guess," I reply, taking a sachet of sugar, a spoon and serviette.

"Hmm." Nick smiles.

"So my snoring kept you awake, hey?"

"Yes, thank you so much. You were even louder than the radio."

"I was enjoying a good sleep until I was interrupted." We both laugh.

"I see the robbery is still front page news."

"Yes, would you expect any more from Wagstaff?"

"Not really, Nick," I reply.

We continue with our drinks and sitting in the service station feels strange after spending the last few days at Nick's farm with no one else around.

Then a thought crosses my mind. "Do you think Wagstaff will start to publish our pictures in an attempt to try and flush out some enemies for reward money?" I ask.

"If he had any evidence he wouldn't have released you on Thursday," Nick replies, taking a sip of coffee.

"Well that's very true, Nick,"

"Wagstaff needs to be killed, doesn't he?" I ask, submissively.

Nick nods, acknowledging my question. "He will never stop until we are caught, dead, or both and I for one have no plans for either yet. I just want evidence from these traitors to confirm how much has been exposed."

"When do you think we will do it?"

"Keen, aren't you, Dean, hey? Let's deal with Thomas and Josef first then see where the trail leads. I haven't heard from Ramone and Carlos for a few days. That concerns me."

"Where do you think they are hiding?" I ask.

"Well, if they have gone back to Brazil they will be dead men, but I can't find out any information yet."

"Why did they leave Brazil, Nick?" I ask.

"That's a very long story," Nick replies.

"Well, we have a long trip." I take a sip of coffee to wash down some of the sandwich.

"True enough, but not here and not now, okay?" I sense Nick is concerned about who might hear.

We finish our drinks and food then begin the walk to the car park as the television station suddenly breaks over to a press conference with Wagstaff sitting behind a table draped in blue cloth material with two men sitting either side. Behind the three men is a large blue emblem of the Metropolitan Police logo as questions begin to be asked from news reporters.

"Director Wagstaff, can you confirm what is the status of the investigation?" one reporter asks.

"Following in depth investigation work from the site of the helicopter crash, I can confirm that it was not a terrorist attack."

"What leads the police to that conclusion?" another reporter asks.

"The type of explosives used along with the accuracy of the missile placement," Wagstaff replies.

"Director Wagstaff, what about the rumours that the money warehouse robbery and the helicopter crash were linked? Can you confirm any more news?" the first reporter asks.

"Yes, I can confirm both are linked. Evidence has been found on both scenes that link the two incidents. We also have some very strong leads and have already held some people for questioning."

"Director Wagstaff, can you confirm if these crimes were part of a secret government agency operation that went wrong?"

"I'm not sure where this information comes from, but what can be confirmed is that there are some strong lines of enquiry and we will very soon be apprehending some of the perpetrators involved."

"How can you say this, Mr Wagstaff?" the first reporter asks.

"Well, these people can't run forever and eventually they will make a mistake and my team and I will be waiting for them. I will be answering no further questions, thank you." Wagstaff can be seen standing and walking out of the room.

The two other men try to avoid any embarrassment by asking if there are any more questions. Both looking at each other, we walk out of the doors and return to the car to continue our journey to Hull. Nick walks to the rear passenger side and takes out a plastic bag. He reaches inside taking out two wigs.

"Here before we continue to Hull put this wig on. It's not much, but it might be enough to hide us through the security check." Nick hands over a black wig.

"I will look like right idiot in this!" I reply.

"You might look an idiot, but you should hopefully be a live idiot."

Climbing into the car, I pull the wig on and rearrange it to look as natural as possible and with no words exchanged between us, I drive away from the service station. I can sense Wagstaff's words have annoyed Nick by his expression, but I also know Nick won't be caught easily and will only be only interested in saving his own skin. Nick keeps adjusting the wig in an attempt to make it look normal.

My story will be a little different and maybe using Archibald's contact is the best option for the escape I need to plan. Reaching Hull Sunday afternoon, after the long drive with almost no words being exchanged between ourselves, we stop at the ferry check in queue and gradually begin to make our way in the car towards passport control. Sitting in the car, it feels like every single security camera and police officer is on the lookout for us both, but it could be just my senses on overload with the tidal wave of emotions from last week. As we reach the passport control, the security has been tightened with eight police officers standing holding machine guns and inspecting every person in each car and I hope that the different coloured hair is enough to hide us.

Nick looks across and winks as one police officer gestures to stop the car and lower the window. "Is this your car, sir?" he asks, looking inside.

"Yes, officer, I have owned it a couple of months," Nick replies.

"What is the nature of your trip overseas?" The officer leans closer towards the car.

"We have a business meeting in Antwerp and will be there a few days. Do you want to see the hotel bookings?" Nick stares back.

"Yes please, sir, and your passport?" He leans back.

"I need to fetch the documents from the boot."

"That's fine, sir, I wanted to check the luggage anyway." He instructs an officer to attend with a sniffer dog.

My heart sinks as Nick climbs out and makes his way to the back of the car. I hope Nick took out the guns and money from the bags, but I'm sure he is not that stupid. 'When did he book the hotel?' quickly rushes through my mind.

The officer can be heard speaking with Nick over our business as the dog sniffs all around the car.

The dog suddenly stops as it reaches my door and I can hear the handler saying, "What is it, Benny? What can you smell, hey?"

My heart sinks even lower as two other officers now begin to take an interest and my mind now kicks into overdrive as I think what the dog might have smelt with the car. Has Nick now set me up and will he use this as an escape plan? But to run from here would be total suicide as the dogs sniffing can be heard getting louder and louder as an officer asks me, "Please exit the vehicle, sir!"

Nick quickly realises what the dog may have smelt and starts to speak with the officer.

"I hit a roe deer a couple of days ago and it got stuck under the car. I called out the local gamekeeper who had to shoot it. Here, I have some pictures on my phone that I can show you."

The officer agrees and Nick takes the cell from his pocket and begins to show the officer.

"What was the name of the gamekeeper and where did it take place, Mr Forster?" The officer stares at him, looking at the passport.

"It was near Six Mile Bottom in Cambridge and the keeper was called Martin Clegg. He promised to cut me excellent joints that I can have in a few weeks," Nick replies

"I bet some smoke from the bullet is still near the door."

"Hmm." The officer begins to walk over as I climb out of the car.

"Six Mile Bottom, you say." The officer lifts his radio and presses the call button.

"Control, can you run a PNC check on a white Passat, reg number AG57 YPT. Also confirm the gamekeeper on Six Mile Bottom in Cambridge and any reported deer road kills, out." The officer lowers his radio and walks around to my side of the car.

"What's your name, sir?" he asks.

"Chris Jackson." I hand over my fake passport.

"You have business in Paris?" he asks.

Nick looks at me quickly as his head shakes very slightly.

"No, officer, in Antwerp as my colleague mentioned." The police radio begins to crackle.

"Sergeant Jones, repeat, Sergeant Jones."

"Yes, Control, come in," the sergeant replies.

"Sarg, the car is registered to MP Projects International Expeditors and has listed owner as Roger Forster. The gamekeeper at Six Mile Bottom, Martin Clegg, has recorded and registered a roe deer road kill on Wednesday last week."

"Okay, thanks Control. I am sorry, gentlemen, to have inconvenienced you but after last week everyone is on the highest security." The officer stands back and walks away.

"Officer, we fully understand and not a problem, you can't be too safe these days and thank you." Nick smiles, walks around and closes the boot lid then begins to climb back in to the driver's seat.

I smile back at the officer with the dog, as he drags it away and then it begins to show attention in a red minibus camper behind us. Lowering myself into the passenger seat, the door is closed and at the same time I take a huge sigh of relief as we start the engine and drive into the hull of the ship, following the directions of the boarding crew. The huge ships engines vibrate through the steel structure of the hull as we park the car and climb out, beginning to walk in the direction of the staircase. The floor of the hull deck is grass green with yellow lines indicating the safe walk routes and the gloss white steel structure has stain lines from where rust is forming between bolts and fasteners. Looking around the hull, people stand from their cars all neatly parked in rows, giving big stretches from their long journeys as the exhaust gases fill the air causing me to cough from the high amounts. I quickly wonder how on earth people can work in here with no form of protection against the harmful emissions. We continue up the central staircase of the ferry until we reach deck level nine and begin the walk along the narrow corridors to our cabins. Nick passes me the cabin key access card with number 9110.

My cabin is reached first and, stopping, I ask Nick, "What time shall we meet up?"

"Well, a quick shower and change, how about thirty minutes in the main bar?"

Nodding in agreement, the card is inserted into the door slot and the handle operated. The door is opened and I walk into the small cabin past the en suite bathroom on one side and small wardrobe on the other. The cabin has two single beds with white sheets with a porthole partly covered with light orange curtains. The light from the porthole makes the small cabin look bigger than it actually is but it's enough for tonight. I place the bag on the left bed and remove the black wig. Beginning to take out the toiletries ready for a shower and then, removing my clothes, I walk into the small bathroom and place the toiletries onto the small worktop surrounding the sink. Then, turning, I look at the shower cubicle that takes up a large corner of the bathroom behind a plain white curtain. Next to the mirror is a safety label that reads, *"Our cabins are protected by heat sensors that will be activated with steam from the shower. Always close the bathroom door."*

Closing the door, I walk into the shower then, drawing the curtain shut, turn on the water. After a few seconds the water is hot and following a refreshing shower I dry myself with the supplied towel and then walk back into the cabin to dress before drinks and dinner. As I dress my thoughts drift to the last few days and the revelations from Nick and my past. My mind searches for the truth but not knowing what is fact or fiction, other than Nick's words, I find it difficult to accept his statements. One fact is true, I remember working at Bennett's then at Harpers and Harpers, but thinking backwards I can't picture my past prior to these memories. I have never really given it much thought until now, but trying to find out the truth now hangs like a heavy weight around my neck. It is clear that Nick may be the only person with the answers is now clearly a different story with information from Archibald and his contacts. This information could also hold the key to the past I long to find.

Nick is a character that is calm and composed on the outside but underneath his skin lies an uncontrolled man that will stop at nothing until he gets his way and with these actions I feel a level of uncertainty when I am around him, making me uncomfortable. 'Why have I joined him on this killing spree?' flashes through my thoughts but a large part of me wants to see and feel what happens and if this was a part of my old life then reliving certain events may bring back the emotional aspects that for now are forgotten. Last week certainly confirmed to me that killing another person either by accident or by premeditated actions is probably the most difficult emotion to live with and having this guilt is a burden for the rest of your life. If what Nick is saying is true then this is the second time I must have lived through this guilty emotion so I find it strange I can't remember the previous experience. I look at my watch to see the thirty minutes is almost over so, quickly slipping on my shoes and then gathering my cell, door access card and wallet, I head down the corridor of the still moored ferry in the direction of the bar. Walking into the bar, Nick can be seen sitting by a table looking through the window and staring at the open sea and I wonder what fills his thoughts at this time.

"So you finally made it? I thought you may have jumped over the side to escape?" Nick asks without even looking at me.

"Well, the thought did cross my mind but I knew you couldn't complete this job without me," I reply, smiling.

"Very true." He turns and smiles, gesturing for me to join him.

We sit watching the people on the quayside walking about as the waitress asks what drink we would like. Both ordering a gin and tonic, we sit quietly and my mind thinks about the few days of training that Nick gave me and I hope that I don't let him down.

The waitress brings the drinks over along with some snack food and places them on the round table as Nick asks, "What time does the restaurant open?"

Looking at Nick, she replies, "Thirty minutes after cast off. Do you want a table reserved?"

"Yes, that would be great, thank you. The name is Jackson." Nick looks at me smiling.

"Oh, so I pay the bill today, hey?" I reply in a sarcastic tone.

"That will be ten pounds, sir, thank you." The waitress smiles.

"Could you reserve a table for tonight?" I reply, taking out my wallet.

"Which restaurant, sir, would you like to dine?" she asks.

"What do you have?" Nick asks.

"A la carte menu or buffet," she answers.

"A la carte please, seeing as he is paying." Nick smiles at me.

"I hope you have some rubber gloves for washing up 'cause I'm not paying a la carte." I laugh, giving the waitress the £10.00.

The waitress looks at me as to answer yes or no so I reply by saying, "A la carte is fine, thank you."

"At what time, gentleman, would you like to dine?" She takes out a pad from her pocket and begins to write down the information.

"As soon as these drinks are over and we cast off." Nick lifts his glass.

"Will 7.30 p.m. be fine?" she asks.

Lifting my glass, I say, "Cheers, that will be fine." The waitress walks away.

"Are you ready, Dean, for what we are going to happen these next few days?" Nick asks.

"I think so, but it was close earlier, thought the police had caught us." I look around the bar casually to see who is close by.

"Never panic, Dean, there is always a way out of everything and having a plan B is critical." Nick takes a sip of his drink.

"I'm just not as confident as you, Nick," I reply.

"Well, someone once told me anything is possible if you put your mind to it and stop at nothing until you get what you want." Nick stares at a couple walking into the bar.

"Really, who was that?" I lift the glass to my lips, taking a sip.

"You!" he answers.

Not saying another word, we continue to sit looking through the windows eating some of the nibble food and sip our drinks. The ship's engines begin to increase, then the ship begins to move, sending vibrations through the super structure and the glasses behind the bar resonate and judder. As the land begins to be left behind the ferry gradually rocks on the water now free of its moorings. Finishing our drinks, we leave the glasses and make our way to the restaurant on the next deck higher, opposite the small casino and duty free shop, which are now both open. Reaching the entrance of the partly filled restaurant, we stand and the feeling of the ship gradually swaying on the water can be felt.

Giving our names, the maître d' lifts out two menu cards and shows the way to a table and, as we walk through the restaurant, both of us scan around the people for any possible signs of threats. We reach a table overlooking the sea through a round porthole window. Sitting each side of the square table, the cutlery is already set along with red and white wine glasses with serviettes neatly folded.

A second waiter walks over to the table, saying, "Good evening, gentlemen, my name Alfredo and I will be serving you tonight." He places a wine list on the table.

"Good evening," we both reply, beginning to open the menus.

"Gentlemen, the soup of the day is cream of mushroom and the fish is salmon served on a bed of asparagus and hollandaise sauce. I will return in few minutes to take your orders." The waiter walks away.

Looking through the menu I don't feel very hungry, but know we have a long trip ahead wanting to reach Berlin as soon as possible. Deciding on a mushroom soup followed by a chicken breast in white wine sauce, I lower the food menu to the table and lift the wine list.

"I will drive the other side if you want a drink, Nick?" I ask.

"Well, that's very good of you, old boy, many thanks." The wine list is passed over.

Nick asks, "What are you eating, Dean?"

"Mushroom soup and chicken breast." I reply.

"Red or white wine?" he asks.

"A light white for me but only a small glass."

"Hmm, white will be fine for me since I'm having salmon and you are paying," he laughs.

The waiter returns. "Are you ready to order, gentleman?"

Nick starts. "The king prawns and then salmon for me please."

"Very good and you, sir?" The waiter turns to me.

"Mushroom soup and then chicken breast."

"Any wine, gentleman?"

"A bottle of the Pinot noir," Nick replies.

"Along with a bottle of water please," I add.

"Very good, gentleman." The waiter removes the red wine glasses.

Travelling out to sea, the ferry gracefully sways on the water. As I look through the windows, the topography of the land melts into the flatness of the shoreline with the sea air filling my lungs. In the distance, the blades of the wind turbines slowly rotate from the sea breeze, causing the red warning lights to flicker against the ever-darkening sky. The sun, now turning orange as it disappears below the horizon, sends its last rays glimmering across the surface of the water, closing another day. My mind now begins to drift to the beginning of a new life as I watch every cloud floating away in the hazy purple sky. The night now begins to take over as the sight of other ships' lights sparkling in the distance compete against the star constellations winking against the black canvas. A new light begins to shimmer on the surface of the water as the hunter's moon glows ever brighter, signifying that the hunt for Thomas and Josef is not far away.

12

As we travel on the ferry, Shaun makes his way towards O'Neil's Irish bar thinking about the information that he will be told and what the outcome could be after less than one week of Chloe and his unborn child being killed. With not sleeping properly for over three days his mind is totally confused and his emotions are racing through his body as the door is opened and he walks into the bar. At the far side of the bar a familiar person can be seen sitting at a table enjoying a late afternoon drink of whisky and Shaun's heart sinks even further.

Shaun, with bowed head, walks over and as before greets the frail old man sitting in a wheelchair with a handshake and, "Good evening, sir."

"Mr Neal, please take a seat," the old man replies.

"So, Shaun, how are you doing? Because you look terrible," the old man asks.

"I've had better weeks, sir," Shaun replies as the red haired barmaid, Kelly, approaches the table.

Looking across at him she asks, "Are you okay, Shaun? You look ill."

"Thanks, Kelly, everyone appears to be saying the same. A large Jameson's and ice," he snaps back.

The old man takes a sip of whisky and then as the barmaid walks away he speaks. "Why haven't I received any field reports for the last few weeks, Neal?"

"I've had a few problems of my own this last couple of days," Shaun replies.

"Really, and what has that got to do with me?" the man asks.

Kelly brings over a large tumbler of whisky and places it on the table, staring at Shaun with a look of despair on her face. He quickly lifts the glass, taking a big sip, saying, "Another one, please."

Shocked, Kelly turns and walks away to fetch another drink.

"I take it from your condition and the amount of whisky you have just swallowed that your problems involve a woman?" the old man asks.

With a redness beginning to develop in his eyes, Shaun nods his head, saying, "Yes Mr McGough."

"You fuckin' idiot, Neal, your task was simple enough, but you have even managed to fuck that up. I stuck my neck out for you and this is how you repay me!" McGough has aggression in his voice, taking a sip of whisky as Shaun turns his glass on the table.

"I will make it right if you just tell me who killed Chloe," Shaun asks.

"Argh, the woman that was killed Monday with her husband, carrying your baby, yes?" McGough smiles across at a shocked Shaun.

"How did you know?" Shaun asks.

"Neal, I may be old but I'm not stupid. I know everything, especially those that work for me. So what would you do to the person that killed your beloved Chloe?" McGough asks, taking another sip of whisky.

"Kill the fuckin' bastard!" Shaun snaps back then takes another big gulp of whisky, emptying his glass.

"Really, so how will you find this person?" The old man looks at Shaun, waving across to the barmaid for his second drink.

"You know me, sir, I'm always resourceful." Shaun tries to smile.

"Really, so where is your target at the moment?" McGough asks.

"He was ill at work on Wednesday and was sent home," he replies, turning the empty glass on the table.

"So where is he now, Neal? Sitting in his flat waiting for his loyal friend to check on him?" McGough takes another sip of his drink.

"Mr McGough, I have done everything that you and this fuckin' agency have requested from me and much more apart from babysitting your precious boy." Shaun glances across towards the bar to see Kelly looking at him.

"I'm sure my precious boy feels ever so much better knowing that his loyal friend looks over him getting drunk?" He stares at Shaun over his glasses and continues.

"Neal, you were given a specific task, but instead you have decided to make the most of your undercover surveillance by fornicating with every woman you have spoken to. This is not what you were hired to do and my patience with you is running out. I've made a mistake in hiring you and I will correct that mistake before the end of today." The old man speaks again with venom in his voice as he finishes his drink and begins to reverse the wheelchair from the table.

"I don't know where Nash is, I haven't been around to see him yet." Shaun tries to smile at Kelly as she lowers the second whisky glass onto the table and walks away.

"Maybe you had better start trying to find Nash and forget your self-pity because I know for a fact that he hasn't been at that flat for over two days now as you drown yourself in guilt." McGough leans on the table slightly.

"What about the person that killed Chloe?" Shaun begins to stand.

"That's simple, Neal, one will lead to the other." The wheelchair buzzes into action as McGough begins to move forward in the direction of the door.

Shaun stands with a look of puzzlement on his face as the words from his handler's mouth digest through his mind as the puzzle is completed and it suddenly clicks into place. "Nash?" Shaun shouts.

The chair stops near the door where two a male agents now stand waiting and looking over his right shoulder, McGough smiling and nodding as Shaun sits back down in his chair.

Kelly comes back to the table and touches Shaun on the shoulder, asking, "What's wrong, baby?" McGough turns the wheelchair around and begins to drive back to the table.

"Just leave me alone, Kelly," Shaun snaps out as the whirring of the chair's electric motors gets ever louder and he shrugs off her hand.

Kelly quickly walks away with tears welling in her eyes as McGough reaches the table.

"Bring Nash to me alive and I will reward you." McGough stares at Shaun.

Shaun, looking back, begins to have tears welling in his eyes replies back, "What do you mean, sir?"

"What reward?" Shaun asks.

"You can have Nash when I've finished and that way we can both get justice." Shaun looks back at McGough with a smile beginning to shape on his face.

Nodding in agreement, Shaun speaks with emotion from his voice. "Okay, sir, you have a deal. I will contact you when his fuckin' body lies at my feet."

McGough, smiling, reverses the chair and makes his way again towards the door where the two agents stand like statues. "Good luck, old boy, and take care of yourself. I will be in touch once confirmation of Nash's whereabouts is known."

Shaun, looking into the whisky glass, begins to turn the tumbler, watching the teardrop of brown liquid running down the clear surface. His mind begins to plot how to catch Nash and safely deliver him to McGough, but also what torture can be inflicted on him. Taking the glass, Neal lifts it to his lips and in one gulp takes the whisky into his mouth and swallows it. Standing, he takes a twenty pound note from his pocket and throws it onto the table as he quickly walks in the direction of the door, completely ignoring Kelly who is standing at the bar sobbing and trying to gain his attention. Shaun, pulling the door open, storms out of the bar with only one thing on his mind: the capture of Nash and the pain he will inflict for killing Chloe.

Nick and I continue eating and drinking whilst in the cabaret lounge, live entertainment begins with a woman singing her adaptations of the latest songs from easy listening music. After paying for our meals we walks towards the cabaret bar area. Reaching the bar we order drinks and walk through to where the glass fronted balcony overlooks the small stage. The singer is approximately twenty-five years old, medium build and quite pretty with short brown hair. Her voice breaks slightly at a few of the high notes, but most of the crowd are half drunk anyway so don't notice. Nick seems very quiet and withdrawn, hardly saying a word as the singer continues through her set and clearly he is deep in thought over how the breach of security from Josef and Thomas talking with Wagstaff has annoyed him. The seriousness of our situation now begins to unfold and the thoughts of extracting information from these traitors overwhelms my emotions with fear and excitement, wondering what pain Nick will inflict on them. Thomas and Josef will now be judged for their actions but deep in the back of my mind it's clear that one day both Nick and myself will also have the same fate, with Wagstaff and his team the people serving the sentence.

My inner confidence grows with every passing hour and I feel as though nothing will stop us from finding out the truth. Looking across to Nick I now feel that we have a strong bond of loyalty between us but also know it could be short lived. I begin to think back to the Friday night when we first met and how much of a threat I felt in that back room of Castro's. Who would have thought barely one week later that we would have carried out a successful robbery, escaped police capture and now be heading to Germany to seek revenge. The last weeks tidal wave of emotions, range from the blackest days after the robbery, with the guilt I felt after killing those people to the highs of evading Wagstaff and his team on several occasions. My thoughts move to the few hours in the prison cell and, not having much time to reflect since that day, I try to scroll back in my mind to remember when I had been in this situation before, but it seems more like an old foggy image and not a true memory. One point is clear, being locked up for years in the four walls of a cell will never be an option for me and the freedom being experienced now reminds me of a life that I once had but why I left it is still unclear.

"Time for bed, Dean, we have a long day tomorrow," Nick announces.

"Yes, very true." His words break my thoughts.

We both stand from the table and, leaving the glasses behind, begin the short walk out of the bar then down the spiral staircase heading along the dull white corridors back to our separate cabins with the occasional swaying of the ferry being felt.

Taking the paper door card from my pocket and placing it next to the lock, I turn and say, "Goodnight, Nick, and I wish you a pleasant sleep."

Looking at me walking past, he smiles, then replies, "Don't let the bed bugs bite, Dean."

Opening the door, I watch Nick continue to walk down the corridor and, stepping into the cabin, I close the door and start to undress ready for bed. With the time quickly reaching ten forty-five, a well-earned sleep is needed before the long day tomorrow. But as I lay in the bed with the casual rocking of the ferry the pictures shown to me by Wagstaff quickly begin to flash through my mind and I start to imagine the blood covered bodies of Thomas and Josef laying on the ground after their interrogation by Nick is over. Trying to shut out these thoughts, I begin to focus on the swaying motion of the ferry that after some time relaxes my mind and I fall asleep.

Awaking in the morning, the weak morning sunshine fights through the sea mist floating above the surface of the water. The blurred image of container ships can be seen moored up, waiting for their turn to unload at the docks with the huge payloads reaching for their place in the sky. We meet for breakfast and, after the waiter has shown us to the table and taken our orders, we start to discuss the plans in more detail.

"Okay, Dean, we need to drive over the border into Germany then plan for a hire car since we need our car for escape back." Nick takes a drink of his coffee.

"Well, we can arrange a car en route," I reply.

"Once we are in Berlin we need to meet my contact, Stefan, who will give me updates of Thomas and Josef along with handing over some weapons."

"Where do you know Stefan from?" I ask inquisitively.

"We go way back to the early eighties and I can vouch for his intel."

"What then?" I ask with excitement in my voice.

"You're looking forward to this, hey?" Nick replies.

"Hmm, yeah, I guess so."

"Well, then we need to wait until our ex colleagues arrive and we will welcome them with open arms."

"Open arms, or open fire?"

"A bit of both, to be honest."

"I want to be in and out quickly before both the authorities and their handlers realise what has happened," Burns replies.

We continue with our breakfast and the thoughts of killing these two guys after all the trouble they have caused feels so exciting with a level of nervousness hanging in my mind. Nick has clearly done this type of work many times before and apparently so have I but it feels strange and fresh like the first day in a new job.

Finishing our breakfasts, we return to the cabins for the long journey ahead and, taking the paper door card from my pocket, I open the door and walk into the small portside cabin. Once all the final pieces of clothing and washroom products are collected, they are placed into the small case, zipping it shut. Lying on the opposite single bed, my eyes are closed and the vibrations coming from the super structure resonate through the whole ferry as it gradually begins to slow as it reaches its place at the Euro port quay. The ship finally lurches to a stop as the ropes take the strain of the ferry and the tannoy system whistles, announcing that we have arrived and passengers can now make their way to the stairwells on car deck five. Standing from the bed, I reach for the bag and, making my way to the door, quickly scan around the cabin for any traceable items. The autumn sun now burning through the sea mist begins to warm my face as it slowly rises higher in the sky. On the other side of the door, people can already be heard walking along the narrow corridors and doors bang shut as they rush for the stairwells.

Opening the door, Nick is already starting to make his way down the pale green corridor along the reddish brown patterned carpet and as he is caught up he turns and smiles, knowing the next part of our journey is payback. Reaching the stairwell on deck eight, the queue of people is already beginning to slowly twist downwards onto the car deck.

Following Burns, we reach the Passat and, as he clicks the remote, it unlocks and the interior and sidelights wake into action, illuminating the dark corner of the ferry deck where we have parked. Opening the rear boot door, the cases are placed inside and we climb into the front seats as the side door of the ferry finally opens, allowing some much wanted fresh air and morning sunshine into the staleness felt inside the ferry deck. As the cars begin to move the deck fills with exhaust fumes, poisoning what little clean air has reached inside the confined space of the hull and the ferry attendant then signals our turn to move. We begin to move forward and my mind fills with what could happen and, lifting my sunglasses, I place them over my eyes. Reaching the outside world from the hull we continue towards customs clearance and passport control. Nick, turning slightly to the left, drives along one of the main central lanes, knowing that these guys will be the quickest with most cars passing this way. He stops behind the queue of three cars and gradually edges forward as finally our turn at the cabin is reached. I open my door window and hand over the two passports. The border patrol office takes them, has a quick look and hands them back with almost no hesitation.

Driving forward, we continue past the customs zone, turning left and following the all traffic road signs. Nick announces, "Well, that was easy enough. Look for the road signs for A15 and A20 and the sign for Osnabruck that will take us towards the German border."

I reply, "Yes, that was far easier than airport trouble."

"Dean, take out my cell from the front pocket of the bag behind and start to look for hire car rental on the German side near the border."

Reaching in the back, I open the front flap and take out his cell. Swiping the front the unlock code is required and Nick says, "6842." So pressing the keypad buttons, the cell is unlocked and, quickly checking the network coverage, I begin to search for car rental companies in North Rhine Westfalen region.

Knowing Nick's taste in cars I look for Audi or BMW deals for unlimited kilometres and, quickly finding several options, find a rental office not too far away from the boarder.

"Okay, have found an Audi A4 TDI deal at Salzbergen Europcar for seventy-five euros per day or four days for two hundred and twenty-five euros with unlimited kilometres."

"That sounds good, so book it online and use the MasterCard in the front pocket."

Reaching back again, I take out the card and book it straight away, starting from that afternoon at 12 p.m. as Nick joins the A20 with signs for the E30 en route for the border.

"Okay, it's booked, Nick."

He replies, "Good, now check for local parking in the area to see where we can leave the car for a few days."

Typing in the request, the slow internet begins to search and after a few seconds several places appear. "There is a department store secure parking, some local general public parking or, wait, this is better, a railway station."

"Perfect, and a foreign car parked for a few days will be fine."

"Sounds perfect. Type the address into the sat-nav system," Nick instructs.

Completing the task, I observe the heavy lines of trucks moving slowly on the opposite side of the road towards the port and watch Nick easily drives past the lines of trucks on our side of the carriageway, sensing he has driven many times on the continent. Keeping well within the speed limits, we continue to follow the sat-nav directions being shown on the system as my mind drifts to what will happen when we catch up with Thomas and Josef. It is clear he will stop at nothing until he gets the answers that are being searched for. My emotions are full both of anticipation and a sense of nervousness after remembering the pictures Wagstaff showed me as I look out across the flat arable land of the Netherlands. Trees and hills gradually begin to form on the horizon as we reach ever closer to the German border and, checking the clock in the car, it has taken just less than two hours. The border signs are quite evident but the sudden increase in the speed of the traffic confirms we are now travelling on the autobahn with several cars now overtaking our what appears to be slow speed.

Quickly glancing across, the speedometer that reads one hundred and sixty kilometres per hour. The sat-nav instructions inform us to leave the A30 and head towards Salzbergen. So, turning off the autobahn, we follow the signs as per the route and join a road lined with trees on one side and open fields on the other. The sun, still shining bright, illuminates all the green fields burning off the last of the morning mist and exposing the freshly cut silage grass covered in storks and herons. The smell of fresh soil fills the car as we pass a tractor starting to plough in the last of the cereal roots with hundreds of seagulls follow behind the cabin looking for a late breakfast snack.

Continuing along the A65, the trees and fields begin to disappear, being overtaken by occasional houses and commercial properties, then passing the sign for Salzbergen we drive into the city, following the railway station signs. Nick sees a sign for a fuel station so, pulling onto the forecourt, he decides to fill up.

"We may not have time when we return so better refuel now. I will buy some bottled water for the long journey."

I nod my head in agreement and pass him the credit card from the centre console where I left it from earlier. He climbs out and walks to the back side of the car, opening the fuel cap. The metallic noise of the pump nozzle being inserted into filler pipe clinks through the bodywork, and then the whirring of the pump as the fuel starts to fill the tank. The smell of fuel fills the inside of the car from Nick's slightly opened door window and after several minutes the pump stops with him knocking the nozzle in the pipe. He closes the cap and walks towards the main office and, entering the building, he collects two bottles of water. Reaching the counter, he hands over the credit card. He can be seen exchanging conversation with the young lady behind the counter and after she hands back the card he turns and walks out. Reaching the car, he opens the door and passes me the two bottles then slides onto the driver's seat. Inserting the key he starts the engine, clicks in his seatbelt then, engaging first gear, we drive away continuing along the same road. Driving past the car hire office we continue to follow the signs for the parking that is indicated five hundred metres away for the railway station.

Nick turns at the infill lane and stops next to the barrier, taking the token from the meter. The barrier lifts, allowing us to drive inside and slowly moving around the partly filled parking lot, his well-trained eyes search for a safe place to leave the car away from cameras near the back of the lot. There is an area with overhanging trees near the right-hand side so, quickly reversing the car into the parking bay three spaces away from the trees, the engine is stopped and we both climb out. Taking the bags, the doors are closed and the car is locked as we walk in the direction of the rental office. Our eyes scan everywhere for any possible threats and the position and type of surveillance cameras fitted near the car park. We cross the almost empty road and reach the rental office car parking with a grey Audi A4 with HH number plates seen in between a red Fiat 500 and silver Skoda Octavia. I open the office door for Nick and, reaching the inside, a young man speaks.

"Guten morgen, wie kann ich dir helfen?"

Nick, speaking in fluent German, replies, "Guten Morgen ich hete gerne ine Reserviet fur eine Auto?"

My mind untangles the conversation that I follow.

"Do you have the booking confirmation?" the man asks.

Nick, taking out his cell, opens the confirmation email. "Yes, 456DTES."

"Argh, yes, you placed the request this morning. You are in luck, I have the Audi as requested."

"All good," Nick replies.

"The booking is four days, correct?" He reaches over the counter for the keys.

"Correct," Burns replies.

"Can I have driving license and identification card?"

Nick hands them over.

"Oh, I see you're English?"

"Yes, is that a problem?"

"No, your German is very good. Are you the only driver?"

"Yes, I am the only driver," Nick replies.

The young man types all the details into the computer and then, handing back the documents, asks, "Do you have the credit card for payment?"

Nick, taking the documents, hands over the credit card.

"Thank you, where are you travelling to?" the man asks.

"We have friends in Osnabruck that we are visiting for a few days."

"Oh, okay sir," he replies, not really interested.

"You have basic cover and excess of nine hundred euros. Do you want to pay an extra ten euros per day and reduce excess to zero with all accident damage covered?"

Nick replies, "Yes, thank you, this may be a good idea." He looks back at me, smiling.

"Sir, I will block a total of five hundred and fifteen euros on the card including the two hundred and fifty euros deposit that will be given on the return."

"Okay," Nick replies as the man hands back the card.

The printer starts to whirr into action as the contract is printed off. After a few seconds, he rips off the paperwork and, lifting it to the counter, begins to explain. "This line shows the person who the contract agreement is with. This section is the driver and this section covers the accident coverage. The last section covers if you are involved in an accident you need to contact the police, or for any speeding offences your details will be sent to the police."

"Fine, no issues," Nick replies.

"Good, now signatures are required here, here and here," He points to the paper document.

"The car has inbuilt sat-nav and is a diesel. The tank is full and needs to be returned with a full tank or you will be charged this amount." He points to another part of the contract showing the refuel costs.

"There is no damage on the vehicle but this scale of measurement will be used, okay?" He indicates to a paper scorecard.

"Dankeschon," Nick replies.

The young man hands over the keys from behind the counter and looks at Nick. "I wish you a safe journey and see you in a few days."

Nick, taking the keys, smiles and turns. He walks towards the direction of the door with me following behind. As he reaches for the door handle the young man suddenly says, "Oh, you also have unlimited kilometres, I forgot to mention before."

Nick, opening the door, replies, "Dankeschon, young, man and wish you a good day."

I walk outside towards the car as Nick closes the office door and clicks the central locking button. As the headlights illuminate, the doors unlock and, walking towards the back of the car parked next to a weld mesh fence, the trunk button is depressed and the lid opens. Placing my suitcase inside the trunk, he joins me and, lowering his bag next to mine, the lid is closed. Opening the front passenger door, the scent of fresh leather engulfs my senses that increase even more from the smell only a new car emits as l climb inside and slide onto the seat. Nick slips behind the driver's wheel and quickly adjusts the seat and mirrors for his comfort before closing the door and pushing the engine start button. The engine roars into action as I pull the door shut, knowing he will be moving forward almost immediately and with a look of anger in his eyes he quickly pulls away from the parking space. We stop by the exit of the parking lot and, joining the road quickly, begin our journey back towards the A2 and Berlin.

"Okay, Dean, set the sat-nav to English and plot us the quickest course to Leipzig city centre. I think there is a Best Western."

"Leipzig? Why Leipzig? I thought we were going to Berlin?"

"Change of plan, old boy, new intel confirms our guys are in Leipzig."

"No problem, Nick, just a bit surprised."

"Well, on the ferry I received some intel with a definite sighting of both in Leipzig so we will pick up supplies from my contact." Nick has a level of excitement in his voice.

As we continue towards our new route my mind plays over how easy it was to understand the German conversation between Nick and the assistant in the car rental office. Like many other recent events, it feels like a jigsaw puzzle is gradually beginning to be constructed in front of my eyes, detailing much information from my past life and with a hunger burning deep down inside to absorb more as though I need to search answers over the truth of what really has happened to me. Knowing for sure Nick is one part of this great big puzzle fills me both with a level of security and at the same time a curse since he is the only person who appears to know what I truly am. But one thing is for certain, I'm the only person who is responsible for my actions and the thoughts of reaping revenge with Nick against Thomas and Josef are top on my list. After all, they also betrayed me with their actions. It fills me with an excitement burning bright like a flaming torch. Nick and I reach the Leipzig Allez main railway station and, parking the car, we walk into the busy station then sit at one of the bars, ordering a beer each and waiting for any news from his contact. Suddenly a message is delivered to his cell and, lifting it from the tabletop, Nick opens the message and with a smile appearing quickly across his face I know the news is good.

"Got the bastard at last!" With one gulp Nick finishes his beer and throws a ten-euro note on the table and gestures for me to move.

Quickly finishing my drink, we both head off in the direction of the hire car with Nick walking at such a fast pace it feels almost like we are running. Throwing me the keys, I unlock the car and, climbing inside, we wait for his informant to arrive. It's already late afternoon and following the long drive from Europort we watch the last of the commuters beginning to disperse from the railway station. A dark blue Mercedes C class slowly drives onto the parking lot as we wait, watching the approaching car.

"Here is my guy." Nick smiles and quickly flicks the headlight switch.

The driver, noticing the lights, continues in our direction. As the car draws alongside our vehicle with the boots parallel to each other, I casually look across at the contact. He is a middle-aged guy with scruffy brown hair and a short beard. Nick and the informant both climb out and meet between the two parked cars, giving each other a big hug. Both begin talking in German. I can follow some of the conversation but not all.

"Hey, Stefan, how is business going?" Nick asks.

"All good, and you? What about the money sorting house robbery? It was all over the news here, were you involved?"

"No, it was too amateur for me," Burns replies.

"So these two men, why are you after them?" Stefan asks.

"They fled the country owing a lot of money to some acquaintances of mine and since I have a German contact I have been approached to find them."

"Are they going back to the UK when you catch them?" Stefan asks inquisitively.

"Maybe in parts!" Nick replies and hands over a brown envelope to Stefan.

"The usual finder's fee I assume is okay, my clients haven't made up their minds on their lives yet. My task is to locate, apprehend and hold until the client decides. Do you have the equipment I asked for?"

"Yes, it's in the trunk."

I look around, watching the commuters going about their usual business then climbing into cars and exiting the parking lot. It's clear with being the only cars left we will quickly become visual targets for anybody looking. Burns, now standing at the back of Stefan's car, leans inside and takes out a folded plastic sheet and tucks it under his left arm then lifts out a rucksack bag and by how he holds it I can see it's heavy with equipment. Stefan then closes the lid and, looking in my wing mirror, two security guards can be seen walking from the railway station in our direction as Burns reaches our car and opens the boot lid, placing the bag and sheet inside. After a few seconds he closes the lid as Stefan has already climbed into his car and starts the engine with the guards about a hundred metres away. Nick returns to the driver side of the car carrying a rucksack.

"Hey, what are you guys doing? The station is now closed," one of the guards shouts in an aggressive German voice.

'Just leave' races through my mind as Nick slowly opens the door and shouts back a reply in German, leaning across the car.

"Yes, gentlemen, my brother had some groceries for me. I was late leaving work. We are going now." Nick waves then smiles and lowers the rucksack into the footwell. He slides into the car and I quickly start the engine as he closes the door, I begin to move away.

"That's all we want is two rent-a-cop pricks now giving shit," Burns snarls.

Stefan has already reached the exit and is pulling onto the main road, accelerating away as we begin to move.

The second guard shouts across, "Okay, but this isn't a meeting place." The guards smile to each other.

"Leave it, Nick, it's not worth an answer to them arseholes."

"His answer will be a fuckin' empty bullet case if he carries on."

Just then a police car pulls onto the car park. Nick, seeing the threat, quickly takes out a handgun from the rucksack and pushes it between the underside of his right thigh and the seat surface. The police car drives past ourselves and stops next to the security guards. I reach the exit and casually drive away from the station in an opposite direction to Stefan, as instructed by Nick.

I constantly scan the rear view mirror and the road in front for any possible threats as my heart feels to be in my mouth from the excitement. Then we continue towards the address given for Thomas. Eventually, we reach a group of modern apartment buildings and I park on a side road close enough to see the main entrance, then stop the engine. In the subdued lighting Nick takes out two pairs of latex gloves and handing one pair to me gestures to pull them on. Reaching back into the rucksack he then pulls out another pistol giving it to me. We then check the handguns and wait for Thomas to arrive. Some of the apartments have the shutters open and the occupants can be seen moving around. My heart beat remains calm and controlled even with every passing car and person as the time quickly moves to an hour. In the faint darkness the image of a person walking in the shadows begins to take the interest of Nick, taking a silencer from rucksack he slowly attaches it onto the barrel threads and I know by these actions, it's Thomas who is approaching. Switching off the interior light, Nick then indicates for us to get out of the car and, after gently closing the doors, we make our way in the direction of the apartment entrance. He gestures at a block of garages on the opposite side of the street and as I gradually cross in the near darkness as the image of the person now becomes more apparent. With his curly dark residing headline and pointed nose there is no confusion over the person being Thomas.

Reaching the side of the garages, I look across to see Nick disappearing into the cover of the hedge by the entrance and with each approaching footstep my heart beat increases with the adrenaline pumping faster. Walking into the main entrance gate of the apartment complex, a single pop is heard from the silenced gun as Thomas collapses to the ground. Running back to the car pushing the pistol into my jacket pocket, I start the engine and drive towards the entrance without any headlights as Nick drags Thomas's lame body out into the street under the cover of the hedge and a large tree. Pushing the button for the boot, the lid opens automatically and, stopping the car, I climb out to assist Nick with the body. Firstly I place the bag on the back seat, then unwrap the plastic sheet covering the inside boot space and taking the cable ties that now rest on the opened sheet pass some over to Burns.

Thomas's wrists and ankles are bound, then with me by his feet and Nick by his arms we lift him into the boot placing him onto the thick plastic sheet. Closing the lid softly, Burns scans around the flats and houses, to see if any attention has been drawn by our actions and, being satisfied, he gestures to move. Making his way to the passenger side, I slide onto the driver's seat and begin to move along the noisy cobbles, switching on the headlights as we make our way onto the main road.

Unscrewing the silencer from the handgun, Nick places it into his jacket pocket, finally pushing the gun behind his trouser belt. Reaching the road junction, we continue straight towards the town of Jesewitz along the B87. We drive out of the city quickly reaching Jesewitz where we continue for the small village of Gostemitz. Entering the village just past the main Catholic Church, he indicates to turn left down a small lane. Driving along the narrow lane, the car headlights illuminate the row of trees down the left side and open fields opposite. We continue along the single lane as another driver wishes to pass, so pulling into a lay-by the car gradually continues past. The male and female occupants stare at us as they pass, wondering who we are with both Nick and I ignoring the temptation to look at them. We drive another two hundred metres then turn into an old derelict farmhouse courtyard with a large barn to the right. Stopping by the large arched doors of the barn and with the engine still running, we climb out and walk towards the back of the car. The boot catch is released and the body of Thomas lays dormant inside. Reaching inside for his feet, he murmurs slightly as Nick grabs him by the arms. The victim is then lifted out and we take him towards the doors.

"Drop his feet and get the door catch, Dean, there's a light switch on the right side of the wall," Nick instructs.

So, dropping his feet, I fumble in the light from the car headlights to open the catch and pull the door open. Feeling along the coldness of the stonewall inside the barn, I finally sense the switch and with a loud *'click'*, light illuminates through the darkness of the building. Walking back out to Nick, I lift his feet and we carry Thomas into the barn. The barn inside has large wooden roof joists that span the complete width of the roof space. To the right of the wooden access door is a large wooden workbench with tools and old cardboard boxes stored on the top. The rest of the barn has old ropes, chains and different farming equipment hanging from the walls from rusty nails with an old grey tractor partly covered by a dark brown sheet in the far left corner. In the far right back corner of the barn are piles or split logs covered in cobwebs as though they have not been touched for years and as we walk on the soil floor dust gracefully rises into the air.

"Place him on the floor below the roof joist," Nick indicates.

Lowering him to the soil floor, Nick walks to one of the main stone columns and, taking a length of rope, walks back and as he does so begins to tie a slipknot into one end.

"Lift his feet and take the shoes off." Nick throws the length of rope over the roof joist.

He attaches the end of the rope around his ankles then quickly checks his body for anything that could be used as a knife then begins to gradually lift Thomas's body up until he is partly suspended upside down with his shoulders still touching the ground.

"Now let's leave this bastard here while we have something to eat." Both turning around, we walk out of the barn in the direction of the door.

With the engine still running, we climb back into the car and drive away from the barn. My mind begins to imagine what possible torture is going to be inflicted onto Thomas. You can see the aggression in Nick's eyes and for sure it will not be pleasant. My body shakes with excitement and nervousness, knowing that this will be something I can't remember experiencing before and the thought of being part of killing another man feels so wrong but we both know it must be done for self-preservation. The fears from last week have now disappeared and with the refresher training from Nick certain parts of my old life begin to fall into place with an added confidence. Driving past a small petrol station, Nick turns onto the forecourt and we climb out, making our way inside removing the latex gloves as we walk. Nick speaking perfect German, ensuring we blend in and not drawing attention asks what food is available. The shop is in the final stages of closing for the night and apart from ourselves there are two men and three women rushing around the store fetching beer and some meat for a late barbeque.

As the food is being purchased, including some bread, cheese and salami, a lonely security guard makes an entrance, probably in an attempt to hurry things along and get everyone out. Bagging the food and returning to the car with hardly a word uttered between us, we then begin to drive away on the journey back to the farmhouse as a solitary police car passes, showing no interest. Continuing along the narrow road we eventually turn back through the entrance and onward to the barn. Stopping by the wooden arched door, I climb out of the car, carrying the bag of food with the darkness of the night now overwhelming my senses and for a few seconds, it makes me feel as though I'm being suffocated. Shrugging off these feelings of fear, I notice Nick has begun to open the door and, walking into the barn, the adrenaline starts to pump around my body making my legs feel a little rubbery with each footstep. Nick reaches for the light switch and with one click the darkness of the night suddenly disappears, revealing Thomas still suspended from the roof joist.

Walking over, Nick pulls back on the gloves and then kicks him in the mid-section, causing him to moan in pain as he says, "There's plenty more for you yet, bastard, don't go asleep on me yet."

Placing the paper food bag onto the top of the old large wooden workbench, I take out the contents and, using the bag as a plate, arrange the food on top. I can hear Nick beginning to unhook the rope and then he continues to lift Thomas off the ground until he is fully suspended. Walking over towards the workbench, he takes out a small pocket knife and, placing it next to the food, gestures for me to start cutting. He lifts a metal tube around one metre long from the side of the bench and casually strolls back in the direction of Thomas who gradually rotates upside down from the twisting action of the rope with an occasional spot of blood dropping from the bullet wound in his stomach that hits the light soil floor below. Standing close to the already blood stained patch of soil, Nick lifts the steel tube and, with both hands as a baseball player, swings the tube into Thomas's stomach causing him to spin on the rope and scream out in agony.

Thomas, screwing his face up in pain, spits out a mouthful of blood and moans, "Please stop, Nick, I did nothing."

"I haven't fuckin' started with you yet, bastard!" Nick grabs him by the hair and punches him in the face.

"Who did you sell me out to you fuckin' traitor?" Nick rams the tube into his stomach again by the gunshot wound.

"Please, Nick, nobody." Thomas winches.

"Let me ask it another way then, what have you been offered to sell me out?" Nick lifts his knee into the face and with a crack breaks his nose.

"Arghhhhh," Thomas moans in agony.

"I thought you guys were tough, you fuckin' pussy," Burns laughs.

As I continue to cut some of the bread and cheese, trying to ignore the brutality that is evident in front of my eyes, Nick continues the torture in a different direction.

"Now bastard, I can do this all night and enjoy every second of it or I can make it easier for you. The choice is yours." Nick paces around the hanging prey.

After a few seconds of silence, apart from his heavy lethargic breathing, Thomas says, "Okay, what you want to know?"

Nick stops in his tracks instantly, replying, "You see, that's just bullshit because he is trying to save his skin, just like in London."

Nick lifts the tube and rests it across the back of his neck and top of the shoulders as he asks again, "Whom have you sold me out to?"

Thomas, coughing and spitting out more blood, answers, "Okay, I tell you, but please let me down?"

"Let you down? I will let you down when I have my answers and not before." Nick lifts the tube from his shoulders and prods him with one end.

Thomas, knowing that he is dammed either way, begins to speak. "Please, I feel faint and giddy."

"So what? Do you really think that I give a shit?" Nick answers, showing no compassion.

"I was approach by government agent who offering diplomatic immunity if I would hand you over." Thomas, with blood covering his face, tries to look towards Nick.

"Go on," Nick instructs in a raised yet controlled voice.

"The agent wanted to know why you had included Dean into the team at such a late stage," Thomas coughs.

"What did you tell him?" Burns asks.

"I say didn't know and thought Dean was a late arrival." Thomas tries to look at me.

"What did this agent look like?" Nick asks.

"He was about two metres tall, around forty years old, smartly dressed." Thomas spits more blood to the floor.

"Fuckin' liar." Nick takes another baseball swing at his side, cracking a couple of ribs.

"No, no, please, I not lie. His name was Preston and there was a woman agent too," Thomas yells in pain, spitting out more blood.

"What else did this agent ask?" Nick continues to walk around Thomas.

"He wants to know about the money sorting warehouse and about the other team members."

"I suppose you sold them out too, yes?" Nick prods at Thomas again with the steel tube.

"Please, Nick, let me down, I feel sick and dizzy!" He starts to cough then regurgitates out blood and food from inside his stomach.

"Did you sell the others out too, you fuckin' bastard?" Nick punches him in the side of the head.

Thomas then, being sick again, coughs and mutters the answer, "I know they approached Josef too, but I did not tell."

"Okay, but let's see what your fuckin' kraut mate will say when I catch hold of him, eh?" Nick walks over to the rope and releases the knot, dropping Thomas to the floor, who lands in his own sick and blood.

Nick then walks over to the far side of the barn and drags an old black metal garden chair from in the shadows to the direction of the battered and broken Thomas lying twisted and moaning with pain.

"Give us a hand, Dean," Nick instructs.

Walking over I pull the latex gloves back onto my hands, then we both lift Thomas from the ground and place him onto the chair as he moans every time we move him.

"Grab that barbed wire and gloves, Dean, from by the bench."

Reaching the bench, I pick up the thick leather gloves then the roll of barbed wire and place them on the ground next to Nick. He immediately pulls on the leather gloves and starts to unravel the wire from the reel. He connects it to the top of one chair leg then unwinds the wire from the reel across the chest of Thomas and then threads it around the opposite chair leg, pulling it tighter. The barbs begin to cut deep into Thomas's chest, but now he is already unconscious from the beatings that he has sustained. Nick continues to bind Thomas to the chair with several loops of wire and without even hesitating walks across to the table. After removing the leather gloves, he starts to eat the food that I have cut and prepared. In all this torture I feel as though nothing seems strange and I begin to eat food with Nick.

"That fuckin' bastard knows more than he is letting on. We need his mate here, then we'll see what happens." I join Nick, nodding my head in agreement as he continues.

"That bastard Wagstaff is behind all this, I know it, Dean, and we'll catch up with him soon enough." Nick stares across at Thomas.

"Why does Wagstaff want you so much, Nick?" I ask, taking a bite of bread.

Nick, smiling, replies, "It's in the past, Dean, and tonight's not the time."

He picks up the pocketknife and, turning quickly, walks out past the door into the night. The noise of a car door being opened and closed can be heard and then the returning footsteps of him. He re-enters the barn and walks straight over to Thomas, holding a small black box in one hand and knife in the other, then begins to sweep over Thomas's body. I join Nick as a familiar bleeping noise is heard from the black box. He slowly sweeps around Thomas's stomach with the bleeping getting quicker and finally stopping near the gunshot wound. Nick inserts the knife and begins to dig out a small black fragment of a broken capsule. Taking the fragment,

Nick lifts it to examine it closer with his eyes, gradually turning it.

"That was a lucky shot; this bastard has a tracker capsule fitted. I knew he had a handler and looking at the design it's British made."

"We need to move quickly. Whoever has planted this will be onto us. Let's get back to Leipzig and track his mate. That way we can get this job done fast and see where we go next."

"What about him?" I ask.

Nick removes the rope from around his ankles and places it around his neck, then begins to tighten it using the joist as the cantilever. "If he wakes up and tries to move and escape he will fall, choking himself. Either way he's a dead man."

We walk towards the door, switch off the light then quickly climb into the car, driving away back towards Leipzig. During the journey in the car, my mind plays over how easy Nick found inflicting pain onto Thomas and at times looked as though he enjoyed it. From my side during the interrogation, I felt quite excited and didn't really show any emotional contact to Thomas, in fact it almost reminded me of someone beating a piece of meat rather than a human being with the pain from Thomas not even registering as wrong after Monday's events. A big part of me senses that this isn't the first time I've been involved with the beating of confessions from prisoners, but another side tells me that I have been on the receiving end and a vivid memory of a darkened room and two men begins to form in my mind like a hazy cloud. The only time I felt any sympathy for Thomas was when he pissed himself just before passing out and I probably knew then his life is over and he will never see another day. But betrayal in this line of work has dire consequences with no prisoners and after all he knew what the outcome could be when he was signed up. Like me, if he didn't know the risks he should have just walked away. My mind thinks about Preston and why he is involved and after thirty minutes of high speed driving we see the main road signs for Leipzig as Nick instinctively continues towards the centre square again where we can begin the next search for Josef. Nick draws the car into a roadside parking place and stops the engine.

"Open the glove box, Dean, there is another silencer along with some mag clips." Nick looks across as the time clicks over to 9 p.m.

Opening the glove box, I reach inside and, even in the darkness of the city, instantly sense the coldness of the steel against my hands and take out the spare mag clips and silencer.

"Hand me a spare clip." Nick offers across his open hand.

Lowering a clip into the palm of his hand, I push the additional mag clip and silencer into each of my jacket pockets then lifting the gun from my jacket, cock back the top slide and click on the safety catch, then I push the gun into my trouser belt hidden by my jacket.

"Take out those two small radios from the door bin, Dean, and hand one over; we will need to split up."

Reaching for the radios, I hand one over to Nick who immediately switches it on and begins to flick through the channels looking for a safe communication network. After a few seconds he reaches a channel with no interference and says, "Okay, Dean, set to channel twenty-six."

Lifting the second radio, I switch it on then set the digital display to twenty-six. Nick stops and lowers the radio as a young couple walk past. He operates the call button that echoes on my handset, then he continues to search through for another channel.

"Okay, thirty-seven is plan B if there is any interference. Don't use names and call Josef Terry. Don't mention mark or target and remember these things only have a two-kilometre radius. Radio silence unless compromised, okay?" I nod in agreement.

"Just remember your training and no hero shit, this guy is a trained killer and we need to take him together and alive!" he commands.

"Okay, Nick, I will follow as you instruct." I am nodding in submission, but deep down wanting to kill Josef.

"Right, let's go!" Nick announces as he opens the driver's door as I follow through the passenger side.

He indicates for me to take the right side of the main square as he begins to casually work his way up the steps to the left. This time my heart is beating a little faster in the hunt for Josef, knowing that he is probably armed and may have already heard that Thomas has disappeared. Reaching the main square of Leipzig, I start to walk around in the warm evening air with hundreds of people still sitting outside the bars and restaurants, enjoying the evening eating and drinking outside while they can smoke and laugh and relax from the pressures of work. The tables and chairs are so close together; it is difficult to walk past without stopping for people to pass the other way with the table umbrellas almost touching.

The people talking so close to each other generate a low humming sound that is deadening the distinctive music floating in the air from a violin being played from a street entertainer near the bung keller. Trying to locate Josef in all of these people will be a nightmare, but I'm certain he will be somewhere enjoying the pretty women walking past. I hear a humming sound coming from behind me so, turning my head to the right, I see a man riding a mountain bike with an iPod plugged into another world cycling along the pavement. Moving slightly to the right, I let him pass by and watch him nearly hit a middle aged couple who are walking in front of me. I continue to walk around the uneven coble stone streets looking at the architecture of the old buildings and checking for possible vantage points that could be used by Josef or myself for sniper positions. Suddenly the radio crackles in my pocket and, finding a quiet doorway underneath some shop balconies, I take it out and reply.

"Receiving over."

"Meet me back at the car, I've located him, out."

"Okay, out."

So, quickly heading back in the direction of the parked car, I can see Nick already standing by the Audi as the rain starts to fall. He unlocks the car and gets inside, waiting for me. Reaching the car, I climb into the passenger seat and look at him in the darkness as the hunt continues.

"Got the bastard, I have seen him entering an apartment building in the old centre."

"So what do you want to do?" I ask inquisitively.

"Well, he didn't see me, but it was pretty clear he was in a hurry. I'm sure he is going to make a run for it."

A message is delivered and Nick, taking out his cell, checks the text. "Okay, Stefan is going to take the front door and we will wait in the street behind. Josef will probably escape through the back exit."

Starting the engine, Nick begins to drive along the dark, narrow, cobbled roads in between the old tall buildings of Hain Strasse. The only noise echoing around the buildings is the splashing of water as the car passes through puddles caused by the still falling rain. The rain droplets hit the windscreen and sparkle as they pass by the illuminated headlights against the street in front. In the shadows, the silhouette of a familiar person can be seen leaving the back of an apartment building.

"At fuckin' last!" Nick proclaims, beginning to gradually accelerate.

The person continues to walk with their back to us, taking no notice of the approaching danger until finally the headlights confirm it's Josef. Josef, now hearing the speeding car through the falling heavy rain, turns and with a look of horror hits the front of the car, letting out a large scream.

Burns releases his foot from the accelerator and, applying the brakes, sharply brings the car to a fast halt with the noise of the impact still echoing through the metal shell of the Audi and ringing in my ears. In the dim light Josef's body can be seen bouncing off the bonnet and smashing into the top right corner of the windscreen, shattering the toughened glass. His limp body then slides down the passenger's side of the car, knocking and banging, finally collapsing into a pile on the wet road with no movement. Nick, in an instant, applies the handbrake and quickly jumps out of the car, leaving the engine on tick over, running around to check if Josef is still alive. As Burns checks the pulse of the lifeless body, the car is filled with the noise of the windscreen wipers scrapping over the broken glass. Opening the door, the cold rain hits my face as I climb out and walk around to the back of the car and grab the remaining cable ties. Nick is already preparing Josef's wrists and ankles to accept the binding that will prevent him from trying to escape. Throwing Nick the bundle of ties, I begin to look around the dark alley to see if anyone has reacted from all the noise and Josef's scream, but the cold metal shutters blank out any of the outside world.

"Help me to lift him inside the boot!" Burns instructs.

Nick finishes binding the wrists and ankles together and we start to lift the body. Suddenly Josef begins to move, making a groaning noise, but from the look of anger in Nick's eyes nothing will save him now. Reaching the back of the car, Burns lifts the wet and bleeding body, throwing him onto the thick clear plastic sheet as I push his legs further inside with Josef's fate now truly sealed. A pair of headlights begins to approach from behind as we climb back into the car and drive away with Josef moaning with pain in the trunk of the car. Nick continues to drive the battered hire car through the back streets of Leipzig and out towards Gostemitz where Thomas is already left bound as the rain begins to ease and finally stop. The roads are littered with puddles that we splash through as we continue en route to the farmhouse. It is clear that Burns can't wait to interrogate the pair of them together, using one against the other to gain the information he wants over Wagstaff. But now it's clear that torture and punishment is what he wants for betraying his trust and loyalty with nothing stopping him. This is part of what Wagstaff had warned me about and how Burns had previously treated friends and colleagues. Either way it's clear that this is not a good time to be on his bad side.

With hardly a word spoken between us, the only noise that can be heard in the car for that thirty-minute journey is the groaning and coughing as Josef as he begins to regain consciousness. The fate of both him and Thomas is quite clear: they will be dead before dawn and I will have played another major part, but this time it feels as though killing these two men feels like payback for Lloyd and the others that died on Monday. These two guys may appear to be innocent, but it's clear Nick is judge, jury and executioner for tonight. My body beings to shake with the anticipation of what will happen tonight and in a strange way an excitement begins to flow, releasing endorphins in my brain from the next adrenaline rush. Looking across to Nick and sensing his body language, I can tell that he is deep in thought. I try to imagine what could possibly be racing through his mind right now, but thinking about what he said over the past few days, it's clear that only pain, anger and suffering of Thomas and Josef fill his hunger.

Turning off the B87, Nick returns down the small narrow tarmac road with the headlights illuminating a short pair of concrete gateposts signifying the driveway to the old farmhouse. Driving towards the derelict barn at the side of the farm, we splash through the deep puddles. Reaching the large wooden doors, Nick stops the car but keeps the headlights shining forward. As we both climb out of the car, the dampness from the earlier rainstorm fills the air and the only sound that can be heard is the eerie cry of a fox screaming that makes the hairs on the back of my neck stand up.

Nick looks across and says, "I'm sure these two bastards will be a good meal for that fox." He gestures for me to open the trunk.

He lifts the pistol, pulling the top slide back to check that there is a bullet in the chamber in case Josef tries to escape. Pushing the boot catch button with a positive click, the lid springs open, revealing Josef trying to move around slightly in the dim light of the trunk with the smell of fresh sick and blood filling our nostrils. Nick clicks the safety catch on the pistol and tucks the gun back into his trouser belt then reaches for the legs of Josef and begins to drag him out of the trunk. Helping Nick, I grab at his belt and can feel the congealed blood touching my fingers as the semi-conscious Josef groans with pain. The wheezing noise that can be heard from his heavy laboured breathing clearly shows that some of his ribs are broken and maybe a punctured lung as we finally lift Josef's body from the car. Dropping his feet to the ground, we drag him towards the direction of the barn with his ankles and wrists still bound. Reaching one of the wooden doors, Nick pushes it open with his shoulder to reveal Thomas lying on his side, still fastened to the chair. As we drag Josef into the barn Thomas starts to speak.

"Nick, is that you?" he asks.

"Shut your fuckin' mouth, traitor!" Nick replies aggressively.

"Nick, I am sorry for what happened, but I was not involved, maybe Josef is the one?" Thomas tries to turn and look at us.

"Well, let's find out, hey, since your good friend is now here," Nick replies, laughing.

Josef is dragged then dropped to the ground next to the chair where Thomas is still bound with barbed wire and Nick, having the look of hatred deep in his eyes, will clearly stop at nothing until the pair of them are dead. He quickly starts to constrain Josef by throwing another rope over the roof joist and, attaching it around his neck, begins to haul him up from the ground until he is in a kneeling position, coughing and shaking. I stand near where Thomas lies on the ground, feeling the excitement as Nick walks across.

With a quick action, he grabs Josef by the neck and, lifting his knee, hits the nose, sending blood across Josef's face, "Now, Fritz, what do you have to say?"

Josef leans forward and instantly starts to choke from the rope around his neck. "Not yet, you bastard, not yet." Nick forces him to kneel straight.

"So, which one of you wankers is going to talk?" He walks over to Thomas and kicks him in the stomach.

"What you talking about?" Josef coughs.

"I'm talking about the silent alarm and why it wasn't deactivated." Nick gives Josef a hand chop around the back of his neck.

"All I want is a name and I will let you live."

"The name of who?" Josef asks, spitting out a mouthful of blood.

"The name of the person who set me up."

"How is Thomas?" Josef asks.

"Well he's alive for now," Nick replies.

"You're an animal, Burns, treating us this way," Josef shouts.

"Betraying my trust makes you such a good character, hey?" Burns gives Josef another hand chop to his neck.

"It was Ramone and Carlos."

"What! You fuckin' liars." Nick is outraged as his face completely changes from anger to disappointment.

357

"You're lying just to save your own fuckin' skin." Nick snaps then lifts up the steel tube from earlier and begins to hit Josef around the body.

"I tell you, it was Ramone and Carlos," Josef coughs, spitting out more blood.

"Who did what?" Nick leans close to Josef's face.

"They said if we help set off the silent alarm, we could all benefit."

"All benefit? Hardly, setting off the alarm could have got all of us caught."

"They said immunity." Josef coughs, then leans sideways and passes out.

"Immunity, not from me!" Nick shouts.

Nick, annoyed and clearly angry, strides across to Thomas who is struggling to breathe with his chest rising and falling, almost panting. Wanting to revenge the betrayal, he takes a handgun that was concealed in his trouser belt and, placing it on the left temple of Thomas, he fires a single round at point blank range, similar to what was seen with Greg before. The sound echoes through the empty barn as pigeons start to flutter around the loft space, shocked over the sudden noise.

Tucking the handgun back behind his belt, he then begins to untie the rope, lowering Josef to the ground. As the rope eases its grip around Josef's neck he starts to cough, regaining consciousness. As he begins to move slightly on the ground, obviously in pain from the car accident and the beating, Nick sees red and continues with the torture, kicking him hard in the stomach, causing Josef to spit out more blood onto the soil floor. Then, bending down, he grabs hold of some hair on his head and turns him to see Thomas dead in the chair.

"Okay, you bastard, what were you saying?" Burns turns and smiles.

Josef, smelling his death isn't far away and realising the mistake he made crossing Nick, then continues, "Ramone mentioned UK government agent who offered a deal."

"Let me guess, the deal was to hand me over, yes?"

"No, the deal to hand over Dean. You were optional." Josef says, trying to move a little.

"Fuckin' kraut liar." Burns kicks him hard in the face.

"Arrgh. No, Nick it's true, the agent wanted Dean." After standing away from the torture, I now move forward, taking an interest now my name is mentioned.

"The name of this so called agent." Nick grabs his hair.

"It was, ergh, Wi—"

"Wagstaff?" Burns announces, trying to finish the word.

"No, it was Wilson," Josef replies.

"Wilson? Surly you mean Wagstaff?" I ask.

"No, it was Wilson, a woman Ramone was sleeping with!" Josef coughs.

"This doesn't make any sense." Nick looks across to me.

"Why would this agent want me?" I lean forward.

"Josef, have you ever seen this woman?" I ask.

"Yes, only once. She has brown hair and is about forty years old."

"This sounds like an agent that works for Wagstaff."

"I fuckin' knew it was that bastard behind it!" Nick proclaims.

"Why didn't he approach Ramone directly like with me? That doesn't make sense," I ask.

"Who cares for now. I have what I want from these bastards so let's go."

Josef coughs and tries to move a little more.

"What shall we do with these guys?" I ask.

"Dean, that's simple." Nick pulls out his gun and shoots Josef straight in the head, killing him instantly and sending another solitary gunshot into the darkness.

I stare across at the two bodies then look towards Nick who, with a smile on his face, says, "That'll teach them, hey? Now grab that fuel tin from by the bench and toss it over the bodies."

As instructed, I fetch the fuel canister as Nick starts to remove the wire from Thomas's body that bound him to the chair. Removing the corpse he places it next to Josef's body on the ground then winds up the hemp ropes, throwing them on top of the bodies, along with some of the logs from the wood-store. Unscrewing the cap from the canister, my nostrils are filled with the distinct smell of diesel and as the liquid is poured over the bodies, its strong aroma fills the barn. Nick takes a cheap lighter from his pocket and as he flicks the striker sparks shower from it with a solitary flame flickering in the dim light of the barn. Bending down, Nick lights some of the hemp rope that quickly catches fire, soaked with the diesel fuel, and within a few seconds a large whoosh is heard as the remaining fuel ignites, filling the barn with a yellowish light from the flames as the clothes then catch alight. Smoke rises into the barn loft space as we exit through the door to collect the plastic sheet from the car boot. The sheet is folded gently, so as not to spill any congealed blood, and is then carried between Nick and myself back into the barn where it is thrown over the now burning mass. It quickly hisses and ignites, melting over the fire, causing blue flames to rise and hiding the smell of burning flesh hanging in the air. Quickly exiting from through the main door, we climb into the car with Nick driving away at high speed. Still feeling shocked over the deaths but also quite relieved that two of the witnesses to the robbery are now dead, it feels like a weight has been lifted and another chapter can begin, but the smell of our clothes is awful.

"Okay, on to Brazil next, Dean. Ramone and Carlos, I'm sure, are trying to hide out there, but they are not clever enough to cover their tracks. We will drop this car off and bounce back over the boarder then drive to Schiphol for a flight from Amsterdam to San Paulo." Nick speaks with venom in his voice.

Burns continues, "Those fuckin' bastards won't get the best of me, I'll fuckin' show them."

Trying to change the subject slightly, I ask, "How are we going to give this car back with all the damage to it?"

"Simple, Dean, we should be back to Salzbergen before dawn so we can drop the car off outside the hire office and post the keys through door. We will be long gone over the border before they even notice."

Continuing out of the village as the time clicks past 1 a.m., we reach the A2 quickly with Nick driving like a man possessed, accelerating the Audi to almost max speed with his foot buried deep into the throttle pedal.

"Can you reach my mobile from the front pocket of my bag?" As instructed I take the cell from the bag.

"Now unlock it and search for Graham White in the contacts. We need a new route including hotels. Maybe the Crown Plaza in Brazil and KLM flights?"

"It's nearly after midnight Nick, will this Graham guy still be awake?" I start to scan through the contacts and find Graham White travel shop.

"He never sleeps, especially when money is concerned."

So, pressing the call button, the sound of ringing can be heard. "Placing the cell next to my ear," Nick asks.

"Nick, how are you, it's a little late?"

"I know, Graham, but this is urgent."

"It's always urgent with you," Graham replies in a strong muffled Yorkshire accent.

"My colleague Dean will explain what we want and the route needs to be planned ASAP." Nick gestures for me to move the cell.

Placing the cell next to my ear, the accent becomes clearer. "Dean? Is that really you, Dean?"

"Hi, Graham, yes, hello. We need a flight from Schiphol to San Paulo and the hotel stay in Crown Plaza for a few days."

"Okay, no problems. What about a stay in Schiphol for a few hours to freshen up if I can't get good flight connections?"

"That's a good idea, Graham, thank you. I'm sure Nick will approve. Which hotel were you thinking?"

"The Sheraton is okay and I am sure it will suit Nick's taste."

"What is he asking, if we want a hotel in Schiphol? Good idea," Nick comments.

"He seems happy with that."

"Some fresh clothes too at the hotel in Schiphol." Nick shouts over.

"Tell him bollocks, I will sort it. What size are you, Dean?" Graham replies.

"Thirty-six waist and forty-four chest, medium build."

"Hey, same as before. It will only be charity shop stuff, not designer," Graham laughs.

Being a little shocked that Graham knows my clothes size, I reply, "Oh right, okay."

"Tell the boss to give me a couple of hours," Graham announces.

Nick shouts across, "I want it sooner than your usual couple of hours reply, Whitey, you owe me," Nick growls.

Graham laughs. "Give me an hour, Dean, I should have a route planned by then and tell him bollocks." The cell goes dead.

"He will sort the route in an hour, he always does. We can ditch the Passat at Schiphol parking, switching the plates so it's non-traceable to us. We will need to wipe this car down and loose the guns. There is roadside service stop in a few more kilometres so we can dump the guns in general waste."

"Take the handguns from the back seat and, after removing the clips and rounds, take them apart. Then using the hand wipes in the front of my bag cleans all the surfaces of the guns, but make sure you wear the latex gloves first."

So following Nick's instructions, I place a fresh pair of latex gloves on my hands and begin to unload and disassemble the guns as Nick continues to drive at speed. The signs for a roads side service stop are noticed at forty-five kilometres then fifteen minutes later, Nick indicates to pull over at the five hundred metre markings. As we pull into the service stop there are a four cars and one van parked under the dull orange lighting. Driving past, he picks a place away from the other cars in a darker section of the tarmacked bays.

"Now take the gun parts and wrap them into that newspaper and place different parts in general waste bins. I will head for the toilets and then buy us a coffee each," he says as he stops the engine and points at the newspaper in the passenger door bin.

Grabbing the newspaper, the different gun parts are wrapped into paper, making little packages. Leaving the car, I walk gradually towards the building, dropping the gun part packages into different general waste bins in a casual manner as Nick locks the car and walks towards the main building in a covering action, making sure no undue attention is drawn to us. The noise of the cars roaring past on the autobahn constantly breaks the short silences even though it's 2 a.m. on a Tuesday morning.

Nick quickly returns with two coffee drinks and we continue our drive to Salzbergen so that we drop of the damaged hire car. Slowly driving towards the hire car offices Nick's eyes scan the area for any cameras, police or people who could identify the occupants of the crashed car. Passing twice past the offices and confirming the area is clear, he stops on side street just short of the drop off area.

"We need to wipe this car down for any prints so you start in the front and I will take out the bag and check the boot area." Nick instructs.

Wiping down the door handles, glove box, steering wheel, gear selector and other instrument dials the car is quickly cleaned.

"What about any fibres in the seats or carpets?" I ask.

"Unless we burn it out, it's pointless really, now you go and walk over to the Passat, then drive opposite the hire car office parking about 50 metres up the road and I will drop this wreck off."

So as instructed, I walk over towards the Passat checking the area for any possible threats. Reaching the car I casually walk around it to make sure all is fine. All the tyres are still inflated and there are no wheel clamps fitted, so opening the door I slide onto the driver's seat and start the engine. In the distance Nick can be seen starting to drive towards the hire car offices. Heading towards the car barrier system I insert the parking card from Monday, but the system is not working and the barrier opens automatically allowing me to exit. Pulling into the kerb fifty metres away from the offices, I watch Nick walk casually to the offices and posting the keys through the letterbox disappears for a few seconds then reappears next to our car.

"I had to hide from the security camera but all is easy, now let's get the fuck out of here!" Burns commands.

Driving away from the kerb and heading out of Salzbergen trying not to drawn any attention the time on the car dashboard clicks over to four thirty am as we continue in the direction of the Netherlands border. After thirty minutes we cross through seamlessly and head in the direction of Schiphol airport with the time fast approaching 5 a.m. Nick's mobile vibrates and pings as a message is delivered.

Quickly reaching over, he unlocks the screen and checks what has been sent. "It's an email from Graham with the next details our flight to Brazil. It's late afternoon so he has booked the Sheraton hotel for us. He has arranged some fresh clothes and cases to be delivered to the main reception." Nick places the cell back on the dashboard.

The sat-nav reads another forty minutes to the airport parking and, with the protocol already established, we need to wipe the car down of any prints and then ditch it. After thirty minutes of driving, signs for Schiphol airport begin to show on the motorway and we turn towards the parking area. Quickly placing baseball caps on our heads to cover our faces, we pull into the car park and then drive to find a secluded area and after several turns of parking levels we reach the fourth floor. Nick gestures to head for an area with limited lighting. Having already taken out the packet of latex gloves, he pulls a pair onto his hands. Stopping the car, he passes some gloves over and then we begin to wipe down the inside of the car, covering the doors, windows, dashboard and centre console. I open the door and, after wiping down the outer handles, quickly wipe the back passenger door card. A plastic carrier bag is removed from the back seat and all the inside is checked before I join Nick who is now opening the boot. A rustling sound is heard as he removes a pair of stick-on number plates and, closing the boot lid, he tears off the old plate then quickly sticks on the new one.

He walks around to the front and repeats the process before I pass him the keys. Locking the car, he leaves the keys on the front driver's tyre then looks at me saying, "Just in case, you never know."

With all the rubbish, number plates and wipe down clothes placed into the plastic bag, we begin to walk down the staircase and towards the airport hotel casually dropping the evidence in a rubbish bin on route. Occasionally glancing around, we continue our progress to the hotel making sure we are not followed. Reaching the hotel, we walk into the lobby and quickly locate the main reception desk.

Confidently reaching the reception, Nick speaks to the lady. "Good morning, we have reservations for two rooms."

"Good morning, gentlemen, can I have your names?"

"Yes, it's Mr Jackson and Mr Forster."

"Let me check. Yes, here we are, and I see we are also holding a case for each of you."

"Yes, that's correct," Nick replies.

"Your bookings are not for very long. How will you pay?" the receptionist asks.

"Credit card." Nick removes it from his pocket.

She lifts the telephone receiver and the word 'cases' can be heard. "Do you need Wi-Fi access?" she asks, replacing the receiver.

"One device each?" Burns replies.

"You have unlimited access and devices with your booking using your surname and room number. Do you want to pay now?"

"Yes, that will be fine, thanks." Nick hands over the credit card.

"Do you want the invoice for International Expeditors Limited?"

"Perfect, do you need a business card?"

"No, sir, I have your details from last time. Okay, gentlemen, here are your keys. Mr Forster you are room one hundred and thirty-two and Mr Jackson I have placed you in room two hundred and seventy-three. I wish you a pleasant stay."

A porter arrives with the cases and, after checking the names on them, we proceed to the lifts and finally the thought of some rest feels great. Pushing the call buttons for floors one and two we enter the lift.

"I'm beat, Nick, after last night." I lean against the lift side.

"Well, we have a few hours rest before the flight so get some sleep. Hey, you did well." The lift stops on Nick's floor.

He walks out and smiles, saying, "Catch you in a bit, okay?"

"Fine, no worries," I say as the doors close.

Still leaning against the side, the lift stops and as the doors open my eyes look at the room signs that require additional focus due to being overtired. Strolling towards my hotel room, I count the door numbers in an almost semi-conscious state until a sixth sense tells me to stop. I look at the door number then the access card and, seeing that both match, insert the card into the slot and the green light confirms the door unlocking. Turning the handle, I continue inside and push the card into the wall slot and stare at the large bed calling my name. I release the handle, closing the door behind, and then collapse onto the bed fully clothed and fall asleep. My sleep is disturbed by the sound of the hotel room guest phone ringing and, still groggy, I lean across to lift it.

"Are you awake, sleepy head? Time to move." Nick's familiar voice can be heard.

"Err, yes, okay. Will just take a shower and change."

"Well, don't be too long. See you downstairs soon."

'That was a quick five hours' crosses my mind as I slowly roll off the bed and stand. I walk over the suitcase that is left by the foot of the bed and lift it to see what is inside. Unzipping the front and flipping it open, I see a clear bag full of toiletries. Some new shirts, underwear, socks, a pair of jeans and some T-shirts. Unpacking a pair of pants and socks from their new boxes, I walk into the bathroom also carrying the bag of personal hygiene products.

I lay the small tins, tubs, and bottles out on the white counter close to the sink and then begin to undress. Walking into the shower cubicle, the warm water hits my naked skin and instantly makes me feel more refreshed and clean. After a shower, cleaning my teeth and pulling on underwear and socks, I return to the bedroom, taking out a new shirt from its plastic wrapper. Pulling the shirt over my body, I quickly check how it looks as I stare into the large dress mirror. After stepping into a pair of jeans and placing shoes back on my feet, I pack away everything into the case ready for the next journey as I turn, open the door and walk out of the room down the corridor to the lift like I have now done many times before. Leaving the keys for the rooms at the reception, we walk into the main departures hall filled with a sense of fear over the security checks that we will need to pass through in order to catch our flight. Trying to blank out these thoughts, we see the security guards standing waiting for flight passengers to arrive.

13

Finally after the long flight from Schiphol the plane begins its descent into Guarulhos International Airport. I am feeling completely relaxed over what will happen over the next few days. As the plane lands, the pilot welcomes us to Brazil and my thoughts now shift towards Nick and how he is going to track Ramone and Carlos in a city with over ten million people. The plane stops on the apron then gradually gets positioned to the air bridge with all the flight crew preparing for the passenger disembarking as the 'fasten seatbelts' signs are switched off. The mad panic of people rushing from the plane starts only after the business passengers leave. Casually collecting our things, Nick and I leave the aircraft and follow the signs heading for the immigration desks. Quickly scanning around the airport, my senses are on high alert for any possible threats, but it appears just another day as I reach the counter and pass my fake passport documents over.

"Good morning, sir, how are you?" the policewoman asks.

"Good morning. I am well, thanks."

"What is the reason for your visit? Where are you staying and how long will you be here, Mr Jackson?"

"I'm here for a few days on business and am booked into the Crown Plaza."

The middle-aged woman smiles and takes out the stamp machine to my passport, saying, "I wish you a good trip and goodbye."

Reaching for the documents, I reply, smiling, with, "Thank you."

I continue towards the exit with Burns not far behind. Walking past the baggage claim area, we reach the exit doors and suddenly are exposed to the crowds of people and blast of warmth from the heat of the Brazilian spring weather. The line of hotel drivers stand with name boards and looking for the Crown Plaza our names can be seen. Reaching the driver, we are greeted and taken to a white Mercedes with the hotel signage across the front doors. Climbing into the back of the car, the leather seats are cooling against the heat as we head towards the hotel that will be our base for the next few days. The driver tries to make small talk, but I can sense Nick is keen to get started with the tracking of Ramone and Carlos so reaching into his case, he takes out a cell phone and after pressing a few buttons the familiar sound of ringing can be heard.

A voice answers and Nick, speaking in fluent Portuguese, starts a conversation. "Marco, how are you? How is business?"

A strong Brazilian voice can be heard responding back quickly with the names of Ramone and Carlos being mentioned several times in the conversation with more conversation flowing and the final word, "Tchau."

Looking across at me, Nick gives a gradual nod, saying, "They have been found."

It's clear from the seriousness in his eyes that death will follow once we catch up with them after their betrayal of Nick.

Once arrived at the hotel, Nick and I walk to the main reception for check in after passing through the security x-ray machines that check our luggage.

"Good morning, gentlemen, how can I help you?" the receptionist asks.

I look at her name badge that shows 'Monika' and, smiling back, Nick replies with, "Good morning, Monika. Yes, we have two double rooms booked for a few nights."

"Yes, sir, what are the two names?" Monika asks.

"Okay, it's Chris Jackson and Roger Forster," Nick replies.

"Yes, gentlemen. Well, welcome to Brazil at this beautiful time of the year."

Monika smiles at the pair of us.

"Thank you," we both reply.

"Can I ask the two of you to complete the checking in card, and if I could have your passports for scanning?" We hand over our fake passports without trying to attract attention.

"Thank you, Mr Jackson. I have room four hundred and twenty-three and Mr Forster room three hundred and seventy-nine," she says as she hands over the door access cards.

Another hotel and set of lifts runs through my mind as we walk towards the doors pressing the call button. A 'ping' sound is heard as the doors open and we enter pressing the floor level numbers.

"Drop the stuff in the room then meet me back in the lobby I want to go straight out looking for these guys okay?"

"Yes Nick no problem." I reply.

The lift doors open on level three and as Nick walks out continuing along the corridor I watch him whilst the lift doors close and it feels like another chapter of my life ends. The lift jolts to a stop on the fourth floor and walking out to check the signage for the room number another chapter begins with the hunt for the brothers. Walking along the thick grey carpeted corridor following the illuminated room numbers, I stop next to the dark brown door and push the key card into the activation slot next to the doorframe and a buzzing sound is heard as the lock mechanism opens the door. I am instantly met by brown and white marble flecked flooring that leads to the king size bed and large suite room with a sofa and office desk. The refreshing air conditioning begins to whirl gracefully, chilling the room as the sixty-inch television suddenly switches on with a note across the screen welcoming Mr Jackson to room four hundred and twenty-three.

Placing the bag on the end of the bed, I walk over to look through the large floor to ceiling windows at the jungle and road network near to the airport and complete any threat assessments and escape routes. Then, turning towards the bag, I unzip the case and take out the toiletries clear bag and walk into the huge en suite bathroom. Checking for towels and cleanness, the bag of products is emptied and neatly placed next to the white ceramic sink in a ritual as though it's been done many times before. Returning to the bag, the few clothes are removed from the case and hung inside the wardrobe before placing the bag on the floor. Finding the TV remote, I sit on the end of the bed, quickly flicking through the channels on the TV looking for any world news to see if we have been mentioned, but no information is given. After a deep sigh of relief, the TV is switched off and I begin the walk down to the lobby and meet Burns to see what today brings in the hunt for Ramone and Carlos.

Waiting in the lobby, Nick twitches and constantly keeps looking through the large hotel windows, waiting for something to happen. Suddenly he stares at a blue Ford Taurus that stops at the main hotel gatehouse. His cell begins to ring and, taking it out from his trouser pocket, quickly he answer with, "See."

Burns gestures for the two of us to walk outside as a very thin pale man with a messy short beard can be seen driving a car towards us. The car stops and the driver climbs, then stands by the driver's side.

Reaching the driver, Nick smiles, saying, "Marco, my old friend, how are you? It's great to see you again." They shake hands vigorously then hug.

"Nick, my friend, it's good to see you again after all these years. You must be Dean?" he asks whilst shaking my hand.

"Yes, Marco. Nice to meet you." We all climb into the car with Nick in the front as I sit behind Marco.

Closing the door, Marco passes out a handgun to the each of us as Nick continues to speak with his informant, confirming the intel over Ramone and Carlos's location. We drive away from the hotel and begin to make our way to the outer slum areas of the favelas above San Paulo city where the search starts. The tension in the air can be cut with a knife as Marco drives the bulletproof Taurus around the narrow streets where lots of ambush points for gangs to carry out hijacking can be seen. Looking at the expressions on people's faces, it is clear that if anything goes wrong we are on our own and a couple of handguns are no defence against AK 47s and rocket launchers. The stories of the gangs in the favelas are well known, being heavily armed and trained well in handling these weapons. With police not even passing through certain areas this is one of the most dangerous places in the world.

Nick starts his story about the two rival gangs in Brazil and the history behind them, mentioning the first organised gang and two founding members of The First Capital Command PCC, Jose Marcio Felicio and his brother who Burns has worked for in the past. Both men were expelled due to them being too powerful and they founded a rival organisation called the Third Command TC. According to the Brazilian police the gangs run the favelas and there are now four principal leaders of the PCC, with Marcos Williams Camacho acting as the main face of the organisation. It's clear Nick wants to carry out a simple grab of the brothers and, even with his gangland connections to The Third Command, I feel this won't be possible, but the confidence in Nick to catch these guys flows inspirational positive energy. It's clear he won't back down no matter who he upsets. After several hours of driving around in the smelly, sticky, warm, humid air, our backs are soaked with sweat generated against the vinyl seat covers of the car. The sun begins to set over the mismatch of buildings as Ramone suddenly appears from a small bar carrying a bottle of beer. The expression on Nick's face changes from the intense scowl seen all day to that of pleasure, knowing Ramone has been found.

Nick looks at Marco and asks one simple question. "Which neighbourhood are we in?"

"This area is under PCC control," Marco replies.

Looking at Nick, smiling, I see the word leaving his mouth. "Perfect."

Nick seems to know a lot of information about Ramone and Carlos and it's clear that this piece of information is the final part of the puzzle for the safe apprehension of them.

"Marco, take us to back to the hotel, okay?" Nick instructs.

Driving away from the Vista da Favela Jaqueline, we continue along the Alameda Ribeiro da Silva in the direction of the hotel. I ask Nick, "What made you so happy earlier?"

Smiling back, he replies, "All in good time, my boy."

Reaching the entrance of the hotel, police and military vehicles can be seen everywhere and my heart begins to sink, thinking that the authorities have found out where we are staying and that we are travelling on fake passports. Our faces must be on every single police and security authority computer system all over the world in an attempt by Wagstaff to find us and, looking at the four armoured personnel vehicles parked outside the main entrance, it's clear they have lots of hardware.

Stopping at the closed barrier to the hotel grounds, Marco asks the security guard, "What's happening here?"

The security guard replies sharply, "Routine guest inspections, there are some important guests at the hotel for a meeting."

Nick looks casually back towards me, giving a wink, and, with a smile, says, "Lucky there's no need to worry about us."

Trying to remain calm, I give a fake smile, but know deep down that if the authorities are after us we have no way of escaping from here and with two men we are after on the run in the favelas, this whole trip is beginning to become a complete nightmare. Nick, though, remains calm and controlled and is not in the least bit concerned over the possible hostile forces that could be waiting for us inside the hotel.

"Don't panic, Dean, everything will be fine," he replies.

Not being convinced and taking a deep sigh, I look out of the side window expecting the worst as four police officers can now be seen standing by the main entrance of the hotel. Marco completes the sign in process and we continue down the ramp to stop outside the hotel entrance as the police stand clenching AK-47 machine guns, awaiting our arrival. With my heart beating faster than ever, and what feels like a mouth full of sand it's so dry, we climb out of the car and make our way to the large mirrored glass entrance doors. Marco drives slowly away and our escape is now closed.

One officer stands in front of our path and casually holds out his hand with his raised palm stopping us. "Your name and room numbers please, sir?" he asks in broken English.

"Roger Forster, room three hundred and seventy-nine," Nick replies quickly.

"Chris Jackson, room four hundred and twenty-three," I answer with a little nervousness in my voice.

The police officer stands slightly to one side and allows us to pass through the large revolving glass door through to the inside of the lobby where police and military personnel can be seen standing everywhere trying to look important. Two men in grey suits lean against the main reception counter talking with the hotel staff management and looking through the recent visitors register. It's clear that with this much manpower something very big is going down, but Nick walks very casual as though it is a normal day at the office. Reaching the elevators, his cell begins to ring and, taking it from his trouser pocket, he answers the call as before, speaking perfect Portuguese and exchanging laughter with the other person. The lift doors open and we walk inside as Nick presses the fifth floor call button. Wondering why this floor has been selected, I look across at him and notice that the fifth floor has business suites so it's clear we are going to meet someone as the lift begins to move and judder. After a few seconds, the movement of the lift comes to a gradual halt as the doors ping open just as Nick disconnects the call.

Walking out of the lift, we are greeted by three more military security personnel who are standing in the corridor cradling machine guns and staring at us with piercing glares. One of the soldiers beckons us to move forward and gestures to lift our arms as they start to pat us down for any weapons. Luckily both Nick and I left the handguns in the car and after the search the main guard points to the direction of the business suite. As we start to walk along the glass-panelled corridor, all the rooms are empty apart from the last one where the silhouette of two people can be seen standing behind the frosted glass. Reaching the final door, a large security guard stands at the end of the corridor and as we approach he taps on the door and, pushing it inwards, holds it open for us to enter.

Walking inside, two very well-tanned men in well-fitting expensive suits laugh and joke with each other, but suddenly stop to look at us. One man is around seventy years old with a head of white hair along with a small white beard. The other man closer to forty has dark brown hair and a clean-shaven face. Nick, as confident as ever speaking fluent Portuguese, begins to make light-hearted conversation as he shakes hands with each of the men and finally introduces me as his colleague. The guard closes the door and my mind returns back to Castro's club and the back room as the older of the two men gestures for everyone to sit around the table. Burns sits closest to the older man and me to the far right. We all take our seats as the black leather chairs squeak as we recline into them, making ourselves comfortable. The younger man looks across at us, both probably wondering why we are here. Around the room, a large floral arrangement of lilies in a grey coloured ceramic vase dominates the centre of the oval frosted glass table, filling the air with its fresh aroma. Next to the vase is a set of drinking glasses presented on a sliver tray with two glass jugs of water filled with ice and lemon slices.

Taking a pair of glasses, one is offered to Nick and the other to the older gentleman who greatly accepts. I lean across and, placing my hand on the glass jug, instantly feeling the coolness from the water touching my palm, sensing the wetness from the condensation on the glass surface. Lifting the jug, the condensation that has formed on the outside of the glass can be seen running down the sides leaving a ring of water on the tray. Filling the first glasses, I continue to fill two more and place them in front of the other man and finally myself.

The main window of the room overlooks the vehicle entrance to the hotel as the air conditioning continues to whirr quietly, sending out waves of cool refreshing air. The late afternoon sunshine penetrates slightly into the room and the sunlight reflects on the stainless steel frames of the other four chairs that remain still neatly placed around the table.

The conversation quickly turns into English. "So, Mr Burns, what can we do to help you?" asks the old man in a frail broken English voice.

"Mr Felicio, firstly I would like to thank you for this meeting. We need to discuss with you a matter of urgency over two family members. As we agreed some ten years ago, both of your brother's sons have been in my care since they had to leave Brazil." Nick continues with Mr Felicio nodding in agreement.

"Last week, however, we were all involved in a robbery to collect money for the next business deal and their actions have caused the death of several fellow team members and also what I fear they may have given evidence to the British intelligence agency over your business dealings in return for safe passage back to Brazil. It is also clear that they have not honoured your family with respect and currently reside in the PCC area of the city."

"Yes, I am aware of this already and it causes me some concern, but family blood is thicker than just money." Felicio takes a sip of water.

"Agreed, Mr Felicio, but are you also aware they have made payment to the PCC organisation for safe hiding here in Brazil?" Nick now lifts his glass to take a drink and continues.

Felicio flinches in his seat with movements confirming he is not comfortable with this news. "That fact I was not aware of and this is disturbing."

"What I'm asking is your permission to collect Ramone and Carlos, gain the information that I require and then, if it suits your demands, deliver the brothers back to you." The chair squeaks as Nick leans back.

Felicio, leaning forward in his chair, speaks, "Mr Burns, I don't think that is the only option you seek? Am I right?"

Nick, very keen to kill the two brothers for their betrayal of him, takes another sip of water then replies, "No, Mr Felicio, I will be honest with you. Keeping these two people alive is not what I seek, but in order to keep our working relationship I will accept this decision if it pleases you."

Felicio knows that Nick is going to kill the brothers regardless of his words but also understands the meaning of trust and loyalty. He stands and walks over to look through the window and with his back to everyone continues to speak.

"Mr Burns, I agree with your words valuing loyalty but Ramone and Carlos have done neither in the past and now it haunts my family name. My brother died knowing that his sons betrayed this family and could never find it in his heart to forgive them, so if their own father can't forgive them, why should I? I remember our conversation over ten years ago when I asked you to care for these brothers and hoped that my brother would have had a change of heart, but this never happened and on his death bed he asked me to terminate them so this decision now lands at my feet."

Felicio, continuing to look through the glass windows, takes a deep sigh. "What happens if I don't want the brothers back in the family?" he asks.

"Well, disposal can be arranged if that is what you request," Nick replies, taking another sip of water.

Just then a knock can be heard on the glass as the guard opens the door to let a waitress into the room carrying a tray of drinks and the smell of fresh coffee instantly fills the heavy atmosphere.

"I took the liberty of ordering coffee for everyone." Felicio turns around as the drinks are placed on the table along with a plate of biscuits.

The drinks are passed around and the tension in the room begins to ease. It is clear that Felicio is not happy with his nephews, but betraying his dead brother's memory will be pulling at his heartstrings. Felicio walks back towards his seat and reaches for a couple of biscuits, placing them in the rim of the white saucer holding the coffee cup and then walks in the direction of his son as everyone else begins to take their seats, now resettled and comfortable with the waitress gone. As the door closes, the conversation continues.

"Are we outstanding any payments, Mr Burns?" Felicio's son asks.

"Yes, I have the money ready with a settlement figure that I'm sure you will be happy with," Nick replies.

"Hmm, what happens if something comes back to us from the nephews?" Felicio's son asks his father as he begins to bite onto a biscuit then takes a sip of his coffee.

Felicio, walking around the room, gradually stroking his short white beard deep in thought as Nick continues to speak. "Mr Felicio, when I have worked for you in the past, there has never been any issue or comeback to your organisation and I am aware that this is your family, so your decision is hard. Why don't I collect the brothers first, deliver them to you and we can question the pair of them together? That way we can both see what is happening and then any final decision over their lives can be made together."

Felicio turns and stares at all of us, then gestures to his son. "My son Caesar understands the true value of loyalty and honestly, that is why he is here today to know that the decision I am going to make is one of the most difficult in my life. I have ordered the execution of hundreds of people over the last sixty years with much of their blood still stained on my hands, but deciding the fate of two family members will always haunt my thoughts and is far more difficult. I loved my brother and over the last fifty years we built our business empire with no compromises so our enemies knew we had no weakness. I will therefore request you apprehend the brothers and once you have gained the information you seek remove the two of them forever." Felicio has redness in his eyes as he speaks.

Continuing to speak, he walks over and places his hands on his son's shoulders. "Please tell them both that they have not only dishonoured the memory of their father but also the name of this family with their actions.

"As for payment, use it for front money to fund your next venture and send only pictures to prove that the nephews have been eliminated forever. This will conclude our business from the casino deal." Felicio walks over to Nick and, after shaking both his hand and mine to confirm the deal is done, he turns and gestures to his son and both of them make their way to the door.

Placing his hand on the door handle, Felicio looks back at Nick and nods his head. "I wish you all the best for the future and look forward to seeing your next project take shape."

Nick, still standing, replies, "Thank you, Mr Felicio, and I wish you all the best. Sorry to bring bad news at this time, but rest assured the problem will be cleaned."

Felicio and his son turn and walk through the doorway and as the glass door closes shut with a ringing sound Nick looks to me with a smile almost from ear to ear. Without even hesitating, he says, "Right, let's get these fuckin' bastards, I'll show them we can't be messed with."

Nick, sitting back down, looks over to me as the importance of this meeting finally becomes apparent with Nick agreeing to eliminate two family members from one of the most powerful gang families in all of the southern hemisphere. In the distance the sound of sirens can be heard as Felicio and his son depart under the close protection of police and military personnel. My thoughts drift towards the statement Nick made over the next job and I begin to think about what more he possibly wants, so taking a drink of coffee I turn and ask him.

"Well, that went better than I expected." I sigh with relief.

"Mr Felicio is a keen supporter so let's tidy the mess up from this job. Come, drink up, let's go and get these guys. They may already know we are here for them."

Both standing, we make our way to the door as the empty corridor greets us with all the police and guards gone. Following a quick lift journey, we make our way to the bedrooms and as we separate Nick looks across saying, "I'm glad you're here with me, Dean. Shall we meet at 7.30 p.m. for dinner?"

The time seen on my watch reads six so, nodding my head, I reply saying, "Yes, sounds good and glad you invited me for dinner, that is." I smile back at him.

Taking the door card key from my trouser pocket, I push it into the slot and the lock mechanism whirrs open as Nick disappears back into the lift. Walking into the room and closing the door behind, the late afternoon sun begins to shine through the window as the air conditioning system begins to squeak into life. Lying on the freshly made bed and closing my eyes, I begin to think about what Nick has just done, bargaining with one of the most powerful men in Brazil for two family members and what could happen next, helping him since losing all confidence in the present team for their betrayal. Another thought crosses my mind. I wonder how many more people does Burns work with. It's clear he is well connected globally, both with government and non-government agencies, and has carried out hired killing in the past, but he also has a dark side and I know that even if Felicio had said no, Nick would still have killed Ramone and Carlos just for payback and to clean up the loose ends. The excitement felt from the killing of Thomas and Josef is becoming addictive and knowing that no one will stop us makes it even more enjoyable.

After the meeting with Felicio and his son, my head begins to figure out the complex relationship Nick has with so many people and the thought of now killing both Ramone and Carlos fills my body with an excitement that I now find difficult to replace with a normal life. But deep down there is a niggling feeling that what we are doing is wrong. Any sane person tries to always look composed and hides these bad thoughts into the darkest of places, but also knows that one day they will surface and walking along the dark road will start again. My mind is still blurred over my past, but a part of me can now remember fighting against my inner demons that twist and turn every thought into a non-logical answer. It is clear that when a person tries to bargain for their life it's such an adrenalin rush and it's hard to find another way to get that same buzz. At the moment, with the support offered from Nick, we are riding high like being on the crest of a wave, but also I know deep down that eventually the wave will hit on some rocks, washing us both out in the process.

Whatever Nick wants from me, our future is not clear yet, but one thing is for certain, I am not the man he remembers. Something has changed inside and over this last few weeks my brain is in overload trying to figure it out what has altered. Maybe I am reading too much into the situation but when you suddenly change from an average Joe to a person involved in kidnapping, torture and multi million pound robberies, there is no going back to a normal life. My thoughts are broken by the ringing of the phone in the room and, as the red button continues to signify that a call is waiting, my body begins to move in slow motion to lift the receiver.

"Mr Jackson?" The ladies voice asks with a Portuguese accent.

After a few seconds of regaining my thoughts, I reply, "Yes."

"Mr Jackson, you have a visitor in the hotel lobby who is asking for you."

Thoughts rush through my mind as I try to think who possibly knows I am here and travelling under a fake name and passport, but there is also a feeling of knowing who this person could be and what they want.

"Mr Jackson, what shall I tell them?" the receptionist asks.

"Tell them I'm coming down to meet them," I reply sharply placing the receiver back.

I look at my watch to see I don't have long before joining Nick for dinner so, hoping this meeting will be short, I make my way to the stairs and walk down towards the direction of the hotel lobby. My mind keeps playing over who could be waiting for me and what they possibly want. Perhaps it's the police or maybe it's Wagstaff's agents. I reach the lobby doors and push them open to reveal the main reception and, walking towards the receptionist, my eyes try to scan for who this person is but I can't recognise anyone at first until a familiar voice speaks out with my name.

"Dean, I thought it was you. What are you doing here?" As I turn, the face seen instantly confirms the voice heard.

Meanwhile, Nick thinks over his plans on how to take Ramone and Carlos, completely engrossed with anger as he paces around his room like a caged animal waiting to escape, taking vengeance against those that have betrayed his trust.

"Sophie? Well, of all the places to meet, what a surprise. What are you doing here?" I ask with a look of shock on my face, noticing that her hair is cut short and dyed black as she begins to walk across.

"Nick contacted me and asked if I could join him here. Is that a problem, Dean?" She stands, placing her hand on my right arm.

I can sense she is shaking, but I am not sure if it's from fear or excitement.

"No problem to me, Sophie," I answer, gradually lowering my arm and walking away slightly, giving her some distance then taking a seat opposite her.

"So how have you been, Dean, after those tragic events? I haven't heard anything from you, are you okay?" she asks, now sitting.

"Yeah, well, I have been busy, you know, and decided to take a few weeks off," I reply with limited interest, looking out the large lobby windows.

"Nick has asked me to join you both for dinner," Sophie announces.

"Really? He never mentioned it to me earlier, but hey, that's his call not mine," I reply with even less interest.

"Are you okay, Dean? You seem very distant." Sophie tries to act concerned.

After listening to this shit for a few minutes I already feel lied to and snap back at her, "Look, Sophie, I don't know what you want and frankly don't care. The person you met all those weeks ago has gone and isn't coming back, so whatever your latest plan is tell Nick that I ain't buying."

Looking at me with tears beginning to well in her eyes, her lips begin to quiver with fear. "Dean, I came here to warn you to get away from Nick as soon as possible. He wants to kill you."

"Oh, really? And why is that?" I ask with an aggressive tone.

"Wagstaff, he believes that you told Wagstaff everything and that is why the robbery went wrong." She wipes a tear from her cheek.

"You seem to be well informed of the whole events Sophie. Maybe it's you that's informed Wagstaff because nothing came from me and you are the only one sitting here that can keep a straight face when lies need to be told," I answer sharply.

"Dean, you have me all wrong. I'm here to help you."

She weeps slightly.

"Sophie, save your crocodile tears for someone else, you introduced me to Nick and that I am grateful but these last few days I have seen true loyalty and your actions in the past don't link that broken chain."

In the faint distance the elevator door can be heard to ping open and Nick emerges in his ever-confident manner and, instantly seeing the two of us, begins to walk over.

"You had better wipe away those tears and act normal," I snap back at her as Nick makes his approach.

"Sophie, how wonderful to see you. I forgot to mention earlier that Sophie will be joining us for a few days, Dean. I hope that it's okay?" Nick asks as he begins to sit in the large leather chair.

"Sure, no problem. It appears I don't have a choice anyway. As long as I'm not the one to take her sightseeing!" I reply, laughing.

"No, Dean, Sophie has her own plans for a few days here, am I right?" he says as he takes her hand, giving it a quick kiss.

"Yes, Nick, you're right. A few days away to visit a couple of friends," she answers with a fake smile.

"Sophie was just telling me about how happy she is to be here with us both, isn't that right?" I lean back in the large chair.

Looking across at me with 'fuck off' written in her eyes, she responds, politely as ever, "Oh, yes, I was so pleased when Nick called, it was just out of the blue."

Nick smiles and pats her knee. "Well, you know me, always thinking of others before myself."

"Sophie was just saying how difficult it was after the robbery and knowing some of the people who died." I place her on the spot at she moves in her chair, feeling awkward.

Nick instantly picks up on the body language and replies, "Sophie is a sweet thing that cares for everyone. I have told her to be more assertive but she won't listen. So shall we have dinner?"

All standing, we make our way to the large open plan restaurant with Nick taking the lead and me at the back. Sophie walks, as ever, with a fantastic movement in high heels, wearing a black slim fitting dress hugging her beautiful athletic body with the smell of Dolce & Gabanna hanging in the air. My mind drifts back to the Friday night we had shared all those days ago and what could have been, but after how she was used by Nick and her betrayal of my trust, my feelings are that I can never believe anything she says. Thinking to the time before the robbery, my life was actually better than it is now, being on the run, living in hotels, old buildings and trying to stay underneath the radar. But once you have been in the focal point for everything it's difficult to turn back time to when my old life as a simple finance manager working in an office was so much easier. Preparing to take seats in the restaurant, Nick gestures to Sophie to sit first as the waiter pushes the chair underneath her with Nick and myself following.

"A la carte menu, Mr Forster?" the waiter asks.

"Yes, perfect," Nick replies, acting posh.

"What would you like to drink, sir?" The waiter stands by the table.

"Don Perignon 1964?" The waiter has a concerned look on his face.

"Don Perignon 1964 sounds good, Sir, but I will need to check."

"It's a celebration, after all, so I hope you have it!" Nick laughs and smiles.

Sophie looks across to me trying to smile but I just ignore her as the waiter begins to hand out the menus. My feelings for her have completely changed from being at the stage of love to now feeling as though I can't even stand to be at the same table eating food with her. I know she didn't make me choose this life, but that doesn't stop the way I'm thinking.

It is wrong to blame her, but after the things that have happened before trust and honesty are very important to me and this feels like a knife in my stomach twisting and turning. The emotions running through my head feel like waves on a seashore that keep washing from one decision to another with a total loss of clear sight. I was once so clearly focused on what I wanted in life, but after leaving my family and friends and losing someone I loved very much, a numbness formed in my heart and mind not letting anyone inside without fear of being hurt again. These thoughts, combined with meeting Nick, carrying out an armed robbery, killing people and lying only ensure that my life will continue to twist down an ever deeper black hole of pain and suffering unless a change is made.

A familiar male voice begins to register in my mind. "Have you decided what to eat yet, Dean?" Nick asks.

"Not quite, but nearly there," I say as one waiter brings over the bottle of champagne and another a bucket of ice and champagne flutes.

"What about you, my dear? What have you decided to indulge your taste buds with?" Nick looks across to Sophie.

"Oh, I don't know, Nick, everything reads so fabulous. What about you?" she asks.

"Filet mignon is always my favourite, but the swordfish sounds good." The waiter begins to pour the five hundred pound bottle of champagne with his hand shaking slightly.

"Don't spill any of it!" Nick laughs.

The waiter tries a false smile but is clearly nervous serving the drink.

"I'm going to have the sea bass," I pronounce.

"Very good choice, sir, if I may say so," the waiter replies.

"What about the swordfish?" Nick asks him.

"An excellent choice also, sir," he replies again.

"I will have the lobster," Sophie replies.

"Of course, madam, what else?" He continues, "May I recommend the seafood platter, this way the three of you could share. It is an excellent light bite starter."

"Yes, that sounds perfect." All nodding in agreement.

Nick lifts his glass as the waiter places the bottle into the ice. "Cheers to you both and what a start to another great day tomorrow." The glasses clink together as we all say, "Cheers."

"Sophie, what are your plans for tomorrow? Rest by the pool or visit your friends?" Nick asks, sipping his champagne.

"I was thinking of meeting my friends for lunch at Carlota. What do you think, is that okay?" Sophie speaks in her polite voice, now fully composed.

"Yes, that's a great idea. It has fabulous food, but please ensure you use a proper driver around here. A beautiful lady like you needs protection. Am I right, Dean?"

"If you say so, Nick, I'm sure Sophie is grown up enough to look after herself." Looking across at her, I give a fake smile and take a sip of my champagne with the bubbles fizzing in my mouth.

"Hmm, I sense some tension between you both here tonight." Nick looks across to us.

"No problem from my side," I reply.

The food starts to be served at the table and the meal continues with Nick obviously sensing the friction between us. He starts to play this against our emotions, talking about how we could make a lovely couple, but Sophie's face clearly shows that something is driving her and that being in our company makes her very uncomfortable as she continues to twitch and move in her seat. The small talk continues, trying to mask the uncomfortable feeling between Sophie and me as the main course is served along with another bottle of champagne. Once the plates are cleared away, Sophie has decided that enough is enough and begins to stand from the table.

"Where do you think you're going?" Nick asks.

"I feel a little tired from the journey and need some rest," she replies.

Nick snarls back, slightly, drunk as he grabs her hand. "You're not fuckin' going anywhere. Now sit down and shut up!"

Sophie, with a look of pain across her face and a tear rolling down her cheek, replies, with distress in her voice, "Let go of my hand, Nick, you don't own me," as she tries to drag it away.

Nick is clearly annoyed over Sophie wanting to leave and, as I feel a little remorse, I ask, "Nick, if she wants to go, let her."

Staring at Sophie, Nick releases her hand and, relaxing back into his seat, lifts the champagne glass and takes a sip. Sophie looks at me, smiles and quickly turns, almost running out of the restaurant.

"Don't interfere in my business again, Dean. That bitch can't be trusted and you have to show her who is boss."

"Sorry, Nick, but earlier you were trying to match us up and now you're telling me she can't be trusted?"

"All women are the same, treat 'em mean and keep 'em keen. At least she looked at you as her hero, hey!" He gulps the last of his champagne then signals to the waiter for the bill. It's clear that after he has a drink, Nick begins to react in an uncontrolled manner and this reaction confirms what I am beginning to sense in that he is unstable and maybe some of what Wagstaff was saying is true. Signing the bill, Burns stands, turns then says, "Goodnight." He walks out of the restaurant.

Still sitting at the table, I continue to think about his reaction to Sophie and wonder what more could happen with Nick's instability as I finish the last of my champagne then begin to question even more about whether this is truly what I want. I leave the restaurant and walk through the lobby onwards to my room where, after entering, I undress and lie in the bed continuously rolling over in my mind conversations and reactions from both Nick and Sophie during the night. I finally fall off to sleep.

14

Awaking in the morning. I dress and stare through the hotel room window at the hillside in the distance, noticing the change from the greenery seen with the forest and trees to the multi coloured apartment buildings. It's clear to see how the human race overtakes its surroundings and with my mind now thinking of breakfast, I continue towards the restaurant.

Walking into the busy room with people everywhere talking and collecting food, Nick is seen sitting at a table drinking coffee. Casually reaching the table, I join him for a light breakfast. Hardly a word is spoken until Nick, seeing the time, gestures that we should leave. Nick and I wait for Marco in the hotel lobby with a strange atmosphere hanging following the discussions from last night and the thoughts of today with the capture of Ramone and Carlos. Nick, on the warpath, will stop at nothing until both men are caught, tortured and finally killed. The betrayal that Nick feels goes much deeper than he shows and something in his dark past must have forced him to react in this way to all the team. Until now he has never spoken openly about the events in his past, but after Sophie left the meal last night in tears there is some deep secrets hidden.

Just then the blue Ford Taurus arrives at the main hotel gates, then, both looking across to each other, we stand and make our way through the revolving doors into the warmth of the morning sunshine as Marco gradually drives the car down to the main hotel entrance and the song birds can be heard singing loudly, welcoming the spring day until an aircraft flying overhead breaks the calming sound. Opening the car doors, Nick rushes for the front and I naturally sit in the back behind Marco. Across the back seat is a blue sports bag and the faint noise of metal can be heard clunking as we drive away as the noise registers in my head of guns clanking together. Then, confirming my curiosity, I look through the open zip to see various gun barrels and bullet magazines.

"Head for the PPC area again," Nick instructs Marco.

As we drive away from the hotel the hatred for Ramone and Carlos can be seen in Nick's eyes as he turns around to look straight at me saying, "Check what weapons we have, Dean."

Leaning over the bag and placing my hands inside, the coldness from the steel is sensed as I start to lift out the weapons with the smell of fresh gun oil engulfing my nostrils. I begin to lay them out on the rear seat, seeing two short stock AK-47's with ten full clips, a pair of colt 45 pistols with six magazines of bullets and finally a sawn off pump action shotgun with a box full of magnum cartridges. All the guns are battered with most of the bluing warn off the metallic parts and the wooden stocks have lumps and scratches taken out of them. Nick requests one of the AKs so, passing the machine gun forward along with five magazines in between the two front seats, Nick takes the weapon from my hands and begins to check over the top slide and safety catch. Next he takes a magazine of bullets and pushes it into the holder with a firm knock of his hand. The gun isn't cocked, but will quickly be ready. I take the other AK and push a loaded clip into the mechanism, clicking on the safety catch. Then, placing it next to the bag, I lift up the shotgun and, opening the cartridge box flap, grab out a hand full of ammunition and begin to push the cartridges against the spring-loaded port underneath the main shotgun action.

As each cartridge clicks past the metal cover, my mind begins to think about what damage could be caused to anyone who gets in the way of the exploding cartridges when they are fired. After making our way through the morning rush hour traffic, we enter the PPC section of the favelas and my heart begins to beat a little faster with the expectation of what will happen. Nick stares through the windscreen, looking like a praying mantis waiting for its prey as we make our way in the direction where Ramone was seen yesterday and then he lifts his hand to indicate Marco to slow down and pull to the right. Looking through the windscreen, the figure of a man can be seen casually making his way past the lines of battered and damaged cars on the opposite side of the road.

"Carlos." Nick speaks calmly and quietly, announcing his prey has arrived.

Nick, holding his hand up, gestures to Marco who begins to move forward as Burns cocks the AK-47's action that slides a bullet clicking into the chamber as he stares at the oncoming prey, finally indicating for Marco to stop. Carlos is wearing a baseball cap, blue jeans, Nike sports trainers and an Adidas T-shirt and has clearly not noticed the slowly moving car until suddenly he raises his eyes to see Nick exploding from the car, shouting, "Get on your fuckin' knees and don't move!" Carlos, taking his hands from his pockets, quickly thinks about running, but Nick, reading the situation, fires a single round into his leg, shattering the femur. Now out of the car and having the second AK loaded, I stand, giving coverage from all four sides as Nick and Marco run over towards Carlos to collect him. I continue to stand between the car door and body as a fast moving vehicle can be heard approaching from behind and, looking in the direction of the engine noise, a green Ford Landau starts to make distance quickly.

"Contact behind, we gotta move now," I shout across, seeing the injured Carlos being dragged along the road kicking and shouting his innocence.

"Shut the fuck up," Nick replies quickly as they reach the back of the car.

The noise of house doors and windows closing can be heard echoing through the quiet streets above us. To the right a car stops ten metres behind us. Quickly staring at the car, the occupants include a driver and three other men that are heavily loaded with machine guns. Nick gives Carlos a big hit in the face with the machine gun stock as Marco starts to open the boot.

"Help Marco with the traitor Dean and I'll see what these fuckers behind want," Nick instructs.

Quickly moving to the back of the car, Marco is already trying to lift the semi-conscious body of Carlos into the open trunk and he looks down to see where the bullet has hit his leg where fractured pieces of bone and muscle flesh show against the blue jeans now stained deep red with blood. Carlos gradually moves his head to reveal where Nick has smashed the gunstock into his face, shattering his nose with blood weeping from the open cut. We lift Carlos into the trunk and cable tie his wrists together. Looking back, Nick can be seen standing next to the parked car with the AK 47 hanging by his side in a non-aggressive stance, but I notice his hand is always on the handle waiting to swing the gun to fire if he is threatened. Nick can be heard laughing and joking with the men in the car, clearly showing that the whole event appears to be quite amusing, but equally a huge tension can be felt in the air as though something could erupt at any time.

Closing the boot lid, the voice of Carlos can be heard saying, "Help me, Dean." I stare around to the heavily armoured gangs of men gathering around our position.

The men, clenching machine guns and pistols tucked in their trouser belts, clearly show we are massively underpowered if anything should start. The nervousness in my body begins to make me shake with a level of both excitement and fear. Nick can be seen shaking hands with the front seat passenger and as he walks back in our direction he is calmly brimming full with confidence as though he has just secured another big deal. That distance of ten metres feels like an eternity as the gunmen stand on the street and others lean slightly over the high building balconies peering at us below. Every pair of gunmen's eyes watch his every step, waiting for any potential threatening behaviour from any of us.

Finally reaching us, Nick gives a wink and then, as in slow motion, speaks. "Phew, that was fuckin' close. Get in the car and let's get out of here now."

Quickly climbing into the car, Marco starts the engine as the other car from behind us drives past with the front passenger, waving his hand through the open window and signalling goodbye. The people standing on the street all suddenly begin to disappear as fast as they arrived with almost no sound and the road begins to feel like any other with all the tension evaporated as though into a transparent mist.

"Drive, Marco. Get us the fuck out of here now," Nick instructs and for the first time with some nervousness in his voice.

"Okay, Nick," he replies.

Looking back at me, Nick continues, "Well, at least I know where Ramone is now, but it wasn't easy. Those boys were just about to open up on us."

"What the hell happened?" I ask.

"These guys are scouts for PPC and clearly we are well into their turf, but I explained the situation and the agreement we have with Mr Felicio." Nick takes a deep sigh.

"Thankfully, even rival gangs have a loyalty and trust between each other and the PPC received a message this morning from Felicio not wanting British government spies in their organisation. So we have been granted twenty-four hours stay of execution to extract them otherwise we will be the next on the list to be hunted." Nick looks forward.

Marco has a look of fear on his face and begins to turn white with shock as he tries to remain calm, probably wondering what has he done getting involved with us. But even in the face of death Nick, although a little unsettled, still keeps controlled and clearly focused on what has to be done. Carlos can be heard moaning in the back of the car as Nick instructs Marco with hand signals to turn left. The streets are completely empty as though word is out that we are searching for someone and, as we drive in between parked cars along narrow roads, four men can be seen standing in the middle of the road. As our car approaches they walk into a house on the right and before we even get level to their position, two of the men throw Ramone into the street. The other two men reappear and hold Ramone on the ground with a machine gun at his head, waiting for us to arrive. As we draw closer, the green Ford Landau can be seen parked. The man standing holding the machine guns is the front seat passenger and beckons us to stop in the street. Marco brings the car to a gradual halt and Ramone can be seen trying to look at the car and who is inside.

Nick opens his door first and the colour from Ramone's face can be seen draining away, almost instantly realising what is now going to happen. Marco climbs out and walks around to the back of the car ready to open the boot lid and as I climb out, Nick has begun to walk over to Ramone and the other gang members. Shaking hands with the leader who cradles a machine gun, two of the other men lift Ramone from the road and push him in the direction of our car, making sure he makes no sudden movements. Ramone's mind must be full of fear as he begins his walk along the road that must feel like he is on death row, going as slow as possible making his last bit of freedom count with every footstep with Nick following close behind, smiling. The four men reach the back of the car as I turn and watch the rest of the street to see if any possible threat is going to be launched, but the other men just stand calmly, sharing a lit cigarette, taking large breaths and trying to blow smoke rings. The boot lid catch clicks and I turn to see the look of horror on Ramone's face when he sees what has already been done to his brother As he looks over to me with help written all over his face, I just turn my head away slightly, pretending to ignore the sign of despair. Marco binds his wrists with a plastic cable tie and Nick instructs Ramone to join his younger brother in the trunk, clearly feeling some level of guilt that Carlos is injured.

As Ramone begins to climb into the trunk, Nick gives him a sharp chop to the back of his neck with the butt of the machine gun and like that the boot lid is closed with a heavy metallic slamming noise, causing the car to bounce. Once again Burns shakes hands with the gang members and then indicates for us to get in the car. Climbing back into the car, we quickly drive away to the secure house where the interrogation can begin. After twenty minutes of driving we cross back over into Felicio's family section of the favelas with Marco driving casually within the speed limit so as not to draw any undue attention. Finally we reach the safe house and, stopping the car close to the front door, we all climb out and make our way to the back of the car. Nick gestures with his hand for Marco to make his way to the door and gain entry while we both are left to handle the brothers. Marco can be seen walking towards the front door as I click open the boot catch. He reaches the door and the faint noise of knuckles knocking on wood can be heard. Suddenly the peacefulness of the late morning is shattered by the sound of a shotgun blast and, looking in the direction of the door, a smoking barrel can be seen protruding through the letterbox as Marco falls almost in slow motion to the ground with most of his head removed.

Looking across with shock on my face, Nick replies, "Don't worry, Dean, it's all part of the plan. We needed to get rid of Marco. He is a leaking ship and could lead other people to us."

Staring back across towards the house, two men can be seen dragging Marco's body through the open doorway into the house and then both turning to walk towards our direction. Reaching the pavement, they both nod at us and then climb into a waiting red car that speeds away and leaves us with a dead Marco and two brothers to deal with. As the boot lid opens Ramone's eyes squint from the sunlight, but he doesn't make any other movements.

"Get out, bastard," Nick instructs as Ramone begins to wiggle and move in the trunk, causing Carlos to moan with pain.

Ramone finally begins to sit upright out of the trunk with blood running down the right side of his neck from where Nick hit him earlier. "Help your lying, cheating brother out too."

Ramone, now standing on the road, leans against the back of the car and lifts his hands to feel the blood on the back of his neck and, looking back at Nick, says, "We both did nothing, boss. We would never be disloyal to you."

"Save it for inside, bastard, and get your fuckin' brother out or you will be back in there with him," Nick snaps then suddenly takes out a knife, and in one quick action cuts the cable tie that binds Ramone's wrists.

Ramone rubs his wrists then reaches into the trunk and starts to speak Portuguese to his brother, who by now is starting to regain consciousness but is in pain from the smashed femur and broken nose. Carlos groans with pain as Ramone begins to pull and try to lift his brother from the back of the trunk. It is clear he is struggling and I begin to move forward to give him some help.

"Leave it, Dean. We have all day to watch him struggle and no matter what pain he feels now it's nothing to what it's going to be soon." Nick looks around to assess if there are any threats.

After what appears to be an age, Ramone finally manages to drag his injured brother from the boot of the car and now, both standing linked arm in arm, they slowly begin the final walk up the small concrete path. Nick pushes the two of them across their backs in the direction of the house doorway as I begin to close the boot lid on the blood drenched plastic sheet then follow the three of them towards the house. The small skull pieces and blood pool from Marco's head have already begun to dry in the warmth of the sunshine as flies begin to land on the red patch of concrete near the front door. Ramone can be seen helping his brother over the small, dark wooden step and, rubbing past the flaking green paint of the front door, he stops next to the body of Marco lying in the small hallway.

"Move inside to the left," Nick commands and the injured brothers step over the body of Marco and continue into the left room.

Walking through the doorway, the hallway is already filled with the buzz of flies landing on Marco's partly removed head with a large pool of blood already collected on the worn red ornate floor tiles. The smell of fresh blood is overwhelmed by the stench of shit and piss from the open sewer seen at the side of the house.

"Close the door," Nick requests and I push the door against the frame hard to slam it shut.

The house is the last one in a row with the start of a hillside to the left and an empty house to the right. The light blue wall paint in the small hallway can be seen peeling and blistering from the rising damp caused by the open sewer and hillside opposite with a staircase made from cheap pallet wood leading upstairs. Stepping over Marco's body, I walk into the room where the others are already standing. The room stinks of rising damp with the pinkish painted plaster walls crumbling from the water ingress. Looking around the room, there is a double sofa, coffee table and pair of dining chairs with another door leading into a kitchen behind. Black stains on the walls can be seen where pictures once hung and the moth eaten net curtains float gracefully in the wind that passes through the broken windowpanes.

"Place your brother on the sofa and sit on this chair," Nick commands as he drags a cheap plastic dining chair to the centre of the room.

After carefully lowering his brother onto the sofa, Ramone sits on the chair and instantly begins to shake with fear of what Nick will do to him and his brother. Nick, still having the AK-47 hanging from his shoulder, walks near to the edge of the room and places the gun on a small coffee table. He then drags the other dining chair closer to Ramone. He takes out some electrical cable, ties and binds Ramone's ankles to the chair legs, then binds his wrists together behind the chair back and finally sits down opposite him.

"Now I'm going to ask you some questions and if I don't like the answer you will die. Is that clear?" Nick leans forward, staring into Ramone's eyes.

Ramone nods his head in agreement as the questioning commences.

"So why did you flee the UK so quickly, Ramone?"

"I know it looks bad, boss, but we were worried after the robbery went wrong and we wanted to leave before the chase was on for us!" Ramone takes a big sigh and lowers his head in shame.

"Really, is that so? And leaving the UK saved the rest of us from getting caught, hey!" Nick grabs his black hair, lifts his head, spits into Ramone's face then stands and quickly walks into the kitchen.

"Dean, you must believe me, we have done nothing wrong!" Ramone looks across as I stand near the window cradling the AK. Nick can be heard throwing kitchen drawers everywhere with the sound of plates and drinking glasses smashing along with cutlery clinking as it hits the hard tiled floor.

Walking back into the room, Burns is carrying a large carving kitchen knife, a hammer and a pair of long nose pliers. "So let's see if Carlos agrees with your little story."

He walks across to Carlos who is lying across the sofa now almost fully unconscious from pain. Placing the hammer and knife on the floor, he grabs one of his hands and, leaning across Carlos's body, quickly attaches the pliers and with a quick wrenching action starts to pull off his fingernails one by one as Carlos suddenly screams with pain, struggling against the attack by Nick and tries to hit him as Ramone begins to cry.

"Nick, please, we are both innocent and have done nothing wrong," Ramone sobs as Burns collects the tools from the floor.

"If you have any love left for your brother Ramone, I will give one more chance to tell the truth." Nick drops Carlos's hand then walks across to grab Ramone by his black hair, pulling his head back.

He punches him across the face, breaking his nose and sending a spurt of blood flying into the air as Ramone grunts with pain. Nick releases his grip and Ramone lowers his head with blood beginning to drip onto the dirty red tiled floor. Staring through the window, a car drives past slowly but shows no intention in stopping as Nick reaches Carlos, treading on the removed fingernails and crunching them against the tiled floor. Ramone tries to look over his shoulder to see what Nick will do next as the large carving knife is pushed into the gunshot wound and gradually twisted with Carlos screaming out in agony. Trying to hit Nick with his bloody hands.

"Stop, stop! All right, I will tell you anything but please leave him alone." Nick retracts the knife and then, walking behind Ramone, places the blood-covered blade against his neck.

"So what do you want to tell me, traitor?" Nick snarls.

"Okay, while we were in the UK an agent, Director Wagstaff, approached us both looking for information about you." Nick removes the blade and Ramone takes a deep sigh of relief.

"Go on, and what did you tell him?" Nick walks across and, placing the tools onto the floor, he sits back in the cheap chair leans forward and picks up a piece of cloth from the floor. He then starts to wipe Carlos's blood from his hands.

"He kept asking about your next job, about Dean and the other gang members." Ramone lowers his head again in guilt.

"Continue." Nick leans back in the squeaky chair.

"Wagstaff said that if we helped him to catch you the government would offer us new identities and immunity, granting us free exile anywhere in the old Commonwealth." Ramone lifts his head to look across at Nick.

"So what was the outcome? Did you and your brother sell me out for a free passport and new life?" Nick stands.

"Nick, I'm sorry, but he was threatening to deport us and inform the Felicio gang. He knew everything about what happened and why we were under your protection." Ramone begins to have tears running down his face.

"Really? I have some information about an Agent Wilson who you were fucking and giving pillow talk to."

Ramone, looking shocked, replies, "Err boss, what do you mean?"

"So all I want to know is if it was you pair that sold me out. Well, your little plan has failed anyway." Nick walks back over to Carlos.

"What do you mean, Nick?" Ramone tries to turn his head to see what is happening with Burns.

"Do you think I would be that stupid to enter Brazil without meeting your uncle? Who, by the way, sends his regards and wants me to relay a message."

"Message? What message?" Ramone asks with nervousness in his voice.

"That your father never forgave you and your brother for betraying the family name." Ramone lowers his head again in guilt, trying not to sob.

Ramone, starting to shake, asks, "What else did he say?"

"Quite simple, you will both never be welcome in his family again." Nick takes the pistol from his belt and beckons me over.

"So, before we kill you both, what else did you tell that bitch? Did you mention anything about the next job?" Nick points across at Carlos and with the sign of death strokes his index finger across his neck, signalling for me to kill him. As instructed, I walk over to Carlos and, lifting the AK, point the gun at his head and then click off the safety catch.

"I don't know what you mean? I never mentioned anything!" Ramone shouts.

With a gradual squeeze of the trigger, the room echoes with a single gunshot as a bullet round is fired into the back of Carlos's head, spraying blood and brain tissue into the air.

"Noo, you fuckin' bastard! No, Carlos, I'm so sorry!" Ramone screams.

Nick stands and, leaning across to Ramone, pushes the end of the carving knife into the side of his neck. "Do it. Do it, you fuckin' psycho." Ramone screams in pain and shock.

"Not yet for you, your suffering is only just starting and for sure you will be begging soon enough for us shoot you." Nick lowers the knife then walks back into the kitchen.

Ramone continues to weep at the death of his brother as I look across with the lump in my throat still trying to digest the torture that Carlos must have gone through and the pain Ramone must now be feeling. Nick can be heard slamming doors in an attempt to find something else to inflict pain on Ramone with me continuing to cradle the machine gun and looking out of the window for any possible threat, not even registering that I killed Carlos. Walking back into the room, Nick can be seen carrying a length of electrical cable. Making his way over to the nearest wall socket, he takes the carving knife and splits the cable ends then, holding one end, throws the cable out into the room, forming a line on the floor towards Ramone. Walking into the hallway, he clicks off the main isolator switch and quickly makes his way back into the room where he starts to push the bare wire ends into the socket. Noticing that the cable is slightly short, he then drags the chair, with Ramone still attached and sobbing, closer to the wall socket.

"What are you doing now, Nick? Please, I have told you everything." Ramone, still trying to protest his innocence, realises what Nick is planning.

"Dean, go into the hallway and operate the electrical switch when I tell you." I nod in agreement with no comment. Nick begins to make off the other ends of the wire to expose the bare copper inside as Ramone begins try and move around in the chair, struggling to escape. Nick punches him in the face again, then begins to wrap one wire around each of Ramone's wrists, tying them off tight. Ramone tries to push him away but Nick reaches across for the handgun and hits him at the back of the neck with the butt.

"Now, you traitorous bastard, this is your final chance to tell me the truth before I pass electricity across your heart and you die a slow and agonising death as a traitor should." Nick spits in his face, places the gun back on the table and walks back in the kitchen, emerging with a small glass bottle.

"Nick, I have told you everything, but you're going to kill me no matter what I say now," Ramone replies.

"Think of it as your last confession." Nick places the brown glass bottle on the coffee table next to the gun.

Ramone looks across at the bottle, curious what is inside. "Okay, I told Wilson you were planning the robbery and that Dean had been approached to help."

"What has Dean got to do with it?" Nick asks, walking around Ramone's chair.

"I was jealous, okay? I was always your number two and within days you made such a fuss of him." I walk back in the room after hearing my name.

"I have information that you have been speaking to Wagstaff weeks ago and not just as Dean arrived." Nick lifts his head by the hair to stare at him.

"No, I only met Wagstaff on the Sunday before the robbery," Ramone answers.

"That's not what the Germans told me, they said you had spoken to them about Wagstaff weeks ago and had been feeding information about my organisation though Wilson." Ramone's face suddenly changes to a look of horror now that he has been caught out.

"After everything that I have done for the pair of you, this is how you repay me. Well, enough is enough of this bullshit, I should have killed you two years ago as your father requested." Nick lifts the bottle from the table and starts to unscrew the plastic lid slowly.

"Do you know what this is?" Nick moves the bottle closer to Ramone's bleeding nose.

Ramone takes a smell of the air and instantly recognises the aroma of sulphuric acid and begins to wriggle in his seat away from the bottle, beginning to beg for forgiveness. "Nick, please, I haven't done anything else!" Nick gradually begins to tip the liquid over his head and as the acid touches his skin it begins to burn his flesh and Ramone screams with pain.

"Okay, Dean, flick the fuckin' switch on this bastard," Nick instructs, starting to laugh and continuing to watch Ramone jumping in agony.

Walking back into the hallway, the house is filled with the shouts of Ramone as the acid burns into his eyes and the deep cut on his nose. Reaching the isolator switch, my mind begins to think about what I am doing in killing another person. Even if he betrayed Nick he did nothing to me, but then my loyalty for Nick overtakes my emotions.

Feeling like a prison guard on death row, I suddenly pull the lever with a large click. A huge blue spark jumps across the metal contacts as the electricity begins to flow.

"Arghh." Ramone's screams fill the room as the electric current enters his body, which starts him jumping and twitching in the seat.

Returning to the room, smoke is already beginning to rise from his body as the smell of burning flesh, similar to pork on a barbeque, starts to engulf the senses. Nick can be seen leaning over Ramone with a huge cigar, lighting it from the flames that have begun to ignite from the sulphuric acid.

He looks back and, smiling, says, "Okay, Dean, that's enough," as Ramone continues to twitch and screams with pain.

Reaching the power lever, I pull the switch off with a mechanical click and a large spark can be seen as the power supply is cut. Returning back into the room, Nick can be seen lifting his pistol from the table to shoot Ramone in the head with him now slumped in the chair as his chest gradually moves, trying to breathe, with the clothes covering his body smouldering from the fire and sick oozing from his mouth, still barely alive.

Nick, placing the gun against his left side temple, begins to speak. "You brothers were like sons to me and this betrayal will never be forgotten." A single round is fired and the bullet path from the exit wound can be seen with a blood mist floating in the air. The shot still echoes in my ears as Nick begins to remove Ramone's body from the chair then disconnects the cables with a tear rolling down his cheek. I walk over and help with moving the bodies, still in shock from what has happened in front of my eyes.

"What are we doing with the bodies, Nick?" I ask cautiously.

"There is a can of petrol in the back room, go and fetch it would you?" I nod submissively.

The kitchen is very basic with an old metal sink and some basic cupboards scattered around the room. Most of the light beige doors either hang from the hinges or are smashed and broken. The cupboard underneath the sink has no doors attached so the red plastic petrol can is easily seen on the lower shelf. Reaching inside the cupboard, the smell of fresh petrol masks the stench of rat urine and faeces that litters the kitchen everywhere along with more rising damp. The broken window is covered by a grey vertical blind, and cracked yellow wall tiles hang with mouldy grout around the sink area. Outside the side of the hill borders the small blue painted bricked yard with rubbish and broken furniture lying everywhere. Lifting the can, I turn and begin to walk back in the living room where Nick drags Marco's body next to Ramone's. With his cell, Nick starts to take pictures of the three bodies before he begins to smash their teeth with a hammer and finally cuts off their fingers with the knife, pushing it against the hard flooring cracking each joint. Handing him the petrol can, he unscrews the lid and begins to pour petrol over the two bodies in the centre of the room before throwing the remains over Carlos still left on the sofa.

The fumes from the petrol begin to make my eyes sting as Nick picks up the machine gun and gestures with his head to walk towards the door. Reaching the front door, he turns and throws the cigar against the base of the sofa and waits until the flames begin to ignite from the fuel poured everywhere and across to the bodies. Closing the door, we quickly walk towards the parked car, watching the smoke beginning to exit through the broken windows as the room catches fire.

As we drive away from the house, the flames begin to lick against the outside walls through the windows as thick black smoke bellows into the sky. Following the executions of the brothers, I feel on such a high now being comfortable with my part in their demise, but the underlying thoughts now in the back of my mind is why Nick flew Sophie over to Brazil for these couple of days and clearly he is manipulating the situation. The feeling of being betrayed does begin to cut deep and Nick sensed this last night over his actions. Arriving close to the hotel, Nick parks the car on a nearby road and gestures for us to climb out then, leaving the keys in the ignition along with the guns in the boot, we casually walk into the hotel grounds through the main entrance gate and security lodge then onto the entrance doors. Hearing a car engine start, I turn around to see the blue Taurus being driven past, clearly a member of the PPC gang collecting the car for disposal. Our flight back to the UK is six and a half hours away and, quickly returning to our rooms, we change and check out of the hotel then wait in the hotel lobby. The hotel car arrives to take us for the airport drop and Nick joins me in the lobby. With Sophie already gone on an earlier flight, Nick tries to break the silence between us.

"So, Dean, are you looking forward to the flight back home?"

"Yes, Nick, a flight back to the UK sounds good."

"I just want to apologise that I flew Sophie here, I thought it might help."

"Not sure with what, Nick, but move on, okay?"

"Agreed, Dean." Nick smiles across to me.

We make our way through the hotel doors in the direction of the waiting taxi and with that end this killing spree, realigning what Nick calls the balance of our lives. I'm sure this incident may come back to haunt me. Lowering the bags into the trunk, the driver closes the lid as we open the rear passenger doors then, climbing into the back of the car, make ourselves comfortable on the seat. The driver enters the car and as we move on the cobbled driveway, I stare through the side window of the car to the hotel, wishing my goodbyes and with that the start of the next chapter in my life. After a short journey, the car quickly reaches the international airport as we make our way to the BA flight terminal. The hotel car stops outside the terminal entrance and, taking our bags from the trunk, we walk into the airport, still travelling on false passports. Both walking calmly but swiftly, we separate and I stand, looking at the flight destination boards as Nick continues towards the check in counters. Opening the small front pocket of my travel case, I take out my flight documents and recheck the time and departure gates along with viewing all the security cameras and giving Nick enough time to reach the business counter.

Noticing that Nick has moved on, I casually begin to walk in the terminal building, heading for the check in counters and passing police officers as I go with my heart beat showing no signs of nervousness that was very different from last week.

Reaching the business counter, the lady speaks, "Hallo. Sir, can I help you?"

I hand over my passport. "Yes, I am booked for the Heathrow flight."

"Ah, yes. Thank you," she says as she takes the document.

Then, after a few seconds clicking the keyboard, "Sir, there appears to be a problem."

My heart sinks as I see the words exit from her mouth and reply, "Really, what?"

"Your seat has been double booked under two names but the same number. That's strange."

"Hmm, I have my e-ticket slip. Will that help?"

"Possibly, sir, if I could look." She lifts the receiver of the desk phone and begins to speak to someone in Portuguese.

Casually looking around, it is noted that there are no police or security personnel nearby in case a sharp exit is needed. Continuing to stand at the counter, a man appears next to the lady and starts to look at my passport and previous flight ticket with KLM.

"Sir, who did the return flight booking for you?" the manager asks as I look at his name badge.

Reaching into my front suitcase pocket, I take out the other documents and find the name of the company. "International Expeditors Limited arranged the flights."

The manager presses a few buttons on the keyboard and from the reaction on his face realises that the error is not mine.

"Yes, that's fine, sir. My apologies for the delay, my colleague will complete your check in."

Breathing a silent sigh of relief, I look at the lady as she prints off the boarding pass and hands it over to me.

"Do you have any luggage?"

"Only this small case."

"That's fine, sir, thank you. Have a good flight."

"Excuse me, where is the business lounge?" I ask.

"Oh yes, sorry, sir. Past security and keep to the left. You have priority lane access and the pin code for the business lounge is 8642," she replies.

"Thank you for the help." Turning, I walk away from the counter.

Blending in and remaining calm and composed is critical for passing through all the security checks and drawing no attention to yourself. As I reach the baggage scanning areas Nick is already on the other side gradually walking to the business lounge where we had agreed to meet. The only things to separate from my case for the scanners are the liquids and small aerosols, so taking the clear bag holding them from the front pocket; they are placed onto the small tray. All the mobiles and other items are still in the front pocket of the case. I wait next in line for the scanner, casually looking around the airport at all the security cameras and police officers as my case begins to pass into the x-ray machine. Standing inside the scanner, the suitcase passes through without any issues and, clearing the checkpoint, I collect it and continue in the direction of the lounge past the busy shops and groups of people talking and laughing. My mind begins to play back what has happened over the last few days with Germany first followed now by Brazil and the evil things I have carried out. The betrayal of Nick's actions inviting Sophie bubbles on the surface like boiling water with my thoughts disturbed by a text message being delivered to my cell. Stopping close to a souvenir shop, I open the front pocket and removing the cell from the case, it's unlocked. I press on the message expecting it to be from Nick asking where I am, but instead it reads:

'Mr Nash, we need to talk. Do you have anyone else you can ask for help?'

Casually looking around for anyone who could be watching me after sending the message, I recheck the text and most importantly the cell number. The number starts +44, clearly showing a UK code with the first thoughts that this must be from Wagstaff instantly filling my mind. Then the cell vibrates and sounds as another cell is delivered.

'Your resent actions have alerted other interested parties.'

It must be Nick testing my loyalty. Or maybe it's Sophie trying to play mind games, one of Archibald's clients or finally it could be Wagstaff. Placing my cell into my trouser pocket and zipping up the suitcase front pouch, I continue to walk in the direction of the business lounge wondering who has sent the text. Agreeing in my mind not to mention it to Nick, I press the buttons for the access code for the lounge door and walk inside, instantly feeling an inner peace in the quietness of the lounge against the hustle and bustle from the airport. Scanning my boarding pass barcode, I continue into the lounge, gradually looking for exits, threats and finally the location of Nick who can be seen sitting in the rows of dark leather armchairs placed in the centre of the room. He casually glances across as I enter, walking over in his direction. My bag is lowered onto the floor against an opposite armchair and, walking over towards the refreshment counter, I fetch some food and drink, noticing that Nick had already poured himself a large whisky on ice.

Deciding to remain focused, the option of a soft drink and some fruit is selected, walking back to the armchair; my thoughts turn to the text message and who could have sent it. Reaching the chair, I place the plate of fruit and glass of fresh orange near to Nick's cell resting on the tabletop. We continue to sit opposite each other without a word being spoken, waiting for our flight to be called. I keep running different scenarios through my mind. Is it Nick testing? Is it Nick asking Sophie? Is it Wagstaff or one of the agents or is it, as the text says, another interested party? With all the things that have happened the last few weeks and the assassinations of the Germans, along with the brothers, maybe another ally in this messed up life is not a bad thing. After some time Nick stands and begins to walk in the direction of the washroom so, using this opportunity, I take the cell from my pocket, unlock the code and type in the words.

'Time and place to meet must be public.'

I wait, holding the cell in my slightly shaking hand and keeping a watch both on the toilet door and the message being delivered screen as Nick suddenly reappears. I know if I make any sudden moves he will instantly pick up on them. Casually switching the cell to flight mode and placing it on the table, he instantly notices it sitting opposite me. He stares across and I sense he is waiting to ask me why the cell is out but he doesn't. Maybe it's me but it's clear his mood over the last twenty-four hours has changed, becoming more withdrawn. Possibly the killing of Ramone and Carlos has affected him as he felt them as sons combined with the death of Lloyd, his close friend, and the betrayal from the robbery. It is perhaps too much or it could be that I am reading too much into the situation, but one thing is clear: the time will come when I will be on my own and finding some new help and support is critical for my own self-preservation after how quickly Burns disposed of Greg.

With the darkness of my actions now hanging deep in my thoughts, our plane is then called for boarding and, feeling like Ramone and his walk to death, I look across to Nick, lift my case and gradually begin to walk towards the departure gate. Reaching the gate, first, business and rewards members are asked to board. Showing the pass, I continue onto the aircraft, finding my seat and placing my luggage in the overhead locker. The air hostesses pass around drinks as Nick can be seen sitting a couple of seats behind as the other passengers continue to board. Finally with the doors closed we begin our journey back to the UK as my thoughts are filled with who sent the text message and what could be waiting once the plane lands. Flying into Heathrow airport after the overnight flight, I feel a little tired, but my thoughts are full of killing the four men in the last few days. I feel very different emotions remembering the Monday morning on the ferry and the excitement experienced over the start of this adventure, but now it feels almost like a normal day and past memories now start to awaken my subconscious.

I sense a feeling from many years ago that now begins to leak again into a new possible future, engulfing my emotions and drowning out the type of person I really am. Nick is now becoming uncontrollable and, although he proclaims about clearly loving this type of life, deep down I sense he feels unhappy. For me the excitement of hunting then killing humans feels wrong and goes against normal human behaviour and emotions, and this thought is possibly the main reason why I disappeared those years ago. My deep thoughts are suddenly broken as the plane bumps onto the runway.

I briefly look across to Nick, who is staring out of the window checking for any possible threats. My thoughts now shift to the aircraft door and whether the police will be waiting for us on the aerobridge and if we can safely negotiate ourselves from this aircraft and back to the farmhouse in one piece as the flight crew prepare to open the doors. Nick already mentioned that he would go in front and we would rendezvous at the Europcar rental stand, trying not to draw attention to ourselves, but this could be easier said than done in one of the busiest airports in the world with security

414

personnel everywhere. I stand from my seat and, lifting my case from the overhead locker, begin the walk from the aircraft with nervousness racing through my body. Reaching the landing jetty, no police stand and as we continue into the airport terminal I pass through passport control without any fear. Nick can be seen walking towards the car rental section near the arrivals hall and I casually follow, looking in occasional shop windows to check in the reflection if anyone follows. Finally walking past the car rental section, Nick is already collecting the keys as I stop to wait. With a simple head gesture we continue towards the parked car area and reach the BMW 3 series that has been hired.

Climbing into the passenger seat after placing the cases into the boot, Nick passes me the keys. Starting the engine, we begin the journey to the farmhouse. The security and comfort offered by my apartment fills my emotions but with all this heat going back there is not an option. As with last week, we continue along the now familiar roads. Heavy rains begin to fall and, finally reaching the farmhouse, the final part of the plan with the capture of Wagstaff fills my thoughts as the car turns onto the gravel driveway. It's clear from our previous discussions that Nick will stop at nothing until Wagstaff is caught and tortured. Stopping just short of the metal gates, Nick jumps out of the car and begins to drag them open. As I stare through the rain soaked windscreen he waves me through quickly and, continuing slowly along the crunching driveway, it feels like months since we were last here. But also, strangely, a warm, welcoming feeling, as though I have returned back home, seems to flow into my body.

Stopping close to the main door of the farmhouse, the engine is switched off and, climbing out of the car, the wetness of the autumn rain can be felt on my face as I walk around to the back of the car. Lifting the two bags from the boot, Nick joins me as we continue towards the direction of the front door. Reaching the door, Burns makes several turns of the key, clicking the heavy mechanism with the faint noise of rain lashing against the windows. The door is quickly pushed open and, walking into the hallway, the silence is broken with each footstep, followed by Nick deactivating the alarm system. We continue to climb up the wooden staircase with the faint scent of musty air filling my nose as the last light of the day tries to break through the rainclouds but the dullness is too overpowering. Reaching the top of stairs, he switches on the kitchen ceiling lights, illuminating the darkness.

After the long journey, the welcoming sight of the sofa and chairs takes over my emotions and, placing the bags next to one of the armchairs, I collapse into the comfort of the leather surrounding my body, giving me a sense of security in the farmhouse. Leaning back with my head resting against the chair, I stare up to the ceiling and then, closing my eyes, the noise of Nick beginning to fill the coffee machine with water echoes through the open plan room. The rustling of a coffee packet can be heard followed by the whirring noise of the coffee machine beginning to warm the water.

His footsteps echo through the room, followed by the sliding noise of one balcony door being opened and finally the sound of geese calling on the lake fills the air. The smell of fresh coffee begins to float across from the kitchen as Nick returns and then, lifting out cups from the cupboard along with taking spoons from the drawer, the drink can be heard being prepared. Footsteps echo as he walks across towards the sofa and, placing two cups of fresh coffee on the table, he then sits on the sofa as the leather squeaks, absorbing his body.

Taking a big sigh, he says, "Well, what an action packed last few days, hey?"

Replying with, "Hmm." I say nothing.

"Let us rest for a few hours then have some dinner, yes!"

I nod in agreement, saying, "Yes, fine, Nick, no problem."

"Is everything okay, Dean?"

"Yes, Nick, why do you ask?"

"You seem a little quiet."

"Just tired with all the travel." Deep down, however, my emotions are beginning to feel very differently. The wind begins to increase outside, battering the rain harder against the windows.

"Okay, after this drink I will go and fetch a few supplies. Do you want anything?" Burns asks.

"No, I'm fine, thanks."

Nick, looking into the eye of the storm, watches the rain battering against the windows as he gradually sips his drink. Finally after several minutes he stands, places the cup in the sink and turns, saying, "Okay, well, see you in about an hour or so."

The sound of his footsteps down each wooden step is followed by the front door being opened and closed. The faint noise of gravel rustling is heard before the engine starts and he drives away. This is my opportunity to check if any messages have arrived so, quickly taking the cell from the case, I unlock the screen and switch off the flight mode button. I continue to sit in the armchair, grasping the cell in my hand and hoping for a message to be delivered in an attempt of holding onto a future that is not fixed.

15

Meanwhile Shaun paces up and down in his apartment, wondering what to do next with his mind completely confused with the threats from McGough and death of Chloe and not knowing what to do first. Seeing Nash's apartment keys hanging up, Neal sees red and snatches them from the hook, deciding to visit the apartment and establish where Nash could have disappeared to without telling his best friend. So, storming out of his own still ramshackled flat, he quickly runs up the staircase in the direction of Nash's apartment. Reaching Nash's door, he inserts the key and gradually begins to open the door and is shocked by what he sees. He begins to walk around the apartment that has been completely cleared of any furniture and possessions, leaving just the blinds and curtains hanging from the windows with a few pictures and pieces of paper lying on the laminate flooring. He walks into the kitchen where all the cupboards have been cleared and looks inside the open refrigerator for any signs, but even all the food has gone. Continuing into the bedroom, all the wardrobes have been emptied, just leaving a few clothes hangers looking as though no one had ever lived there.

Shaun walks back towards the front door. Looking around the living room and remembering some of the good times he had there, still shocked, he begins to walk back to his own apartment, wondering what to do next. His cell vibrates, signalling a message has been delivered. Taking out his mobile, he unlocks the screen and checks the message sent from a familiar number that reads, 'Nash, just arrived back in the UK at Heathrow airport.' Neal, reaching his own apartment, kicks his way through the rubbish and walks into the bedroom, taking a box from the wardrobe. He places the box on his bed and unclips the lid to reveal a semi auto pistol and two magazine clips. Lifting out the gun, he takes a clip and inserts it into the pistol handle, pulling back the top slide. Fear and anger can be seen deep in his eyes as he storms out of the apartment, heading for the garage. Reaching his car, he starts the engine and races out of the basement in an attempt to try and head off Nash but, with Burns planning, he and Nash are already long gone.

Agent Briggs sitting at his desk continues his search tracing back Nash's life from old electoral records, birth certificates and finally traces back old addresses with no clear pattern forming. He collects information from schools and colleges and finally universities until a complete picture of Nash's apparent life is established. After placing some clothes in his car, he starts to drive from London towards Knutsford, Cheshire trying to please his mentor, Wagstaff. The first address to investigate, taken from the handwritten notes in his black book, is the old family home. He parks outside the 1950s' detached house and notices the curtains moving slightly. Climbing out of the car, he walks along the cracked and broken tarmacked driveway. Reaching the door, he makes his presence known by banging the large, black lion-headed knocker firmly.

Briggs stands by the door, looks around the overgrown front garden with grass and weeds everywhere and waits for any sounds inside but nothing is heard. He knocks on the door again, knowing that the curtains moved and this time also announces that it's a police detective. "Hello, sir, this is Detective Briggs and I would like to ask you a few questions." He shouts.

A small whirring noise can be heard and then, as agent Briggs tries to look through the frosted glass in the front door, the locks start to be opened. A frail old man supported by walking sticks opens the door slightly and says, "Hello, Detective, do you have any identification?"

Agent Briggs reaches into his jacket and, taking out his warrant card, shows it to the man. With shaking hands the old man takes the warrant card and checks the details. "Please enter," the old man announces and fully opens the door.

Walking into the old house, Agent Briggs follows the man down the entrance hall and into the living room. The house has old pictures on the walls and the threadbare carpets do little to protect the flooring underneath having most of the pattern worn away. The two men reach the living room and the old man gestures for Briggs to sit on the old floral patterned settee. The old man then lowers himself into an old leather chesterfield armchair next to a fireplace with the last remaining ashes still smouldering. Then Briggs takes out a small black notebook from his pocket and begins to ask a few questions.

"Would you mind confirming your name, sir?" Briggs asks.

"Yes, Detective, my name is Gordon Humphries," he replies.

"Okay, sir, and can you confirm how long you have lived here?"

"Well, a very long time. Probably since 1952."

"Okay, sir, thank you but our records don't show you living at this address, but it could be a mistake." Briggs scribbles a note into his book.

"Well, young man, I assure you I have lived here since then. I can fetch the deeds if you like?"

"No, sir, that won't be necessary. It must be a mistake. There is no need for that," Briggs replies.

"So what is the problem, Detective?" Humphries asks.

"There is no problem. I am just trying to establish if anyone called Dean Nash has ever lived here."

"Dean Nash, hmm. Well, that's a name from the past."

"So you know Mr Nash, sir?" Briggs leans forward, interested.

"Well, I certainly I know of him. What has he done?"

"I am looking for him to assist with some of our ongoing enquires," Briggs replies.

"Enquires into what, Detective Briggs?" Humphries asks.

"I'm sorry, sir, I can't divulge that information at this time."

"So I guess you are checking out his old schools and colleges, hey, to build up a profile. That sounds like a murder case. Interesting."

"I'm sorry, sir, but you seem to know a lot about police techniques. Were you with any force?"

"Yes, I was once with a force. Are you here on your own, Detective?" Humphries moves in his seat to get more comfortable.

"Yes, sir, I thought it was pointless for two officers to travel from London here."

"Hmm, that could be a mistake."

"A mistake? Why, sir?" Briggs starts to become nervous and twitches in his seat.

Just then two men burst through another door with silenced handguns. "Well, I imagine that it is you who has been looking through all those old records in an attempt to find Nash, leading you here first. Am I right?"

"What is this, Mr Humphries? Do you realise that I am a serving officer!" Briggs tries to act tough but deep down he is shaking with fear.

"Do you realise, young man, that I only need to click my fingers and you are dead? Who gave you permission and authority to look into Dean Nash's files?"

Briggs, now shaking with fear, knows he has nowhere to hide and replies, "Well, it was my boss Intelligence Director John Wagstaff."

"Argh, John Wagstaff, another name from the past. Does he know that you are here?"

"Err, no, why?"

"Well that's another mistake, young man, not telling your commanding officer your whereabouts."

Briggs, now sensing his fate, tries to act tough again, replying, "Well, all cars have trackers now so all our movements are monitored."

"You really think that will save you?" Humphries smiles as he clicks his fingers and the two men shoot Briggs dead in a volley of shots.

Briggs's body falls on to the floor next to a threadbare rug where the two men quickly holster the guns. One man, dressed in a dark grey suit and brown hair about 40 years old, feels through the clothes of Briggs and removes his car keys, then begins to walk out of the house as the other man, around 50 years old and dressed in a dark blue suit, rolls Briggs inside the old carpet material. The man then lifts the limp body of Briggs and drags it into the hallway and then onwards to the back garden where the other man is waiting with a white bag of powder. The pair of men can then be seen dropping the body into a pre dug hole and finally the top flap of rug is opened by one of the men. The man dressed in the dark grey suit, then scatters a bag of quick lime over Briggs's body.

The flap is turned back over and then both men begin to cover the body with shovels full of soil and rubble as the old man supervises from the kitchen doorway of the house, leaning against the frame for support. Once the carpet and body are covered, the man dressed in dark blue, can be seen walking towards the precast concrete garage and, opening the door, then unlocks a car boot and reaches inside to take out a clean pair of shoes. After changing the shoes, he walks into the garage then starts the engine and reverses out a blue Jaguar car. The second man walks back to the house and helps the old man into the car. After changing his shoes, the grey suited man then walks down the drive and the sound of a car engine is heard as he drives Briggs car inside the garage. Climbing out, he closes the garage door and walks back to the house checking that the doors are locked. Quickly looking around to make sure no witnesses have seen the events, he climbs into the front passenger side of the car and all the men gradually drive onto the main road with not a single word uttered between them.

"Jeremy, will you take me home now?" the old man asks.

"Yes, Mr McGough," he replies.

I sit relaxed in the armchair listening to the last of the rain hitting the windows waiting for a reply from my message and now think it must be a contact from Archibald. I also know that this could be my only option to escape from Burns. After what feels like an eternity my thoughts are broken by a message being delivered.

'Mr Nash, there is much I can do to help your situation. Burns wants to kill you! We must meet?'

I read the message several times to recalibrate what has been sent and after digesting the options I send a reply.

'I am interested in what you would like to discuss. When could we meet?' I press send.

I quickly look at my watch to check the time since Nick went out, and placing the cell on the arm of the chair, I wait for a reply. Then the sound I was dreading: a car on the gravel driveway. I know Burns returning will affect the answer being read. Switching the cell to silent I place it back in the bag, stand and walk over towards the balcony with a sick feeling in my stomach, confirming the thoughts I have had all along. Nick can be heard parking the car then the doors open and close followed by a few steps on the gravel and finally the front door opening. My heart sinks even deeper knowing that the decision to give up my old life and start this new one, although it sounded exciting those few weeks ago, now already starts to feel like a my soul has been ripped from my body and the trust I had for Nick combined with this latest information confirms no one can be trusted. Nick's footsteps reach the top of the staircase as I continue to look over the balcony, listening to the sounds of the wildfowl on the lake. Shopping bags are heard being placed on the worktops and he joins me on the balcony. It must be obvious to him that I am not happy but he ignores the signals or pretends not to see them.

Nick asks, "What do you want to eat?"

"I don't mind, really. I'm not that hungry."

"Hmm, okay. I will make something light. How about a simple salad?"

"Yes, fine, okay," I respond without any eye contact.

He walks back into the kitchen and begins placing the bags of the food into the refrigerator. The rustling of plastic can be heard as he starts to prepare the salad as I continue to think about what I have done. This was not the life I was looking for, but now I am stuck until I can change the odds in my favour and it seems that the contact is the only option for my escape.

I walk into the kitchen to join Nick, who has finished preparing the salad, as he asks, "Are you feeling a little rested now? I can't wait to get Wagstaff."

"What then, Nick? What happens after we kill Wagstaff? What happens then?"

"That's simple. We move onto the next job," he replies.

"So are we always going to be on the run?" I ask as we walk towards the dining table then, sitting on the chairs we continue our conversation.

"Well, after this next job we will never have to worry again."

"Strange, you said that about the last job and here we are!"

"I never said it would be easy!" Nick snaps.

"No, but you also said we wouldn't be running like hunted fugitives." I place the cutlery on the table.

"It's Wagstaff. Trust me, once he is dead, we can bury our tracks and be gone."

"Oh, and killing the director of Intelligence for Great Britain won't bring any undue attention, hey!" I speak with a raised voice.

"Dean, please give me a chance to prove it. I haven't been wrong so far."

"Apart from being on the run you are right, but I don't want to live constantly looking over my shoulder."

"Dean, guys like us will always be looking over our shoulder for the bad things we have done in the past. Do you really think that after our previous missions, we could simply have a normal life with a wife, family, little house and rose garden? Get serious man, you're a trained assassin with enemies all over the world."

Nick continues, "For you to escape once from that life and disappear for years was a miracle and for you to do it again, well it has never been done." Nick stares across at me.

"How long was I missing, Nick?" I ask more calmly, trying to gather information over my past.

"Altogether about eight years and we all thought you were dead after your last op went so wrong."

"What was the op?"

"Top secret, Dean, all we knew was that you had gone over to Turkey to extract a female operative who had intelligence over a rouge terrorist group from Syria."

Nick takes a drink of water. "We all thought you were crazy to volunteer, but the confidence you had to parachute in at night and complete a daytime extraction was madness."

"So what happened?" I ask.

"The woman got to the pickup point with bullet wounds and later died and you were never seen again. A few agents went in to try and find you but all were killed."

I try to look back into my past thoughts to establish what happened but the memories are not there. "So how did I get back here?"

"You were acting strange before you volunteered and the cardinals didn't want to send you, apart from one guy."

"Who was that guy?" I ask, wondering if it could be the contact.

"There were some cardinals who were never known and he could have been one of them. Now have you calmed down a little from earlier?"

"Yes, thanks." I am still unsure of his actions and he knows more than he lets on.

"I need your help with this next job, then. That is it no more." Nick smiles.

Feeling a little more relaxed, I continue with the salad and we enjoy the afternoon. My mind searches for the past memories that Nick talked about but nothing seems to register. One thing is for sure and the message over Burns wanting to kill me is information causing my mind to lose direction, not knowing what is fact or fiction. I must meet this contact to see what they can offer even if just for my sanity. Walking back into the kitchen, the plates are placed into the dishwasher.

"I'm going to work on the plans for Wagstaff's capture, do you want to help?" Burns asks.

"No thanks, I need a little rest." So, turning, I walk down the staircase back to the room from last weekend. Reaching the room, I lay on the bed and fall asleep. Nick continues to work on the final points of the plan to kidnap Wagstaff in the finite detail.

Waking up wondering what the time is, I stand and leave the bedroom to begin the walk back up the staircase. As I reach the top Nick can be seen slumped over the dining table, asleep, with his head resting on his arms with papers and documents underneath. I walk over and gently touch his shoulder. That instantly causes him to jump up and in the process I turn slightly, fall and hit my head on one of the dining chairs, knocking myself out. The next thing I remember as I open my eyes is Nick standing over me with the feeling of wetness on my head. My head feels like a sledgehammer has hit the side and, as I gently lift my right hand, the wetness is from a water soaked cloth Burns placed on my head.

Gradually Nick helps me to sit up then finally, he supports me as I sit on one of the dining chairs with him constantly asking, "Are you okay? It was my fault."

Still feeling very groggy, I ask, "How long was I out?"

"Well, for a few hours, it must have been a strong knock. How many fingers can you see?" He waves three in front of my eyes.

"Err, six, or are you just a mutant? Only three," I reply.

"Phew, you had me worried for a bit."

"My head feels like it has been used as a football." Even with the pain something is different as Nick fetches me a glass of water then places it in front of me.

"Well, that's most of Saturday gone. What were you thinking trying to wake me up?" Nick explains.

"My bad I guess." My thoughts are starting to become clearer.

"Do you want me to make you something to eat?" Burns asks.

The message I received was right, but the last thought that stabs at my heart is that of a cardinal saying, "You, my boy, are too big for this operation and if you get caught, I for one will not arrange your release, you are an expandable asset to this country." His familiar voice on the phone stings deep.

Standing, I walk downstairs. "Where are you going, Dean?" Nick asks, concerned.

"Need a change of clothes and then I will eat something, okay," I reply.

Reaching the bedroom and closing the door, I take out the cell from the case and see a message has been delivered. Opening the screen, the message is from the same number previously seen, so clicking open, I read the message.

'We can meet Sunday afternoon if that works for you?'

Knowing this is my only option, I write a reply. 'Okay, will give you a call tomorrow afternoon.'

In a few minutes a reply is delivered. 'Very good, Mr Nash.' And with that message the wheels are in motion to another possible chapter.

After changing my clothes and washing my face, I walk back up the stairs to continue with the Wagstaff capture plan and, sitting near to Nick by the dining table, pull out a chair and stare at Burns.

"Now that I've regained my focus, I'm sure you were planning to show me the Wagstaff kidnap plan."

"Yes, yes, it's here but are you feeling up to it?"

"Ready as ever," I reply.

Nick starts to explain the plan as my past thoughts begin to ignite memories and confirm my worst fears of what Burns has been telling me. I remember some of the Turkish operation and being locked in a torture room for information much like we had done with Thomas and Josef with partial thoughts on how I managed to escape. I decide to keep this information to myself as one vivid memory returns and that conversation I overheard where Nick's voice explains how he wants to kill me.

"Well, how are we going to capture him? It won't be easy, I bet he has personal trackers and things like that," I ask.

"Dean, not a problem. We will hit him with a Taser gun that will act like a signal jammer. That way he will be unconscious and we can carry out a full body scan." Nick speaks calmly and is composed.

"He has agents guarding him all the time." I ask.

"Dean, everyone is vulnerable at some time of the day and just when you least expect it!"

Nick continues, "I have been tracking Wagstaff's movements for months so we can get him Sunday morning when he walks to the local shop for his newspaper."

Looking at Nick I ask, "So who's doing the driving and the shooting?"

Nick starts to laugh. "I've wanted to shoot that bastard for years, so you're not having that glory now!"

"What about transport?" I ask.

"Already sorted, I have arranged a white hire van," he replies, still smiling.

As Nick and I continue the details of Wagstaff's kidnapping, I begin to search for more answers as past images of people's faces and places start to filter back into the medial temporal lobe sections of my brain, but how much of it is fact and fiction is difficult to decipher at this time with my head still feeling as though it has been hit by a large hammer. After the conversations with Burns and Archibald, it is possible my subconscious is looking for any answers to fill in the blank pages of my past life, placing any parts of a story to make a memory. The reason behind why so many of my memories were missing in the first place and who erased them is the biggest mystery. It is clear the one reason why I was comfortable with Burns's company is due to our past together and my subconscious would have recognised this. Knowing that he wants to kill me shows his betrayal in my loyalty and now, after I helped him remove the other gang members, it's clear Burns will kill me when he can get the chance. Maybe helping to kidnap Wagstaff could be a good idea to see if any details are leaked. With my life now changed so much, if Wagstaff isn't stopped he will always be hunting me so learning more about him should give me an edge and hopefully some advantage in the future once I can remove the threat of Burns and continue with my new life. My mind focuses back to the present time and keeping Nick entertained is the best option as the conversation continues.

"So how quickly do you think the armed response officers will be scrambled once we take him down?" I ask.

"I reckon we have about four minutes to knock him out and get moving," Burns replies.

"You say the Taser will act like a signal jammer? How long do we have after the shock?"

"My, Dean, you have serious questions tonight. It must be that knock to your head, eh?"

"No, Nick, I just want to make sure our backs are covered," I reply, smiling.

"Well, we have about thirty minutes once the voltage supply is stopped, but the tracker will be difficult to remove since it's probably deep inside his mid-section. So easier to stun him again," Burns answers.

I sit staring at Burns with an anger beginning to grow inside as the chaos around me starts to draw me deeper into the darkness of an ugly past. With every minute my mind searches for any reason to react to his words in an aggressive manner, but keeping calm is critical for the next couple of days until I have spoken with the contact on Sunday afternoon. My thoughts change to how I can escape from Burns and make contact on the Sunday and ultimately who the person is along with what they can offer. Burns must sense my inner anger being in such close proximity and his presence starts to feel like a bad taste in my mouth. My mind, hungry for information, tries to search for any old memories of these feelings before with only flitting images that keep disappearing.

After Burns finishes running through the plan, it's clear I must kill him to escape from this life and I begin to kick myself for raising my head up again from the simple life I had managed to make. The feelings of missing something from my life all those weeks ago confirm this past life I walked away from, but how can I disappear again? Nick begins to prepare some food for dinner and, as with other times, before we dine we just make small talk and basic conversation but there is an excitement in his voice and the kidnapping of Wagstaff fills his every word. As for me, the kidnapping of Wagstaff could lead to a better understanding of my old life and hopefully a method and plan for my future. After finishing the meal, we tidy away the dishes, plates and cutlery then retire to our separate bedrooms deep in thought over what could happen tomorrow and each of us wanting to capture Wagstaff for our own reasons. After a restless night's sleep I awake to the noise of Burns walking around upstairs and, after washing and dressing, I join him for a quick coffee and toast before we make moves for the day ahead. As with last night there is a solitary quietness between us as though that missing link of friendship we had before is now beginning to break as we start to drift apart, wanting different things.

16

Nick and I walk out from the protection of the farmhouse and make our way to the car, closing the large oak front door with a definitive thud. The car is covered with early morning dew as the birds sing the autumn chorus and the dampness in the air touches the skin on our faces. Taking some kitchen roll from his pocket, Nick wipes the condensation from the windows as I walk towards the front gates along the gravel driveway to open them. Burns has hardly said a word this morning and I can tell from his body language he is deep in thought as he opens the door and lowers himself in to the driver's seat then, turning the key, starts the engine. The door is closed with a loud thud as I reach the gates and, placing my hand on the catch, the coolness of the steel from the morning air can be felt touching my skin. Opening the gates with a gradual creaking sound the noise of the car moving along the gravel can be heard. The car approaches and drives through. Closing and locking the gate, I climb into the front passenger seat to be greeted with some slight warmth from the heaters as Nick says, "A bit fresh in here this morning, hey." The heater switch is clicked down a setting, reducing the whirring noise.

Nodding my head in agreement, we begin another chapter in my new life and the kidnapping of a government agent director that will certainly end in his death and for us promotion to the top of Britain's most wanted list and being hunted all over the world. We start to travel along the narrow country lanes, splashing through puddles formed from last night's rain along the roads heading for a small lock up garage and the white hire van needed for the kidnapping of Wagstaff. My thoughts drift towards what Wagstaff may say and the actions he could carry out, being an ex-solider. Nick has the Taser gun ready in his pocket that we will use to stun him and knock out any tracking devices that could be hidden in his body. Continuing along the narrow lane, we reach the main road in Nuthurst, beginning the drive back into London for the direction of Caterham. As we reach the outskirts of Caterham, Nick turns right near a petrol station and heads for a row of lock up garages. The garages are all prefab concrete with the steel doors painted differently in groups.

Stopping at the last green door, Nick looks across and asks me, "Dean, take this key and unlock the doors. The van is open and keys are under the sun visor. You back it out and I wait."

So, climbing out of the car and closing the door, I walk over to the garage and insert the silver key into the padlock. The lock clicks open and I unthread the ring through the black hasp and staple catch to pull open the wooden doors. The morning sunshine reflects inside the concrete garage to reveal a white ford transit van with Hertz rental stickers across the back. Nick parks the car and waits for me to reverse the van into the open. Walking to the front, I push the button and open the door lock. I climb up into the driver's seat quickly and my nostrils are filled with the smell of new plastic and, looking into the back, I notice it's covered in thick white sheeting. It's clear that Wagstaff will be killed and covering the van confirms no traces are left. Tilting the sun visor, the keys drop into my right hand and the engine finally starts after several seconds of trying. Reverse gear is engaged as the van begins to move backwards. My nervous breathing causes water vapour in the cabin and condensation to form on the cold windscreen. Looking at the dashboard, the heaters are switched on, filling the van with a squeaking noise from the electric fan starting to run.

Light illuminates the back of the van as the morning rays of sunshine shimmer through the rear windows making it difficult to see as the lumpiness of the cold engine causes vibrations to pass in to the steering wheel at low speeds. The van is parked next to the hire car and Nick drives it into the empty garage. After a few seconds he emerges carrying a small black bag, closes the doors and re feeds the padlock through the catch clicking it shut.

He walks across to me and, climbing into the cabin, places the black bag in the footwell. "Okay, Dean let's get that bastard Wagstaff. It's payback time at last." He speaks with an aggressive tone in his voice.

Driving away from the lock up garage, I ask Nick, "Which direction?"

His simple reply still echoes in my mind. "Keep heading towards Tilford where that fuckin' traitor lives." More aggression is felt with his cold answer.

Beginning the journey to Tilford, Nick already knows that Wagstaff fetches his Sunday newspaper at 7.45 a.m. from the local shop next to the pub The Barley Mow, so his plan is to be ready and be parked along the route for the kidnap. Quickly looking at my wristwatch, the time clicks over to 6.30 a.m. and we start to leave the busy suburbs of Caterham, heading into the countryside along the A22, heading for the M25. After fifty minutes of driving, passing through small villages along the A3, we finally pass the village sign for Tilford.

Nick starts to give directions. "Okay, slow down and drive past the school on the left then take the second right opposite the red phone box. The shop and local pub are next to each other so we can wait down the small lane until he appears."

He continues, "I will get out and walk up behind Wagstaff, hitting him with the Taser. At the same time you bring the van up slowly with the side door already open so you can stop and help drag him inside."

Nick makes it sound so easy and trouble free as I turn into the lane opposite the phone box. The lane is very narrow and has a gentle slope just wide enough for the van to pass, but I need to turn around and park close to the top near the junction.

So, pulling into a gateway, the van is reversed and turned around to drive back up the lane. Nick starts to fidget around in the black bag between his feet, taking out two thin waterproof overalls, gloves and masks. He pulls on a pair of the latex gloves and reaches inside the bag for the final item, a silenced pistol that he checks, loads a round into the chamber and clicks on the safety catch. The look in his eyes it that of sheer hatred and anger as he places the pistol on the dashboard.

"Okay, Dean, stop a little short of the junction in that small gateway, we need to get these overalls on." The time clicks to seven twenty-five.

Both climbing out of the van, we step into the thin blue overalls and, pulling on the pair of gloves, I take one of the plastic masks and pull it over my face.

My nose is filled with the smell of cheap vacuum formed plastic as the thin elastic band cuts into the back of my head. The close contact of the plastic instantly starts my skin sweating and causes the mask impression to stick onto my face. Nick fits his mask and, as with me, it distorts his face in an attempt to hide his identity. Sliding open the side door of the van, I attach the lock in place and see the time on my wrist watch clicks onto seven thirty-five. My heart begins to beat a little faster as seven forty reaches closer and with every second my hands begin to shake more and more.

"It's only natural for your hands to shake. After all, it's not every day you kidnap a government agent. Patience is the thing as all things come to those who wait." Nick stares into the distance.

The figure of a person begins to appear in the distance and with a distinctive limp we both know it's him walking along the pavement. "Wagstaff, you fuckin' bastard," Nick mutters under his breath.

"Okay, Dean, you give me twenty seconds then start the van." Just then a young child can be seen running behind Wagstaff.

"Is that kid with Wagstaff?" I ask.

"Fuck it, must be his grandson. Well, it's too late now, he comes with us too!" Nick replies.

"Are you fuckin' serious? Taking Wagstaff is bad enough, but his grandson as well? That will just start a nationwide search," I say, raising my voice to Nick.

"Dean, we can use the grandson as leverage to get answers from Wagstaff and then release him somewhere later, okay," he replies with excitement in his voice.

I know deep down that when Wagstaff is taken, his grandson will go too and both will die, but now being in this deep means a whole new ballgame. If kidnapping is required to find out who sold us out then so be it. Nick quickly walks up the lane as I count twenty seconds and begin the van engine crawling along the lane. Reaching the junction, Nick is seen suddenly grabbing the grandson with his left arm and with the right hand taking out the Taser gun from his pocket as he shouts something to Wagstaff that causes him to turn around. The large figure of the target hits the ground shaking as Nick holds the trigger, sending fifty thousand volts into his body with the little boy beginning to cry in shock, still being held.

Pulling the van level to the pavement, Nick throws the little boy into the back and then starts to lift Wagstaff into the open side door even before I have the chance to climb from the front seat. Jumping to the pavement, I grasp Wagstaff's legs and lift him into the van as Nick continues to make his way inside. The boy, curled in one corner of the van, cries and it echoes through the steel van body. Finally lifting Wagstaff's huge body into the van, I slide the door, slamming it shut. Running around to the driver side door, I climb onto the seat as Nick reaches into the black bag, taking out a roll of gaff tape as the van begins to pull away from the curb.

Wagstaff's newspaper can been seen gently flapping in the breeze, still lying on the pavement.

The little boy screams and shouts in shock. "Granddad, Granddad what's happening?" but Wagstaff is stunned from the Taser shot.

A ripping noise can be heard as Nick, in a single action, pulls off a length of gaffa tape, wrapping it around the boy's eyes followed by his mouth, then finally binding his wrists together and shouting at the boy to be quiet and still. Making his way over to Wagstaff, the limp body is turned over with tape applied to bind his wrists, ankles and, as with the boy, his eyes and mouth.

Now climbing into the front of the van, he removes his mask and looks at me. "Okay, Dean, take off your mask and head for the warehouse from Monday. Don't drive too fast, the last thing we want is attention."

As the boy sobs in the back of the van I ask, "What are we going to do now?"

Burns replies quickly and calmly as agreed, "We find out from Wagstaff who sold us out then kill him." He shows no signs of remorse in his voice.

My head is filled with what he will do, not only to Wagstaff, but his grandson. The two prisoners lie in the back of the van with Nick sitting on the front seat with a smug grin covering his face as though he has just won the lottery. Driving back towards London, there are no cars on the roads until in the distance in front of us two sets of blue flashing light can be seen racing in our direction.

Nick, seeing the approaching police cars, quickly indicates with his hand saying, "Turn left down that small road."

Filled with dread over what pain Burns will subject Wagstaff to during his torture, in order to now get his answers, we stop the van and wait for the police to drive past. After a few minutes Nick instructs for the van to be turned around and we turn back onto the main road as another car can be seen in the distance leaving the village.

Meanwhile Shaun, following a tip off address from McGough, drives to check out a small village. He is so engrossed in how to kill Nash, with plotting and scheming different ideas that he doesn't realise how close his target is from being found. He drives around Caterham but after checking every street begins the head back towards London following a white van. Rage and anger flow through his body with every passing second. Eventually, Neal grabs his mobile and sends a message to McGough, 'Nash is nowhere it's a dead end!' The van he is following slows and turns onto a derelict warehouse area near the River Thames. Shaun suddenly realises who the driver of the vehicle is and can't believe his luck seeing Nash's face. Not believing his luck, Neal keeps his distance and stops near some bushes by the pavement, watching as the van gradually slows and come to a halt near to a large roller shutter door. He stares intensely as Nash can be seen climbing from the driver's seat and walking towards a wooden side door and finally entering the building. Shaun's legs begin to shake with adrenaline as his eyes are now fixated on Chloe's killer. He watches as the roller shutter door begins to open. Nash reappears then walks back to the van.

Stopping in his tracks, Nash gazes across towards the direction of where Shaun has the car parked behind some tall bushes. Sensing nothing, he climbs back into the van and drives it into the warehouse. Once the van is fully inside, the engine noise stops and the roller shutter doors begin to close. Burns jumps out of the van onto the wet concrete floor and, waving his arms beckons me to follow, Wagstaff can be heard beginning to awake from the Taser gun volts. Climbing out of the van, Nick can be seen pulling open an internal door next to the small office and he switches on a light, illuminating a staircase leading to a cellar.

Nick shouts across, "Get the kid from the back and take him down into the cellar. I will get Wagstaff ready."

Climbing from the van, I walk around and slide the door open with a mechanical thud. Wagstaff can be seen beginning to move as Burns appears then injects some fluid into his neck with a small syringe taken from a small shelf by the cellar door. It is clear that this kidnapping has been in Nick's thoughts for some time as parts of the puzzle continue to click into place. The young boy in a slumped position shakes and sobs, leaning against the back doors of the van that causes the metal structure to vibrate. Climbing fully into the back, I place my hands around his small body and start to lift him out. I can feel the coldness of his body after resting against the steel van doors. Beginning to move, the boy shakes his head, trying to talk, but the tape prevents any words from being spoken. His light body is easy to move as I lift him to the side door.

My thoughts drift towards what Burns will do with the boy and the guilt feels worse than the helicopter crash. Maybe it's because it's more personal with actual one to one contact. Taking a deep sigh and coughing slightly to clear my dry dusty throat, I lift him out from the van and start to carry him in my arms down the staircase. The slippery concrete steps are difficult to walk as I begin to slowly make my way towards the subdued lighting being emitted from in the cellar room. A single light bulb flickers like a candle in the breeze from the fluctuating electrical supply. At the far side of the room is a dirty black armchair and, still carrying the sobbing child, I walk over and lower him onto the damp, smelly fabric. The guilt of bringing the child into this situation begins to stab at my insides, sending pains into my stomach and making me feel sick.

Nick shouts from upstairs, "You ready to give me a lift?"

Leaning towards the boy, I whisper, "Don't worry, everything will be fine," as I touch his left shoulder.

"Just coming now," I shout back to Nick.

Reaching the top of the staircase, Burns has almost dragged Wagstaff's body out of the van by placing his hands under the arms and now only the legs are left balancing by the sliding doors. Walking over, I climb into the van and take the weight of the legs as Nick begins to walk in the direction of the doorway and then we start down the stairs for the cellar. We reach a circular area dimly lit under the solitary light bulb and lower the huge body onto the cold, wet floor. Walking to another part of the cellar, Nick collects an old wooden chair and places it directly in the centre of the illuminated circle.

"You go back upstairs, close the van doors and bring me the black bag from the van," he instructs with a look of excitement in his eyes.

Nodding my head in agreement, I turn quickly and stare at the boy to make sure he is still safe in the chair and make my way back up the slippery stairs. Nick notices me quickly checking Wagstaff's grandson and scowls back at me. I know it's going to be a difficult task to try and save his life. Reaching the top of the staircase, I quickly walk towards the large wooden doors and push them shut. I continue towards the van, where I reach inside, lifting out the bag. Through the unzipped top I notice some of the contents including screwdrivers, pliers, cut throat razors, and hammers.

My mind is suddenly filled with a flashback of a room with a table full of similar tools and dim lighting. Freezing in my tracks, the smell of the musty air inside the derelict building and wet concrete replay in my mind as though it was yesterday and, with a shudder running down my spine, goosebumps appear on my skin and the hair stands on the back of my neck as though I have been in this situation before. Trying to refocus my thoughts back to today, I quickly turn and climb down the stairs, closing the cellar door as I go with the tools clanking together with each step.

The last few weeks have shown a side to me that I never thought possible with helping Burns kill the other team members, but today feels different with the certain death of

Wagstaff and probably his grandson seeming so different. What happens after today remains unknown, but the repercussions will be felt forever, not just with Wagstaff's family but all the government agencies knowing that no agent is safe. Reaching the basement, Nick his threaded a rope through a hook in the ceiling and is lifting Wagstaff up into a standing position with the rope tied around his neck in a noose like a hangman. Wagstaff is still unconscious from the injection of sedative but his lips and face are beginning to turn blue from lack of oxygen. The chair is slid underneath Wagstaff's body and Nick releases the rope, dropping the lifeless body slumping into the chair. The gaffa tape binding Wagstaff's wrists and ankles is cut and then fresh is reapplied wrapping around his ankles to the chair legs and then his wrists to the arms. With the noose still attached, Burns sticks another syringe into Wagstaff's neck with the antidote and after a few seconds Wagstaff begins to regain consciousness and starts to twinge and move slowly.

Slapping him across the face, Nick starts the interrogation. "Wakey, wakey, sleepy eyes."

Wagstaff, still moving slowly, tries to speak but can't due to the gaffa tape and in one quick action Nick rips the grey tape off. With his eyes still covered Wagstaff tries to look around and with a groggy voice asks, "Where's my grandson, Burns? Is he safe?"

"He is quite safe, John, but your life, well, that's another matter." Burns looks across to the grandson.

"Burns, I fuckin' knew it. Leave my grandson alone, he has nothing to do with this. If you harm him it will be your last mistake," Wagstaff threatens.

"Save your threats, John. I've heard them all before and now I'm hardened off to them." Nick leans forward, spitting in Wagstaff's face.

"What do you want, Burns? I knew you were always a piece of shit, but kidnapping a young boy is the last straw."

"Oh really? Maybe this time I want to be caught to explain to the government about all the tidying up work I have done for you in the past, covering your tracks." Nick walks to the bag of tools.

"What happened in the past is long gone now, Burns, and none of your threats will save your life. There's a bounty on your head so large every trophy hunter will be after a slice." Wagstaff continues to move his head around.

"Good. Bring them all on. Besides, I have trained most of them so I know what to expect!" Burns takes out a cutthroat razor.

"Not all of them, Burns. Nash is something different." Wagstaff smiles.

Nick places his index finger across his lips and, looking across to me, says, "Nash? Nash who?"

"You know who, Burns. Dean Nash, he helped you with the warehouse robbery on Monday last week, your new little puppet. I bet he is here right now."

"Don't know anyone called Nash or about a robbery on Monday." Nick walks back to Wagstaff.

"So what's this all about then? A Sunday morning chat? You could have had tea this afternoon if you wanted to talk, but you want to act like an animal as always," Wagstaff growls.

Nick takes the razor and, in a sweeping action, slices across Wagstaff's chest. Blood begins to ooze out onto his white shirt. "An animal is what your government made me."

"Argh." Wagstaff slumps slightly in the chair.

"Is that all you have?" Wagstaff, clearly in pain, smiles with a brave face.

"For a bastard like you I have a lot more." Burns snaps back then punches him in the left side of his mouth, bursting his lip, then in the knife cut, Burns sees the tracker in

Wagstaff's chest, so removing it, he throws it to the ground and crushes it with his foot.

Wagstaff spits out the blood from his mouth and continues to talk. "I guess you want to know which one of your handpicked team set you up from the robbery?"

"What robbery? Wagstaff, I don't know what you're talking about," Nick replies.

"Burns, I know it was you. It has your name written all over it so let's stop fuckin' around." Wagstaff spits more blood from his mouth.

Burns, knowing he can't hide it any more, and in fact wanting to boast over the robbery, replies, "Well, seeing as your tracker and wire have been removed and there is no one else here other than us, and seeing that you're going to die, I have nothing to lose. So yes, I planned the robbery and carried it out." Nick walks around the chair.

"Your planning was very good with the airport and you almost had us fooled, but it's a shame your team let you down in the end."

"Go on?" Burns listens intently.

"Lloyd dead, Paul dead, Greg, Vernon, Ramone, Carlos and those two German contractors. Nash is the only guy still alive, and finally you. How does that sound?" Wagstaff coughs.

Waiting outside, Shaun's emotions are completely clouding his judgement as he tries to control the anger welling from deep inside, talking to himself, saying, "Keep calm, that fucker will pay." McGough's words keep replaying over and over in his mind as he takes the pistol from the glove box. In a single action he pushes the clip into the handle and pulls back the top slide, loading a round into the chamber.

Clicking on the safety catch, he stares at the gun, looking at the blackness of the barrel and action with the feeling of fresh oil that coats his hands. Murder now flowing though his veins, he pulls the handle, opening the door. With a swift movement he leaps out of the car, closing the door behind. After quickly looking at the bag of equipment resting across the back seat, he quickly checks to see if anyone else is watching, he turns, walking towards the direction of the warehouse. He pushes the pistol into the rear of his trouser belt, pulling the leather black jacket over to cover it as his mind boils with killing Nash, but what to do after hasn't even properly registered. Reaching the wooden side door, Shaun waits a few seconds for any possible noise from inside the building, but hears nothing. Assuming the coast is clear, he places his hand on the door and begins to open it very slowly with all his senses on full alert.

Taking the pistol from the belt, he continues to open the door with voices and shouting coming from inside the building but muffled as though behind a door. Now fully entered into the building, Shaun closes the door gradually and sees the white van parked with voices shouting out again as Neal stares across in the direction of an area to the far side of the building. Looking closer in the subdued lighting, he sees a door with a faint illuminated halo from around the edges and slowly he begins to make his way to the direction of the door as several unfamiliar voices can be heard followed by what appears to be a yelling sound. Freezing in his tracks, Shaun stops and wonders what is happening behind the door and clearly from his experience some form of interrogation is taking place. Another scream and large thud can be heard as Shaun's heartbeat increases with the thoughts of what is happening as more shouting takes place. Shaun now decides to open the door to see what is happening behind it. His shaking hand rattles the door handle as he begins to turn the mechanism, opening the door.

"Wagstaff, you fuckin' bastard," echoes from behind the door as Neal continues to pull it open.

Now with the door fully open, a wooden staircase can be seen leading downwards in the direction of the voices.

Closing the door behind, Shaun continues down the staircase in the direction of the voices and low lighting. 'Thud, thud floats through the air along with the name 'Wagstaff' being spoken by a posh English voice as Shaun gradually makes his way down each step one at a time, trying not to draw attention to himself. His back is pushed hard against the wall and his partly shaking hand is holding the pistol in front. He walks towards the ever-increasing light with each footstep closer to the noise and finally his eyes are filled with the sight of an old man strapped to a wooden chair underneath a light bulb with another man towering over him. At the far side of the darkened room is Nash staring at the whole gruesome event. Shaun's mind is full of only one thing, killing Nash. As he begins to lift the pistol gradually in the direction of him, the older man standing near the hostage strapped to the chair suddenly turns and sees Shaun. A shot rings out in the basement.

"Argh," can be heard as the bullet hits the flesh of a person. Suddenly, in the confusion, a second pistol is fired as a volley of return shots hit the wall next to Shaun, sending concrete dust and particles flying into the air as Burns dives to the ground, taking cover next to Wagstaff.

"I'll kill you, Nash, you fuckin' bastard!" Shaun takes two more shots.

"Is that you, Shaun? What the fuck is going on?" I shout across, drawing a pistol from inside my jacket.

"Fuck you, Nash. I know it was you. Don't try to hide what has been done. McGough has told me all about it!"

Nick, crouching behind the beaten and bleeding Wagstaff, who is now severally injured with a bullet hole in his right shoulder, shouts across, "Who is this fuckin' idiot, Dean?"

"It's Shaun, my friend, but I don't know what his problem is."

"Well, one thing is certain, he will be a fuckin' dead ex-friend in a minute." Nick reloads his gun and takes another couple of shots.

Lifting my gun, I see Shaun's right leg and, taking a shot, hit him cleanly just in the thigh muscle. As he screams in pain he fires off the several more rounds, hitting Wagstaff two more times as he tries to stumble back up the stairs to escape. Following quickly behind, I run past Nick and run up the stairs to try and catch him. Reaching the top of the stairs, I stop briefly by the door and begin to open it as Shaun takes another couple of shots, hitting the doorframe and sending wood fragments flying in the air. The gunshots ring through the empty building. Not returning fire, I gradually open the door to see Shaun already exiting to the outside and, quickly assessing that taking a shot is too risky, I allow him to leave. Running to the side door and slowly pulling it open, Shaun can be seen hobbling over towards the tall bushes where earlier I sensed being watched. A car engine is started. The squealing sound of tyres is then heard as a white Audi A4 car driven by Shaun leaves the area at high speed in the opposite direction. As I watch him disappear, I turn and return back to the building, entering through the side door, closing and locking it before making my way down the stairs to the basement. Reaching the bottom of the stairs, Burns can be seen pointing the gun in my direction, standing next to Wagstaff.

"Well, your friend has done a great fuckin' job, Dean! Hitting Wagstaff twice with stray bullets."

"Is he still alive?" I ask.

"Arrgh," can be heard as Nick checks Wagstaff for still being alive.

"Just about, but his grandson is dead." Nick gestures.

Quickly walking past Burns, I reach the young boy and see where a bullet has hit him in the chest with fresh blood covering his white T-shirt.

"Fuck. Fuck, this boy was innocent," I shout.

"Who's McGough?" Burns asks, still pointing his gun at me.

"What? How the fuck do I know, Nick? I have never seen Shaun that crazy before. Why are you pointing that gun at me?"

Nick, feeling betrayed, clearly wants to tidy all the loose ends with only Wagstaff and myself the last two who know about the robbery. My mind remembers how quickly Burns killed Greg with a couple of bullets to the head and, sensing my end is close, I slowly begin to lift my gun in the direction of Burns as a final shot rings out. Burns drops to the ground but quickly stands and heads towards a door at the back of the basement as the sound of police sirens becomes louder and louder. Turning around, I hear Wagstaff coughing and walk over towards him.

Wagstaff whispers, "Nash? Are you there, Nash?"

I stand over him saying, "Yes, I'm here, Wagstaff."

"My grandson, how is my grandson, Dean?" Wagstaff asks.

"I'm sorry, John, I couldn't save him," I reply, having a lump in my throat now, holding his hand.

He coughs out a mouthful of blood and begins to cry then starts to speak in a broken voice. "I found out about you, Nash. Burns needs to be stopped or thousands of innocent people could die."

"What do you mean, John?" I ask as the police cars' tyres screech to a stop outside.

"I knew you weren't an account, you are much more than that, and I am sorry that I couldn't stop Burns sooner." He coughs again and grips my hand tightly.

"I wanted to recruit you to work for me. But now get out of here, find McGough and kill Burns. Will you do that for me and revenge the death of my grandson?" Noises of police officers smashing the doors can be heard echoing through the building.

"Yes, John, I will do that for you. I'm sorry about your grandson." Wagstaff takes one final gurgling breath and dies as footsteps are heard on the concrete surface above.

Lowering Wagstaff's hand, I turn and run for the back doorway, grabbing a hand grenade that was dropped on the floor by Burns. Then I flee along the damp, dimly lit corridor, following Burns's escape route. The police start to smash down the upper door of the basement as I run through the maze of passageways under the building. Seeing a steel door, it is pulled shut behind myself and then, clicking the handle to lock it, the grenade is stuffed behind it after pulling the firing pin. Continuing to run along the damp slippery corridor, my mind is full of what has happened but escape is the most important thing to focus on now. Further back down the passage, the police have reached the bodies of Wagstaff and his grandson. The commanding officer checks for any pulse but, fearing the worse, sends a message of the sad news. The remaining officers continue down the escape corridor and after a few seconds, they reach the steel door blocking their route and start to bang against the steel skin, sending an eerie echo along the empty corridor. I only have about ten seconds before the grenade will explode and then thankfully turning around the last corner in the distance is a halo of light around a door casing at the end of the building, shining bright as I take a sigh of relief.

Suddenly the whole building echoes as the grenade dislodged from the steel door explodes, sending a dust cloud racing through the narrow passage. With a huge roaring noise behind me, I'm engulfed as the blast hits me hard in the back whilst shoulder barging against the outer door. The door flings open followed by me and a massive cloud of concrete dust. Without stopping I continue running in a straight line heading for the River Thames with dust still floating in the air and from my clothes. Reaching the bank, I jump head first into the water that instantly washes away the dust. The coldness and strong current of the Thames isn't noticed until almost half way across when I begin to tire as the adrenaline from the escape starts to wear off.

In the distance a police boat siren can be heard racing along the Thames towards the back of the warehouse as police officers finally manage to break through the side fencing and are seen running to the back of the building, trying to help their colleagues from the tunnel. With these actions my footprints are hidden by all the busy foot traffic left on the settled surface, hiding my escape.

Finally reaching the opposite bank of the river slightly out of breath, I slowly begin to drag myself out. After standing, I begin to walk along the footpath, scanning around for any possible threats as rain begins to fall. The already soaking clothes cling to my skin and the coldness from the water starts to sap the warmth from my body. I walk past a parked car and notice a jacket on the back seat. Quickly looking around for any people, the door handle is tried, but it won't open. Taking the pistol from the back of my trousers, I break the glass window with the butt and, reaching inside to take the jacket, at least I am sheltered from the cold rain. Continuing to walk along the footpath, I pull the green jacket on and zip it up as my thoughts race over what to do next. Clearly Wagstaff wanted me to kill Burns and now for sure the missing contact name must be McGough. I take out my mobile from the trouser pocket and thankfully it is still working. Then, beginning to flick through the contacts, the unknown person's number is found. As the rain continues to fall, the call button is pressed and, with more past thoughts clearer in my mind, I realise that for the second time in my life I need to sign a deal with the devil for my soul as the familiar voice of McGough answers my call.